xMCiRR

Susanna Gregory was a police officer in Leeds before taking up
an academic career. She has a ~~~ ~~~

and thrilling atmosphe~~~ ~~~ detail
Lancash~~~ *~~~trangler*

D1492958

Also by Susanna Gregory

The Matthew Bartholomew series

The Thomas Chaloner series

SUSANNA GREGORY

A

MASTERLY MURDER

sphere

SPHERE

First published in Great Britain in 2000 by Little, Brown and Company
First published in paperback in 2001 by Warner Books
This edition reissued in 2017 by Sphere

3 5 7 9 10 8 6 4 2

A CIP catalogue record for this book
is available from the British Library.

ISBN 978-0-7515-6940-7

Typeset in Baskerville by Palimpsest Book Production Limited,
Falkirk, Stirlingshire
Printed and bound in Great Britain by Clays Ltd, Elcograf S.p.A

Papers used by Sphere are from well-managed forests
and other responsible sources.

MIX
Paper from
responsible sources
FSC® C104740

Sphere
An imprint of
Little, Brown Book Group
Carmelite House
50 Victoria Embankment
London EC4Y 0DZ

An Hachette UK Company
www.hachette.co.uk

www.littlebrown.co.uk

For Aggie Lewis-Jones

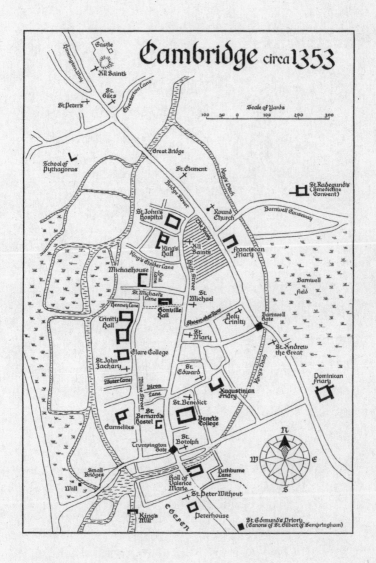

Cambridge circa **1353**

Scale of Yards
100 50 0 100 200 300

Castle
All Saints
St. Giles
Huntingdon Road
Chesterton Lane
St. Peters

Great Bridge
School of Pythagoras
St. Clement
King's Ditch
St. Radegund's (Benedictine Convent)

Bridge Street
St. John's Hospital
Round Church
Barnwell Causeway

King's Hall
XII Saints
The Jewry
Franciscan Friary

King's Childer Lane
Michaelhouse
Pilgrim Lane
High Street
Barnwell Field

St. Michael's Lane
St. Michael
Henney Lane
Gonville Hall
Shoemaker Row
Barnwell Gate

Trinity Hall
Holy Trinity
St. Mary
St. Andrew the Great

Clare College
King's Ditch
Dominican Friary

St. John Zachary
St. Edward
Water Lane
Milne Street
Piron Lane
Augustinian Friary

St. Benedict
Carmelites
St. Bernard's Hostel
Benet's College
Trumpington Gate
St. Botolph

N
W   E
S

Small Bridges
Mill
Luthburne Lane
Hall of Valence Marie
St. Peter Without

King's Mill
Peterhouse
St. Edmund's Priory (Canons of St. Gilbert of Sempringham)

PROLOGUE

Cambridge, January 1349

A SILVER MOON SLANTED ITS BRIGHTNESS INTO THE muddy streets of the Fen-edge town. The clear weather had brought a biting cold, so that even huddled inside his thick warm cloak, Master Wilson of Michaelhouse shivered, and his fingers and toes were so chilled that he could barely feel them. There was a dusting of frost over the rutted filth of the High Street, and the numerous potholes were glazed with a crust of ice, cunningly concealing the slushy mess of raw sewage and rubbish that waited to ooze around carelessly placed feet.

Usually, so late in the evening, the town would be still, the silence broken only by the occasional bark of a dog or the footsteps of the night-watch as they patrolled the town. But, that January, England was in the grip of a terrible disease that had rolled relentlessly across Europe, killing old and young, rich and poor, and the good citizens with the bad. The agonised gasps of the dying and the wails of the bereaved shattered the peace, and in many houses lights burned in the chambers where the sick lay.

Wilson shuddered and drew his cloak more closely around him, stepping quickly over the huddled form of a beggar who lay in the street. Whether the man was merely sleeping or whether he had succumbed to the plague, Wilson could not tell and was not inclined to find out. He hurried on, leaving the High Street to make his way towards the Barnwell Causeway and St Radegund's Priory, where his lover awaited him.

A shriek of despair from the house of Sheriff Tulyet made his blood run cold. So far, the numerous Tulyet clan had been fortunate, and not one of them had been affected by the foul sickness that turned healthy people to blackened, stinking corpses within a few hours – or days, if they were unlucky. But the pestilence was showing no signs of weakening its grip on the town, and Wilson suspected it had been only a matter of time before the Sheriff's family lost someone to it. He slipped quickly into the shadows when he saw two people emerging from Tulyet's house. He recognised them as his Michaelhouse colleagues Matthew Bartholomew and Brother Michael, one a physician and the other a Benedictine monk. Physicians were all but useless against the plague, and people gained far more comfort from the ministrations of the clerics, who were at least able to grant them absolution before they died. Wilson was sure that Brother Michael had been a greater solace to the Tulyets than Bartholomew and his ineffective remedies could ever hope to be.

He pressed himself back into the blackness of a doorway as the two scholars walked past. By day, Wilson kept to his room, seeing no one and running the College by yelling through the firmly closed door. No one knew how the plague spread, but Wilson had heard that people who hid themselves away from the victims were more likely to escape infection than those who walked freely among them. Wilson did not want Bartholomew and Michael to speak to him: even meeting their eyes might be enough to give him the disease. He also did not want them to know that he left his room each night to meet with the lovely Prioress of St Radegund's Convent. Living in isolation was all very well during the day, when his business was with the rough assortment of men who were Michaelhouse's scholars and servants, but once night fell, and darkness enveloped the town, Wilson longed for the warmth of human contact and found he needed the companionship and understanding that only the Prioress could provide.

When the trudging, exhausted footsteps of Bartholomew and Michael had faded away and he was alone again, Wilson left his hiding place and continued along Bridge Street. From a house in front of him came a sudden shaft of golden light as a door was flung open. There was no time to duck into the shadows before Adela Tangmer, the vintner's daughter, dashed out and saw him. Before he could stop her, she had seized his arm, her ugly, horsy face white with shock and grief.

'Please help me. My mother is dying and she needs a priest.'

Wilson tugged his arm away quickly and took several steps back, trying to distance himself from her. 'I am sorry, but I cannot help you. I am not a friar.'

'But as a scholar of the University you have taken holy orders and can therefore grant absolution to the dying. My father told me that you absolved Mayor Horwoode's wife only last night. Please! My mother does not have many moments left to her.'

'I am sorry,' said Wilson, trying to edge around her without coming too close. 'But Mistress Horwoode's was a special case.'

'My mother's is a special case,' pleaded Adela. 'She once committed adultery, and she needs to confess before she dies or she will spend eternity in Purgatory. Only you can help her.'

'No,' said Wilson firmly, starting to walk away. 'I am in a hurry.'

'I will pay you any amount you ask,' called Adela desperately, as he began to stride up the street.

Abruptly, Wilson stopped and turned to face her, shaking his head in disbelief. 'Do you think I would risk my life for money? It would not be much use to me if I were to catch the contagion and die.'

'I have a pomander filled with special spices that you can place over your nose and mouth,' said Adela immediately. 'And I will lend you my charm – it has been dipped in the holy well at Walsingham and if you wear it, you will be quite safe.'

Wilson hesitated, so Adela quickly unfastened a healthily heavy purse from her belt and handed it to him. He weighed it in his hand, and then nodded reluctant agreement. He passed from the cracking cold of the January night into the mellow warmth of the house, and then followed Adela into the fearsome hell of a plague victim's death chamber.

Late September 1353

The autumn sun drenched the fields of ripe corn and barley near the river in a haze of scarlet and gold. Beyond the dusty yellow of the crops were the water meadows, great swaths of marshy grass lined with trees that were tinged amber and orange as their summer foliage began to turn. Across the river were the towers and the thatched and tiled roofs of the University's Colleges – Michaelhouse, Trinity Hall, Gonville, Peterhouse and Clare.

The sounds of a fine day were in the air. The exuberant shrieks of children who played in the river's murky shallows mingled with the bleat of grazing sheep and the distant jangle of bells announcing the office of terce. The air was rich with the scent of freshly mown hay, the crops that still awaited harvesting, and the ever-present sulphurous odour of the River Cam. A lark twittered in the pale blue sky high above, while nearer to the ground, a pair of pigeons cooed contentedly in the ancient oak trees that stood sentinel near the old mill.

Two men strolled along the winding path that ran past the mill and then on to the little village of Newnham Croft beyond. One wore the distinctive blue tabard that marked him as a Fellow of Bene't College, while the other wore the grey habit of a Franciscan friar. They walked slowly, enjoying the peace of a Sunday afternoon away from their various duties and obligations.

'What has been happening at Bene't this week?' asked the friar, leaning down to pick a grass stem on which to chew. 'Does it still seethe with arguments and plots?'

'Of course,' said the scholar. 'And work on the new accommodation range progresses so slowly that I wonder whether we will be long in our graves before it is completed. If I had known I would be living in an unfinished building for three years, I am not sure I would have accepted a Fellowship at Bene't.'

The friar smiled. It was not a pleasant smile, and there was more malice than friendship in it. 'I heard a story about one of your Bene't colleagues the other day. He sold several bracelets to Harold of Haslingfield, the goldsmith.'

'And?' asked the scholar when the friar paused. 'What of it? Were they stolen property?'

The friar raised his eyebrows in mock surprise. 'Stolen property? What kind of men do you admit as Fellows of Bene't College, if you can so blithely ask me that sort of question?'

The scholar sighed irritably. 'You know very well what

kind of men are at Bene't. Tell me about this jewellery.'

'You are not the only one to question its origins. Harold the goldsmith was offered such an attractive price for these trinkets that he took them to his fellow guild members and to the Sheriff, to see whether anyone might recognise them as the proceeds of crime.'

'Well?' snapped the scholar, when the friar paused again. 'Were they?'

The friar shrugged, knowing he was infuriating his companion with his trickle of information, but enjoying the sensation of power it brought. The scholar wanted to know what was being said about his College and since the University was so unpopular with the citizens of Cambridge, listening to the friar's idle chatter would be the scholar's only opportunity to learn what the town thought of Bene't.

'No one could say,' the Franciscan replied carelessly. 'The Sheriff and the honourable members of the Goldsmiths' Guild said no such items had been reported as stolen, and that was the end of the matter.'

'So why are you telling me this?' demanded the scholar irritably. 'That one of my colleagues sold a goldsmith jewellery that was not stolen is hardly an intriguing topic of conversation.'

The friar gave his secretive smile, unperturbed by the scholar's prickliness. 'I am informing you that a Fellow of Bene't is dabbling in the gold market. I assumed you would be interested.'

Suddenly, from across the river drifted a mournful, mysterious noise that made both men gaze at each other in alarm. It was a discordant, grating, chilling sound, like dozens of tomcats on a moonlit night, and it stilled the laughing voices of the playing children as abruptly as if a bucket of cold water had been dashed over them. Even the pigeons were momentarily startled into silence.

'What in God's name is that?' breathed the friar, looking around him uneasily.

'Nothing – in God's name,' said the scholar, beginning to laugh, his bad temper at the friar's piecemeal revelations forgotten. 'Those inharmonious tones come from the Michaelhouse choir. They practise on Sunday afternoons.'

'Well, that must keep the congregation's numbers down,' said the friar, crossing himself hurriedly. 'I am surprised they are allowed to disturb the peace like that on the Sabbath.'

'Michaelhouse probably bribes the Sheriff to turn a deaf ear. But never mind those caterwaulers. Did you hear about the Bursar of Ovyng Hostel? He has been drunk in the Brazen George three times this week!'

'No!' said the friar in scandalised glee. 'Has he really?'

The scholar nodded. 'And the word is that Ovyng's philosophy teacher is so poorly sighted these days that he cannot even make out the titles on the books he uses in his classes. The Master pretends not to notice, because the philosopher is an old friend, but is it fair of him to take the fees of students and then abandon them to the care of a man who can no longer read?'

The friar shook his head disapprovingly, although his eyes gleamed with spite. 'I should say not. It is disgraceful!'

'And one of our porters told me that an Ovyng student stole – *stole* – a plum cake from the baker in Bridge Street yesterday. What kind of men enrol in the University these days? Thieves, frauds and drunkards!'

'Especially the so-called scholars at Ovyng and Bene't,' said the friar, and both men laughed.

Their voices clattered on, malicious and vindictive, as

they continued to walk towards Newnham. Concealed behind the clump of oak trees near the path, two more men wearing the blue tabards of Bene't College regarded each other sombrely.

'You see?' asked one of the other bitterly. 'He does not care who he chatters to, or what he says about our College. He is a wicked gossip, and, if he is allowed to continue unchecked, he will do Bene't all manner of harm.'

His colleague nodded slowly. 'Then we will have to ensure that does not happen,' he said softly, fingering the dagger at his side.

CHAPTER 1

'IF YOU DO NOT KEEP STILL, HOW CAN I PULL THE sting out?' asked Matthew Bartholomew of Brother Michael in exasperation.

'You are hurting me!' howled Michael, struggling as the physician bent over him again with a small pair of tweezers. 'You are jabbing about with those things like a woodpecker on a tree. Have you no compassion?'

'It is only a bee sting, Brother,' Bartholomew pointed out, bemused by the fuss the Benedictine was making. 'And if you sit still for just a moment I can remove it, and all your terrible suffering will be over.'

Michael regarded him suspiciously. 'I have heard of bee stings proving fatal to some people. Are you trying to tell me something in your discreet, physicianly way?'

Startled, Bartholomew laughed aloud. 'It would take more than a mere bee to make an end of Brother Michael, the University's Senior Proctor and valued agent of the Bishop of Ely – although I have never witnessed such drama in all my life. Even children do not squall and shriek like you do.'

'That is probably because they do not understand what you are about to do,' said Michael haughtily. 'Well, come on, then; get it over with.'

Imperiously, he thrust a flabby arm at Bartholomew and turned his head away, eyes tightly closed. Once he had deigned to be co-operative, it was a simple task for the physician to pluck out the offending sting and then daub the afflicted area with a salve of goose grease and juniper berries, although the monk accompanied the operation with an unremitting monologue of complaint.

They were in Bartholomew's medicine store at Michaelhouse, the College at the University of Cambridge where they held their Fellowships. It was a small, dimly lit chamber, more cupboard than room, that was always filled with the bitter-sour aroma of various potions and salves. Every available scrap of wall space was covered by overloaded shelves, and the workbench under the window was stained and burned where ingredients had spilled as they had been mixed.

It was a damp, gloomy November day, and clouds sagged in a lumpy grey sheet across the small town and the marshy expanse of the Fens beyond. University term was well under way, and Bartholomew could hear the stentorian tones of his colleague Father William, who was teaching in the hall across the courtyard. Bartholomew was impressed. The previous year a generous benefactor had paid for the windows in the hall and the adjoining conclave to be glazed, and for the Franciscan friar's voice to carry through the glass to the other side of the College indicated an impressive degree of volume. Bartholomew wondered how the other masters could make themselves heard above it.

'Right,' he said, as he finished tending Michael's arm. 'That should heal nicely, if you do not scratch it.'

'But it itches,' protested Michael immediately. 'It is driving me to distraction.'

'It will itch even more if you keep fiddling with it,' said Bartholomew unsympathetically. 'How did you come to be stung by a bee anyway? It is the wrong time of year for bees.'

'Apparently not for this one,' said Michael stiffly. 'I bought a cake from a baker in the Market Square, and the thing decided to share it with me. No amount of flapping and running seemed to deter it, and so I was reduced to swatting it when it landed. Then it had the audacity to sting me.'

'If the bee was crushed, you had the better end of the bargain. But we have been away from our students long enough. I want mine to learn about how Galen developed the Hippocratic theory of the four humours, not about how the Devil founded the Dominican Order, which is what Father William seems to be bawling to his students – and to the world in general – this morning.'

'Is he really?' asked Michael, half startled and half amused. 'I have been in such agonies with this sting that I have not even heard our Franciscan fanatic today – and that should tell you something of the suffering I have endured.'

Bartholomew frowned. 'William should be more discreet about his dislike of Dominicans. Master Kenyngham told me last night that one of our two new Fellows – due to arrive today – is a Dominican.'

'I expect Kenyngham told William, too – hence this morning's bit of bigotry. You know the Franciscans and the Dominicans in Cambridge loathe each other, Matt. They are always quarrelling about something they consider desperately important – usually something the rest of us neither understand nor care about.'

'I hope William and this new Dominican will not turn Michaelhouse into a battleground,' said Bartholomew with feeling. 'We have managed to remain pleasantly free of squabbles between religious Orders so far, and I would like it to remain that way.'

'It might spice things up a little,' said Michael, green eyes gleaming as he contemplated the intrigues of such a situation.

'It would not,' said Bartholomew firmly, replacing the jar of salve in his bag and washing his hands. 'William does not have the intellect to embark on the kind of clever plotting you enjoy – he is more of a fists man.'

Michael laughed. 'You are right. But you have missed your chance to enthral your students with lurid descriptions of bile, phlegm and blood this morning, Matt, because the porter will ring the bell for the midday meal soon. Hurry up, or there will be nothing left.'

He had shot from the storeroom and was crossing the courtyard to be first at the table, before Bartholomew could reply. The physician smiled at the fat monk's greed, finished tidying his chamber, and followed at a more sedate pace. He shivered as he walked across the yard to the hall. A bitter north wind blew, bringing with it the promise of yet more rain, and perhaps even snow. He had just reached the porch when Cynric, his book-bearer, came hurrying towards him, shouting to catch his attention.

'You had better come with me, boy,' said Cynric breathlessly. 'I have just found Justus dead near Dame Nichol's Hythe, on the river.'

'You mean the Justus who is John Runham's book-bearer?' asked Bartholomew, startled. Justus had served dinner at high table only the previous evening. 'How did he die? Did he drown?'

Cynric looked uncomfortable. 'It is not for me to say – you are the physician. But come quickly before the poor man's corpse attracts a crowd of gawking onlookers.'

Bartholomew followed him out of the College and down the lane to the ramshackle line of jetties that lined the river bank. They turned right along the towpath, and headed for the last pier in the row, known as Dame Nichol's Hythe. Dame Nichol was long since dead, and the sturdy wharf she had financed was now in a sorry state. Its timber pillars were rotting and unsafe, and huge gaps in its planking threatened to deposit anyone standing on it into the sluggish brown waters of the River Cam below. The bank behind was little more than a midden, cluttered with discarded crates, broken barrels and scraps of unwanted clothing, and the fetid mud was impregnated with human and animal waste. The whole area stank of decaying, wet wood and sewage.

In the summer, the wharves – even Dame Nichol's – were hives of activity, with barges from France and the Low Countries arriving daily, loaded with all manner of exotic goods, as well as the more mundane wool, grain and stone for building. In the winter, however, the colourful bustle of the tiny docks all but ceased, and that day only a few shabbily dressed bargemen laboured in the chill wind, slowly and listlessly removing peat faggots from a leaking flat-bottomed skiff. Two gulls watched Bartholomew and Cynric with sharp yellow eyes, waiting for them to be gone so that they could resume their scavenging for the discarded fish entrails and eel heads that lay festering and rank in the sticky muck of the towpath.

Cynric's fears that Justus's body would attract hordes of intrigued townsfolk were unfounded: the toiling bargemen – and even the birds – were not interested in it. Life was hard for many people following the Great Pestilence that had swept across the country, and it was not uncommon for desperate souls to end it all in the murky depths of the river. Justus lay disregarded and uncared for amid the scrubby weeds and filth, no more popular or remarkable in death than he had been in life.

Justus had been the servant of a Michaelhouse Fellow

called John Runham, although Bartholomew had always been under the impression that they did not like each other. He could understand why: Runham was smug, condescending and arrogant; Justus was self-absorbed and dismal.

'I found him when I came to buy peat for the College fires,' explained Cynric. 'I noticed a stray dog sniffing around, and when I came to see what it had discovered, I saw Justus. At least, I assume it is Justus. He is wearing that horrible tunic Justus always donned when he was not working.'

Cynric had a point about the corpse's identity. The bizarrely patterned garment of which Justus had been so fond was all that could be immediately identified, because a thick leather wineskin had been pulled over the body's head and then tied tight under the chin with twine. Bartholomew crouched down and undid it, noting it had been knotted at the front in the imperfect, haphazard way he would expect from a suicide. He drew it off, hearing Cynric's soft intake of breath as he saw the dark, swollen features of the dead book-bearer.

'Well, it is Justus right enough,' said Cynric grimly. 'I would recognise those big yellow teeth anywhere. Did he kill himself?'

'It looks that way,' said Bartholomew, inspecting the wineskin. It was a coarse, watertight sack, designed to hold cheap brews for those not able to afford the better wines that came in casks. Because the bag had been sealed with resin to make it leak-proof, it was also air-proof, and once the rope had been tightened around the neck, it had suffocated the wearer.

'Justus was never a contented man,' said Cynric, regarding his fellow book-bearer pityingly. 'He was always complaining about something. And he envied me my happiness with Rachel.' He gave a sudden and inappropriate grin. 'Married life is a fine thing, boy. You should try it.'

'Perhaps I will one day,' said Bartholomew vaguely, unwilling to indulge in such a discussion when one of the College servants lay dead at his feet. 'But first, I want to be certain that Justus killed himself, and that no one gave him a helping hand into the next world.'

'But why would anyone do that?' asked Cynric, surprised. 'He had nothing worth stealing, because he spent all he earned on wine or ale. None of his clothes are missing as far as I can see, and here is his dagger – not a very valuable item, but one that would have been stolen had he been murdered for his possessions.'

Bartholomew inspected the dead man in more detail, checking for signs that Justus might have been involved in a struggle. He examined the man's hands, but they were unmarked and the fingernails showed no evidence that he had clawed at an assailant. Ignoring an exclamation of disgust from Cynric, Bartholomew sniffed cautiously at Justus's mouth, and detected the pungently sweet odour of alcohol – far stronger than he would have expected had the smell come simply from Justus having a wineskin over his head for a few hours.

The front-tied knot on the bag, plus the fact that Justus had probably been in his cups when he had died, suggested to Bartholomew that the servant had drunk himself into a state of gloom and had chosen suffocation with the wineskin as a reasonably easy death. Justus was seldom without wine to hand, so it was not inconceivable that he should choose such a method to dispatch himself. And, as Cynric had pointed out, Justus was a naturally miserable man who was given to moods of black despair.

Poor Justus, he thought, sitting back on his heels and gazing down at the contorted features that lay in the mud in front of him. Life as book-bearer to a demanding and ill-tempered master like John Runham could not have been especially pleasant, but Bartholomew had not imagined it was bad enough to drive a man to suicide. He wondered what aspect of Justus's existence had caused him to end his life in such a pathetic way and to select as unsavoury and grimy a spot as Dame Nichol's Hythe in which to do it.

While Cynric went to summon porters to carry Justus's body to St Michael's Church, and to report what had happened to Brother Michael, who as Senior Proctor would need to give a verdict on the sudden death of a University servant, Bartholomew waited, gazing down at the body that lay in front of him.

It was damp from dew, and stiff, suggesting that it had been there for some hours. Bartholomew supposed that serving dinner at Michaelhouse the evening before had been one of the last things Justus had done. He racked his brains, trying to recall whether Justus had seemed more morose than usual, but the book-bearer was so habitually sullen that Bartholomew was not sure whether he would have noticed anyway.

It was not long before Michael arrived, bustling importantly along the river bank, and more breathless than he should have been from the short walk from his College.

'Suicide?' he panted, scratching his bad arm. 'I am not surprised. Justus was a morose beggar, and was always moaning about something. I have never met a more gloom-ridden man – and that includes all the Franciscans in my acquaintance! Well? When did he do it?'

'I cannot tell specifically, but probably last night.'

'He served us dinner last night,' said Michael thoughtfully. 'And shortly after that I saw him leave Michaelhouse with a full wineskin dangling from one hand. Could I have been the last person to see him alive?'

'Possibly,' replied Bartholomew, sorry that he had not been aware of the extent of Justus's misery before it had led to such irreversible measures. The community of scholars and servants at Michaelhouse was not large, and someone should have noticed Justus's sufferings and tried to help.

Michael glanced around at the insalubrious surroundings of Dame Nichol's Hythe and gave a fastidious shudder. 'He could have picked a better spot than this to spend his last moments on Earth.'

'I imagine the quality of the scenery was not uppermost in his mind,' said Bartholomew. 'He probably saw this only as somewhere he would not be disturbed.'

Michael nodded. 'Few people wander here after dark. Well, it is obvious what happened: Justus came here alone last night intending to drink himself into oblivion, became overly despondent – as he often did when he was in his cups – and decided to do away with himself.'

Bartholomew could see no reason to disagree with him. 'The cord was fairly taut around his neck, but not so tight as to leave a mark. He must have knotted it there, and then slowly slipped into unconsciousness from lack of air. There is no damage to his hands, so he did not fight against it.'

'And he is still in possession of his clothes and dagger, which suggests to me that he lay undisturbed until Cynric found him this morning,' concluded Michael. 'Poor man.'

Cynric arrived with two porters and a stretcher, and Bartholomew and Michael began to walk back to Michaelhouse while the servants followed with the body. Bartholomew noticed that the corpse had been covered as an automatic mark of respect, although a filthy horse-blanket hastily snatched from the stable had been used. There would be little mourning for the book-bearer, and Bartholomew wondered whether any of his colleagues would even bother to attend his burial.

'Come on, Matt,' said Michael, taking his arm, and hauling him along with surprising speed for a man who looked so flabby. 'We can still make the midday meal if we are quick! I was only able to grab a lump of bread before you sent for me.'

'A missed meal will do you no harm,' said Bartholomew, eyeing the monk's substantial girth critically. 'It might even prove beneficial. I do not think it can be healthy to be so fat.'

'What nonsense you speak sometimes,' said Michael scathingly. 'Being a Master of Theology, the Senior Proctor, an adviser to the Bishop of Ely . . .'

'Spy for the Bishop of Ely,' corrected Bartholomew.

'. . . and a Fellow of Michaelhouse is a tiring business, and I need all the sustenance I can lay my hands on. Anyway, how did you come by this ridiculous notion that well-built men are unhealthy? Even a half-wit can see that the people who are ill most frequently are those who do not have enough to eat. Nearly all your patients are skinny people with appetites like sparrows.'

'But most of my patients are poor. The poor tend to be thinner than the rich, because they cannot afford the luxury of gluttony.'

'Well, there you are then,' said Michael triumphantly. 'Everyone knows the poor are subject to more diseases than the rich, and you have just acknowledged that poor people are thin. *Ergo*, being thin makes you susceptible to a greater number of illnesses. You are a strange sort of physician, Matt, always flying in the face of logic to form your own peculiar theories. No wonder your medical colleagues are convinced you are a heretic.'

'I do not have many medical colleagues left,' said Bartholomew dismally. 'Those who survived the plague have either died or moved on to more lucrative positions. Only Master Lynton from Peterhouse and Robin of Grantchester remain.'

'You should not claim Robin of Grantchester as a colleague,' advised Michael. 'First, he is a surgeon, not a physician. And second, he kills more people than he saves. I hear he is going to amputate Master Saddler's leg today, even though Saddler will gain more from a priest than a surgeon, from what I am told.'

'Robin plans to operate?' said Bartholomew, surprised. 'Saddler will not survive if he does. Amputation might have saved him two weeks ago, but not now. Robin is a fool to try.'

'He is a fool with three shillings in his pocket,' said Michael. 'He always collects payment in advance – if he did the honourable thing and only charged patients who lived, he would starve. And speaking of starving, there is the bell for the midday meal.' He beamed happily, Justus and the unsavoury image of Cambridge's surgeon firmly pushed from his mind as he anticipated happier things. 'We are just in time.'

Leaving the monk to hurry to his meal, Bartholomew went to wash in the basin of water that always stood on the floor of his room. It was a peculiarity of his that he always rinsed his hands after touching corpses, much to the disdainful amusement of his less fastidious colleagues. As he scrubbed them dry with a piece of sacking, he gazed out of his window.

In the dull, metallic light of November, the College looked stark and comfortless. With the exception of the hall and conclave, none of the windows had glass, and the scholars were faced with two choices: to close the shutters and have a room that was cold and dark, or leave them open for one that was very cold but light enough to see in. To compound the problem, Michaelhouse only provided fuel for fires in the communal rooms, not for individual chambers. Some scholars could afford to buy their own wood, but Bartholomew, with nothing but his Fellow's salary of four marks a year, could not. His training as a physician might have made him rich, but he found it more satisfying to treat the diseases and ailments of the poor, than to dispense purges and astrological advice to the wealthy. The fees paid by the few who could recompense him for his services only just covered the expenses incurred in providing for his less affluent clients.

He finished drying his hands and walked outside to the courtyard. The College was looking decidedly shabbier than it had done a year before, and parts were in desperate need of maintenance. Michaelhouse's founder had originally intended the yard to be cobbled, but somehow this had never transpired, and the rectangular patch of land enclosed by the hall, conclave and kitchens at one end, the porters' lodge and a sturdy wall at the other, and flanked by two opposing ranges of rooms where the scholars lived, was little more than a square of churned-up mud, the treacherous slickness of which was legendary throughout the town.

The hall itself was a handsome building, and had once been the home of a wealthy merchant called Roger Buttetourte. Buttetourte had used only the best materials, and his mansion had been built to last. The same was not true of the accommodation ranges, however. Michael's room, which was above Bartholomew's, had such a large hole in the roof that his students complained the moon shone through it and kept them awake. Bartholomew's own chamber had walls that ran dark with mildew, while the plaster fell away in rotten clumps, exposing the damp stones underneath.

Bartholomew picked his way across the quagmire of the yard, and climbed the steep spiral staircase that led to the hall. It had been a long time since breakfast, and, like Michael, the other scholars were hungry, so Bartholomew found he was the last to arrive. The high table, where the Fellows sat, was on a dais at the south end of the hall, while at right angles to it were two long trestle tables for the students and commoners. Every scholar was already at his place, standing behind the benches with his hands clasped in front of him as he waited for Master Kenyngham to say grace.

Beaming benignly, the Master waited until the physician reached his seat, while Michael sighed impatiently, his eyes fixed on the freshly baked bread. Bartholomew's students nudged each other and grinned; their teacher's absent-mindedness when he was engaged in medical matters often meant he was late for meals and it had become something of a joke with them.

As Bartholomew came to stand between Michael and Father William, he saw that two seats, which had been empty since a pair of Fellows had left to take up posts in Westminster Abbey, were occupied. He realised that the newcomers must be their successors, and studied them with interest.

One was the Dominican friar whom Master Kenyngham had mentioned the previous evening. He had a pale face and hair that stood up in a peculiar comb around the edge of his tonsure, and there was a fanatical gleam in his eyes. Bartholomew felt his heart sink. Here was no compliant cleric who would turn a deaf ear to the insults hurled at him and his Order by the belligerent Franciscan Father William, and the physician sensed that it would not be long before the two men found something to argue about.

The other newcomer wore the white robes of a Carmelite, and Bartholomew's spirits sank even further. Even if the Dominican and the Franciscan managed a truce, one of them would be bound to initiate some kind of dispute with the Carmelite. There were several Orders of mendicant friars in Cambridge, each of which loathed the others, and Michaelhouse had now managed to appoint representatives from three of them. He supposed he should be grateful that Kenyngham, who was a Gilbertine, and Michael, who was a Benedictine monk, usually remained aloof from the unseemly rows in which the others engaged with such fervour.

But the Carmelite, unlike the Dominican, did not look like the kind of man who enjoyed dissent. He was short and round, with a cheery red face that was creased with laughter lines. He smiled at Bartholomew when he saw he was being assessed, and Bartholomew smiled back, liking the merry twinkle in the man's eyes and the fact that he was not too overawed by Michaelhouse's formality to acknowledge a new colleague with a gesture of friendliness.

While Kenyngham flicked lovingly through his psalter to select the reading of the day, Bartholomew leaned around Father William and tapped the lawyer, John Runham, on the arm.

'I have some bad news,' he whispered. 'Your book-bearer is dead.'

'Dead?' asked Runham, startled. 'I do not think so! Justus served my dinner last night.'

'He died after that. Cynric found his body near Dame Nichol's Hythe this morning.'

'Damn!' muttered Runham, gazing at him irritably. 'What did he do? Jump in the river?'

'He tied a wineskin over his head,' said Bartholomew, feeling sorry for Justus in having a master who cared so little for him. Bartholomew would not have taken news of Cynric's demise with such casual indifference. 'He suffocated.'

Runham gave a mirthless smile. 'That sounds like Justus. If he had to take his own life, wine would have been involved somehow. Curse the man! Now I will have to find a replacement and I am busy this week. What a wretched inconvenience!'

'Especially for Justus,' retorted Bartholomew before he could stop himself. How Runham received the news of his book-bearer's death was none of his affair, and it was not for him to be judging his colleagues' relationships with their servants.

'Especially for me!' hissed Runham vehemently. 'You know how difficult it is to find reliable staff these days – we have the Death to thank for that, carrying off so many peasants. Justus could not have chosen a worse time to abandon me. I am willing to wager he did it deliberately.'

Shaking his head crossly, he turned to face the front, leaving the physician repelled by such brazen self-interest. He hoped Runham would remember that it was his responsibility to bury his dead servant, and that he would not leave the corpse to fester in the church for days until he decided he had sufficient time to undertake the necessary arrangements.

'Are we ready?' asked Kenyngham, cocking his head questioningly at Bartholomew, who realised that he had not assumed the attitude of prayerful contemplation usually required when the Master intoned the reading of the day. He bowed his head, and Kenyngham began to read, pausing at random moments to reflect on the sacred words in a way that had Michael sighing in hungry impatience. When Kenyngham had finally finished – or had paused sufficiently long to make his listeners suppose he had – there was a scraping of chairs and benches on the rush-strewn floor as the Fellows and students took their seats.

Kenyngham, however, remained standing, his psalter still open in his hands. For several confusing moments, no one spoke or moved. The servants were loath to begin bringing the food to the tables if their saintly Master were still in the throes of his prayers, while the scholars, who knew Kenyngham might continue to read until he had completed the entire book unless stopped, shot each other uneasy glances. Michael was the only one hungry enough – or irreligious enough – to remind the Master that he was not alone in an ecstasy of religious contemplation, but in his hall with the entire College waiting for its dinner.

'The food is getting cold,' he stated baldly.

Startled, Kenyngham glanced up from his psalter and regarded Michael in surprise, clearly having forgotten entirely where he was. He gazed around the hall at the watching scholars.

'Ah, yes,' he said, recollecting himself. 'I have an announcement to make.'

Another long pause ensued as his eyes slid downward to the hallowed words of the psalter, which were apparently more demanding of his immediate attention than his six Fellows, eight commoners and forty or so students.

Blind Father Paul smiled indulgently. 'That man is a saint,' he whispered in admiration. 'His whole existence is taken up with spiritual matters.'

'He is short of a few wits,' murmured Runham unpleasantly. 'I swear he barely knows where he is most of the time – unless it is in a church. It is not good for the Master of a College to be so ...' He hesitated, deliberating what word would best describe the eccentric Master of Michaelhouse.

'Unworldly,' suggested Bartholomew.

'Holy,' countered Paul.

'Odd,' stated the loutish Ralph de Langelee flatly, a man who had decided to become a scholar because his duties as spymaster for the Archbishop of York were not sufficiently exciting. He entertained high hopes that the scheming and intrigues in the University might furnish him with the adventure and exhilaration he craved. For the most part, he had not been disappointed.

'Unsuitable,' finished Runham firmly.

'What did you want to tell us, Master Kenyngham?' prompted Michael, eyeing the food on the platters near the screen at the far end of the hall.

Kenyngham cleared his throat, then beamed paternally at the assembled scholars. Before his mind could wander again, William almost snatched the psalter from him. Closing it, he laid it on the table. Kenyngham patted him on the head, as an adult might do to a child, much to the friar's consternation and the students' amusement.

'You may have noticed that we have two new faces at the high table,' said Kenyngham, gesturing to the Dominican and the Carmelite who sat on his left.

'Welcome, welcome,' said Michael, waving a hand that was more dismissive than friendly. When Cynric placed a basket of bread in front of him, he immediately selected the piece that was significantly larger than the rest. His colleagues, however, were more interested in the newcomers than in the rough bread baked from the cheapest flour the College could buy, or the thin bean stew that was now being distributed in greasy pewter bowls by the servants.

'Master Thomas Suttone,' Kenyngham continued, indicating the Carmelite, 'comes to us from Lincoln, where he has been vicar of one of the parish churches. He will teach the trivium – grammar, rhetoric and logic.'

'Good,' said William with feeling. 'I have been forced to teach the trivium since Alcote met his untimely demise in the summer, and I am heartily sick of it. Now Suttone can take over, and I can concentrate on what I am best at.'

'And what, pray, is that?' asked Langelee archly. 'Unmasking warlocks among the Dominicans?'

'When I was with the Inquisition . . .' began William hotly.

'We are pleased to have you at Michaelhouse, Master Suttone,' said Bartholomew quickly, before William could start down that track. The friar's tales of his ruthless persecution of 'heretics' in France were enough to put even Michael off his food, and Bartholomew did not want the new Fellows to wonder what they had let themselves in for on their first day.

'I am delighted to be here,' said Suttone, his red face breaking into a happy smile. 'As parish priest in Lincoln, my duties included teaching the city's children, who were lively and curious, but I missed the maturity and depth of adult minds, and I am looking forward to many hours of academic debate and disputation at Michaelhouse.'

'Lord help us!' whispered Langelee in alarm. 'He sounds like one of those thinking types.'

'This is a University,' replied Michael under his breath. 'We are supposed to harbour "thinking types" in our Colleges.'

'Lincoln,' mused William, regarding Suttone with suspicion. 'That is a heathen place, I hear.'

'It cannot be heathen,' said Bartholomew, smiling. 'It has a magnificent cathedral.'

'So does Paris,' replied William, pursing his lips as if

no more needed to be said on that matter. He turned his attention back to Suttone. 'Runham's book-bearer comes from Lincoln. You may find you have mutual acquaintances.'

'Excellent!' began Suttone. 'I will . . .'

'I hardly think that my wine-loving book-bearer and a Carmelite friar would have enjoyed the same company,' said Runham dryly.

'Especially not now,' muttered Michael, exchanging a glance with Bartholomew as they both thought about the sorry figure found dead on the river bank.

'Actually, Justus is—' began Bartholomew.

'Runham is right. Justus is a man more fond of taverns than churches,' said Langelee, reaching for his own cup, as if in sympathy. 'So, unless you like your ale, Suttone, I doubt you will have come across each other.'

'And John Clippesby, our second new Fellow, hails from Huntingdon,' said Kenyngham, speaking quickly before the conversation ran away from his introductions completely. 'He will teach astronomy and music.'

'*Music?*' queried William in disapprobation, making it sound like some disgusting vice. 'We have never had anyone teaching music at Michaelhouse before.'

'Then it is about time someone started,' said Father Paul, smiling sightlessly to where he thought the Dominican might be located. 'Music can be a wonderful thing.'

The other Fellows said nothing, but none of them looked at Michael, whose choir had managed to put most of them off that most noble of arts. The students murmured their own greetings to the two new-comers, to which Suttone responded with a friendly smile and Clippesby's intense face assumed the kind of expression he might have used had someone accused him of molesting his mother. Bartholomew wondered whether he was entirely sane – it would not be the first

time that a madman had been foisted on the University
by an Order that did not know what else to do with him.
Needless to say, Kenyngham did not notice Clippesby's
strange reaction to the students' affable greetings, and
continued with his announcement.

'Masters Suttone and Clippesby will be formally admitted to the Society of the Holy and Undivided Trinity,
the Blessed Virgin Mary and St Michael – to give us
our official name – on Saturday evening. That is in two
days . . . no three days . . .' He frowned in thought.

'It is the day after tomorrow, Master,' said William
irritably. 'Today is Thursday.'

Kenyngham nodded his thanks. 'And we will celebrate
the occasion with a feast.'

Michael almost choked. 'A feast? You cannot just snap
your fingers and have a feast! It takes planning and
preparation to arrange a decent feast. All we will have
on Saturday will be more of this miserable bread and
a double helping of this even more miserable stew. We
need at least a week to organise something worthwhile.'

'And I should like to take this opportunity to give you
a little more news,' Kenyngham went on, oblivious to
Michael's displeasure. 'I propose to resign as Master of
Michaelhouse on Saturday. Our two new members can
join our other Fellows – Brother Michael, Fathers William
and Paul, Doctor Bartholomew, and Masters Runham and
Langelee – in selecting one of their number to become
our next Master.'

Predictably, the gentle, unassuming Kenyngham was surprised and dismayed by the chaos that erupted following
his announcement, and was bewildered by the raised
voices and objections to his proposed retirement. It
took some time to restore order, at which point – in a
moment of rare common sense – he hastily signalled to

the Bible Scholar to begin reading, effectively preventing any further discussion during the meal.

When the last remnants of the food had been consumed by a scowling Michael, Kenyngham rose to say another grace, but was prevented from leaving the hall by the vicelike fingers of Father William, who seemed about to embark on an argument there and then, with all the students watching the dissension between their seniors with open interest.

'I suggest we Fellows adjourn to the conclave for an emergency meeting,' said Runham, before the friar could begin a diatribe. He turned to the two bemused newcomers. 'Perhaps you might care to join us. You will, after all, be expected to vote for the next candidate for the Mastership, so you had better see for yourselves what is on offer.'

He gave them a smile that was far from genuine, and Bartholomew immediately saw that the vain and pompous Runham intended to have his own name put forward as Kenyngham's successor. The physician grimaced: it was not an attractive proposition. Runham's cousin, Thomas Wilson, had been Master of Michaelhouse during the black days of the plague, and he had not been a popular Head of House. The similarity between the two men was such that Bartholomew could not imagine Runham would be any better.

He was about to follow the other Fellows into the conclave when Cynric arrived, breathing hard from a sprint across the courtyard. Since his marriage to a local seamstress at the end of the summer, contentment had added a ring of fat to the Welshman's waist, and he was now considerably less agile. He was also happier than Bartholomew had ever seen him, and he and Rachel Atkin were settling down to a life of domestic bliss that delighted them both.

'There has been an accident,' Cynric gasped. 'Someone has fallen from the scaffolding at Bene't College and hurt himself. One of their porters has come to ask if you will go. He is waiting for you at the gate.'

'I will come with you,' said Michael, following the physician towards the spiral stairs.

'There is no need,' said Bartholomew, giving the monk an admonishing look as he gave his bad arm a vigorous massage.

'There is every need,' muttered Michael, scratching his arm a second time just to prove he was master of his own itches. 'I do not want to spend the afternoon locked in the conclave with the likes of William, Langelee and Runham, all telling me to vote for them as our next Master.'

'You will have to do it eventually,' said Bartholomew. 'If not this afternoon, then later.'

'Later is better,' said Michael. 'By then, they will have aired their views – several times, I would imagine – and I will have escaped the worst of it. And anyway, I need a little time to consider my own campaign before I lock horns with the others.'

'You intend to stand, then?' asked Bartholomew, not at all surprised that an ambitious man like Michael should consider the Mastership of Michaelhouse a suitable prize for his talents.

Michael nodded. 'Of course. I am easily the best person for the task, and I do not want to lose just for the want of a little preparation.'

'What do you mean by "preparation"?' asked Bartholomew uneasily, suspecting that Michael's strategy might well involve some less than honest tactics.

'You will see,' said Michael enigmatically. 'But I should come with you anyway. A person injured or killed on University property is the business of the Senior Proctor, as I am sure you know by now.'

'I most certainly do,' said Bartholomew, not without rancour, for he had been dragged into all kinds of intrigue and murder by virtue of being the Senior Proctor's close friend.

'What about our meeting?' called Langelee indignantly, as they left the hall. 'What about discussing this decision of Master Kenyngham's?'

'We will have to gather later,' said Runham, casting predatory eyes over the newcomers, so that Bartholomew sensed he intended to make good use of the delay by winning their support for himself. 'We cannot discuss such a significant issue with a quarter of our membership absent.'

'When, then?' demanded William belligerently. 'This is important. We cannot postpone our discussion until Matthew decides he has no more pressing visits to patients.'

'Then how about after dinner tonight?' suggested Father Paul. 'William is right – we should meet as soon as possible to talk about this.'

'I am busy this evening,' announced Langelee importantly. 'I told you last week that I have been invited to dine with the Duke of Lancaster at Bene't College.'

'You certainly did,' muttered Michael nastily. 'At least six times that I recall.'

'I was invited – by the Duke himself, actually – because of my powerful and prestigious connections,' Langelee explained to Clippesby and Suttone, apparently deciding that Runham should not be the only one to start an immediate election campaign. 'You see, before I decided to make a name for myself as a scholar at Michaelhouse, I was in the service of the Archbishop of York. I know all kinds of influential people.'

'What Langelee is saying,' said Michael, noticing Suttone's bemusement at this unasked-for confidence, 'is that he is on intimate terms with archbishops and dukes, and that you should bear this in mind when you come to vote for our next Master. Essentially, he is soliciting your support, although in the hallowed halls of Cambridge, this is usually conducted with a little more subtlety.'

'I can be subtle,' objected Langelee indignantly. 'But I can also be direct, which is what this College needs. No one likes all this underhandedness and subterfuge . . .'

'I do,' said Michael.

'. . . and what we need is a Master who will be honest, candid and sincere,' Langelee continued.

'That should narrow the choices then,' mumbled Father Paul, uncharacteristically facetious.

'And that man is me,' concluded Langelee, favouring his colleagues with a blazing grin. 'I would make you a splendid Master.'

'It is refreshing to hear such confidence in one's own abilities,' said Runham dryly. 'But we need to arrange a meeting to elect a successor first. Since you are dining with royalty tonight, can I suggest that we meet after breakfast tomorrow morning?'

'I have business with my Prior then,' said William grandly. 'Business of a *religious* nature,' he elaborated, glancing meaningfully at Clippesby and Suttone to make sure they understood that while Langelee might have royal connections, his own influence lay where it really mattered – with the Prior of one of the most powerful Orders in Cambridge, not to mention God.

'I heard he has been summoned by his Prior to be reprimanded for fanning the flames of hostility between the Franciscans and the Dominicans again,' whispered Michael to Bartholomew, his eyes glittering with amusement. 'If William decides to stand for Master, you will have the opportunity to elect yourself an experienced and competent rabble-rouser.'

'Then I suggest the best time to meet is before the admissions ceremony on Saturday,' said Runham smoothly. 'I cannot see that the election of a new Master will take long, and I do not think we will delay the beginning of the feast unduly.' He smiled graciously at Suttone and Clippesby. 'But before then, perhaps I can show you around our College? And then I will answer any questions you might have over a cup of wine in my room.'

'Oh no, you do not!' protested Langelee, outraged. 'I know what you are trying to do! You are attempting to win the votes of these two, so that *you* will be elected Master!'

Runham looked hurt, and Michael gave a vicious snigger as he watched the exchange.

'Take one each,' he called, as he followed Bartholomew down the stairs. 'Then you will be even.' He chuckled as he walked across the yard. 'I feel almost sorry for Runham and Langelee. They are already entertaining high hopes that they will be elected. How can they even begin to imagine they have a chance when *I* intend to be Michaelhouse's next Master?'

'Do you indeed?' said Bartholomew. 'And what makes you think that those few – very few – of us Fellows who do not intend to make a bid for power ourselves will vote for you?'

'Voting!' exclaimed Michael disdainfully. 'This election will not be decided by voting.'

'It will, Brother,' said Bartholomew. 'That is how we elect Masters at Michaelhouse – by each Fellow writing the name of his preferred candidate—'

Michael made a dismissive sound. 'And I accused Langelee of being unsubtle! The Mastership of Michaelhouse is far too important to leave to that sort of chance. And the issue will not be decided on Saturday, either.

That is far too soon. I must see what can be done to delay matters.'

'I do not want to hear this,' began Bartholomew.

'No,' said Michael thoughtfully. 'It is better that you do not know my plans in detail. I do not want you revealing them to the opposition.'

'You mean you do not trust me?' asked Bartholomew, startled and rather hurt.

Michael sighed. 'I trust you in most things – more than I trust myself sometimes. But you do not have a clear grasp of University politics, and there is too much at stake to risk you inadvertently telling someone something he should not hear. But while we stand here, your patient is waiting. We should go before you dally so long that he needs my services rather than yours.'

As Bartholomew opened the door to his storeroom to collect his medicine bag, he saw three of his students in the courtyard and told them to read specific sections from Galen's *Prognostica* to the others, ignoring their obvious disappointment at losing what they had anticipated would be a free afternoon following Kenyngham's unexpected announcement.

'None of the other masters are making their students work today,' said Sam Gray sullenly, shoving his hands in his belt when Bartholomew tried to hand him the book.

'None of the other masters have students who have failed their disputations as many times as you have,' replied Bartholomew tartly. 'And, as I have told you before, there are plenty of students who will willingly take your place should you fail again.'

Gray said nothing, knowing that the shortage of physicians following the plague meant that newly qualified medics could pick and choose from the lucrative opportunities available, and that if he wanted to make his fortune, he would do well to stay with Bartholomew.

'He will read to the fourth-years, and I will read to the others,' said Tom Bulbeck, one of Michaelhouse's brightest scholars, who would soon be leaving to take up a position as house physician to the powerful Bigod family in the city of Norwich – a prestigious appointment that made Sam Gray green with envy.

'Or, if you like, I could show them how to dissect a rat – like you did last year,' offered Rob Deynman, Bartholomew's least gifted student. 'I remember how to do it exactly. You take a rat and a sharp knife, then cut through the stringy stuff to reach the purple bits—'

'No,' said Bartholomew hastily. 'Just listen to the Galen. And if any of my patients come, please fetch me – do not try to deal with them yourself.'

'Yes,' said Gray with spiteful glee. 'Look what happened last time – Agatha the laundress's teeth have been the talk of the town since you laid hands on them.'

Leaving them before *that* discussion could begin in earnest, Bartholomew hurried across the courtyard to the gate, where the Bene't College porter was waiting for him. Michael, having donned a handsome fur-lined black cloak against the winter chill, was not far behind.

'You took your time,' grumbled the porter, who had been slouching against the wall. 'Had to finish your meal, did you, while a man lies dying?'

'We will have none of that insolence, thank you very much,' said Michael sharply. He glared at the man, inspecting him closely as they walked up St Michael's Lane towards the High Street, where Bene't College was located. 'I know you. Our swords have crossed before.'

The man looked shifty. 'You probably met my brother, Ulfo. People say there is an uncanny resemblance between us.'

But Michael was not an easy man to fool. 'No, it is *you* I have encountered before.' He snapped his fingers. 'I remember now! You pummelled a student half to death last winter, and he made an official complaint against you for grievous assault.'

'I did not lay a finger on him,' snarled the porter angrily. 'He lied!'

'So your College said,' concurred Michael. 'The case was dropped, if I recall correctly.'

'Justice was done,' said the porter unpleasantly, so that Bartholomew had the impression that justice had not been done at all – at least, as far as the battered student had been concerned.

Michael scratched his arm thoughtfully. 'Osmun,' he said. 'That is your name.'

'So?' demanded Osmun aggressively. 'What of it? What has my name to do with you?'

'Let us hope it has nothing to do with me,' said Michael coolly. 'I do not want the likes of you warranting the attention of the Senior Proctor and his beadles again.'

His tone held a warning that Osmun was not so stupid as to ignore. He glowered at the monk, and began to walk more quickly as they neared Bene't College, effectively ending all further conversation.

Bene't was the newest of the University's colleges, and had been founded the previous year by wealthy townsmen in the guilds of Corpus Christi and St Mary. Its official name was the College of Corpus Christi and the Blessed Virgin Mary, but most people called it Bene't College because it stood on land that adjoined St Bene't's – or Benedict's – Church.

The two guilds intended their foundation to rival splendid Colleges like the Hall of Valence Marie and King's Hall, and masons and carpenters were busily erecting fine new buildings for the Master of Bene't and his scholars. A hall and one wing had already been completed, but the range that bordered the High Street was still under construction, and comprised a precarious shell of four walls clad in a jumble of scaffolding, ropes, pulleys and platforms. Seeing its haphazard nature and its proximity to the road, Bartholomew was surprised that there had not been an accident before.

'Bartholomew!' came an urgent voice from a group of people who stood in a tight huddle at one corner of the unfinished building. 'Here! Quickly.'

Bartholomew hurried forward when he recognised Master Lynton, the physician from Peterhouse. Lynton was a kindly man, with a halo of fluffy white hair that always reminded Bartholomew of a dandelion clock. He had done well for himself in his profession, and his patients were invariably the wealthiest and most influential people in the town – Lynton would never consider doctoring anyone unable to pay. His ideas on medicine, however, were conventional in the extreme, and he and Bartholomew seldom agreed on treatments or diagnoses. Bartholomew would have liked Lynton better had he been anything but a physician.

Bartholomew pushed his way through the fascinated onlookers, and crouched next to Lynton, who was trying without success to stanch the bleeding from a wound in the chest of a man who lay in the mud. Bartholomew took one look at the rapid, shallow breathing, the bluish lips and white face, and the awkward angle of the man's legs that indicated a broken back, and knew Lynton's efforts were futile.

Although there was nothing he could do to save the man who lay in a distorted heap at the base of the scaffolding that surrounded Bene't College, Bartholomew tried to make his last moments on Earth as comfortable as possible. He dribbled a concoction of poppy juice and laudanum between the blue lips, and took a clean compress from his medicine bag – always carried looped over his shoulder – to stem the bleeding from the chest wound.

Lynton sat back with a sigh of relief. 'Thank you, Bartholomew,' he said, flexing his bloodstained fingers and wiping them on his tabard. 'Now we should set about bleeding this poor fellow.'

'I think he has lost more than enough blood already,' replied Bartholomew, wondering how Lynton could possibly imagine that bleeding could hold any benefits for the dying man – other than perhaps to hasten his end.

'Will he live?' asked one of the spectators unsteadily, fixing Bartholomew with anguished eyes. Like the man who lay dying, he wore the distinctive blue tabard that marked him as a Fellow of Bene't College. He crouched next to his colleague, helplessly rubbing one of the cold, limp hands.

'If we make an incision in the foot, the blood will drain down and will lessen the flow from the chest,' said Lynton with great conviction. He pushed Bartholomew's hands away from the compress and applied the required pressure himself. 'I will stem the bleeding here, while you make the cut. You are the one who dabbles in cautery, not me.'

'But I do not practise phlebotomy,' said Bartholomew. 'And it will make no difference to this man anyway. A priest will be able to do more for him than physicians.'

'But we must save him,' protested Lynton. He glanced at the dying man, and then leaned towards Bartholomew confidentially, keeping his voice low. 'His name is Raysoun, and his friend is John Wymundham, both Fellows of Bene't. They are two of my most lucrative patients.'

'I am sorry,' said Bartholomew, also in a whisper. 'But there is nothing we can do. Raysoun's back is broken, he has already lost too much blood, and he is having difficulty breathing.'

'But I cannot afford to lose him,' said Lynton insistently. 'You must do something.'

Bartholomew could think of nothing to say, and instead glanced up to indicate to Michael that he should prepare to give Raysoun last rites. As the monk readied himself, the man's colleague – Wymundham – grabbed Bartholomew's shoulder in a grip that was unexpectedly strong for a man who gave an initial impression of being somewhat effete.

'You cannot give up on him!' he cried desperately. 'Look! His eyes are opening! He lives!'

Raysoun was gazing blankly at the sky, but his eyes were unfocused and Bartholomew thought him too badly injured to be aware of his surroundings. Wymundham bent close to him, gripping the hand he held so fiercely that Bartholomew was certain Raysoun would have objected, had he been able to feel it.

'Everything will be all right,' Wymundham whispered comfortingly. 'You had a fall, but you will live to make theologians of our students yet.'

'You must bleed him before it is too late, Bartholomew,' said Lynton, although with less fervour than before. 'I sent for the surgeon – Robin of Grantchester – but he is busy amputating a leg and cannot be disturbed. You must do it.'

'But Raysoun is dying,' said Bartholomew softly. 'Nothing we can do will save him, and if we bleed him, all we will do is risk causing him pain.'

Lynton gazed down at his patient, and Bartholomew thought he was going to argue. But the older physician merely nodded – as though he had known the futility of any treatment, but was just going through the motions – and then climbed to his feet and moved away, leaving Raysoun to Michael. Bartholomew went to stand next to him.

'What happened?' he asked, while Michael began intoning prayers for the dying. The injured man's friend seemed about to shove the monk away, but instead began exhorting Raysoun to stand up and walk back inside the College with him.

'Apparently, he fell from the scaffolding,' said Lynton. 'No one saw it happen, but the carpenters say he was clambering about up near the roof shortly before a passer-by found him lying in the road.'

'If he fell from the scaffolding, then why is he bleeding from his chest?' asked Bartholomew. 'It looks to me as though he landed on his back, not his front.'

Lynton pointed to a bloodied metal tool that lay on the ground. 'This was embedded in him when I arrived. I imagine he must have impaled himself on it as he fell.'

'But how?' asked Bartholomew, puzzled.

'I do not know,' said Lynton, a little impatiently. 'But look around you. The builders have scattered their implements very carelessly – I can see at least two more of those pointed things from here.'

'Awls,' said Bartholomew. 'Carpenters use them for making holes in wood.'

'Whatever,' said Lynton, uninterested. 'But the workmen should be forced to take more care. I will have a word with the Sheriff about this when I finish here – that half-finished building is dangerous. It is only a matter of time before someone is hurt by falling scaffolding.'

'You are right,' said Bartholomew, glancing up at the ramshackle array of planks that sheathed the growing College. 'Perhaps part of the road should be closed until the work is completed.'

'I will see what I can do,' said Lynton with a sigh. 'But it is a shame such precautions are too late for poor Raysoun.'

On the ground, Wymundham seemed to be having some kind of conversation with the dying man, putting his ear close to his lips. Michael lowered his own voice, aware that Raysoun might be making a confession that could mean a shorter sojourn in Purgatory. Bartholomew was surprised that Raysoun was even conscious, but supposed that a few moments of clarity before death were not impossible.

'I will miss him,' said Lynton, crossing himself as Michael smeared chrism on the dying man's forehead and mouth. 'I prescribed a weekly purge that was temperate in the first degree – very expensive.'

'Why?'

'To soothe his liver after he had over-indulged his penchant for wines.'

'He drank heavily?' Bartholomew had certainly noticed the smell of drink on the dying man as he had administered the medicine, and the half-empty wineskin that lay nearby had not escaped his attention, either.

Lynton made a curious gesture – half nod, half shrug. 'Recently he did. It did not agree with him, which is why he was obliged to summon me so often. But regardless of what he meant to me financially, it is hard to watch a man die knowing I am powerless to save him. It reminds me of the Death, which claimed so many of our patients, when all our years of training and experience as physicians were worse than useless.'

Bartholomew did not reply, because, for once, he understood Lynton's sentiment completely.

Raysoun took a deep, rasping breath before a rattle in the back of his throat told the silent onlookers that he had breathed his last. Wymundham stared down at him in disbelief, then released a blood-chilling howl of grief. Sensing that he might become hysterical, Bartholomew took his arm and quickly guided him back inside his

College, intending to deliver him into the hands of colleagues who would look after him. Michael and Lynton could deal with the body of Raysoun. He looked around for the porters, but they had joined the crowd outside, and so he walked with Wymundham across the courtyard to the building that was clearly the hall.

Bartholomew had never been inside Bene't before, and was impressed by the sumptuousness of those buildings that had been completed. The walls were made of good-quality stone purchased from the quarries at Barnack near Peterborough, and were a pleasing amber hue. Inside, the floors of the hall were polished wood – not just flagstones strewn with dried rushes like Michaelhouse's – and were liberally scattered with fine wool rugs. Large chests with handsome iron bindings stood at one end of the room, while the tables at which the scholars ate and which they used for lessons were carved from oak that had been buffed to an impressive sheen.

Wymundham slumped in a chair at the high table and put his head in his hands, sobbing loudly. Bene't was deserted, so Bartholomew went behind the serving screen, and found a jug of wine and some cups. He filled one and took it back to Wymundham, urging him to drink. Eventually, the man's weeping subsided, and he rubbed away his tears with a hand stained with his friend's blood. Bartholomew saw a basin filled with water on one of the windowsills, dipped a napkin in it, and gave it to the scholar so that he could clean his face. At Bartholomew's silent kindness, Wymundham began to weep afresh. The physician sat with him, waiting for him to compose himself.

Wymundham was not an attractive man. His narrow face had a rather vulpine look about it, and his small eyes were bright and beady. His mannerisms were fussy and effeminate, and under his scholar's tabard he wore hose of soft blue wool, so that his legs reminded Bartholomew of those of an elderly nun.

'I am sorry,' said Wymundham, wiping his nose on the napkin. 'It was the shock.'

'It is all right,' said Bartholomew gently. 'Is there anyone I can fetch to be with you? One of the other Fellows, perhaps?'

Wymundham shook his head. 'That will not be necessary, thank you. I am perfectly recovered now. As I said, it was the shock of seeing poor Raysoun die that distressed me. We were good friends. We were the first Fellows to be admitted to the College last year, you see.'

'If it is any consolation, I do not think he felt much,' said Bartholomew. 'In fact, it is likely that he did not even know what had happened to him.'

'Oh, he knew,' said Wymundham with sudden bitterness. 'He told me. Just before he died.'

'Told you what?' asked Bartholomew, confused. 'That he knew he had fallen?'

'That someone had killed him,' said Wymundham harshly. 'That is what shocked me, even more than seeing him lying there in all that blood.'

'You mean he told you that someone had murdered him?' asked Bartholomew, bewildered. 'But Master Lynton said he fell—'

'Someone stabbed him with one of those builders' spikes, and then shoved him off the scaffolding,' interrupted Wymundham, pursing his lips and regarding Bartholomew with bird-like eyes. 'That is what he told me as he died.'

'He may have been rambling,' said Bartholomew, wondering whether grief had turned Wymundham's mind. 'I had given him a powerful medicine to dull any pain he might have felt.'

'He was not rambling,' said Wymundham firmly. 'He sounded perfectly clear to me.'

'Then who pushed him?' asked Bartholomew, still doubtful. 'And why?'

Wymundham shrugged his thin shoulders. 'Our College is not a happy place, and the Fellows are always quarrelling and fighting.'

'You think one of the Fellows pushed Raysoun to his death?' asked Bartholomew, startled.

'That is what he told me,' said Wymundham, raising one of his fluttering hands to his face. 'And it is dreadful. Quite dreadful.'

'Did he say which Fellow?'

Wymundham gave a pained smile. 'Oh, yes. But when I became a member of Bene't College I swore an oath of allegiance, and I take it seriously. I will tell the Senior Proctor what Raysoun whispered with his dying breath, because I will be legally obliged to do so, but I should not gossip about it to anyone else.'

'Then shall I fetch Brother Michael for you?' asked Bartholomew.

Wymundham shook his head. 'I am not ready to face him yet. And I expect I look perfectly hideous. I will sit here quietly for a while and compose myself. Brother Michael will come to me when he has seen poor Raysoun's body removed to the church.'

Bartholomew refilled the cup, noting that Wymundham had regained some of his colour and that his hands were now steadier.

'You have been kind to me,' said the Bene't man, giving Bartholomew a weary smile. 'And you seem a sensible sort of fellow. I would very much like to confide in you, but it is better if I do not burden you with our unsavoury secrets – better for you, that is.'

'Brother Michael will be here soon,' said Bartholomew,

thinking Wymundham was absolutely right: he had no desire to be drawn into the murderous politics of another College and he certainly did not want to know who had killed Raysoun. 'You can tell him, then.'

'A divided College is a dreadful thing,' said Wymundham, almost to himself. 'You have no idea what it is like.'

'No, but I think I may be about to find out,' said Bartholomew, thinking about Kenyngham's resignation and the repercussions it would have. 'But if one of your Fellows *has* been murdered, then the whole town will know about it before long. It will be impossible to keep something like that quiet – you saw the crowd that had gathered around Raysoun's body.'

'You underestimate the power of the University,' said Wymundham, laying a hand on Bartholomew's knee and squeezing it gently. 'But I am sure you will learn.'

Bartholomew was only too aware of what the University could do in the town, probably far more so than the mincing, effeminate creature who sat opposite him dabbing at his eyes with the napkin with one hand, and with the other firmly clasped on the physician's knee.

'But you should go back to your students,' said Wymundham, releasing him abruptly. 'And I must prepare myself for the interrogation of the Senior Proctor.'

CHAPTER 2

L EAVING MICHAEL TO SEE RAYSOUN'S BODY TAKEN to the church and to interview the grieving Wymundham, Bartholomew left Bene't College, and started to walk slowly back to Michaelhouse. It was a market day, and he could hear the lows of cattle, the bleats of sheep and the squeals of pigs all the way from the High Street, not to mention the frenzied yells of the stall-keepers as they vied with each other to sell their wares.

His hands were stained red with the blood of the dead scholar, so he went to rinse them in the ditch that ran down the side of the High Street. The water that made his fingers ache from its coldness was probably tainted with sewage, offal and all manner of filth, but Bartholomew considered them all preferable to the blood of what promised to be a murdered man.

'Do I see you washing in the town's sewers?' came a cheerful voice from behind him. 'That is unlike you.'

Bartholomew turned in pleasure at the sound of his sister's voice. 'Edith! I thought you were at home, in Trumpington.'

Edith Stanmore, like her brother, had black curly hair, although hers now had a sprinkling of silver in it. Ten years older than Bartholomew, she was as different from him as it was possible to be, despite their physical similarities. She was ebullient, unfailingly cheerful, and firmly believed the world comprised only two kinds of people – good ones and bad ones.

'I love the peace of my husband's country manor,' said Edith, watching him scrubbing his hands in the murky water. 'Usually, I prefer it to the noise and muck of the town. But Oswald spends most of his time here with his business, we have a very efficient steward to run the estate, my son is studying in Oxford, and my little brother is far too busy healing the sick to walk the two miles to visit his boring old sister.'

'That is not true,' protested Bartholomew. 'You know I like to see you.'

'Yes? Then why do you not come more often? The last time you visited me was in September – before term started.'

'Really?' asked Bartholomew, genuinely surprised. 'I did not realise it had been so long.'

'So I gathered,' said Edith dryly. 'But the point of my rambling explanation is that I am bored in Trumpington, and so I travel to Cambridge with Oswald most days.'

'Most days?' queried Bartholomew, astonished. 'I have not seen you . . .'

'But I have seen you. Running here, dashing there, always much too preoccupied to stop for a leisurely chat with the wife of a mere merchant.'

'Never,' said Bartholomew firmly.

'But it is true,' she said, laughing. 'In fact, this is the first time I have even been able to catch up with you, you move so fast. But what are you doing, kneeling there in the filth? Preparing to wage war on the town again for the vileness of its ditches and streams?'

'Not this time,' he said, standing up and shaking his hands to dry them. 'And I have had enough of medicine for today anyway.'

'You tended the man who fell from the scaffolding and died?' asked Edith.

Bartholomew nodded. 'Were you there, then, among the onlookers?'

'No, but I heard people talking about it at the Trumpington Gate. Bene't should be forced to make that scaffolding safe. I said to Oswald only yesterday that someone was bound to injure himself on it soon. But you look as though you need a diversion from this, not a discussion of it. How is life at Michaelhouse?'

Bartholomew sighed, not certain that the change of topic was for the better. 'Kenyngham plans to resign on Saturday, which means that we will have to elect someone else as Master. I dread to think who it will be.'

Edith agreed wholeheartedly in the blunt fashion he found so endearing. 'Men of integrity and honour are a bit thin on the ground at Michaelhouse. Who will stand, do you think?'

'Michael already sees himself as the victor. Meanwhile, I am sure William, Langelee and Runham intend to provide him with some stiff competition. Fortunately, I imagine Paul knows he is too old, and the two Fellows due to be admitted the day after tomorrow are too new.'

'You would make a good Master,' said Edith fondly.

'I would make a terrible Master,' said Bartholomew, smiling at her loyalty to him. 'I would spend all our money on new cesspits, better drains and clean rushes for the floors, and have us bankrupt within a month. But I wish Kenyngham had waited. Thomas Suttone, one of the newcomers, seems a pleasant man, and may make a better Master than William, Langelee or Runham.'

'And Michael?' asked Edith curiously. 'He is your closest friend. Surely you will support him?'

Bartholomew hesitated. Michael had certainly assumed so, but Michael was a man who thrived on intrigue and subterfuge, and Bartholomew had always hoped that Michaelhouse would provide him with a haven from that sort of thing. Under Michael's Mastership, the College was likely to be the focus of more connivance and treachery than Bartholomew cared to imagine. But the alternatives offered by any of the others were almost too awful to contemplate.

'Yes,' he said finally. 'I will vote for Michael.'

'Well, I hope his other supporters are a little more enthusiastic,' she said wryly. 'If his dearest friend has such obvious reservations, what chance does he have of securing the confidence of those who see only his pompous and selfish exterior?'

'He is a good man,' said Bartholomew, immediately defensive. 'Well, most of the time.'

'He is not popular with everyone,' Edith pointed out. 'Not only that, but Oswald has heard that he has been indulging in secret meetings with scholars from the University of Oxford.'

'I sincerely doubt it,' said Bartholomew. 'Michael has always been very firm about his disdain for our rival university, and anyway, he has far too much to do in Cambridge to indulge in plots with Oxford. And what is wrong with Oxford, anyway? I studied there, and so does your son.'

'I have no feelings about the place one way or the other; I am only repeating what I was told. But do not look so gloomy, Matt. At least we can be sure that no one will be stupid enough to vote for that horrible Runham.'

'Langelee would be worse,' said Bartholomew.

'I am not so sure,' said Edith. 'But if you choose not to support Michael, you should vote for William. He will agree to anything when he is drunk – if you can bear to listen to his gruesome stories about the Inquisition – and all you will need to do, if you want something, is to ply him with wine each night. You need not even invest in a good-quality brew, because William will drink anything.'

Bartholomew laughed, enjoying his sister's easy company. He took her arm and began to walk with her along the High Street. He could have returned to his duties in the College, but Kenyngham's announcement had dismayed him, and he did not want to be plunged back into the intrigues that would be brewing as ambitious hopefuls lobbied their colleagues for votes. Instead, he strolled with Edith to the Market Square, where they bought hot chestnuts that they ate as they watched the antics of a knife-thrower.

'How does he do that?' asked Bartholomew, trying to gain a better position to see the nature of the trick he was certain was involved. 'It is not possible to be so consistently accurate.'

'Oh, Matt! Must you be so analytical?' cried Edith, poking him in the ribs with an elbow. 'Just enjoy the spectacle. And speaking of enjoyment, have you seen Matilde recently?'

Bartholomew shook his head. 'I have seen very little of her since I returned from Suffolk in June. Kenyngham gave me an additional six students this year, and I have been struggling to try to fit in all the lectures they should have. I cannot recall ever having been so busy.'

'There were rumours that you were sent to Suffolk in the first place because of your friendship with Matilde,' said Edith bluntly.

'A friendship with a prostitute is not something the University encourages,' said Bartholomew, suspecting that the stories held a grain of truth, and that his colleagues had indeed contrived to send him away from the town to allow time for his relationship with the pretty courtesan to cool. 'It is particularly frowned on for Fellows, who are supposed to be setting a good example to the students.'

'It seems to me that these additional six students are no accident, Matt. Your friends are trying to keep you occupied, so that you will have no time to pursue a life outside their stuffy halls.'

Bartholomew realised she was probably right, and smiled at himself for being so naïve, knowing he should have seen through his colleagues' machinations.

'You should marry, Matt,' said Edith, regarding him critically. 'Or you will turn into one of those dreary old men who are only interested in the food and drink they devour at high table.'

'I hope not,' said Bartholomew with a shudder. 'Michaelhouse is not noted for the quality of its fare. I should be in a sorry state indeed if I lived only for that.'

She shot him an anxious, sidelong glance. 'You are not thinking of taking the cowl, are you, as Michael is always trying to persuade you to do?'

'No,' he said, turning his attention back to the knife-thrower. 'I would not make a good monk.'

'Then give up this life at the University, and practise medicine in the town – with real people, not drunkards, gluttons and power-mongers, who either loathe women or like them too much. And marry! You are a handsome man, and it is a waste for you to be celibate.'

'But in order to marry, there needs to be a compliant woman, and there do not seem to be many of those around.'

'Then I shall find you some,' said Edith, sensing a challenge. 'Leave it to me.'

'No, thank you,' said Bartholomew in alarm, knowing from past experience that the ladies Edith was likely to consider would be wholly unacceptable. It was not that he was fussy – he was an easygoing man who invariably found something to enjoy in most people's company – but he did not want to spend his evenings in stilted conversation with someone who had nothing to discuss but the price of fish or the state of her wardrobe.

'I can think of several,' said Edith, ignoring his objection. 'Please do not try to pair me off with the first available

female you encounter,' he pleaded. 'Michaelhouse may
have its disadvantages, but I am happy there. I do not
want to be trapped in a loveless marriage.'

Edith pursed her lips. 'You should put more trust in
me, Matt. I know what I am doing.'

He regarded her uncertainly, not at all sure that she
did.

While Bartholomew tried to distract her with some
coloured ribbons being sold by a chapman, Edith began
a sweeping search of the Market Square to see whether
she could locate a suitable partner there and then. He saw
her eyes linger briefly on the substantial figure of Adela
Tangmer, the daughter of an immensely wealthy vintner,
and felt his spirits flag. Adela's consuming passion was
horses, and Bartholomew, who knew little more about
them other than that they had four legs and a tail,
suspected he would be a bitter disappointment to her.
Even discussing the price of fish held more appeal to him
than endless monologues about fetlocks and foaling and
the merits of deep chests.

But, with relief, he recalled that Edith did not like
Adela Tangmer, and even the prospect of seeing her
brother happily married would not induce her to recommend Adela to him. Edith considered Adela overbearing,
and disliked her mannish ways. However, Adela had a
half-sister who was very different, and Edith had extolled
the virtues of Joan Tangmer on a number of occasions.

He was relieved when Edith's gaze moved on. To his
horror, though, he saw her look rather keenly at the
willowy form of old Mistress Mortimer, the long since
widowed mother of the town's spice merchant, who was
easily old enough to be Bartholomew's grandmother. He
saw Edith give an almost imperceptible shake of her head,
although he could tell that Mistress Mortimer had by no

means been permanently discounted as a prospective sister-in-law. Edith then began to assess the three young step-daughters of Mayor Horwoode, the oldest of whom was barely past puberty.

'No,' said Bartholomew firmly, as Edith opened her mouth to speak.

'Hello, Matthew,' came a loud, braying voice behind them that made them both start. It was Adela Tangmer. 'And Edith, too. What brings you from the country to the town? Rat poison?'

'I beg your pardon?' asked Edith suspiciously. She was not the only one to be nonplussed: Bartholomew also had no idea what Adela was talking about.

'Rat poison,' repeated Adela. She put her hands on her hips and regarded Edith and Bartholomew askance. 'Do not tell me that you did not know the Franciscan friars always sell their famous rat poison on the last Thursday of the month? I thought the sale of one of the most vital commodities known to man was an event of national significance!'

'I do not think about rats very often,' replied Edith archly. 'But my husband usually lays in a store of the Franciscans' poison, and I leave such matters to him.'

'I would never trust a man with something so important,' declared Adela. 'If I left the purchase of rat poison to my father, we would be overrun and eaten alive in a week! And, of course, I have the nags to think of – they do not appreciate rats in their hay at all.' She gave them a grin full of big yellow incisors.

'What a handsome dress,' said Edith, looking down at the unattractive brown garment that fitted Adela's heavy body like a sack around corn. 'It suits you very well.'

Bartholomew held his breath, certain that Adela would know she was being insulted. Adela, however, took Edith's words at face value.

'Well, thank you. It is a little faded, but it is one of my favourites. It is excellent for riding, because the grease in it means the rain runs off instead of soaking through, and it is much more comfortable than the tight garments that are so fashionable these days. Do you not agree, Matthew?'

'It has been some time since I went riding in a dress,' said Bartholomew, 'so I am not in a position to say.'

Adela roared with laughter and gave him a hefty slap on the shoulders that made his eyes water. 'I heard your husband bought that new filly from Mayor Horwoode,' she said to Edith conversationally. 'She will be a good investment for him – she is a sweet-tempered beast.'

'Speaking of sweet tempers,' said Edith, 'Matt was just saying that he felt the men at the University should see more of the town's women.'

'I was not,' said Bartholomew, startled. 'I—'

'It is a good idea,' continued Edith, cutting across him as though he had not spoken. 'It would make them all less aggressive, and they would have a more rational view of life. Him included.'

'Good breeder,' said Adela.

Bartholomew and Edith gazed at her uncomprehendingly.

'The filly,' said Adela. 'She will be a good breeder. I can always tell, you know. It is all to do with the shape of the flanks.'

'Will you and your sister Joan be going to watch the mystery plays outside St Mary's Guildhall next week?' asked Edith, giving Bartholomew a none too subtle dig in the ribs, prompting him, he presumed, to display some kind of interest in accompanying Joan.

'Lord, no!' said Adela, hands on hips. 'I have a foal due soon – an unusual time of the year, but there it is. No predicting nature, eh, Matthew?'

'But Joan . . .' began Edith.

'Joan is betrothed to Stephen Morice, so I imagine he will take her,' said Adela carelessly. 'He is a wealthy man and a burgess, too. It is a good match, and it is about time she stopped mourning for the husband she lost to the plague.'

Edith shot Bartholomew a withering look that implied the impending marriage was his fault for not acting sooner.

'You will miss her when she goes to live with Morice,' said Bartholomew, who knew that Adela, Joan and their father Henry Tangmer all shared a house on Bridge Street.

'More than you can possibly imagine,' said Adela fervently. 'My father has been urging us to marry for years, and now she is betrothed, I will have to bear the brunt of his complaints alone. But I suppose that is the way of families. Does Edith nag you about your reluctance to select a spouse, Matthew?'

'She does,' agreed Bartholomew.

'I do not,' said Edith, at the same time.

Adela looked from one to the other in amusement. 'Actually, I am pleased to have run into you, Matthew,' she went on cheerfully. 'Do you have any tried and tested remedies for ending unwanted pregnancies?'

Once again, Bartholomew and Edith gazed at her speechlessly. Her voice had been loud, and one or two people had overheard. It was hardly a matter for bellowing across the Market Square, and abortion was not looked upon kindly by the authorities. If Bartholomew was caught dispensing that sort of treatment, losing his licence would be the least of his worries.

'It is not for me,' Adela bawled, giving her braying laugh when she saw what they were thinking. 'One of my old nags is pregnant, and I do not think she will survive bearing another foal. I am fond of her, and do not want her to die.'

'Sorry,' said Bartholomew, keenly aware that people were still looking at them. 'I have no idea what would end a pregnancy in a horse.'

'Just tell me what you recommend for people, then,' pressed Adela, undeterred. 'I often use human remedies on my horses – and sometimes they even work. Perhaps I could give you some of my horse cures, and you could adapt them for use on your patients. That would be jolly.'

'Not for my patients,' said Bartholomew, edging away.

'Do not be so narrow-minded,' Adela admonished him. 'But you can always let me know if you change your mind. You know where I live. Goodbye.'

She strode away, an eccentric figure in her old-fashioned wimple and unflattering dress. The handsome blue riding cloak and well-made leather shoes were the only indication that she was a woman of some wealth. When she was out of earshot, Bartholomew started to laugh.

'Not her,' said Edith, laughing with him. 'I do not want a sister-in-law who will raise that sort of topic at the dinner table. Now let me see.' She began to scan again.

'I must go,' said Bartholomew quickly. 'My students . . .'

He faltered, looking across the Market Square to the Church of the Holy Trinity. He was considerably taller than Edith, and so she could not see what had made him stop speaking mid-sentence. She craned her neck and stood on tiptoe, hoping that a woman had smitten him with her charms at first sight.

'What is the matter? Who can you see?'

Bartholomew's gaze was fixed on a figure in a blue tabard who slunk along the back of the church, weaving between the grassy grave mounds. John Wymundham, Fellow of Bene't College and friend of the lately deceased

Raysoun, looked around him carefully, before opening the church door and disappearing inside.

'That is odd,' said Bartholomew. 'That was Wymundham. His friend has just died – murdered, he says – and he was supposed to be talking to Michael about it.'

'Oh no, Matt!' cried Edith in dismay. 'Not murder again! Now you will never have time to meet the ladies I select for you.'

'Every cloud has a silver lining,' he said, grinning. 'But I am not involved in this – all I did was tend Raysoun as he lay dying. Solving the crime is Michael's work, not mine.'

'So, why were you staring at Wymundham with such intense interest?' asked Edith, unconvinced.

'Wymundham said he would wait for Michael in Bene't College, but here he is, wandering around the town.' Bartholomew shrugged. 'I suppose it means nothing. Perhaps Michael was too busy to see Wymundham today, and agreed to interview him another time.'

But it seemed strange that Michael would not want to discover from Wymundham who Raysoun claimed had killed him. Bartholomew glanced up at the sky. More time had passed than he had realised since he had met Edith. Perhaps Wymundham had already spoken to Michael, and felt the urge to sample the calming effects of a few prayers.

However, Edith was right – the affair had nothing to do with him, and he should not waste his time thinking about it. She had already dismissed Wymundham and his dead friend from her mind, and was pulling her brother's arm, leading him to where a fire-eater was entertaining an entranced crowd. Bartholomew forgot Wymundham and Raysoun, yielded to her insistent tugs, and spent the next hour trying to ascertain why the fire-eater was not covered in burns.

*   *   *

The following day was typically busy for Bartholomew. He rose long before dawn to spend some time on his treatise on fevers, working quickly and concisely in the silence of the night, using the light from a cheap tallow candle that smoked and made his eyes water. At dawn, he walked with the other scholars to St Michael's Church, and then ate a hasty breakfast before being summoned to the hovels where the riverfolk lived, to tend a case of the sweating sickness.

After that, he dashed back to the College to start teaching in the hall, ignoring the admonishing glare shot at him by Runham for being late for his lecture. His younger students were restless and unable to concentrate on their lessons, obviously far more interested in speculating on which of the Fellows might succeed the gentle Kenyngham as Master.

His older students were not much better, and he could see their attention was wandering from the set commentary on Galen's *De Urinis*. Bartholomew was not particularly interested in contemplating the ins and outs of urine on a cold winter morning, either, but it had to be endured if the scruffy lads assembled in front of him ever wanted to be successful physicians.

When the bell rang for the midday meal, Cynric came to tell him that he was needed at the home of Sam Saddler, a man afflicted with a rotting leg. Bartholomew had recommended amputation two weeks before, but Saddler had steadfastly refused. Robin of Grantchester had finally relieved him of the festering limb the previous day, and Bartholomew was astonished that Saddler had survived the surgeon's filthy instruments and clumsy stitching. Saddler's hold on life was tenacious, but Bartholomew knew it was a battle Death would soon win. The flesh around the sutures was swollen and weeping, and angry red lines of infection darted up the stump of leg.

Bartholomew always carried a plaster of betony for infected wounds, but Saddler's state was beyond the efficacy of any remedy that Bartholomew knew about, although he spent some time trying to help. He prescribed a syrup to dull the pain, and warned Saddler's two daughters to be ready to send for a priest within the next two days.

On his way back to Michaelhouse, he saw Adela Tangmer, arm in arm with her father, although who was leading whom was difficult to say. Adela strode along in her customary jaunty style, but the vintner walked stiffly, every step suggesting that something had deeply angered him. Bartholomew tried to slip past unnoticed, but Adela was having none of that.

'Hello, Matthew,' she boomed across the High Street, making several people jump. 'We have just been to a meeting of my father's guild, Corpus Christi. What a dreadful gaggle of people – all arguing and bickering. They need to get out more – do a bit of riding and see the world.'

'Bene't College is at the heart of it,' muttered Tangmer furiously. 'I wish to God the Guild of St Mary's had never persuaded us to become involved in that venture.'

'Why?' asked Bartholomew curiously.

'We were doing perfectly well in establishing a modest little house of learning, but that was not good enough for the worthy people of the Guild of St Mary,' said Tangmer bitterly.

'They brought in the Duke of Lancaster as a patron,' explained Adela. 'He donated some money, but we have just learned that there are strings attached.'

'You mean like a certain number of masses to be said for his soul?' asked Bartholomew. 'Similar conditions were imposed by Michaelhouse's founder, Hervey de Stanton. We are obliged to say daily prayers for him.'

'I wish that were all!' muttered Tangmer. 'Prayers cost nothing, especially if someone else is saying them.'

'The Duke wants Bene't to rival King's Hall and the Hall of Valence Marie for splendour,' said Adela. 'The only problem is that his donation will not cover all the costs, and so the guilds of Corpus Christi and St Mary are obliged to provide the difference. And money spent on Bene't would be better spent on good horseflesh.'

'Do you think of nothing but horses, woman?' asked Tangmer in weary exasperation. 'You should marry – that would concentrate your mind on other matters.'

'I do not want to marry,' said Adela with the same weary exasperation. 'I like my life the way it is.'

'What about you, Bartholomew?' asked Tangmer, eyeing the physician up and down speculatively. 'You are not betrothed, are you? Adela would make a fine wife for a physician.'

Adela closed her eyes, although whether from embarrassment or because the topic of conversation was tiresome to her, Bartholomew could not tell.

'She certainly knows her remedies for equine ailments,' he agreed carefully. 'But Fellows are not permitted to marry, Sir Henry. I regret to inform you that I am not available.'

'Pity,' said Tangmer. 'I shall have to think of someone else.'

'Do not trouble yourself, father,' said Adela. 'If I decide I want a man, I am quite capable of grabbing him for myself.'

Bartholomew was sure she was. He made his farewells, and resumed his walk to Michaelhouse. As he approached it, a thickset figure uncoiled itself from where it had been leaning against the wall. It was Osmun, the surly porter from Bene't College.

'I have been waiting for you,' he said, moving towards

Bartholomew in a manner that was vaguely threatening. The physician took two steps backward, and wondered whether his book-bearer would hear him from inside Michaelhouse if he shouted for help.

'What do you want?' he asked uneasily. 'Is someone ill?'

'If they were, I would not send for you to help,' replied Osmun nastily. 'I would rather call on Robin of Grantchester.'

'I do not have time for this,' said Bartholomew, trying to edge past the man. He recoiled at the stench of old garlic and onions on Osmun's breath as the porter suddenly moved forward and grabbed a fistful of Bartholomew's tabard.

'Runham's servant Justus was my cousin,' he hissed. 'He was my uncle's son, and he came to Cambridge from Lincoln because I said there were opportunities to be had here. But now he is dead. He killed himself with a wineskin.'

'I am sorry,' said Bartholomew, shrugging Osmun's dirty hand from his clothes. 'I did not know you were related.' He refrained from suggesting that a little family support might not have gone amiss when Justus was in some of his more gloomy moods.

'I want his personal effects,' Osmun went on. 'He had a nice tunic and a dagger. He spent all his money on wine, but I will have his clothes and that knife he always carried.'

'I will inform Runham,' said Bartholomew. 'We did not know he had any kinsmen in the town.'

'We did not see much of each other,' said Osmun, almost defiantly. 'But as his closest living relative, I am entitled to his things. Make sure they are sent to me.'

'Very well.' Bartholomew paused, his hand on the latch to the wicket gate. 'As Justus's next of kin, you may find yourself responsible for his burial, as well as his personal effects. I am sure Runham will be delighted to be relieved of that particular duty.'

'Oh, no,' said Osmun confidently. 'I checked all that before I came here. Justus's burial is Michaelhouse's responsibility, because he was Runham's servant. You just make sure that fat lawyer understands that. I know my rights.'

He turned and strode away, leaving Bartholomew alone. The physician had only just closed the gate, when Cynric came to greet him, telling him he had been asked to visit Sheriff Tulyet's home as soon as possible.

Abandoning hope of getting anything to eat, he trudged back through the muck of the High Street to the handsome house on Bridge Street where Richard Tulyet lived with his wife and child.

Bartholomew liked Tulyet, a small, energetic man whose boyish appearance belied a considerable strength of character and a rare talent for keeping law and order in the uneasy town; he found he was looking forward to paying a visit to the Sheriff's neat and pleasant home.

Tulyet's son, a lively youngster of three with quick fingers and an inquisitive mind, had managed to insert a stick of his father's sealing wax in his nose, and it was stuck fast. While the anxious parents hovered and offered unhelpful advice and Baby Tulyet screamed himself into a red-faced fury, Bartholomew struggled to extricate the wax in one piece.

When it was done, and the child was all smiles and false innocence in the comfort of his loving mother's lap – although the physician saw chubby fingers already reaching for his father's official seal – Tulyet offered Bartholomew some refreshment in the small room at the back of the house that he used as an office.

'I would keep this locked, if I were you,' said Bartholomew, seeing in the cosy chamber an impressive array of sharp, heavy, sticky, dirty and fragile objects that would provide Baby Tulyet with hours of dangerous delight.

'I will, from now on,' said Tulyet, handing Bartholomew some rich red wine in a carved crystal goblet. He prodded at the fire that burned merrily in the hearth, and indicated for the physician to make himself comfortable. Bartholomew sat, stretching his hands to the flickering flames.

The Sheriff gave a huge sigh, and took a substantial gulp of wine, before collapsing heavily into the chair opposite. He wiped an unsteady hand over his face, shaken by his son's howls of fright and pain. Evidently considering the traumas of parenthood more terrifying than mere law enforcement, he changed the subject.

'I hear your scholars are murdering each other again, Matt. I am glad it is Brother Michael's task to investigate matters involving the University and not mine. You academics seldom commit good, simple crimes – you always seem to go in for convoluted ones.'

'Who told you a murder was committed?' asked Bartholomew, surprised. 'I did not think Raysoun's claim was common knowledge yet. Or do you mean Justus the book-bearer? He committed suicide.'

'I was referring to the Franciscan who was killed this morning,' said Tulyet, eyeing him askance. 'My God, Matt! How many deaths have there been in that festering pit of crime and disorder that you see fit to call a place of learning?'

'Just the two,' said Bartholomew. 'Well, three, I suppose, if you say a Franciscan has died.'

'Three deaths! In less than two days!' exclaimed Tulyet, appalled. 'As I said, give me good, honest town criminals any day. But have one of these "hat-cakes". My wife bakes them for me because she thinks I am too thin for the good of my health.'

Tulyet's wife was an excellent cook, and her husband's wealth meant that she could afford to use ingredients beyond the purse of most people. The cakes were tiny hat-shaped parcels of almond pastry filled with minced pork, dates, currants and sugar, and flavoured with a mixture of saffron, ginger, cinnamon and cloves. They were overly sweet, but Bartholomew was hungry. He took a second.

'So, what do you know about this Franciscan?' asked Bartholomew. 'Are you sure his death was suspicious?' He took a third cake.

'His name was Brother Patrick and he was stabbed in the grounds of his hostel, apparently. Given that he was knifed in the back, suicide has been ruled out, although there were no witnesses.'

'Then it might have been a townsperson who killed him – in which case, the matter is for you to investigate, as well as Michael.'

Tulyet shook his head. 'It happened on University property to a University member. This murder is all Michael's.'

'Which hostel?' asked Bartholomew, reaching for the last cake.

'Ovyng, I believe.'

'Ovyng belongs to Michaelhouse,' said Bartholomew absently. 'But speaking of Michaelhouse, I should go unless I want to be late for this afternoon's lectures. Let me know if there are any problems with your son's nose, Dick, but I do not think there will be.'

'Good,' said Tulyet, following Bartholomew down the stairs and across the hall to the main door. 'We are lucky he is always so well-behaved for you – he is terrible with Master Lynton.'

Bartholomew, recalling the violent struggles and the

ear-splitting howls of rage and indignation, decided he did not want to see Baby Tulyet being 'terrible'. He made his farewells to Tulyet, and hurried back to the College, where the bell to announce the beginning of the afternoon lectures had already stopped ringing. He clattered into the hall late, feeling sick from the number of hat-cakes he had eaten, and found it hard to muster the enthusiasm to talk about urine inspection.

Father William had also heard about the murder of one of his Franciscan brethren in Ovyng Hostel, and was busy holding forth about the Devil's legion – referring to the Dominicans – who stalked the holy streets of Cambridge. Given that Tulyet had said there were no witnesses to the murder – and certainly nothing to suggest that the Franciscan's killer was a Dominican – Bartholomew considered William's comments ill-advised and dangerous. He noticed that Clippesby, the new Dominican Fellow whose sanity seemed questionable, was listening, and did not seem at all amused to be classified as an agent of the Devil by the ranting Franciscan.

William had an impressive voice, and his words thundered around the room, making it almost impossible for the others to teach. Master Kenyngham asked him to moderate his tones twice, but the volume gradually crept up again as the friar worked himself into a frenzy of moral outrage. Father Paul listened to his fellow Franciscan's speech with growing horror.

Michael was also late for his teaching, although his small band of dedicated Benedictines and Cluniacs – who had already committed themselves to life in the cloister – were not the kind of men to cause a riot in the hall if left unsupervised, as Bartholomew's secular students might. They sat in a corner near the window, reading from a tract written by St Augustine, discussing its layered meanings in low, refined voices.

Michael stopped to mutter in Bartholomew's ear as he passed. 'A friar from Ovyng has been murdered. Someone stuck a knife in his back, and his body was found in the garden this morning. Unfortunately, there are no witnesses. The killer might have been another student, I suppose – bitter jealousies are always rife in the hostels.'

'And the Colleges,' added Bartholomew, thinking about the troubles Wymundham had intimated were rampant at Bene't, not to mention the spectre of the forthcoming election for Michaelhouse's new Master.

'True,' said Michael. 'But, I confess, I hold little hope that I will discover who killed Brother Patrick – unless someone confesses to the crime. I could question the Dominicans, I suppose, but that would only give them an excuse to march against the Franciscans, and then who knows what mischief might occur?'

'Are you going to ignore it, then?' asked Bartholomew, surprised. 'A man has been murdered, Brother. You cannot just pretend it did not happen.'

'I will not pretend it did not happen,' snapped Michael crossly. 'But I do not see how I can proceed on the scanty evidence I have. Brother Patrick had only been at Ovyng since the beginning of term, and no one knew him well. I imagine he allowed himself to become embroiled in a fight with some apprentices and ended up stabbed.'

'You should try asking questions in the taverns,' suggested Bartholomew. 'You know the apprentices would brag if they had killed a scholar.'

Michael gave a heavy sigh. 'I would never presume to tell you to jab a knife into a boil to drain away the evil humours, so you might at least do me the courtesy of assuming that I know perfectly well how to investigate a murder. I have been Proctor for three years now.'

'My apologies, Brother,' said Bartholomew. 'Of course you know what you are doing.'

'I have beadles in taverns all over the town even as we speak,' continued Michael testily. 'I could have done without a murder today, though. I wanted to concentrate on my bid for the Mastership and I have not had a moment all day to work on my plan.'

'Brother Patrick should have been more considerate,' said Bartholomew facetiously. 'He should have waited until after Saturday to get himself murdered.'

Michael glowered at him, but then relented. 'I am sorry, Matt. Of course I am doing all I can to track down this killer, and of course it has prior claim to my attention – that is what is making me angry. If I were a less conscientious man, I would abandon the investigation to my beadles and set about having myself elected. But I am not, and I spent the morning looking for a killer, instead of having words in friendly ears.'

'Matthew!' bellowed William irritably. 'Do not stand there chatting with Michael while your students run wild, man! I cannot hear myself think with all their racket.'

The hall erupted into a chaos of catcalls and cheers, as the students expressed their view of William's comment. Their masters, who without exception found the friar's loud diatribes disruptive, grinned at each other, and made no attempt to silence the din. William stood with his big red hands dangling at his sides and looked around him in genuine bewilderment.

Michael wiped away tears of laughter with his sleeve, his bad temper forgotten. 'That man is priceless, Matt! I would not be without him for the world. It has been a long time since I have had anything to laugh about.'

Bartholomew, thinking about the murdered friar at Ovyng, the killing of Raysoun from Bene't College, the suicide of Justus, and the impending battle with

William, Runham and Langelee for the Mastership of Michaelhouse, imagined it might be a while before an opportunity arose for Michael to laugh again.

The following day was equally busy. Teaching finished early on Saturdays, but Bartholomew had no time to enjoy a free afternoon with his colleagues in the conclave – nor did he have any desire to do so, with those Fellows who intended to make a play for the Mastership being uncharacteristically affable. Even Runham, who usually made no secret of the fact that he disapproved of Bartholomew's work with the poor, was politely interested in it, and went so far as to present him with a basket of eggs to aid the recovery of the riverman with sweating sickness. Runham had never shown such generosity or compassion before and his transparent motives did not make Bartholomew any more inclined to vote for him.

Bartholomew spent most of the afternoon pulling the teeth of a man with an inflamed jaw, and then was called to the Castle, where one of Sheriff Tulyet's soldiers had suffered a deep cut during sword practice. It was almost dusk by the time he had finished, but Cynric was waiting with yet another summons from a patient when he returned. He set off in the fading light, nodding to people he knew as he went, and shivering as the chill wind cut through his clothes. The air held the promise of rain, and it was not long before it was falling in misty sheets.

The patient was called Rosa Layne, and she was dying because there were too few trained midwives in Cambridge to deal with the number of pregnancies. Some unscrupulous women took advantage of this and claimed qualifications and experience they did not have; one of them had tended Rosa. By the time the charlatan had acknowledged her incompetence and suggested that a physician should be summoned, it was too late for

Rosa. Before Bartholomew arrived, the bogus midwife had vanished into the darkness.

There was little Bartholomew could do. The baby had twisted in the womb, but had needed only to be turned and then helped out. The self-appointed midwife had dallied so long that the baby had died, and then had dallied more while the mother slowly bled to death. It was not the first time Bartholomew had been called to try to save a dying woman after other people had all but killed her, and he always experienced a wrenching frustration that they had not contacted him earlier. It was not common for a male physician to be called to what was considered the domain of women, but Bartholomew was earning something of a reputation as the next best thing to a midwife, and delivering babies was something he rather enjoyed, although he would have been regarded as peculiar had he admitted so.

He gave Rosa a sense-dulling potion and sent one of her children to fetch a priest. It was not long before her shallow breathing faltered to nothing, and all that could be heard was the appalling Latin of the parish priest, the hacking cough of one of her watching children, and the contented snuffles of the pig that seemed to occupy the best half of the house.

Dispirited, he trudged through the rain to Michaelhouse, and arrived sodden and bedraggled just as the bell rang to call the Fellows to their meeting in the conclave. Hastily, he dragged off his wet clothes and donned dry ones, kicking his leaking boots into one corner and pulling on some shoes that would make him look a little more respectable for the ceremony after the meeting that would admit Michaelhouse's two new Fellows. Cynric had already laid out the red gown Fellows were obliged to wear on special occasions, along with the impractical floppy hat that went with it. Bartholomew tugged them on, polished his shoes on the backs of his hose, and ran across the courtyard, his splashing footsteps splattering mud up his legs and on the robe Cynric had cleaned with so much care.

The other Fellows were waiting for him. The conclave was a pleasant chamber, and the new glass in the windows meant that light still flooded in, while the bitter breezes of winter were kept out. Because nights came early in November, the shutters were closed and a huge fire blazed in the hearth, sending flickering yellow lights across the ceiling. One of the students with a talent for art had painted the walls with scenes from the Bible, and someone had even provided a tapestry to hang above the fireplace.

Still chilled from his soaking, Bartholomew appreciated the stifling heat in the room, but wondered how long fires would be allowed to burn at Michaelhouse once the new Master was in office. Langelee and William both seemed to delight in conditions most men would consider miserable, while Runham had a streak of miserliness in him that might well lead to some radical economies. Bartholomew's only hope for a comfortable winter was Michael, who had no patience with the hair-shirt mentality of some of his colleagues. Michael appreciated his creature comforts, and would never deprive anyone else of theirs merely to assert his personal authority.

'There you are, Matt,' said Michael, as Bartholomew walked in. The monk had his sleeve pushed up, and was giving the arm that had been stung by the bee an energetic scratch. 'Where have you been? We are ready to start, and you are the last to arrive.'

'As usual,' muttered Runham.

Smiling apologetically, Bartholomew closed the door and looked for somewhere to sit. The chamber was equipped with an eccentric assortment of stools and chairs, most of them cast-offs from wealthy benefactors. Michael, Runham, William and Langelee – the most senior Fellows – had already taken the best places near the hearth, leaving the newcomers Clippesby and Suttone to make do with stools by the windows. Master Kenyngham stood at the door, as though contemplating a quick escape, while blind Brother Paul had been led to his customary seat near the wall.

'Osmun, the porter at Bene't, claims to be Justus's cousin,' said Bartholomew to Runham, recalling guiltily that he had agreed to pass on the porter's demands the day before, but had forgotten. 'He wants his tunic and dagger.'

'He is welcome to them,' said Runham. 'He can collect them whenever he likes – and he can arrange for Justus to be buried, too, since they are related.'

'Have you not done that yet?' asked Paul, sounding a little disgusted. 'Justus died two days ago.'

'The weather is cold, and the corpse lies in the church porch,' said Runham dismissively. 'There is no hurry, and I have been preoccupied with more important matters.'

'Regardless of Osmun's kinship, it is still Michael-house's responsibility to bury Justus,' said Kenyngham. 'It would not do to have the townsfolk thinking we do not care about our servants.'

'There are better ways to spend Michaelhouse's funds than on funerals for suicides,' said Ralph de Langelee. 'If Justus has living kin, then let them pay for his burial. If I were Master, I would not throw away College money when it could be used on something more worthy – like improving the wine cellars.'

Bartholomew noted with dismay that it had not taken long for the Fellows to bring the discussion around to the matter currently closest to their own hearts – who was to be the next Master.

'I do not know why my decision to resign has caused such consternation,' said Kenyngham in genuine bewilderment. 'My retirement cannot be a surprise to you. I was present when our College was founded almost thirty years ago, and I am no longer a young man. I long to be free of administrative duties, and want nothing more than to spend my time in prayer and a little teaching.'

'It would be better if you delayed a while,' said Paul reasonably. 'We are not yet ready to choose another Master.'

'I was hoping that Roger Alcote would succeed me,' Kenyngham went on, as if he had not heard Paul. He made the sign of the cross and muttered a prayer for the soul of the man who had been one of Michaelhouse's least popular members. 'But Alcote has gone on to better things, and you must select another.'

Michael paused in his scratching to gesture towards the two newcomers, who sat watching the proceedings with wary interest. 'How can you expect Clippesby and Suttone to decide who would make the best Master? They do not know us.'

'But there are only six of you to choose from,' Kenyngham pointed out. 'John Runham, Michael, Matthew, William, Paul, and Ralph de Langelee – although I anticipate that not all of you will want the responsibility of the Mastership.'

'If you put it like that,' said Langelee, standing and puffing out his barrel chest as he leaned a brawny arm along the top of the fireplace, 'I feel morally obliged to offer my services to the College. I am not a man to shirk responsibility.'

'Oh, Lord!' groaned Michael under his breath to Bartholomew. 'I will resign my Fellowship before I allow Michaelhouse to be ruled by *that* ape in a scholar's tabard.'

'Meanwhile, *I* am keen to continue my saintly cousin's good work,' said Runham, leaning back in his chair and inspecting his fingernails casually. 'You all know that I am a man of my word – when I first arrived here and discovered the paltry tomb that had been provided to hold my noble cousin's mortal remains, I made a vow that I would not rest until that had been rectified. I am sure you have noticed that my efforts have come to fruition, and that the late Master Wilson now lies in a tomb fit for a king.'

'We certainly have noticed!' muttered Michael to Bartholomew. 'That vile monstrosity is the talk of the town. People come for miles around just to smirk at the wretched thing. I have never seen such an example of bad taste in all my days.'

'It *is* bad taste to erect a tomb for Wilson that outshines the one for our founder,' Bartholomew replied in an undertone. 'And all I can say is that Runham cannot have seen his cousin for a long time, if he considers the man to have been saintly and noble. Wilson was a nasty, greedy—'

'What are you two whispering about?' demanded William. 'I was just telling everyone that it is time a *Franciscan* was elected to the Mastership. And since I am the only Franciscan here – other than Paul, that is – it should be me.'

'A subtle election speech, Father,' said Michael dryly. 'Of course, I might say the same for the Benedictines: we have had friars aplenty in the Mastership since Michaelhouse's foundation, and it is high time there was a monk at the helm. However, this is not the basis on which I offer my services. You should recall that I have better connections with secular and religious authorities than anyone else here and you know I can make Michaelhouse the richest and most powerful College in the University.'

He threaded his fingers together and placed them over his ample paunch. Bartholomew smiled, considering Michael's election speech no more subtle than William's.

'All this is true,' said Langelee, sitting down and leaning back in his chair, assuming the pose of a man who knows some secret he is about to enjoy divulging. 'And I would vote for you myself, all things being equal. However, certain information has come to light that precludes me from supporting you. You, Brother Michael, have been doing things you should not have been, and I have written evidence to prove it.'

In Michaelhouse's conclave, everyone looked at Michael, whose eyes narrowed as he listened to Langelee's accusation.

'What are you talking about?' the monk snapped testily. 'I can assure you that there is nothing sinister or shameful in *my* past.'

'I was not thinking of your past,' said Langelee smoothly. 'I was thinking of your present.'

'What present?' demanded Michael irritably. 'Do not speak in riddles, man. If you want to accuse me of something, then say what it is. However, before you make a fool of yourself, I should warn you that I am as untarnished as a sheet of driven snow.'

'Before coming to Michaelhouse, I was an agent for the Archbishop of York,' said Langelee smugly. 'I have maintained the connections I made in his service – including several at the University of Oxford. I have irrefutable evidence that you have been engaging in clandestine dealings with scholars from Oxford with the express purpose of causing damage to Cambridge.'

'Do not be ridiculous,' said Bartholomew immediately. 'Michael is the Senior Proctor, and would never do anything to harm the University.'

But his sister had mentioned Michael's alleged dealings with their rival university only the previous day, he recalled with an uncomfortable feeling. He wondered what shady dealings the monk was involved in this time.

'I said I have evidence,' said Langelee, drawing a sheaf of parchments from the leather pouch he wore on his belt. 'Here are letters from Michael to William Heytesbury of Merton College, Oxford.'

'William Heytesbury,' said Bartholomew, impressed. 'I have heard of him. He is a nominalist who wrote *Regulae Solvendi Sophismata*. It is mostly a lot of tedious logic, but the last chapter is devoted to physical motion, and is a fascinating—'

'It is entirely predictable that you should find the natural philosophy more interesting than the logic, Bartholomew,' said Runham nastily. 'You have an inferior mind that is unable to grasp the finer points of the arts so clings to the physical universe.'

'There is no need for rudeness,' said Paul curtly. 'I, too, found the last chapter of Heytesbury's work the most engaging.'

'None of you should have been reading it,' said William frostily. 'It is pure heresy.'

'We were discussing Michael's disloyal relations with Merton,' said Langelee, seeing Paul preparing to engage William in what might prove to be a lengthy disputation. He waved his documents aloft triumphantly. 'Now is not the time to debate nominalism. But now *is* the time to learn what Michael wrote to Heytesbury of Merton.'

'How did you get those?' demanded Michael, gazing at the documents aghast and evidently recognising their authenticity.

Langelee gave a pained smile, although his eyes were victorious. 'A friend discovered them in the possession of a messenger bound for Oxford. He was actually looking for something relating to my Archbishop, but he passed these to me when he saw they were from a scholar at Michaelhouse.'

'I am sure there is nothing in them to prevent Michael from standing as Master,' said Kenyngham gently. 'Put them away, Ralph. We do not want to pry into Michael's personal affairs.'

'Then you should,' said Langelee. 'They discuss giving our University's property to Oxford.'

'But not Michaelhouse property,' objected Michael. His face was pale, and Bartholomew saw that Langelee's revelation had badly shaken him. Michael was usually able to bluff his way out of uncomfortable situations with bluster and sheer force of personality, but the physician could sense that his friend had already lost this battle.

'Will you not deny Langelee's accusations, Brother?' asked Paul, astonished. 'I did not believe him. I thought he had fabricated the story to discredit you.'

Langelee thrust the documents at him with a gloating smile. 'Look for yourself, Father. Michael's writing is unmistakable.'

'Paul is blind, you oaf,' snapped Runham impatiently, leaning forward to snatch the scrolls from Langelee. 'Give them to me.' His eyebrows went up as he inspected the parchments. 'Well, well. This is indeed Brother Michael's distinctive roundhand.'

'This is not how it seems . . .' began Michael, although his voice lacked conviction.

Langelee raised a thick, heavy hand. 'No excuses. It is here – in ink – that you plot with Oxford men to deprive Cambridge of valuable assets. You are not the kind of man we want as Master of Michaelhouse, Brother.'

'Perhaps it would be better if you withdrew your name,

in the light of these discoveries,' suggested Kenyngham warily, gazing at the offending documents Runham passed to him. 'I am sure you will prove your innocence in time, and there will be other opportunities for the Mastership in the future.'

Michael said nothing, and assumed a nonchalant pose, although Bartholomew could see the anger that seethed in him. He wondered why the monk had not made a convincing denial, or at least had tried to vindicate himself. Despite Langelee's 'evidence', Bartholomew was certain Michael would do nothing to harm the University he so loved.

Kenyngham passed the documents to Bartholomew. They were unquestionably written by Michael, and offered the Oxford nominalist several properties that belonged to Cambridge in exchange for certain information that was carefully unspecified, although the letter made it clear that both parties knew exactly what was on offer.

Bartholomew gazed at Michael uncertainly. Michael refused to meet his eyes, something that almost certainly indicated guilt. Sulkily, Michael snatched the missives from Bartholomew and thrust them into the fire. Langelee gasped, and tried to retrieve them, but the flames were already turning creamy parchment to black, and there was nothing he could do but watch them turn to cinders. But, as far as Michael was concerned, the damage had been done.

'So, we have Langelee, Runham and William who have offered to stand for the Mastership,' said Kenyngham in the silence that followed. 'Michael is disqualified. What about you others? Paul?'

'I do not wish to be considered,' said Paul, his opaque blue eyes gazing sightlessly around the room. 'Not because I could not do it – my blindness gives me an advantage over the rest of you in that I hear and notice things you do not – but because I have decided to return to my Franciscan brethren in the Friary.'

'You cannot do that!' shouted William, leaping to his feet in outrage. 'That will leave me as the only Franciscan here. I will be outvoted in everything, and the College will become a pit of debauchery and vice!'

'Chance would be a fine thing,' breathed Langelee.

Paul smiled at William. 'I doubt that will happen, Father. But I, like Master Kenyngham, am old, and I long to spend my days in contemplation and prayer – not teaching bored youngsters about grammar and rhetoric when they would rather be doing something else. So, at the end of term, I shall vacate my room and leave you.'

'Eight Fellows plus a Master was too many anyway,' said Langelee breezily. 'Seven is better.'

'That man has all the charm of a pile of cow dung,' muttered Michael to Bartholomew, eyeing Langelee with intense dislike. 'Paul is the best of us. The College will be a poorer place without him, and the students will miss his kindly patience.'

'I expect Matthew's duties as a physician will preclude *him* from standing for the Mastership,' said William hopefully.

Bartholomew was about to agree, when Michael spoke.

'Nonsense. Matt has students who are now sufficiently trained to relieve him of some of his work, and he has been at Michaelhouse for ten years. He knows the College and is all a Master should be. We will have him, if I cannot stand.'

Bartholomew was too astonished to object.

'I agree,' said Kenyngham, smiling at the physician. 'Matthew would make an excellent Master – firm, but not inflexible, and his dedication to his teaching and his writing will ensure that Michaelhouse continues its tradition of academic excellence. He would be my choice, certainly.'

'It is true he would be a fair and thoughtful Master,' said William reluctantly. 'And I would rather have him than someone from a rival Order. Matthew is my choice, too.'

'I am not from a rival Order,' Langelee pointed out, a little angrily. He was red-faced, and Bartholomew wondered whether he had been drinking, preparing with false courage for the meeting that might make him a powerful man. 'What about me?'

'But I do not like you,' said William baldly. Michael's snort of spiteful laughter was loud in the otherwise quiet room. 'I do like Matthew, however – well, most of the time. I do not approve of his dealings with harlots, but he seems to have forsaken them these days.'

'But I do not want to be Master,' said Bartholomew, as soon as he could find a gap in the conversation that seemed to be taking place as though he were not present. 'William was right – my duties as physician claim too much of my time. And if anyone thinks I can leave my patients to the ministrations of students like Rob Deynman, he only need look at Agatha the laundress's teeth to see that I cannot.'

'True,' agreed Kenyngham, shaking his head in compassion. 'Poor woman.'

Michael raised his eyebrows. 'You have three votes out of a necessary five to make you Master, Matt. Consider very carefully before you decline.'

Bartholomew shook his head. 'Thank you, but no. I was given additional students this year, and, since Father Philius's death last winter, I have had more patients than ever to see. And there is my treatise on fevers – I will never finish it if I take on extra College duties.'

'I knew you would not agree, but it was worth a try,'

said Michael softly. 'You would not have been as good as me, but I could have guided you along the right paths.'

'You mean you could have ruled Michaelhouse by telling Bartholomew what to do,' said Runham, overhearing. 'Bartholomew's election would have made you Master in all but name.'

Michael gave him a contemptuous glare.

'So,' said Langelee with satisfaction. 'To summarise: Michael, Paul and Bartholomew have declined to stand, which leaves William, Runham and me. It is clear which one of us is the outstanding candidate.'

'Is it?' murmured Michael in Bartholomew's ear. 'Who will you choose, Matt? The bigoted friar who would have us all burned for heresy for holding beliefs that do not directly reflect his own; the cunning lawyer whose most memorable characteristic is his smug pomposity; or the Archbishop of York's spy-turned-academic, who is more lout than scholar, and who stoops to using cheap tricks to eliminate the best man for the task?'

'Michaelhouse will not thrive under the Mastership of any of them,' Bartholomew whispered back. 'It is a case of selecting the least of three evils.'

'I suggest we make our decision now, and then announce it after the admissions ceremony,' said Kenyngham. 'We are all present, and I am sure we all know which candidate we want to elect.'

'It is not my place to speak when I am not yet a Fellow,' said Suttone, his red, cheery face serious. 'But I feel I am not in a position to make a decision of such importance to the College. If you will excuse me, I must abstain.'

'Well, *I* will not abstain,' said Clippesby, glaring at Suttone as though the Carmelite had tried to cheat him of something rightfully his. 'And it is obvious to me whom we should choose.'

'Oh, Lord, Matt,' groaned Michael under his breath.

'Another opinionated bigot! Why do they all have to come to Michaelhouse?'

'Suttone seems a decent man,' said Bartholomew.

'He does,' agreed Michael in a whisper. 'But I do not like Clippesby!'

Clippesby glared around at the assembled Fellows, his oddly intense gaze lingering on the muttering Michael. 'I do not want a disgusting Franciscan as Master and I do not approve of men who smell of strong drink at breakfast – as Langelee did this morning. So, I choose the lawyer.'

'Well!' drawled Michael, as an embarrassed silence greeted Clippesby's statement. 'You are a man who does not mince his words.'

'Are all Fellows' meetings this acrimonious?' asked Suttone nervously. 'Only I was led to believe that the hallowed halls of the University of Cambridge were places of learned debate and enlightenment.'

'Where on God's Earth did you hear that?' asked Langelee. His eyes narrowed. 'I know! Oxford! Our rival scholars are trying to make us sound tedious and dull! "Learned debate and enlightenment" indeed!'

The Michaelhouse Fellows processed into the hall in order of seniority. Master Kenyngham led the way, followed by Michael and William, and then Bartholomew with Father Paul clinging to his arm. Langelee and Runham walked together, while Clippesby and Suttone brought up the rear. The students were already standing at their places, waiting in tense anticipation to learn which of the Fellows would be their new Master.

The inauguration of new Fellows was a special event, and an extravagant number of candles had been lit, so the hall was filled with a golden glow. The fire blazed and crackled, sending flickering shadows across the painted ceiling. The usually bare wooden tables were covered in cloths – old, yellowed and stained ones, but cloths never-theless – and the College silver was displayed on the high table. To mark the occasion, some of the students had even washed and donned clean gowns. The atmosphere of tense expectation and muted excitement reminded Bartholomew of Christmas. He wondered whether the students would look quite so cheerful when they learned who had been elected Master. He suspected they would not.

'We have gathered this evening to witness the swearing in of two new Fellows,' intoned Kenyngham mechan-ically, gesturing for everyone to sit. 'I will read the foun-der's statutes and the newcomers will be asked to obey these rules, and to defend zealously the honour and usefulness of the house.'

Michael gave a huge, bored yawn, and reached out to take a handful of nuts from the silver cup that had been placed in front of him. Langelee had somehow contrived to have his goblet filled with wine before anyone else, and was gulping it noisily. Bartholomew saw his students, Gray and Bulbeck, exchange a look of amusement at Langelee's tavern-style manners, while Deynman had to look away to prevent himself from laughing out loud.

'The new Fellows must listen carefully to the statutes and ordinances made over time by the Masters and scholars,' said Kenyngham, reciting the familiar words without much interest.

'I am sorry Langelee did what he did,' said Bartholomew softly to Michael.

'So am I,' said Michael. 'I was looking forward to being Master of Michaelhouse. Unfortunately, Kenyngham's announcement was sudden, and I did not have the opportunity to prepare myself properly. Langelee acted before I could put my own plan into action.'

'And what plan was that?' asked Bartholomew warily.

Michael puffed out his cheeks, noting the uneasiness in his friend's face. 'Nothing as underhand as the trick Langelee played on me. I was merely going to suggest the election be postponed for a month, to allow Clippesby and Suttone to make their decisions with the benefit of knowing each of the candidates.'

'And during the interim, you would have ensured that only one candidate was able to stand?' asked Bartholomew.

Michael nodded, unabashed. 'It would have been done with discretion and cunning – not like Langelee, who has all the subtlety of a mallet in the groin – and no one would have known that it was I who started the rumours that besmirched the reputations of the others.'

'Then you made a grave error of judgement, Brother. You assumed that your rivals would be equally subtle in their strategies, but you should have known Langelee and William better than that. Runham did: he is a clever man, but he saw such tactics would not work, and he engaged in the same kind of brazenness employed by Langelee and William.'

'All right, all right. You do not have to rub it in,' said Michael irritably. 'I admit I was ill-prepared. This is all Kenyngham's fault. He could not have resigned at a worse time, when I have the Bene't death and Brother Patrick's murder to investigate. My Junior Proctor is in Ely, and I am overwhelmed with work.'

'What is this business with Master Heytesbury of Merton?' asked Bartholomew curiously. 'Offering Oxford something at Cambridge's expense does not sound like something you would do, but that letter was definitely in your handwriting.'

Michael gave a grim smile. 'Of course I am doing nothing that would damage Cambridge – quite the contrary, in fact. Say nothing to anyone else, but my Bishop and I devised a scheme whereby we would sacrifice a few small properties in exchange for some information that will gain us a good deal more.'

'Now that *does* sound like you.'

Michael sighed. 'Thank you. But Langelee's interference may have destroyed all hopes of a successful outcome, not to mention the fact that the delicate nature of the arrangements meant that I could not justify why I was dealing with Heytesbury at all. But in time my plan will become known, and then he will be revealed as the fool he is. Meanwhile, I must suffer in silence. But I will have my revenge on Langelee, never you fear.'

Bartholomew knew perfectly well that Michael would not readily forgive Langelee for thwarting him in his ambitions, and that Langelee would pay dearly. He just hoped he would not have to play a part in it – wittingly or otherwise. Contemplating the ways in which Langelee would be forced to pay the price for his actions seemed to put Michael in a better mood, and he even began to enjoy himself.

'The new Fellows shall also swear not to intrigue or promote litigation contrary to the utility of the house,' droned Kenyngham, reading from the dog-eared copy of the statutes and ordinances.

'That is my favourite one,' whispered Michael to Bartholomew. 'It says that intriguing and promoting litigation are perfectly acceptable, just as long as they are not to the detriment of the College. Our founder was blessed with a stroke of a genius when he wrote that.'

Bartholomew wondered how the founder had managed to produce such dry and antiquated phrases. Perhaps it was because he had been a lawyer.

'They shall swear not to reveal the privy plans of the Fellowship to anyone outside,' Kenyngham went on, with a casual, but unmistakable, glance at the hour candle that stood above the hearth.

'We do not have any privy plans,' muttered Michael somewhat grumpily. 'More is the pity. I could have seen to that, had Langelee not interfered. The only business we have discussed recently is whether we should borrow two marks from the endowment to have the latrines cleaned. I hardly think the outside world will be falling over itself to hear about that kind of decision – even though it took us most of the afternoon to reach, thanks to you.'

'It was important,' whispered Bartholomew defensively. 'Clean latrines are essential for the students' good health – and ours.'

'You do have some odd ideas, Matt,' said Michael, taking another handful of nuts with one hand and scratching his arm with the other. 'No wonder half the scholars in Cambridge think you are mad. We do not eat in the latrines, you know, or sleep in them. In fact, most of us spend as little time as possible in them, given their state.'

'Then my point is proven. And do not scratch, Brother. You will give yourself an infection.'

'If you think our latrines are bad, you should see the ones at Bene't!' said Michael, ignoring the advice. 'I was obliged to pay a visit there the day before yesterday, while I was dealing with the Fellow who fell from the scaffolding – Raysoun.'

'Speaking of Bene't . . .'

'I thought we were speaking of latrines,' said Michael with a snigger. 'Or do you consider them one and the same? That porter who came to fetch you – Osmun – is a nasty piece of work. I remember the student who complained he had been assaulted. The case against Osmun was dropped, but I am sure he was guilty.'

'The Bene't porters are notorious for being rough,' said Bartholomew. 'I think they pride themselves on being the surliest, rudest, most belligerent men in Cambridge.

But did you discover who killed Raysoun? His friend, Wymundham, did not tell me.'

Michael gazed at him in surprise. 'No one killed Raysoun, Matt. He fell off the scaffolding: his death was an accident.'

'Was it?' asked Bartholomew, startled in his turn. 'But what about his dying words? What about Wymundham's claim that Bene't is an unhappy College with bad feeling among the Fellows?'

'Where did you hear this?' demanded Michael. 'The Master of Bene't told me that the Fellows are all good friends who rub along extremely well.'

'Perhaps Wymundham was confused,' said Bartholomew, growing confused himself. 'He was deeply shocked by the death of his friend; it may have unbalanced him and made him say things that are not true.'

'Or perhaps Master Heltisle was lying to me,' said Michael thoughtfully. 'I suspected there was something odd going on in that place – there was an atmosphere of goodwill and cheer that struck me as forced and painful. So, what exactly did Wymundham tell you?'

William gave a hearty sigh to register his disapproval of the muttered discussion that was taking place during the reading of the statutes. None of the other Fellows seemed to care. Father Paul and Runham were engaged in a discussion of their own, while Langelee seemed well on the way to drinking himself into oblivion. Clippesby and Suttone were listening intently, but after all it was the first time they had heard the statutes read.

'Did Wymundham tell you nothing about Raysoun's last words?' asked Bartholomew.

'What last words? I was kneeling next to him, giving him last rites, and I heard no last words. I saw Wymundham leaning over him, but although Raysoun's eyes were open, he did not look aware to me.'

'But did you speak to Wymundham?' pressed Bartholomew.

Michael shook his head. 'It took rather a long time to have the body removed from the High Street because the parish coffin had been loaned to St Botolph's Church, and we had to wait for it to be retrieved. By the time I was ready to interview Wymundham, the man had disappeared. Rather than wait indefinitely for him to return, I decided to see him later.'

'So, did you?'

'No. I have been too busy. The stabbed friar in Ovyng Hostel – which *is* a murder – has taken all my time. I thought Raysoun's death was accidental, and so did not consider its investigation urgent.'

'I saw Wymundham going into Holy Trinity Church on Thursday afternoon,' said Bartholomew thoughtfully. 'It was not long after I had left him at Bene't, and he was looking quite furtive – furtive enough to make me notice him.'

'So, was he furtive because he had lied to you about these so-called dying words of Raysoun's?' mused Michael, resuming his scratching. 'Or because he really does have a secret to tell, and he is afraid someone might not like it?'

'You two might at least make a pretence at paying attention to the ceremony,' hissed Father William in a voice loud enough to carry to the other end of the hall. Bartholomew saw Deynman's shoulders quaking with laughter.

'Sorry,' he said.

'Are you talking about the Bene't Fellow who fell off his College scaffolding the day before yesterday?' William asked, apparently not objecting to the discussion if he were included. 'I ask because I know the Junior Proctor is in Ely this week, and I thought you might need a little help during his absence. I have a good deal of experience of these matters, following the events in Suffolk earlier this year.'

'Your help with that was very much appreciated,' said Michael smoothly. 'We would never have managed without you.'

'I know,' said William. 'So, did you tell the Chancellor about me? I hope you said I would make a splendid Junior Proctor. I know a vacancy will arise soon, and I would like to be considered.'

'I told him everything,' said Michael, favouring the friar with an ambiguous wink.

'Did you?' asked William, not certain whether this was a good thing or a bad. 'But of course, if you do not need me to assist you with this affair at Bene't, perhaps I can look into the terrible crime that was perpetrated at Ovyng yesterday – the vicious, wicked murder of an innocent Franciscan by Dominican devils.'

'No,' said Michael firmly. 'Leave that well alone, please. I do not want you charging into the Dominican Friary and accusing people of murder.'

'But I would be justified in doing so,' argued William hotly.

'Very possibly, but we have no evidence to support such a claim, and I do not want any more friars murdered in tit-for-tat killings – including you, Father.'

William grumbled to himself as Michael turned his back on the friar and gave his attention to Bartholomew. 'So what else did Wymundham say to you?'

'Just that Raysoun whispered with his dying breath that someone had stabbed him with an awl and then pushed him from the scaffolding, and that Bene't's Fellows fight among themselves.'

'Really?' mused Michael. He tapped his knife thoughtfully on the table, drawing an irritable glance from

Runham. 'I will speak to Wymundham first thing tomorrow morning – it is too late to go tonight. And I will want you to look at Raysoun's body for me, too. Now that you have raised suspicions about the nature of his death, we need to know whether Raysoun fell on this metal spike as Lynton claimed, or whether he was stabbed, as Wymundham believes.'

'I will not be able to tell you that,' said Bartholomew in alarm. 'How can I? A stab wound looks the same whether it was inflicted by a person or whether it was the result of falling on a sharp implement.'

'You will find a way,' said Michael complacently.

CHAPTER 3

'AND EACH NEW FELLOW SHALL PAY DUE RESPECT to every senior, and by senior is understood to mean any Fellow admitted before him,' concluded Kenyngham, reading the last of the statutes with a sigh of relief.

'Hear, hear,' agreed Michael, banging on the table with the handle of his knife, and waking at least one bored scholar that Bartholomew could see. He wondered if it had in fact been the monk's intention to waken Langelee, who jumped and gazed around him blearily.

'Do you swear to observe all these rules, in the sight of God and the Holy Spirit?' asked Kenyngham of Clippesby and Suttone, who were now standing in front of him.

The two swore, and then watched as Kenyngham took a quill and wrote their names in the great book of the Fellows of the Society of the Holy and Undivided Trinity, the Blessed Virgin Mary and St Michael. When he had finished, and the wet ink had been sprinkled with sand to dry it, Clippesby and Suttone each bent to kiss its red leather cover.

'Now comes the unpleasant part of the ceremony,' muttered Michael, as all the Fellows stood, and prepared to receive the kiss of peace from the newcomers. 'The only people I will kiss all day transpire to be a red-faced Carmelite with whiskers like a donkey, and a Dominican fanatic with the eyes of a madman. It would be a good deal more enjoyable if they were women.'

'Women will never be admitted to a Cambridge college,' announced Father William, exercising his annoying habit of overhearing certain parts of conversations not intended for his ears. 'It would open the door to the Devil – the sort of thing they would do at Oxford.'

'Perhaps that is why Michael is soliciting the good graces of the Oxford men,' suggested Runham. 'I cannot imagine why else he should deign to associate himself with that rabble.'

'I can see I will never be allowed to forget this,' muttered Michael bitterly.

'It *would* be nice to have women in the College,' said Bartholomew absently, leaning forward to kiss Clippesby, who favoured him with an odd look at the comment. 'Some of the midwives I have met are highly intelligent, and—'

'You meet altogether too many women,' interrupted Father William sanctimoniously. 'And your obsession with them exceeds the bounds of normality.'

He grabbed Clippesby roughly by the front of his habit and jerked him forward to plant a heavy kiss on either cheek. Scrubbing his face in distaste, Clippesby moved on to Michael, who favoured him with the most perfunctory of welcomes before sitting down again.

'Let the feast begin,' announced Kenyngham, clapping his hands to attract the attention of the servants who hovered at the back of the hall.

'Why not tell us who is to be the new Master first?' asked Gray. His comment had been intended only for Deynman and Bulbeck, but his voice was loud enough to carry, and other students nodded their agreement. Bartholomew strongly suspected that Kenyngham had chosen to delay his announcement so that everyone could have the opportunity to enjoy themselves before the axe fell.

The out-going Master pretended not to have heard Gray, and the feast commenced, accompanied by some hastily learned songs from a reduced version of the College choir. The feast's short notice meant that only the best singers were invited to perform, which therefore excluded most of them.

The cooks had not managed too badly, considering the lack of preparation time. First, there was a dish of hare cooked with white grease. Michael mopped up the warm lard remaining in the serving bowl with generous helpings of the soft bread baked specially for the occasion, making Bartholomew feel queasy. When he remarked that too much of the fat would make the monk sick, Michael merely replied that it was to make up for the fact that he would not be eating any of the leeks and sops in wine, on the grounds that they were green and that he did not allow green foods to pass his lips.

It was a familiar refrain, and one that Bartholomew no longer tried to argue against. When Michael had retrieved the last globules of grease from under the rim of the dish, the next course arrived, comprising whole pikes poached in ale, parsley, cinnamon and vinegar: these looked impressive, but were difficult to eat because of the bones. William, who had a penchant for fish giblets, was presented with a large dish of the pikes' steamed entrails from a cook who believed the Franciscan would be Michaelhouse's next Master, and was keen to curry favour. With Michael scoffing his grease-impregnated bread on the one side, and William gorging fish intestines on the other, Bartholomew began to wish he were somewhere else.

Finally, there were fried fig pastries – small rolls of light pastry filled with a mixture of minced figs, saffron, eggs, ginger and cloves cooked in a hot skillet that spat with yet more white grease. Michael ate four and then complained that his innards hurt. Bartholomew ate one, and found it heavy, sticky and overly rich.

The College's wine cellar had been broached to ensure there was plenty of liquid with which to wash the food down. Most of it was a dark, tarry brew that Bartholomew thought tasted more like medicine than wine. The first sip made him wince, and when he had finished the whole cup his head spun and his stomach felt acidic. But the oily meal had made him thirsty, and he did not object when Cynric refilled his goblet.

The powerful drink had its customary impact on the Fellows. Kenyngham's head began to nod as he listened to some dull monologue by Runham, and Bartholomew saw it would not be long before the gentle Gilbertine fell asleep. Michael, red-faced and sweaty, was sharing detailed knowledge of the town's whores with a startled Suttone. To Bartholomew's right, Father William was slapping Clippesby on the shoulders in a comradely manner and regaling him with tales of his happy days in the Inquisition. Clippesby's expression turned from indignant to appalled, and then to hunted. Bartholomew studied the Dominican, who sat twitching uneasily under William's heavy arm, and wondered yet again whether he was wholly in control of his wits.

The student, Sam Gray, reeled towards Bartholomew, with the dull-witted Rob Deynman, equally intoxicated, at his heels.

'I hope it is you,' he slurred. 'You and Brother Michael are the only two Fellows who would make Michaelhouse any kind of Master. Any of the rest would be disastrous.'

'Quiet, Sam!' said Bartholomew, casting an anxious glance down the table to where his colleagues sat. 'You will need to be a lot more prudent than that if you want a future here.'

Gray gazed at him in horror, his eyes suddenly focused

and clear. 'Do not tell me you did not stand!' he breathed.
'Do not tell me you would let your College go to the Devil,
rather than take its reins yourself! You swore a sacred
oath to do all you could for it.'

'I think you had better sit down before you say something you might regret,' said Bartholomew quickly, sensing Gray's indiscreet opinions were about to land them
both in trouble. 'And take Deynman with you – he is
about to pass out.'

Gray caught the staggering Deynman, and together
they weaved their way back to their places. Gray dumped
Deynman on the bench and sat talking in a low voice
to Tom Bulbeck, who kept shooting nervous glances
towards Runham, William and Langelee. Bartholomew
knew they had good cause to be concerned: everyone
would find Michaelhouse a different place once the lax
rule of Kenyngham came to an end.

He rubbed his temples, feeling the onset of a dull
headache from the wine he had consumed – not much
by anyone else's standards, but it was powerful stuff, and
he was not used to it. Cynric slopped yet more of it in his
master's cup, his uncharacteristic clumsiness indicating
that the servants had also availed themselves of the brew
that flowed so freely from the cellars.

In the Master's chair, Kenyngham was sound asleep,
the fingers of one hand curled around his beloved psalter,
and the fingers of the other clutching an empty goblet.
Bartholomew stood unsteadily and went to wake him,
because no one was permitted to leave the feast before
the Master, and the Master looked set to sleep until the
following morning. He wanted Kenyngham to announce
his successor and quit the hall, so that Bartholomew could
go to bed and leave the merrymaking to those with more
robust constitutions.

Kenyngham opened bleary eyes and pulled himself

together. A vague hush came over the hall as he stood, although not even his announcement was sufficient to rouse Deynman from his drunken slumber.

'And now I am sure you are all keen to know who will be your next Master,' said Kenyngham sleepily. Gradually the murmur of voices subsided, and even the servants clattering the dishes behind the screen at the back of the hall were quiet.

'It was not an easy decision,' said Kenyngham. 'We had three excellent candidates who were prepared to stand – namely Father William, Master Runham and Master Langelee. Since the statutes say that a Fellow is not permitted to vote if he is a candidate, and Thomas Suttone decided to abstain, we were left with five Fellows eligible to vote.'

He stopped speaking for a moment, and leaned down to take a gulp from his goblet of wine. He was not the only one. Scholars all around the hall fortified themselves for the bad news they sensed was coming – how could there be good news with those three candidates up for selection? The atmosphere of tense anticipation was oppressive.

'Brother Michael and Doctor Bartholomew voted for William; Father Paul voted for Langelee; and Master Clippesby and I voted for Runham.'

'Paul should have voted for me,' muttered William bitterly. 'We are brother Franciscans.'

'The statutes say that the candidate with the fewest votes should stand down and select one of the others. So, Langelee withdrew and voted for Runham. And Paul, freed from his first choice, selected William. But that meant a deadlock, with Runham and William having three votes each, so I was compelled to insist that Suttone make his choice.'

'Then the new Master was effectively chosen by a

man who does not know either candidate from Adam?' whispered Gray, drink making him incautious. 'That is a bad precedent!'

'Suttone voted for Runham,' said Kenyngham. 'And so I declare that John Runham is now duly elected as the next Master of Michaelhouse, effective immediately.'

In the hall of Michaelhouse, the silence continued after Kenyngham had made his announcement. There was no cheering or exchange of pleased glances. Runham was a good teacher, but he was not liked, and his arrogance and smugness had alienated almost as many people as had his cousin's before him. Runham either did not notice or did not care. He stood as Master Kenyngham sat, and produced a sheaf of notes. Bartholomew gaped, astonished that the man could be so confident of his success that he had prepared a speech.

'That Dominican – Clippesby – will be sorry he voted for *him*,' muttered William furiously in Bartholomew's ear. 'He will not enjoy being in Michaelhouse under the Mastership of a lawyer.'

He would have enjoyed it even less under a Franciscan, Bartholomew thought. William did not like Dominicans, and Dominicans usually did not like him. The physician rubbed his head again as the strong wine made the room reel and tip.

'I do not think I can stand this,' said Michael, eyeing Runham's bundle of papers with dismay. 'After what Langelee did to me, being forced to listen to Runham gloating over his success is more than any mortal should be forced to bear. If I pretend to faint, will you catch me?'

'And then Father William can carry us both out insensible,' said Bartholomew, smiling. 'You fainted and me crushed.'

'Get ready then,' said Michael, raising a hand to his forehead. With a shock, Bartholomew saw he was serious.

'I cannot catch you, Brother,' he whispered urgently. 'You are far too heavy, and you will hurt yourself – and me.'

'Nonsense,' said Michael. 'Here I go.'

He started to raise his ponderous bulk from his chair, clutching at his head dramatically as he did so. Runham was clearing his throat and shuffling his parchments as he prepared to make his first official speech as Master of Michaelhouse. Michael had just opened his mouth to emit a groan, when there was a commotion at the far end of the hall. A porter was gesticulating urgently towards Cynric. The book-bearer listened to his message, and then pushed his way past the rows of students to the high table. Michael sat again, waiting with interest to see what was of sufficient import for Cynric to risk incurring the wrath of a Master about to make his inaugural speech.

'One of your beadles is here,' the Welshman whispered to Michael.

'Now that I am Master, there will be no interruptions of meals,' said Runham sharply. 'And that goes for you, too, Bartholomew. You were late twice yesterday because you put other demands above your College responsibilities. Meals at Michaelhouse will be sacrosanct from now on – they are occasions when the Bible Scholar will read to us for the good of our souls, and when we will reflect in silence on our lives and how we must strive to make them better.'

'How tedious,' murmured Michael. 'I certainly would not have inflicted that upon the good men of Michael-house.'

'Perhaps Runham was not such a bad choice after all,' said William, nodding approvingly.

'I cannot wait until after meals, if I am summoned by a patient,' said Bartholomew, appalled. 'The person might be dead by the time we are finished.'

'Then you will have to reconsider your vocation,' said Runham harshly. 'Your choice is clear: you either live here and abide by my rules or become a town physician. You cannot do both.'

'But—'

'Enough!' snapped Runham. 'From now on, I will have no debates at high table and no one will question my decisions. What I say is final. You have a week to make up your mind whether you will choose College or your external interests – and the same choice is available to anyone else who does not like the way I plan to rule Michaelhouse.'

'But Matthew's treatment of the poor is good for relations with the town,' Kenyngham pointed out. 'That is why I have allowed him to continue. The townsfolk appreciate the fact that we can help them in this way, and are more inclined to view the University in a positive light.'

'Rubbish,' said Runham dismissively. 'The town rabble hate and envy us, and Bartholomew's sordid obsession with their diseases makes no difference one way or the other.'

'That is not true!' cried Father Paul, as angry as Bartholomew had ever seen him. 'And in these times of need following the Death, we must do all we can to help the poor, not deprive them of the one man who provides them with free treatment for their ailments.'

'Then he should follow his conscience and leave Michaelhouse,' snapped Runham. 'At least then he will be able to pursue all the town whores who take his fancy without fear of recrimination.'

'That is unfair,' argued Paul, his expressive face dark with fury. 'Matthew has been—'

'Since you see fit to question me within moments of my appointment, perhaps you might care to resign your Fellowship now, rather than wait until the end of term,' said Runham icily. 'I will have your personal effects sent to the Franciscan Friary first thing tomorrow morning.'

'Now just a moment—' began William, outraged that a fellow Franciscan was under attack.

'And that goes for you, too,' said Runham, rounding on him. 'You are a stupid, belligerent fanatic, who has no place in a University.'

'Even as Master, you have no authority to deprive people of their Fellowships,' said Michael quietly. 'It is against the statutes, because Fellows are elected in perpetuity.'

But he could make their lives so unpleasant that they would not want to stay, thought Bartholomew, eyeing the new Master with dislike.

'I have no wish to remain in Michaelhouse, if its new Master wishes us to ignore the town's poor and selfishly concentrate on ourselves,' said Paul coldly. 'I will leave tonight.'

His chair scraped on the floor as he stood and made his way towards the staircase; the other Fellows and students watched him aghast. The hall had never been so silent; even the customary rustle of rushes around the scholars' feet was stilled. Bartholomew started to rise to protest, but Michael seized his arm and dragged him back down. The movement did not escape the attention of Runham, who glared at them with his heavily lidded eyes. Bartholomew clenched his fists. He was not normally a man moved to violence, but the sight of the smug expression on Runham's amply jowled face made his blood boil, and he felt an almost irresistible urge to leap across the table and wrap his hands around the man's throat.

'What did my beadle want?' asked Michael of Cynric in the tense silence that followed. He glanced up at Runham challengingly. 'I assume you do not object if urgent *University* business occasionally encroaches on a College meal? Or shall I inform the University's Chancellor and the Bishop of Ely that I have been forbidden to fulfil my obligations to them as long as you are eating?'

Runham glowered at him with undisguised loathing, and made no reply. While he could bully some of his Fellows, he was scarcely in a position to take on one with the backing of such powerful men as the Chancellor and the Bishop – at least, not yet.

'The beadle has come from Mayor Horwoode's house,' said Cynric in a whisper, intimidated by the fact that everyone in the hall was listening to what he had to say. 'Apparently, Horwoode has found the body of a scholar from Bene't College in his garden.'

'A student?' asked Michael.

Cynric shook his head. 'It is said to be a Fellow by the name of John Wymundham.'

The golden aura of the beadle's lamp formed a hazy halo as Bartholomew, Michael and Paul followed it up St Michael's Lane and turned left along the High Street. Mayor Horwoode lived near Sheriff Tulyet, and his home was a large, stone-built house set attractively between the Round Church – built to resemble the Church of the Holy Sepulchre in Jerusalem – and the Franciscan Friary.

Michael strode next to his beadle, scratching his stung arm in silent agitation as he considered the events of the evening. Bartholomew walked behind, with Father Paul clinging to him; a bundle of the friar's belongings swung over his shoulder. Normally, Cynric would have been with them, too, scouting behind in the shadows of the night and enjoying the nocturnal foray. But Cynric was now a married man with other commitments, and he had returned to his own home on Milne Street as soon as his duties at the feast were over. Bartholomew felt vulnerable without the book-bearer's comforting presence.

Shadows flickered at the edge of his vision. At least part of it was due to the strong wine but some was the speculative scrutiny of petty thieves and vagabonds, and Bartholomew was glad of the presence of the beadle and his sword. He sensed that at least one would-be robber had melted away into the shadows when he saw the glint of unsheathed metal.

Bartholomew stumbled over one of the many potholes that pitted the street, almost dragging Paul down with him. Somewhere in the silence a dog howled mournfully, answered by another in the distance. The night was cold, and a dank mist had rolled in from the Fens, filling the town with a dirty whiteness that carried in it the scent of the sea and the rich, rotting odour of the marshes.

'You do not have to leave Michaelhouse,' said Bartholomew to Paul. He knew his words were slightly slurred from the wine. 'Runham does not have the authority to force you to go before you are ready.'

Paul pursed his lips. 'I want no place in a College run by a man like Runham. To be frank, I knew that if he won the election, I would not want to remain at Michaelhouse. That was why I said I would resign before we voted – so as not to look churlish.'

'But William might have won.'

'He might,' said Paul. 'But William is not the kind of man who would rule the College with wisdom and understanding, either. The least of the three evils was Langelee – at least he can be manipulated.'

'He can?' asked Bartholomew uncertainly.

Paul nodded. 'All you need to do is to make sure he believes that any suggestions you put forward originated with him – if he feels something is his own idea, he will be more than happy to see it through. But Runham is too clever for such tactics. He is vicious, arrogant and mean-spirited, and life is too short for me to want to spend any of it in his company.'

Bartholomew was surprised. He did not like Runham, but was astonished that a gentle man like Father Paul had taken against him so strongly.

'Thank you for speaking up for me,' he said. 'I am sorry it ended the way it did.'

'I am not,' said Paul. 'I do not want to see the College I love disintegrating under the filthy claws of that lawyer. I will be happier in the Friary.'

'We are here,' said Bartholomew, gazing up at the substantial walls that kept the Franciscan friars in and the town – and the Dominicans – out.

Paul hammered on the gate and then turned his milky eyes towards Bartholomew. 'You will visit me here? You will continue to ease the pain in my eyes with that lotion you devised for me?'

'Of course,' said Bartholomew. 'Assuming the Emperor lets me out, that is.'

'In a week, that might be immaterial,' said Paul. 'You might not be a member of Michaelhouse by then. But you must not let him force you to do something you do not want, Matthew. Fight him.'

A grey-robed lay-brother answered the door and ushered Paul inside. When the gate had closed behind them, the rage at Runham's cavalier behaviour towards the old Franciscan began to boil inside Bartholomew again. Michael touched him on the shoulder.

'Will you come with me to Mayor Horwoode's house to see about this body he found? Then I will walk back to

Michaelhouse with you. There have been outlaws in the town again, and it is not safe for a man to be alone.'

'Master Runham only gave me permission to see Paul to the Friary,' said Bartholomew bitterly. 'What will he say if he learns I have disobeyed his order to return to the College immediately?'

'He can say what he likes,' said Michael indignantly. 'But he will not know unless you tell him.'

'I do not think I will be much use to you tonight,' said Bartholomew. 'I have had too much of that strong red wine.'

'So have I,' admitted Michael, although he did not appear to Bartholomew to be drunk. 'But I never let that interfere with business. Come on.'

'How could Runham do that to Paul?' blurted Bartholomew angrily. 'Paul has been a loyal College member for years.'

'I will think of some appropriate way to repay him,' vowed Michael. 'He will not get away with this.'

'Such as what?'

'I am working on it,' said Michael vaguely. 'I need to think of a way to avenge myself on Langelee first. But when I turn my attentions on Runham, I will hit him where it hurts – his reputation and possibly his pocket. So, keep your fists to yourself until I have had time to devise a plan. I do not want him applying to the Chancellor to have your Fellowship annulled because you have deprived him of his teeth or broken his nose – much as he might deserve it.'

'Runham may be right, you know,' said Bartholomew as they walked. 'It might be better if I resigned my Fellowship and concentrated on being a physician.'

'That is arrant nonsense,' said Michael brusquely, again scratching his bad arm. 'You would never survive without your Fellow's stipend. The few patients who pay you cannot subsidise the rest of your practice, and I cannot see you abandoning the poor to do horoscopes for the wealthy. And what about your teaching? You have always said it is important to train new physicians to replace the ones who died during the pestilence.'

'If you keep aggravating your arm like that, you will end up with an infection,' said Bartholomew, watching as the monk's scratching became more and more furious. 'Let me see.'

'No,' said Michael, pulling his arm away impatiently. 'Here we are: Horwoode's house.'

Horwoode's home was one of the finest buildings in the town, with a red-tiled roof and a near-perfect plaster-wash of saffron yellow. It was surrounded by a large walled garden, the far end of which was bordered by the King's Ditch. The walls were almost twice as high as Bartholomew stood tall, and he imagined it would not be an easy matter to climb over them.

'This is a terrible shock,' said Mayor Horwoode, as they waited for a servant to kindle a lamp. His mammoth wife, Gerta, was with him, and she put one of her substantial arms around his shoulders to warm him as he shivered in the chill of the night.

He was a man in early middle years, whose prematurely balding head was fringed with a circlet of bushy grey hair. As Mayor, he was reasonably successful, because he had a talent for delaying decisions for so long that they no longer needed to be made. But while people were grateful that plans to extend the Castle at the town's expense had been shelved, they were concerned about delayed repairs to the Great Bridge and the postponement of dredging the festering open sewers in the High Street.

'First Raysoun and now Wymundham,' said Horwoode. 'I still cannot believe it.'

'You know them?' asked Bartholomew, surprised that

the town's Mayor should stoop to a friendship with mere scholars.

'We were acquainted,' corrected Horwoode. 'Besides being Mayor, I am also master of the Guild of St Mary, one of the two societies that founded Bene't College. Raysoun and Wymundham were Fellows of Bene't.'

'How did Wymundham come to be in your garden?' asked Michael. 'Did you invite him there?'

'I most certainly did not,' said Horwoode indignantly. 'I do not want scholars in my home. They are a slovenly, dirty brood – it must be from reading all those books.'

His wife cleared her throat meaningfully, and Horwoode seemed to realise that he was addressing two of the 'slovenly, dirty brood'. He smiled, revealing a set of small white teeth, and did not seem to be in the slightest discomfited by his gaffe.

'Here we are,' he said cheerfully, as his servant finally managed to ignite the pitch on the torch. 'Now I can show you Wymundham's body.'

He took the light, and began to lead the way along narrow stone paths that wound between vegetable plots. At the beginning of winter they were mostly empty, with the exception of a few scraggly cabbages. The herb garden was full, though, brimming with sage, rosemary and mint, their rich scents mingling with the earthy aroma of a nearby compost heap.

Horwoode walked deeper into his domain, until Bartholomew began to wonder whether they were going to meet the King's Ditch – the filthy, stinking canal that swung around the eastern side of the town in a great arc and formed part of its defences. No sooner had the thought passed through his mind when something loomed up out of the darkness in front of them. It was the great bank of the Ditch itself, heavily leveed to prevent flooding.

'Here,' said Horwoode, stopping at a shape on the ground. 'This is him – John Wymundham.'

Bartholomew knelt beside the limp form, and saw that it was indeed the scholar who had been so distressed at the death of his colleague two days before. The body was damp from the evening dew, and the eyes were open and glassy. The mouth was agape, the tongue slightly swollen and dark, and a slight cut on one lip showed where a tooth had been broken. There was no other wound that Bartholomew could see – no stab marks or crushed skull or signs that Wymundham had been strangled – and he was not wet enough to have drowned.

'How did you come to find him?' asked Michael of Horwoode, while Bartholomew examined the body. 'He is a long way from your house, and no rational man chooses to wander about in gardens after dark.'

Horwoode regarded him oddly. 'Well, I do, as a matter of fact. I like the peace of these grounds and the solitude they offer – no step-children whining at my heels or townsmen wanting favours. I met Henry Tangmer, the Guildmaster of Corpus Christi, earlier today. He is refusing to donate more funds for Bene't's buildings, and it was not a congenial encounter. I walked down here after he had left, to let the peace of the garden soothe my ragged temper.'

'When was this?' asked Michael.

'Perhaps an hour ago,' said Horwoode. 'I sent for your beadles immediately. Wymundham is a scholar and so his death is the concern of the proctors, rather than the Sheriff. It gave me quite a fright stumbling over a corpse in the dark, I can tell you!'

'When was the last time you came to the bottom of the garden?' enquired Michael. 'I ask only so I can ascertain how long the body has been lying here.'

'About three days ago,' said Horwoode. 'No one else in my household uses the garden in the winter, so questioning them is unlikely to help you, although you are welcome to try.'

There was something puzzling about the body in front of him, and Bartholomew struggled to control his wine-befuddled wits to concentrate. He was sure Wymundham had died because he had been unable to breathe – the blueness of his face and the swollen tongue attested to that. The physician climbed unsteadily to the top of the bank and looked around. There was no evidence of a struggle, and there was nothing there that Wymundham could have used to suffocate himself.

'So, you are saying that Wymundham's body might have been here for as long as three days,' Michael was asking, as Bartholomew skidded down again.

'No,' said Horwoode impatiently. 'He could not have been here *before* Raysoun's death, because I hear he was present when Raysoun fell. His colleagues were concerned when he did not appear for the meal that night – the Duke of Lancaster was guest of honour, you see.'

'I do not see,' said Bartholomew, puzzled. 'What does that have to do with it?'

'No Fellow wanting advancement in the University fails to capitalise on an opportunity to mingle with royalty,' explained Horwoode, clearly surprised that Bartholomew did not know this. 'The Fellows had been looking forward to the visit, and that Wymundham missed it did not bode well for his safety.'

'But he had just seen his friend die,' Bartholomew pointed out. 'Not everyone feels like attending a feast after a shock like that.'

'I do not see why that should have prevented him from making the most of the occasion,' said Horwoode. 'Indeed, the incident might have worked in his favour, because he would have had an interesting tale to attract the Duke's attention.'

'How did Wymundham's body get here, do you think?' Michael asked, seeing Bartholomew about to argue. Just because the physician might have balked at a good night out after the sudden death of a colleague, did not mean that others would have done the same – especially given that the event in question was an opportunity to meet the Duke of Lancaster.

Horwoode shrugged. 'I really have no idea. Since he lies near the Ditch, I assume he came via the water. My walls are high and difficult to scale. I suppose he was on the bank, and he lost his balance and fell.'

'What makes you think he fell?' asked Bartholomew, looking up from the body. His head swam at the sudden movement, and he felt himself topple slightly.

Horwoode regarded his lurch with disapproval. 'I am only offering a suggestion.'

'Did you look at the body when you found it?' asked Bartholomew.

Horwoode sighed. 'Of course I looked at it. I wanted to be certain the man was dead before I went for help.'

'What do you mean by you "wanted to be certain the man was dead"?' pressed Bartholomew curiously, tipsy enough to be incautious.

Horwoode fixed him with a hostile glare. 'Why are you questioning me? I sent for the Proctor, not you. And you are drunk! I can smell wine on your breath and you can barely stand without reeling.'

'I am not drunk . . .' began Bartholomew, although he knew he was not exactly sober.

Horwoode overrode him. 'I have been more than patient. You can carry Wymundham's body back to Bene't and that will be an end to the matter as far as I am concerned. The University can make enquiries if it likes, but they will not involve me. It is neither my fault nor my responsibility that this silly man chose my garden in which to die.'

He snapped his fingers to his servant, who took Wymundham's legs, leaving the beadle to struggle with the torso. Horwoode strode away.

'You have done an admirable job of making enemies for yourself tonight, Matt,' said Michael mildly. 'First you anger the new Master of your College, and then you antagonise the Mayor of your town. If Runham manages to prise you out of Michaelhouse, you will need to stay on Horwoode's good side if you want to practise medicine in Cambridge.'

Bartholomew sighed and grabbed at the monk as he tripped over a root in the dark. 'I should not have come. I told you I had drunk too much wine.'

'So, what did your examination of the body reveal?' asked Michael. 'And do not say that you cannot know for certain until you have looked more closely, or that your wine-sodden mind could make no sense of what you saw. I want to know your suspicions now.'

'I do not think he fell from the Ditch's bank. I think someone held something over his face and smothered him until he was dead, pushing so hard that a tooth was snapped in the process.'

They stumbled through the dark garden and took their leave of the Mayor. Horwoode held open the gate for them, and slammed it shut after they left, making a sound like a clap of thunder that started several dogs barking.

'I wonder what the truth behind this is,' mused Michael as they walked. 'What was Wymundham doing at the bottom of Horwoode's garden in the dead of night?'

'He may not have been there in the dead of night,' Bartholomew pointed out. 'He was not at the Duke's feast on Thursday – the day that Raysoun died – and so it is possible that the body could have been in the garden since then.'

'It seems an odd place for Wymundham to go, though,' said Michael. 'Horwoode suggested that he does not encourage familiarity with the scholars of the College he helped to found, and it did not sound as though visiting Fellows would be made welcome. I do not understand why Wymundham should be found dead there of all places.'

'Perhaps Horwoode is lying,' said Bartholomew with a shrug that made him stagger. 'Perhaps he asked Wymundham to meet him in his garden, so that he could prevent Wymundham from telling anyone what Raysoun said with his dying breath.'

'But that implies Horwoode had something to do with Raysoun's accident,' said Michael. 'And I think that highly unlikely. The Mayor, of all people, should know that good relations between the town and the University are vital for all concerned.'

'Then I wish he would pass that on to Runham,' said Bartholomew gloomily.

'Forget Runham. But are you certain Wymundham was murdered? Are you sure you are not looking for evidence of a crime because you believe Wymundham was carrying some sordid secret, whispered to him by Raysoun – a secret *I* did not hear him reveal, I might add?'

'It was dark by the Ditch and I could barely see, but I think I am right in saying Wymundham was smothered. But for now all I want to do is return to my damp little chamber in Michaelhouse and dream up ways to pay back Runham for what he did to Father Paul.'

Michael shook his arm, unused to seeing his friend so bitter. 'Do not dwell on that, Matt. I assure you I am quite capable of thinking up a way to extract revenge that will leave us untainted. If you had your way, you would have us both hanging from the Castle walls as Master-killers.'

Bartholomew sighed. 'So what do we do now? Is it too late to go to Bene't to make enquiries about Wymundham?'

Michael laughed softly. 'Are you offering to help me? How unusual! I am invariably obliged to beg, bully or wheedle your assistance in matters of this nature. But, much as I would like to take advantage of you, there is little we can do tonight. I would rather talk to the Bene't men in the cold light of day.'

Bartholomew nodded. 'I suppose I will be better at that when I am sober, too.'

'Good. If Wymundham was murdered, then we cannot afford to make mistakes because you should have exercised more self-control with the College's wine. Actually, there was enough of it to ensure the "celebrations" continue for at least half the night. Do you want to return to take part in them?'

'I do not,' said Bartholomew firmly. 'Aside from the fact that I see nothing to be joyous about, that wine was overly strong.'

'That gruesome brew is known to the student fraternity as "Widow's Wine",' said Michael. 'Surely, you have heard of it? It is the cheapest, strongest and nastiest drink money can buy – guaranteed to render you insensible after five glasses and probably dead after ten.'

'I had four,' said Bartholomew. 'Are there any taverns open?'

Michael laughed softly. 'You *are* drunk, my friend! I have never before known you to suggest that we break the University's rules and go carousing in the town's inns.'

'I do not want to carouse; I just want to sit somewhere warm and forget about Michaelhouse.' He became aware of Michael's hand moving rhythmically in the darkness.

'Do not scratch, Brother. You have already made your arm worse.'

'It itches like the Devil,' complained Michael. 'I thought it would ease once you had extracted the sting, but it did not.'

'I will give you a salve to relieve it,' said Bartholomew. He glanced up, aware that the sky was tipping and swirling unpleasantly. 'Look, there is Matilde's house with the candles lit.'

'That means she is awake, then,' said Michael gleefully. 'Come on, Matt. I have not enjoyed a drink with her for a while, and she serves a better brew than you will find in any tavern.'

'We cannot visit her now,' said Bartholomew, horrified. 'It must be nearing midnight.'

'So?' asked Michael. 'Neither of us wants to return to Michaelhouse yet, and I often drop in on Matilde at the witching hour. She will not be surprised to see me.'

'You do?' asked Bartholomew, startled. 'You live dangerously, Brother! What would your Bishop say if word was leaked to him that his best agent was frequenting the houses of prostitutes in the middle of the night?'

'He would probably assume I was there on his business,' said Michael. 'Matilde is an excellent source of information with her network of whores.'

'And would he be right to assume such a thing?'

Michael laughed and gave him a soft jab in the ribs. 'Do I detect a note of jealousy, Matt? You had your chance – the woman is far more fond of you than you deserve, and yet you will not take the plunge and give her what she wants.'

'I hope you do not . . .' Bartholomew faltered, uncertain how to put his question.

Michael laughed and poked him again. 'I am a monk who has sworn a vow of celibacy.' He gave a leering wink that was at odds with his claim, and, before Bartholomew could stop him, was across the road and down the dark alley in The Jewry to where Matilde's house stood. He knocked on the door and waited. Low voices that had been murmuring within stopped abruptly.

'She has company,' said Bartholomew, backing away. 'We should not have come.'

When Matilde answered the door, he was already half-way back up the alley, chagrined that they might be interrupting the town's loveliest prostitute while she was entertaining clients. His feelings towards Matilde were ambiguous. While he considered her the most attractive woman he had ever set eyes on, her profession made any serious relationship with her difficult. Still, she was a good friend, and he had missed their long, intelligent discussions and shared confidences since his extra students and his ever-expanding treatise on fevers had claimed most of his spare moments.

He heard Matilde's exclamation of pleasure when she recognised Michael, and saw the monk ushered inside her house. Before she could close the door, Michael poked his head around it and called to the shadows.

'It is safe for you to come in, Matt. Matilde's visitors are only some of her sisters.'

Bartholomew smiled sheepishly; the town's prostitutes usually referred to themselves as sisters, much as members of the town's guilds referred to themselves as brethren. Like a reluctant schoolboy on his way to lessons, he slowly retraced his footsteps down the alley and entered Matilde's pleasant home.

Matilde's home in The Jewry had changed since Bartholomew had last seen it. The walls had been painted in an attractive diamond pattern of red and yellow, and there were matching tiles on the floor, partly covered by thick wool rugs. She had a new table, too, a handsome piece carved from pale oak, and there was a delicately wrought bowl of spun silver standing on it. Bartholomew wondered whether they were gifts from grateful clients.

Matilde stood in the middle of the room holding a jug of wine. Yet again, Bartholomew was struck by her beauty. She had long, straight hair that shone with health and cleanness, and her simple dress of cornflower blue accentuated the exquisite curves of her slender body. Unlike others in her trade, she used no paints on the delicate pale skin of her face, and her complexion was smooth, soft and unblemished.

She was entertaining two other women, both of whom Bartholomew had treated for various illnesses in the past. One was Una, the daughter of a sergeant at the Castle, and the other was Yolande de Blaston, the wife of one of the town carpenters who knew all about his wife's nocturnal activities and felt nothing but grateful appreciation for the extra money she could earn to help support their nine children.

Matilde was surprised to see Bartholomew. She froze in the act of pouring Yolande a drink when he stepped across her threshold, and regarded him with arched eyebrows.

'And to what do I owe this unexpected pleasure?' she asked. 'Do you want me to supply information about the latest murder you are investigating? Or do you need me to arrange support for digging a new town rubbish pit or cleaning the wells?'

Bartholomew was taken aback by the coolness in her voice, and wondered what he had done to offend her. Meanwhile, Michael squeezed between Yolande and Una on a cushioned bench that was barely large enough for two, and settled himself comfortably, fat legs thrown out in front of him, and his arms stretched along the back of the seat, almost, but not quite, touching the shoulders of the two women.

'Right,' said the monk, favouring Matilde with a contented beam as the two women giggled. 'Do you have any of that good Italian wine you shared with me last time I was here?'

Bartholomew regarded him suspiciously. 'And when was that?'

Michael flapped a dismissive hand. 'I do not recall precisely. But as it happens, Matilde, you are right – there is a case that you might be able to help us with.'

'I thought there might be,' she said, leaving to fetch the wine from the small parlour at the back of the house. 'That is the only reason *he* would visit me these days.'

'You seem to be out of favour, Matt,' said Michael once she had gone.

'Small wonder,' said Yolande, treating Bartholomew to an unpleasant look. 'He only ever comes to see her when he wants something. She was telling us only last night that he had not visited her in almost two months, and now he turns up only to see whether she knows anything about some horrible University crime. But, since he is here, I have a swollen foot that he can look at.'

'And I have painful gums,' added Una. 'It is good he came tonight – now I will not have to rise early in the morning to go to see him.'

'You want me to examine you now?' asked Bartholomew unenthusiastically, wishing they would not talk about him as though he were not there. And anyway, with the room revolving around him in a way that was making him feel sick, he did not feel he should be doctoring anyone.

'You are a physician and here are two charming ladies who need physicking,' said Michael contentedly. 'Where lies the problem? Get on with it, man!'

Bartholomew was kneeling on the floor with Yolande's

foot in his hands when Matilde entered with the wine. He glanced up, then grabbed at Yolande's knee as the sudden movement upset his precarious balance.

'You have had more than enough wine already, Matthew,' she remarked, as she handed Michael his cup. 'You are drunk!'

'He has imbibed four cups of Widow's Wine,' explained Michael.

'That is an apprentices' brew!' said Matilde incredulously. 'Why would a perfectly sane adult who values his health drink Widow's Wine? Was he trying to do away with himself?'

'Do not be so hard on it,' said Una. 'I like a drop of Widow's Wine myself on occasion.'

'The occasion must be when you are too drunk to know what is good for you,' said Matilde, unimpressed. 'Personally, I would never touch the stuff. I have heard that it is brewed with pine resin to give it its strength, and that a dead fox is added to the vats to improve its flavour.'

Bartholomew felt more sick than ever.

'That is why it is popular with young men,' said Yolande. 'My husband's apprentices love it. It is cheap, strong and, after the first cup, its taste does not matter. Were you two out on the town, then, indulging in a little debauchery to break the monotony of all those books you read?'

'We elected two new Fellows tonight,' said Bartholomew. 'After the ceremony, we had a feast.'

'With Widow's Wine?' asked Matilde, laughing in amused horror. 'Is that how Michaelhouse scholars choose to celebrate?'

'I cannot imagine what Master Kenyngham was thinking of,' agreed Michael. 'I suppose he was offered a few barrels cheaply, and did not know its reputation. It is powerful stuff. I, too, feel a little more merry than I would usually do after a mere nine cups.'

'So, which is the latest murder you are investigating?' asked Yolande, as she watched Bartholomew bend carefully to resume his examination of her foot. She snapped her fingers. 'It must be the one where the Franciscan was stabbed in the grounds of Ovyng Hostel.'

'That is one of them,' said Michael. 'I do not suppose any of the sisterhood saw someone fleeing the scene of that little crime, did they?'

The three women shook their heads.

'But it was probably another scholar,' suggested Una helpfully. 'It has all the hallmarks of an internal killing.'

'Really?' asked Michael drolly. 'And what would those be, pray?'

Matilde made an impatient sound at the back of her throat. 'You know very well, Michael. When townsmen kill a scholar, it is nearly always in the heat of the moment, during or after a brawl. But this friar was killed silently and quickly, with no witnesses. It was clearly no spontaneous attack, but a carefully planned murder – an academic murder.'

Michael looked thoughtful. 'You may be right. But I have absolutely nowhere to start with this one – Brother Patrick was fairly new to Ovyng Hostel, and had no time to make serious enemies. And he came from a tiny friary in a part of Norfolk that no one has ever heard of, so I doubt a quarrel could have followed him here.'

'Perhaps he saw something he should not have done, and was killed in order to ensure his silence,' suggested Una.

'But you just said the killing bore the hallmarks of a carefully planned execution,' said Michael. 'That does not tally with Patrick seeing something and an assailant deciding he should not live to tell the tale. Saw what, anyway?'

'It is more likely that he *heard* something,' said Matilde thoughtfully.

'What do you mean?' asked Michael. 'Did you know Brother Patrick?'

'Only by reputation,' said Matilde carefully.

'But he had only recently arrived at Ovyng Hostel,' said Michael. 'How could he have a reputation?'

'It does not take long to establish one,' Matilde pointed out. 'One of the sisters entertained him on several occasions and was astonished at the amount of gossip he knew, even though he had only been in the town for a few weeks.'

'Patrick was a gossip?' asked Michael.

'Quite a shameless one,' said Matilde. 'From what I could tell, he and our sister spent most of their time together engaged in a scurrilous exchange of information. That is why I suggested that he may have been killed because he had heard something someone did not want him to know.'

'But gossips seldom know secrets worth much,' said Michael. 'Because they *are* gossips, people do not tend to confide in them, and they only have access to information that is common knowledge. I do not think his loose tongue would have been sufficient reason to kill him.'

'My experience tells me otherwise,' argued Matilde. 'No one likes a gossip – especially if his tale-telling harms you or your loved ones.'

'What is the other case you have?' asked Una, watching Bartholomew manipulate Yolande's foot with the exaggerated care of the intoxicated. 'You said the friar's death was one of the ones you were working on – what is the other?'

'Is it the one where the baker killed the potter in the

King's Head?' asked Yolande. 'Or the one where the surgeon Robin of Grantchester is accused of murdering Master Saddler by chopping off his leg on Thursday afternoon?'

'Neither of those,' said Michael.

'Robin has been charged with Saddler's murder?' asked Bartholomew, looking up in horror. 'But Saddler was ill anyway. His leg should have been amputated weeks ago, but he refused to allow anyone to do it.'

'You medical men always stick together,' said Una in disgust.

'You will not have to amputate my leg, will you?' asked Yolande nervously.

'Hardly,' said Bartholomew. 'All that is wrong with you is that your shoes are too tight – you need to buy a larger pair.'

'Oh, very practical!' said Matilde crossly, her hands on her hips as Bartholomew stood up. 'And where is she supposed to find the money to buy new shoes with nine children to feed?'

'Slit them,' said Bartholomew. 'The shoes, I mean, not the children. Give them to me; I will do it for you.'

'You will not,' said Matilde, snatching the shoe away from him. 'You are drunk and I do not want you wielding knives in my house. Her husband will do it for her tomorrow.'

'So, which murder are you investigating?' asked Una, opening her mouth so that Bartholomew could inspect her sore gums. Resting a hand on the wall, he leaned over her, hoping he would not slip and end up in her lap.

'It is not murder,' said Michael. 'At least, I do not think so. A scholar fell from the scaffolding surrounding Bene't College two days ago.'

'Oh, that,' said Yolande, disappointed. 'My husband told me about it – he is one of the carpenters who is working on Bene't. He told me that Raysoun was so miserly that he was always climbing up the scaffolding to make sure that none of the workmen were slacking. Because Raysoun was no longer young, and because he liked a drink or two – just like you, Doctor Bartholomew – my Robert said it was only a matter of time before he fell.'

'Really?' asked Michael.

Yolande gave a grin, revealing yellowed stumps of teeth. 'Have I helped you, then?'

'You may have done,' said Michael thoughtfully. 'His friend, Wymundham, has just been found dead near the King's Ditch – in Mayor Horwoode's garden, to be precise.'

'I am sure the Mayor had nothing to do with it,' said Yolande immediately. 'I have visited him every Friday for years and know him well. He is too indecisive to kill anyone.'

Michael laughed. 'I have never heard that used as a defence before, but I will bear it in mind. But no more of murder, ladies. It is delightful to sit and enjoy some congenial companionship. I was saying only tonight that Michaelhouse would benefit from a little female company now and again.'

'It certainly would,' said Matilde fervently. 'I have seldom seen such an unprepossessing array of people – especially that revolting Runham.'

'Do not speak ill of him,' said Michael, in tones that suggested they should. 'Runham was elected Michaelhouse's new Master this evening. Kenyngham has retired.'

Matilde regarded Bartholomew in dismay, as though he were responsible for electing Runham single-handed. 'What possessed you to select a man like that, Matthew? He will be a tyrant.'

'I did not select him,' said Bartholomew tiredly,

straightening up from his inspection of the inflamed gums. 'Una, there is a rotten tooth that needs to be pulled. Robin of Grantchester specialises in pulling teeth, or I can come to your house and do it tomorrow. You decide.'

'She will think about it,' said Matilde, before Una could reply.

'She means we will see whether you are sober tomorrow,' translated Yolande mischievously. 'But we have a lot of business to discuss, so if you two have finished your wine, perhaps you would allow us to get on with it, or we will be here all night.'

Matilde opened the door and waited for Michael to extricate himself from the women on the bench. As soon as Michael had levered his bulk into the street and Bartholomew had followed on unsteady legs, she closed the door, plunging them into darkness.

Michael and Bartholomew began the short walk along the High Street, towards their College. Michael hailed one of his beadles, patrolling to prevent students from causing mischief in the town, to light their way with his lantern. It was raining and the streets gleamed in the faint glow of the lamp. Bartholomew raised his face to the cooling drizzle and wondered when he had last been so drunk. The thick-bellied clouds that slouched overhead seemed to roll and froth before his eyes, and the ground tipped and swayed. He promised himself that he would never touch Widow's Wine again: it was no good for men used to watered ale.

'You are not in Matilde's good books,' said Michael. 'That will teach you to be remiss in visiting your friends. They do not like to feel that they are second best to spotty students and lancing boils.'

Michael's beadle walked next to them, holding his

lantern high so that the scholars would not trip in the treacherous potholes and fissures of the High Street.

'All is quiet tonight,' the beadle reported conversationally to Michael. 'We had to pay a visit to Bene't College earlier, though.'

'Bene't?' echoed Michael immediately. 'Why? Not another death, I hope?'

'It might have been,' said the beadle. 'But we got there in time. Osmun the porter was fighting with one of the Fellows. We have him in our prison.'

'Osmun!' said Michael, shaking his head as they turned into St Michael's Lane. 'If Bene't has any sense, they will dismiss the man before he does anything else to disgrace them. He is a lout.'

The beadle agreed. 'None of us like him – he drinks in the King's Head, and is always causing trouble. He is not the kind of man any respectable College would employ.'

'It is difficult to get good staff these days,' said Michael. 'Labour has been scarce since the Death took so many people. I suppose Bene't feels itself lucky to have porters at all.'

'It should not feel itself lucky to be hampered with *those* porters,' said the beadle with feeling. 'They are the most offensive gatekeepers in the town, and no one can match them for rudeness or their love of brawling. But they are loyal, I will grant them that. They challenge anyone who utters the merest criticism of Bene't. I heard Osmun claimed to be Justus the book-bearer's cousin. Is that true?'

'Why should it not be?' asked Bartholomew.

The beadle peered at him, as if trying to tell whether the question had been asked seriously. He apparently decided it had, and his tone was condescending when he replied. 'So that he could get Justus's tunic and dagger. Why else?'

'That would be a risky thing to do,' objected Bartholomew. 'He might be given a used tunic and a blunt dagger, but he also might have found himself obliged to bury Justus – and that would cost more than anything he was likely to inherit.'

'Michaelhouse is obliged to do that,' said the beadle promptly.

'And Osmun's claim is true anyway,' said Michael. 'I checked with the Master of Bene't, who told me that Osmun brought Justus to him a year ago and asked if he might become a porter.'

'I expect they refused because Justus was not rude enough,' said the beadle with a chortle.

'Bene't did not have the funds to take on more staff, according to the Master,' said Michael. 'So Justus went to work for Runham at Michaelhouse instead.'

'Working for Runham would lead me to kill myself, too,' muttered the beadle fervently, as he stepped ahead to light the way over a particularly treacherous section of the road.

Finally they reached Foul Lane, the muddy runnel on which Michaelhouse's main gate stood. Bartholomew's head was pounding, and he wished he had never set eyes on the Widow's Wine. Michael also did not look well; Bartholomew could see that his face was pale in the dim light of the beadle's lamp.

'This damned arm,' muttered Michael, giving it another vigorous scratch. 'It is driving me insane. I shall be as mad as Clippesby if it does not cease this infernal itching.'

'Let me see,' said Bartholomew, stopping to pull up the monk's sleeve. He staggered slightly as he tried to focus in the feeble glow from the light.

'Are you sure you are capable?' asked Michael, stretching out his good arm to steady the physician. 'I have never seen you so intoxicated.'

'Look what you have done!' cried Bartholomew in dismay, when he saw the red mess the monk had created with his eager fingernails.

'You should have given me something to alleviate the itching,' retorted Michael irritably, tugging his arm away. 'I am not made of marble. No normal man would be able to resist such an agony of itches.'

'If you had let it be, it would not have irritated you so,' said Bartholomew. He rummaged in his medicine bag for a salve. 'Let me put this on it – it should help.'

'Will you treat me here, in the street?' asked Michael in amusement. 'We are only a few steps away from the College gate.'

'I can apply ointment on self-inflicted sores just as easily here as I can in Michaelhouse,' said Bartholomew tartly, slapping a healthy daub of the soothing plaster of betony on to the inflamed skin.

'What is that?' asked Michael, stiffening suddenly. Instinctively, he pulled Bartholomew away from the middle of the lane to the scrubby bushes that grew along the College's east wall. The beadle quickly doused his lamp.

At first Bartholomew could see nothing. The familiar lane with its tall wall and great gate seemed deserted, and the town was absolutely silent. And then he saw what Michael had spotted. Someone was very slowly and carefully opening the wicket door in Michaelhouse's front gate from the inside. A curfew was imposed by the University on its scholars, and students were not supposed to be out after dark. Needless to say many of them found inventive ways to avoid being incarcerated for the night, and it seemed Bartholomew and Michael were about to witness one such bid for freedom.

'We are not the only ones who do not want to be in Runham's new domain tonight,' whispered Michael, smiling mischievously. 'Let us hide here and see who it is. Then I will have my beadle pounce on him, and give him the fright of his life!'

There was not one escaping scholar, but two – dark-cloaked figures bundled up against the rain, who moved silently and furtively as they closed the door behind them.

'Walter must be on duty tonight,' remarked Bartholomew. 'He is the one who sleeps, and the students know they can come and go as they please.'

'Who are they, can you see?' asked Michael, peering down the lane and chuckling to himself.

Bartholomew could not. His vision was too unsteady, the night was too dark, and all Michaelhouse scholars tended to look the same in black tabards and cloaks with hoods that covered their heads and faces. He shivered, feeling the rain soak through his clothes to form cold patches on his shoulders.

'Come on,' he whispered. 'It is freezing here, and I am tired.'

'Wait,' instructed Michael, narrowing his eyes as he squinted in the darkness. 'I want to see who it is.'

'Well, I do not,' said Bartholomew. 'You are being unfair, Brother. No scholar in his right mind will want to spend time in Michaelhouse while Runham is still revelling in his new-found power. Those two are only doing what we have done – looking for a way to be elsewhere.'

'But, Matt—' whispered Michael urgently.

Bartholomew ignored him and pushed his way out of the bushes, walking openly towards the two figures. When they saw him, they started in alarm, but did not make any attempt to run away. Knowing that they would not be able to recognise him, he pushed back his hood so that they could see his face.

'I have just returned from seeing Father Paul to the—' he began.

What happened next was a blur. As soon as he began to speak, one of the figures rushed at him and gave him a hefty shove in the chest that sent him staggering backward, then raced on down the lane before turning towards the river. Startled and indignant that a student should dare to strike a master, Bartholomew grabbed the second man as he made to run past, determined that he should not escape. But the student was stronger than he anticipated, and Bartholomew was uncoordinated. A second shove sent him crashing to the ground. All he could hear were the sounds of running footsteps in the distance.

'Matt!' Michael's anxious face hovered above him. 'Are you hurt?'

'Damn!' said Bartholomew, sitting up and feeling the thick mud – and worse – that clung to his cloak. 'I only had this cleaned last week. Did you see who they were?'

'My beadle has gone after them,' said Michael. 'But I would not hold out too much hope of an arrest, if I were you. They are young and fast, and he is old and slow.'

'Did you see their faces?' asked Bartholomew, clinging to Michael for support as he climbed to his feet. 'They were not Gray and Deynman, I hope.'

'Of course they were not,' said Michael scornfully. 'Do you think either of that pair would push you over? But I did not see their faces – I do not even know if they were our students.'

'They were wearing tabards and cloaks,' said Bartholomew.

'So do lots of men,' said Michael. He gave a sigh of exasperation. 'Why did you not wait, as I told you? I had a feeling that they were not merely a couple of disgruntled students sneaking out for a night on the town. They did not have the demeanour of lads playing truant, and I had the distinct impression that their business was more important than a jug of ale in the King's Head.'

'What do you mean?'

'What I say,' said Michael. 'That there was mischief afoot tonight, and you blundered into it before we could see what it was.'

chapter 4

THE FOLLOWING DAY WAS COLD AND GLOOMY, and a thick pall of mist hung over the town, smothering it in a blanket of dampness that stank of the river and of the filth that lay thick along the High Street. Bartholomew woke with a start when Walter the porter's cockerel began its croaking call directly outside his window. He threw open the shutters and hurled a glove at it, grumbling under his breath as the animal strutted away. Bartholomew would not have minded if the bird had kept its crows for morning, but it made its unholy racket at any time of the day or night, when the fancy took it.

Bartholomew's ill temper at being so rudely awoken was not improved when he became aware that he had a thumping headache. His stomach felt empty and acidic, his throat was dry and sore, and his best cloak was clotted with muck from where he had been pushed into the mud by the fleeing scholars.

The beadle had returned with a hang-dog expression to report that he had lost his quarry, and Michael dismissed him to warn other patrols to be on the lookout for the black-cloaked pair. Angry, Michael had woken the surly porter to berate him for sleeping while people wandered in and out of the College. Walter's sullen self-justification was mixed with a sickening sycophancy that Bartholomew found hard to fathom, until the porter revealed that Runham had already sacked a number of College staff, and Walter was afraid he would be next. With curt instructions that he might have a better chance of keeping his job if he did not sleep every night, Michael had abandoned the porter to his guilty anxiety and stalked across the yard to his room.

The monk was just climbing the stairs to his chamber on the upper floor, when a shadowy figure had emerged from the hallway to demand why it had taken Bartholomew so long to escort Father Paul to the Friary. It was Runham, checking his colleagues' comings and goings. Bartholomew was too weary to feel indignant, and wanted only to lie down, but Michael was outraged enough for both of them. Bartholomew shoved his way past the new Master, while Michael remained in the hall, telling Runham in ringing tones that must have been audible in the Market Square what he thought of a man who lurked in dark corners in the middle of the night to spy on his Fellows. Bartholomew threw off his damp clothes, dropped on to his bed, and knew no more until his abrupt awakening by Walter's annoying bird the following day.

It was Sunday, and Bartholomew's turn to help officiate at the mass that took place just after dawn in the College church. When he saw that the sky had begun to lighten, he hopped across the icy stones in his bare feet to wash and shave in the cold water that Cynric left for him each night. For the first time in years, however, Cynric had forgotten, and the jug was empty. Tugging on his boots, Bartholomew splashed through the courtyard mire to draw water from the well behind the kitchen, shivering in the chill of early morning.

Teeth chattering, he doused himself with the freezing water in the dim light from the open window. He groaned when he heard an ominous tear as the clean shirt he hauled over his head stuck to his wet skin, then ripped it more when he did not take the time to dry himself. He grabbed a green woollen jerkin that his sister had given him, and that was definitely not part of the uniform Michaelhouse scholars were expected to wear, and then covered it with his black tabard. He was late by the time he had finished dressing, so he ran across the yard to the gate, skidding in the slick mud and almost falling.

Still fastening his cloak pin, he was sprinting across the High Street before he realised that Father Paul was supposed to be conducting the mass that morning – and Paul had been unceremoniously expelled from Michaelhouse the previous night. Bartholomew had taken minor orders, which meant that he could take certain services, but he was certainly not qualified to perform a full Sunday mass. He was about to run back to the College to wake Michael, when he saw that candles were already burning inside St Michael's Church. Surprised, he pushed open the door and went inside.

John Runham knelt at the small altar he had erected near his cousin's tomb. He was red-faced and breathless, and Bartholomew saw he had the altar pulled a little way from the tomb and was cleaning behind it with a bundle of feathers tied on a short pole. Bartholomew felt the anger rising inside him even looking at the tomb and its pompous creator but he forced down his ire as he closed the door and walked towards the high altar.

St Michael's Church was a lovely building. It was small and intimate, and had been rebuilt especially for Michaelhouse by the College's founder. There were fine paintings on the walls, the ceiling was picked out in blue and gold, and the stone tracery in the windows was as intricate as lace. In the midst of all this beauty was the late Master Wilson's tomb, an edifice that Bartholomew was not alone in considering to be the nastiest creation in Christendom.

When Thomas Wilson had died during the plague

four years before, he had given Bartholomew money to pay for a splendid tomb to house his mortal remains. Bartholomew had been tardy in fulfilling his promise, and by the time he had commissioned a mason to carve the grave, Wilson's bequest had devalued dramatically. Instead of the glorious affair he had envisaged, Wilson had been incarcerated under a plain slab of black marble with a simple cross carved on the top.

Then Wilson's cousin had come to Michaelhouse. John Runham had been appalled to discover his kinsman housed in something so stark, and immediately set about rectifying the matter. The elegant black slab was now topped by a life-sized golden effigy, and the plain stone rectangle that formed the body of the tomb was hidden by painted panels that blazed with gilt, reds, greens and blues. Unusually, Wilson's statue was not lying on its back gazing longingly heavenward, as was the current fashion, but had been sculpted propped up on one elbow, looking towards where the scholars stood for prayers. Either Runham had modelled for it, or he had given very clear instructions to the mason, because the likeness of the carving to the dead Master Wilson was disconcertingly accurate, and more than once Bartholomew had experienced the uncomfortable sensation that Wilson was actually watching him.

In front of the tomb was a small but sumptuous altar, so that the scholars could kneel to pray for Wilson's soul – although it was not used by anyone except Runham. Bartholomew walked past it, hoping Runham would be too engrossed in his cleaning to notice him. He had almost reached the high altar at the eastern end of the church, when the new Master spoke.

'You are late.'

'I know.' There was nothing more Bartholomew could say. He had no excuse to offer, and he was not prepared to apologise to Runham – he did not want to start the day with a lie.

'You will pay the customary fine of fourpence to me after breakfast,' Runham went on. 'And next time you are late, the fine will be a shilling. You have sacred duties to perform, and I will not permit idleness and irresponsibility to interfere with them.'

Bartholomew saw he would have to ask his colleagues to wake him in the future. He was a heavy sleeper, and usually only stirred when something disturbed him. He would be in desperate financial straits if he were obliged to pay Runham a shilling three times a week.

'It will not happen again,' said Runham softly.

His voice was vaguely threatening, and again Bartholomew did not reply. He noticed that Runham had already lit the candles, found the right place in the Bible for the daily reading, changed the holy water in the stoop, set out the psalters, and arranged the sacred vessels that were required for the mass. In fact, Runham had already done all that Bartholomew was supposed to do in his capacity as priest's assistant.

Bartholomew glanced out of the window. It was still not fully light, and he knew he was not more than a few moments late. He could only suppose that Runham had deliberately arrived early enough to perform all Bartholomew's chores, to drive home his point. It seemed petty, and the anger that Bartholomew had been fighting since he had first seen Runham beautifying Wilson's tasteless little altar began to claw its way to the surface again.

'You took advantage of my leniency last night,' said Runham, laying down his cleaning rod and assuming a mien of religious contemplation. 'You were told to return immediately after delivering Father Paul to his Friary, but you remained out much longer, and came back reeling and stinking of wine.'

'I drank nothing after I left the feast,' replied Bartholomew. 'And I had two patients to attend – one with an injured foot and the other with swollen gums.'

'I trust you did no harm by treating them when you were barely able to stand,' said Runham unpleasantly. 'It would not be the first time a physician left a patient dead because of an over-fondness for wine.'

'They both survived my ministrations,' said Bartholomew, determined not to allow Runham to provoke him. 'But speaking of the dead, when do you plan to bury your book-bearer? I see poor Justus's body still lies in the porch. It has been there since Thursday.'

'I expect I will find a few moments to tend to that this week,' replied Runham, patently uninterested in his book-bearer's mortal remains. He moved to one side so that there was room for the physician to kneel next to him, and changed the subject. 'Perhaps you would join me in a prayer for my cousin's soul.'

Bartholomew could hardly decline – no matter what he thought about Runham's kinsman – so he dropped to his knees and clasped his hands in front of him, hoping that a prayerful attitude would serve to convince Runham to leave him alone. He felt the other man watching him, so he closed his eyes and pretended to be lost in his meditations.

There was a powerful, sickly-sweet scent around the tomb that made Bartholomew want to avoid inhaling too deeply. He had noticed it before, and Michael claimed that proximity to Wilson's private altar always made him sneeze. Runham often placed flowers nearby, and Bartholomew could only assume that the new Master invariably chose the ones with the strongest scents.

'You did not like my cousin, did you,' said Runham, so quietly that Bartholomew thought he might have misheard. He opened his eyes to look at the Master in surprise.

'I built his tomb,' he said levelly.

'That is what I mean. The tomb you raised was a disgrace, and unfit for a man of my cousin's mettle. He would have liked the one I provided much more.'

'I am sure you are right,' said Bartholomew, knowing that the hideous structure Runham designed would certainly have appealed more to Wilson's inflated sense of self-importance. He closed his eyes. 'And now that you have rectified matters, there is nothing more to be said.'

'Have you made your decision?' asked Runham, still in the same soft voice.

Bartholomew opened his eyes again. 'What decision?'

'About whether to become a full-time physician for the town. I am sure that life as a layman will suit you much better than life as a scholar. And anyway, I find medicine sits oddly with the other subjects we teach – law, philosophy and theology.'

'But a good deal of medicine *is* natural philosophy,' said Bartholomew. 'And it also overlaps with astrology, mathematics and geometry.'

'But you do not teach your students astrology, do you?' pounced Runham. 'You claim that reading your patients' stars is a waste of time, and your students would do better to tell their clients to wash their hands before eating, and not to drink water from the river.'

'I did once,' admitted Bartholomew. 'But I have learned that if a physician provides what his patients expect from him, they are more likely to be cured. I suppose the mind has a powerful influence over the body in some people, and belief in a remedy's efficacy will aid recovery.'

'That sounds like heresy to me,' said Runham, eyes narrowing. 'Notions like that do Michaelhouse no good

at all. I do not want you in my College, Bartholomew,
and I do not want you near my saintly cousin's tomb.'

'You asked me to kneel here,' said Bartholomew indignantly. He fought down the urge to retort that he did
not want to be near Wilson's revolting tomb, but contented himself with nodding curtly to the new Master
and heading for the high altar, to try to expunge some of
the murderous impulses he felt towards Runham. When
he had gone, Clippesby emerged from behind a pillar.

'You see, Clippesby?' asked Runham, looking up at the
wild-eyed Dominican. 'Bartholomew is a dangerous man,
and his heretical ideas will pollute the minds of our more
impressionable students.'

Clippesby nodded quickly, his gaze darting here and
there as though he suspected he were not the only one
skulking in the shadows and eavesdropping.

'I heard what he said, Master Runham. I distinctly
recall him claiming that he deliberately created a paltry
tomb for the martyred Wilson, and he gleefully admitted
to teaching his students how to heal using the Devil's
wiles.'

'Well, he did not go quite that far,' said Runham,
regarding the Dominican uneasily. 'But you seem to have
the right idea. Remember what you heard, Clippesby –
I might need your testimony one day. And now our
scholars are arriving, and I must ready myself to take
my first mass as Master of Michaelhouse.'

As he watched Runham preparing himself for the
service, Bartholomew wondered why the lawyer had
suddenly turned so hostile. Although they had never
liked each other, they had always been polite, and
Bartholomew had even treated Runham free of charge
on a number of occasions for the unpleasant flaking
of the skin that seemed to run in his family. Wilson
had been similarly afflicted. But now he was Master,

Runham had dispensed with his veneer of civility, and had become openly antagonistic. Was his rudeness simply a ploy to induce Bartholomew to resign his Fellowship, so that Michaelhouse would no longer offer the study of medicine to its students? Or did Runham hold a genuine grudge against Bartholomew for not creating his cousin a suitably monstrous tomb?

The physician sighed and looked up at the ceiling, just beginning to glitter as the early morning light started to catch the gilt. He had the distinct feeling that his existence was about to change dramatically, and he knew he was powerless to do anything about it.

Still immersed in his reverie, it was halfway through the mass when Bartholomew realised that Michael was not in the church. He was not unduly worried, because the monk often missed services when he was engaged in University business, although he hoped there had not been yet another death to claim the Senior Proctor's attention. There were already four corpses for him to provide verdicts on: Raysoun, who had tumbled from the Bene't scaffolding; his friend Wymundham, whose death so soon after Raysoun's was an uncanny coincidence; Brother Patrick, stabbed in his hostel's garden; and Justus, still lying in a rough parish coffin as he awaited the burial it was Runham's duty to provide.

Bartholomew glanced to the porch where Justus's body lay covered by a piece of coarse brown sackcloth. As a suicide, Justus would not be buried in the churchyard, but would be relegated to unconsecrated land. Since the plague, the number of suicides among the poor had risen: many preferred to kill themselves quickly than suffer a lingering death by starvation. In fact, there were so many of them that a plot had been provided near the Barnwell Causeway. It was a desolate place hemmed in by scrubby marshland vegetation, and was prone to attack by wild animals. Unless Runham used his influence, it would be Justus's final resting place, too.

Whatever Bartholomew might think about Runham as a man, he had to admit that his masses were impressive. The lawyer injected a note of grandeur into his phrases, accentuated by the natural pomposity of his voice, so that the words seemed to take on a new and deeper meaning. And he had brought beautiful patens and chalices with him when he had first been admitted to Michaelhouse, along with a dazzlingly white altar cloth and some scented candles.

Not all Michaelhouse Fellows were in a state to admire Runham's exquisite performance, however. Some of them clutched their stomachs, and most were white-faced, suggesting that Bartholomew had not been the only one to have imbibed too much Widow's Wine the previous night. William looked particularly grim; his heavy face was unshaven and there were red rims around his watery eyes. Even Kenyngham, seldom a man to over-indulge, seemed subdued and pasty-faced.

Michael's choir – minus their leader – was a sorry affair. Missed cues, flat notes and indistinct words were the least of their problems. Knowing they had performed poorly, they shuffled their feet and hung their heads as the mass came to an end.

Michael was fiercely devoted to his singers, who afforded him moments of great pleasure and spells of agonised embarrassment in more or less equal measure. It was the largest assembly of musicians in Cambridge, and owed its size entirely to the fact that the College was in the habit of recompensing participants with bread and ale each Sunday. It comprised local men and boys with a smattering of co-opted scholars that justified it being called the Michaelhouse Choir. Master Kenyngham had possessed the good sense to understand that the choir helped to promote peaceful relations between the College and the town, and that the variable and unpredictable quality of the music was something that just had to be endured for the sake of concord. A glance at Runham's grim face, however, told Bartholomew that the new Master did not intend to follow Kenyngham's example of leniency and tolerance.

'Your performance today was a disgrace,' he announced to the assembled singers, once the mass was over. 'I have never heard such a miserable sound purporting to be music. From now on, your services are not required. Those of you who are Michaelhouse scholars will be under the leadership of Clippesby – the new Fellow of music and astrology.'

Clippesby stepped forward amidst gasps of disbelief. Michael had been master of the choir for more than a decade, and had devoted a huge amount of his spare time to making it what it was – a good deal better than it might have been.

'These people have served the College faithfully for many years,' said Kenyngham with quiet reason, taking Runham by the arm. 'We cannot dismiss them now.'

Angrily, Runham shook himself free. 'You are no longer Master, and in future please keep your opinions to yourself. I have made my decision: the choir is disbanded.'

'But Brother Michael has been teaching us a *Te Deum*,' objected old Dunstan the riverman, his jaws working rhythmically over his toothless gums. 'We have been practising for weeks, so that we will be ready to sing it at Christmas.'

'Then you should have considered that before you embarrassed the College with your dismal racket today,' snapped Runham.

'But it was only because Brother Michael was not here,' protested Isnard, the burly bargeman who liked to think he sang bass. 'We are better when he conducts us.'

'Michael is unreliable and too wrapped up in his other interests,' said Runham. 'That is why I am absolving him of the responsibility and conferring it on Clippesby. Michael is not a musician in any case – he is a monk with a smattering of theology, who spends most of his time politicking with the Chancellor and the Bishop, and meddling in affairs that do not concern him – even to the extent of fraternising with Oxford scholars, if Langelee is to be believed. Where is he this morning, anyway?'

No one knew, and Runham, raising an imperious hand to quell the cacophony of questions and recriminations that rang through the nave from the dismissed choir, prepared to lead his black-garbed scholars back to Michaelhouse for breakfast. Bartholomew did not join them. He wanted to remain in the church for a while, to let the silence and solitude calm his temper before he was obliged to spend more time in the company of the new Master. There was also the fact that Runham would be expecting Bartholomew's fine of fourpence and the physician was determined to make him wait for it.

'But what about our bread and ale for today?' cried Dunstan in a quivery, distressed voice. 'It is all I will get – my daughter cannot spare me food on Sundays, when all her children are home.'

'I cannot, in all conscience, squander College resources by paying for inferior services,' said Runham pompously, processing out of the church with his scholars streaming behind him. His voice came back distantly. 'There will be no bread and ale for you today – or ever again.'

Pandemonium erupted as the outraged choristers began to argue among themselves, voices raised in accusation and recrimination. Then Isnard became aware of Bartholomew, still standing in the chancel.

'Your College cheated us!' he declared furiously, advancing on the physician. 'You let us sing today, knowing that we would not be given our bread and ale.'

Bartholomew thought that was possibly true as far as Runham was concerned, although the choir had done themselves no favours with the diabolical quality of their singing. He did not know how to answer.

Isnard strode forward and grabbed him by the front of his tabard, while his angry friends gathered around in a tight circle. Too late, Bartholomew realised he should not have stayed in the church and that the choir would not care whether he condoned the Master's actions or not. He would be battered to a pulp because he wore a black tabard, and only later, when tempers had cooled, would the singers question whether he had really been party to Runham's decision. He struggled, but the press of people was too great, and Isnard's grip too tight. He closed his eyes tightly, waiting for the first blow to fall.

'Leave him be, Isnard,' came Dunstan's reedy voice, miraculously cutting in over the others'. 'That is no cur of Runham's. That is Doctor Bartholomew, who set your leg for you last year.'

Isnard hauled Bartholomew to one side, so that he could see his face in the pale light that filtered in through the east window. 'So it is!' the bargeman exclaimed, releasing the physician so abruptly that he stumbled. Helpful hands stretched out to steady him. 'Sorry, Doctor, but all you scholars look the same in those black uniforms – especially in the gloom of this godforsaken place.'

'I have never liked this church,' agreed Aethelbald, Dunstan's equally ancient brother, looking around him in distaste. 'It is cold and dark and sinister – as though devils lurk in its shadows.'

'Especially now that one is buried here,' said Dunstan, pointing with a wizened finger at the glittering monstrosity of Wilson's tomb.

As one, the choir crossed themselves vigorously and gazed around, as if they imagined Wilson himself might emerge from his grave and drag them all down to the depths of Hell.

'Wilson was a sinful, wicked man,' said Aethelbald. 'During the plague, he lurked in his room by day to avoid contamination, but at night he slipped out to meet his lover.'

'Did he?' asked Isnard, interested in this piece of gossip. 'Was she a whore, then?'

'She was,' said Aethelbald with conviction. 'She was also Prioress of St Radegund's Convent, God rot her black soul.'

'And he stole from people,' added Dunstan, not wanting Aethelbald to have all the attention.

'Really?' asked Isnard, fascinated to hear that a man with as fine a tomb as Wilson's had been so unscrupulous in life. 'What kind of things did he take?'

'Anything, really,' hedged Dunstan. 'Money, jewels, clothes. Am I not right, Doctor?'

Bartholomew swallowed. He was not aware that Wilson had been dishonest, but he had been secretive, and while Bartholomew could not see him climbing up guttering in the dead of night to burgle a house, he could certainly envisage him cheating someone, or indulging in a little creativity while doing the College accounts.

'I have not . . . I do not . . .' he began falteringly.

'He does not know,' said Aethelbald, waving a dismissive hand in Bartholomew's direction. 'He was out physicking the sick during the plague, and had no idea what the Master of Michaelhouse did in the privacy of his rooms. But it is common knowledge in the town that

Wilson had great piles of stolen gold and silver there when he died.'

Then common knowledge was mistaken, Bartholomew thought to himself. He had been in the room when Wilson had died, and there had been no gold and silver – stolen or otherwise – that he had seen. Like many stories about the plague, telling and retelling had resulted in ever more flagrant digressions from the truth.

'I have never heard about any of this,' said Isnard dubiously. 'If it is common knowledge, then how come I did not know?'

Dunstan shrugged. 'You obviously frequent the wrong taverns. If you want to hear stories about the University, you need to be in the Brazen George, not the King's Head.'

'I shall remember that,' said Isnard. He turned to Bartholomew and returned to his original grievance. 'But your College cheated us. It might not be your doing, but someone will pay for it.'

'Here,' said Bartholomew, taking his purse from his side and handing it to Isnard. 'You are right, and I am sorry. It is not much, but it is all I have, and should buy enough bread for everyone.'

'But not ale,' said Isnard, regarding the meagre contents of Bartholomew's purse with disappointment. 'We do not want your money, Doctor. We want to see that fat, pompous ass strung up on the walls of his own College, so that we can watch the life slowly choking out of him.'

'That is dangerous talk,' said Bartholomew, alarmed by the chorus of vehement agreement that rose around him. 'I know you are angry, but perhaps Michael will be able to persuade Runham to reinstate you. Do not do anything that might jeopardise that.'

'He is right,' said Dunstan reluctantly. 'We should all go home and meet again tomorrow, when we are better able to think clearly. If we march on Michaelhouse now and drag Runham from his breakfast trough to execute him, we might never be employed as choristers again.'

With relief, Bartholomew saw the choir accept this cold logic, and they began to disperse. One or two of the smaller children were crying, and Bartholomew suspected that Dunstan would not be the only one going hungry that day.

'But we will never accept that mad-looking Clippesby as our leader,' Aethelbald called over his shoulder as he left. 'We will only have Brother Michael.'

'I will tell him,' promised Bartholomew.

'Do not tell Michael – he knows that already – tell that pig Runham,' said Isnard. 'It is *he* who needs to know.'

Bartholomew leaned against a pillar when the door closed behind the last of them. Despite the coldness of the day, he was sweating and the back of his shirt was sodden. He took a deep breath, wondering what other evils Runham would perpetrate in his time as Master – if the man managed to survive that long.

Bartholomew had not been sitting alone in St Michael's Church for more than a few moments when a familiar voice spoke softly at his side. He looked up to see Master Kenyngham standing over him, his face white in the gloom. He was puzzled to see that the gentle Gilbertine was shaking, and that tears glistened on his cheeks.

'Thank the Lord you are all right,' Kenyngham whispered unsteadily. 'I thought they were going to kill you where you stood – in God's holy church!'

'What are you doing here?' asked Bartholomew, standing to take the friar's arm and lead him to a bench at the back of the nave, so that the old Master might sit and compose himself.

'I came to find you,' said Kenyngham in a voice that

was dull with shock. 'I had just entered the church when I saw that mob close in on you and – God forgive me – I was too afraid for my own safety to come to your assistance. I was so paralysed with fear that I could not even find the voice to cry out to make them stop.'

'But you are not well,' said Bartholomew kindly, recalling that Kenyngham had been as pallid and unhealthy as the rest of the scholars in the church that morning. Kenyngham was also unused to the violent effects of the infamous Widow's Wine. 'You are pale.'

'That was our choir, Matthew!' cried the friar, distraught. 'They were men and boys who have enjoyed our hospitality for years, and who have joined their voices with ours to rejoice in the glory of God.'

'They joined their voices with ours in order to earn their bread and ale,' said Bartholomew bluntly. 'And it was fury at the injustice of losing it that led them to contemplate violence. These are hungry people for whom the College provides a valued service – not the other way around.'

'Were they right?' Kenyngham asked suddenly. 'About Master Wilson, I mean. Did he really seduce the Prioress of St Radegund's?'

'I do not know if "seduce" is the right word,' said Bartholomew, 'but they had an understanding.'

'Horrible!' exclaimed Kenyngham, putting his hands over his face. Bartholomew could not help but agree: the notion of the smug Master Wilson pawing any woman, religious or otherwise, was repellent. 'And the stolen property? Is it true that the whole town knows Wilson was a thief?'

'I do not think so,' said Bartholomew. 'Wilson was not a good man, but I never heard anything to suggest that he did anything dishonest – although it would not have surprised me if he had.'

'Wilson was less than scrupulous with some people,' said Kenyngham reluctantly. 'I encountered discrepancies in his accounting when I became Master, and a number of people approached me and asked whether various items had appeared in the College coffers after Wilson had died.'

'You mean Wilson *was* a thief?' asked Bartholomew, vaguely amused.

'I did not say that,' said Kenyngham carefully. 'The accounting inconsistencies were possibly honest mistakes, and he may have had nothing to do with the missing items. It is wrong to speak ill of the dead, especially in a church, where the mortal remains of the man we are maligning lie so close to hand.'

'I had no idea he stole,' mused Bartholomew. 'I thought he was just unpleasant, vindictive and scheming.'

'Really, Matthew,' admonished Kenyngham. 'The poor man may be in Purgatory at this very moment, repenting his evil deeds so that he may move on to a happier place. Saying such dreadful things about him will not help. And anyway, to speak ill of the dead might encourage their tortured souls to come and haunt us.'

'Then Wilson would have been rattling his chains in the depths of the night long before this,' said Bartholomew practically. 'Or perhaps the problem is that so many people have spoken ill of him, he does not know whom to haunt first.'

'Matthew!' cried Kenyngham, genuinely distressed. 'Enough! I would never have started this conversation had I known the way it would end. I only wanted to know whether the town was aware of the less saintly aspects of Wilson's character.'

'If the townsfolk really believed Wilson was a thief, you would have heard about it long before today,' said Bartholomew. 'But now that Runham is Master, he will have less time to spend venerating Wilson's memory and the malicious rumours will soon die away. Do not worry, Father.'

Kenyngham gave a shuddering sigh. 'I suppose you are right. But Runham's incumbency has not started well at all. What will Michael say when he hears the choir is no longer his? I went to break the bad news to him, but I found I could not.'

'Where did you see him? At breakfast?'

Kenyngham shook his head. 'He did not appear for breakfast, and I was worried. Have you noticed that Michael seldom misses a meal?'

'I have noticed, yes,' said Bartholomew slowly, when Kenyngham paused, obviously expecting an answer to what was hardly an astute observation.

'So I went to see if he was in his room.'

'And?' asked Bartholomew, when Kenyngham paused again.

'And he is unwell,' said Kenyngham. 'That is why I am here. I remembered you had not joined the procession that walked back to the College, and so I assumed you must have stayed here for some private prayer. Then, when I entered, and I saw that our choir had turned from a heavenly throng to a band of would-be killers . . .'

He faltered, and Bartholomew resisted the urge to laugh. He wondered whether anyone but Kenyngham would be so other-worldly as to see the likes of Dunstan, Aethelbald and Isnard as a heavenly throng.

'What is wrong with Michael?' he asked. 'Was it the Widow's Wine? I had four glasses, and they made me reel like a drunkard, but he claims to have downed nine. I am surprised he even knew where his feet were, let alone used them to walk to Mayor Horwoode's house.'

'It was not the wine,' said Kenyngham. 'He was complaining that his arm hurt, and he wanted me to fetch you. You had better go to see him. I will stay here for a while, to contemplate on what I have learned from this experience.'

He took a deep breath and clasped his hands in front of him, his eyes fixed on the Great Bible that sat on the lectern in the sanctuary.

'Have you learned that you would have done better to vote for Father William?' asked Bartholomew, smiling in an attempt to lighten the Gilbertine's gloom. 'Or better still, that we should have ignored Langelee's accusations and elected Michael?'

Kenyngham did not smile back. 'I have learned that I should never have resigned in the first place,' he said. Tears began to flow again. 'God forgive me! What have I done?'

When Bartholomew arrived back at Michaelhouse, Cynric was just leaving, and his face was as black as thunder. Everyone else was at breakfast, summoned by the shrill little bell that hung near the porters' lodge. Usually, there was someone scurrying late to the hall, but no one dared to take that kind of liberty with Runham in charge, and the courtyard was empty.

'Where are you going?' asked Bartholomew in surprise, seeing his book-bearer cloaked, gloved and carrying a bundle over his shoulder. 'I thought you were on breakfast duty today.'

'I was, boy,' said Cynric in a muffled voice. 'But Master Runham has just informed me that he no longer needs my services and I have been dismissed from Michaelhouse.'

'What?' exclaimed Bartholomew, aghast. 'But he cannot do that! He—'

'Whether he can or cannot, he has, and that is an end to it,' said Cynric, pushing past the physician and heading for the lane.

'No,' said Bartholomew firmly. 'Even a Master cannot dismiss a servant without the other Fellows' consent. You are not dismissed, Cynric.'

'He had their consent,' said Cynric bitterly. 'Langelee and Clippesby agreed to support Runham in his "economies", although at least William tried to prevent me from being thrown out like a dirty rag.'

'But Langelee and Clippesby alone are not enough,' protested Bartholomew. 'Runham needs the votes of the majority of Fellows to pass a decision like that.'

'Father Paul, you, Brother Michael and Master Kenyngham were absent at the breakfast meeting, and that newcomer – Suttone – abstained again on the grounds that he does not know enough of the College to decide such matters, although I could see he was uncomfortable with the notion of throwing loyal men out on to the streets. But with Clippesby and Langelee voting with Runham, your fine new Master had his majority.'

'But you cannot just go,' said Bartholomew in horror, grabbing his servant's arm. 'Come with me to see Runham now. We will sort this out—'

'The decision has been made,' said Cynric, looking away. 'You are too late, boy.'

'But you have been here for years – as long as I have,' protested Bartholomew, still holding Cynric's arm.

'Right,' said Cynric, giving him a rueful smile. 'It was you who brought me here and got me this position, and I am grateful. It has been a comfortable life, all told, and I came to meet my wife through you. But it is probably time I went on to different things. Rachel wants me at home more, and your brother-in-law – Rachel is his seamstress, as you know – has offered me a position as captain of the mercenaries he hires to protect his goods.'

'Oswald is trying to steal my book-bearer?' asked Bartholomew, stunned that Edith's husband would encourage Cynric to leave him without discussing it first.

Cynric gave a reluctant grin. 'I suppose he is.' He became serious. 'That business you dragged me into in Suffolk this summer was a nasty experience, and my Rachel has been urging me to leave you in case something similar happens again. You do seem to attract that kind of trouble.'

'Cynric, I am so sorry,' said Bartholomew, appalled that the events in a remote country village should have had such a traumatic effect on his book-bearer and immediately feeling responsible.

'It was not your fault I fell under that curse, and you did risk your life to have it lifted. But Rachel is right: it is time I settled down and got a real job.'

'But how will we manage without you?'

Cynric smiled again. 'It is for the best, lad. I did not relish the prospect of working for Runham. None of the servants like him – especially after what he did to Father Paul last night. Even Agatha the laundress is thinking of taking a position she was offered at Bene't College.'

'Not Agatha!' groaned Bartholomew. 'But wait, Cynric, you cannot just leave like this . . .'

'I am only going around the corner,' said Cynric, squeezing his arm in a rare gesture of affection. 'And I will come if you need me – remember that if Runham plagues you too much.'

Bartholomew was torn. On the one hand, Rachel had a point, and it was unfair of Bartholomew to oblige Cynric to take part in some of the adventures Michael foisted upon him, although Bartholomew had always been under the impression that Cynric had enjoyed them. On the other hand, Bartholomew could not imagine life without Cynric's loyal, comforting presence.

'I will visit you,' he promised the book-bearer, taking his hand and clasping it warmly.

Cynric gave a lopsided smile. 'You will not. Mistress Matilde and your sister both claim you are an unreliable and infrequent guest. But I will seek you out and we will spend time in each other's company. I will see to that.'

With another brief smile, Cynric was gone, making his way up the lane to Milne Street, where Bartholomew's brother-in-law had his substantial cloth business. With a heavy heart, Bartholomew climbed the stairs next to his room, which led to the chamber Michael shared with two Benedictine students. The door was ajar, and he walked in after tapping gently.

Michael was pale and sweat beaded his face. The root of the problem was the sting in his arm, which had been scratched raw by the monk's ragged, dirty fingernails. Pale red lines ran from the wound to his shoulder, showing where the infection had spread.

'You took your time,' said Michael feebly, as Bartholomew knelt next to him and felt the monk's forehead with the back of his hand. 'I asked Kenyngham to fetch you hours ago.'

'There was trouble at the church,' said Bartholomew vaguely. Michael looked curious, but Bartholomew started to ask questions about his illness, not wanting to tell him about the choir's revolt or that his services as music master had been dispensed with by the odious Runham while he was unwell.

He was surprised by the speed at which the infection had taken hold of Michael; the wound had not seemed so serious the night before. He sincerely hoped his drunkenness had not prevented him from making an accurate diagnosis.

He clattered down the stairs to his storeroom, to gather the necessary potions and salves. He reached for the water that Cynric always left for him, but the jug was empty and Cynric was no longer in the College. Cursing, he walked across the courtyard to collect some of the near-boiling water from the great cauldron that always steamed over the kitchen fire. Agatha the laundress levered her bulk from her wicker chair by the hearth and came to help him.

'I will bring this,' she said, hoisting the heavy bucket in one meaty hand, as if it contained nothing but air. 'You cannot manage it with all you are already carrying, and anyway, it is weighty.'

'Let me take it, then,' offered Bartholomew. 'You carry the medicines.'

Agatha eyed him up and down critically, and apparently decided that she was the stronger of the two. Without a word, she set off across the courtyard at a cracking pace that had him concerned that she would slip in the mud and scald herself. But they arrived at Michael's chamber unscathed, and she lingered in the doorway, watching him work.

'That Runham has dismissed virtually all the College staff except for me,' she said, folding her formidable arms across her equally formidable chest. 'He dares not get rid of me, because he values his manhood.'

'Pity,' said Michael from the bed. 'I would like to see him lose it.'

Agatha gave a screech of raucous laughter that echoed across the yard and that Bartholomew was certain would be audible in the hall, where the scholars would be sitting in silence as they ate their breakfast.

'He has ordered Kenyngham out of the Master's chambers this morning, so that he can move in,' she said, sobering slightly.

'God's blood!' exclaimed Michael, horrified. 'He is not wasting any time, is he!'

'You both need to be careful of Runham,' Agatha advised. 'He is a dangerous man. He wants to dismiss all the old Fellows, then fill the vacancies with his own lickspittle – like that Clippesby.'

'Clippesby?' asked Bartholomew, quickly making a small incision in Michael's arm to drain away the infection while the monk's attention was on Agatha. Michael yelped in pain, and shot Bartholomew an accusing look.

'He has become Runham's henchman,' said Agatha in disapproval. 'Personally, I do not believe the man is sane, which is why he thinks Runham is some kind of god, I suppose. Clippesby follows Runham everywhere, and runs all his errands.'

'That is because Justus, his own book-bearer, died,' said Michael. 'Runham is too mean to pay for a servant, so he is using the pathetic, ingratiating Clippesby as his menial. Serves him right!'

'Yes!' said Agatha viciously. 'The pair of them deserve each other.'

'Have you done anything about Wymundham?' asked Michael of Bartholomew.

'Me?' asked Bartholomew, startled by the question. 'What should I have done?'

Michael sighed irritably. 'I am lying here helpless, and there are deaths that need to be investigated. There are Wymundham's and Brother Patrick's – and Raysoun's, according to what you heard Wymundham claim.'

'But it is not my place to look into such matters. I am not your Junior Proctor.'

'Do not be so pompous, Matt,' said Michael. 'With me indisposed and my Junior Proctor in Ely, there is no one else I can trust. And anyway, it is Sunday and you have nothing else to do. Just go to Bene't and ask to speak to Simekyn Simeon, who is one of the Fellows. I arrested him for drinking in taverns a few weeks back but then let him go, so he owes me a favour. He will tell you the secrets behind Bene't College's façade of friendship and harmony.'

'Oh, Lord!' muttered Bartholomew weakly.

'And then slip across to Ovyng Hostel to enquire if anyone has more information about the death of Brother Patrick.'

'No,' said Bartholomew firmly, deciding to take a stand before Michael's demands took too much of his time. 'I cannot take on *all* your work as well as my own.'

'Shame on you,' said Agatha disapprovingly. 'These poor scholars lie murdered, and you are more interested in writing that over-long book and teaching the likes of that Rob Deynman than in seeing justice done.'

'Quite,' agreed Michael immediately. 'So prove otherwise and do as I ask. Visit Ovyng, and see whether the Principal has any more to tell you about Brother Patrick.'

'But you have your beadles,' protested Bartholomew. 'Send one of them.'

Michael raised his eyes heavenward and exchanged a weary grimace with Agatha. 'I cannot send any of those ruffians to deal with the likes of Fellows and Principals. You know that. I doubt the Principal of Ovyng or the scholars of Bene't would even allow my rough beadles into their presence. I need another scholar – a man of standing in the University, like you.'

Agatha gave Bartholomew a heavy tap – more of a thump – on the shoulder. 'Do as you are told, Matthew. Poor Michael is ill, and cannot do it himself.'

'You are a good woman, Agatha,' said Michael, leaning back in his bed and closing his eyes. 'At least there is one person in Michaelhouse I can trust to put personal convenience second to honour and justice.'

'All right, all right,' said Bartholomew wearily, feeling powerless under their dual assault on his sense of obligation and friendship. 'I will visit Ovyng later today.'

'Good,' said Agatha approvingly, treating him to another eye-watering slap on the back. 'Justice will be served.'

When Agatha left, Bartholomew finished working on Michael, piling him high with bedclothes and feeding him water and potions that he hoped would break the fever. By mid-morning the monk seemed slightly better, although he claimed he was not. Reluctantly, Bartholomew left Michaelhouse to visit Ovyng Hostel, to enquire whether anything new had been discovered about the murder of Brother Patrick.

Ovyng stood opposite Michaelhouse, at the junction of Milne Street and St Michael's Lane. It was a large building that housed about fifteen students, all of them Franciscan friars. By the standards of most hostels it was comfortable, with a pleasant chamber on the upper floor for sleeping, and a hall on the ground floor that served as lecture room and refectory. It was located in a large garden, which was still producing scraggy end-of-season vegetables for its scholars' meals.

Bartholomew knocked at the door and asked to see the Principal. He was shown to a tiny room at the back of the house where the Principal had his office, and given a cup of the splendid malty ale that was brewed in the nearby Carmelite Friary. The Principal, a solemn, humourless man with neat white hair, sighed sadly, and told Bartholomew what he had already told Michael: that Brother Patrick's body had been discovered the previous Friday morning in the garden, and that he had been stabbed. There were no witnesses to the murder, and no one at Ovyng had the faintest idea why anyone should have taken against Patrick.

'How long had Patrick been at Ovyng?' asked Bartholomew, sipping the ale.

'Since September,' said the Principal. 'He was not among the most popular of our students, but he was not unduly disliked.'

'Unduly?' asked Bartholomew, surprised. 'You mean he was disliked, then?'

The Principal grimaced, as if annoyed with himself for the inadvertent slip. He hesitated, then nodded reluctantly. 'Patrick was a gossip, and enjoyed spreading spiteful tales about the others. It is not a pleasant pastime, but not one that warranted his death.'

Bartholomew rubbed his chin. Matilde had mentioned that Brother Patrick was a gossip, and had even suggested that his loose tongue was the reason for his death. 'What kind of tales did he tell?'

The Principal raised his eyebrows, grimly amused. 'If I were to tell you that, I would be no better than him, would I?'

'I am not asking you so that I can tell everyone I meet; I am asking you because these tales may be connected to his death.'

'I doubt it,' said the Principal. 'But the kind of thing he seemed to ferret out were matters like our Bursar's occasional illicit visits to the Brazen George for a drink, or the fact that our philosophy tutor hides the fact that he cannot see to read these days, or that one of the students once stole a pie from a baker. His stories contained nothing very damning, but they were irritating and sometimes embarrassing for those concerned.'

'Do you think it is possible that Patrick discovered something really incriminating, and was killed to ensure he did not tell anyone else?'

The Principal gave a smile that was more sad than happy. 'I do not think anyone at Ovyng has a secret of that magnitude. Feel free to ask all the questions you like, but remember that my scholars are all friars – not novices, but men who have taken their final vows. Ovyng is not like Michaelhouse, where the secular sits uneasily with the religious, and we do not involve ourselves in the squabbles and fights that the rest of the University seems to enjoy.'

'Except the ones with the Dominicans,' remarked Bartholomew wryly.

The Principal's grave smile did not falter. 'That is different, Doctor. We are Franciscans: it is our sacred duty to expose the lies and deceits of the Dominican Order.'

'Then perhaps Brother Patrick was killed by a Dominican,' suggested Bartholomew.

'It would not surprise me,' said the Principal. 'But if that is the case, then Patrick's love of gossip has nothing to do with it, and his death was an act of simple savagery by a rival Order.'

'You are not planning to take revenge, are you?' asked Bartholomew, slightly anxiously.

The Principal sighed. 'It was a course of action we considered in the distressing moments immediately following the discovery of Patrick's body. But we are friars, not town louts. We unanimously decided that any vengeance should be left to the Senior Proctor and his men. Instead, we have hired an additional porter to guard our gates at night and ensure all our doors are locked.'

Bartholomew stood. 'Thank you for your time, Father. I hope Brother Michael will find the person who killed your scholar.'

'So do I,' said the Principal sincerely. 'But Patrick's body lies in St Mary's Church and will be buried tomorrow. I understand you have some skill in examining corpses. Come with me now, to see if you can uncover some clue that the rest of us might have missed.'

Bartholomew felt he could not easily refuse such a

request, so he walked with the Principal to St Mary's, where he spent some time examining the body of the young friar. The case was as straightforward as he could imagine: there was a small, circular hole in Patrick's back, where something had been driven into it, and that was all. The wound was deep and certainly would have been almost instantly fatal, and there was no other mark on the body, suggesting that the attack had been quick and decisive, and the friar had not been given a chance to do anything to defend himself.

The only puzzling thing was the shape of the injury. Most knife wounds were slit-shaped or ovoid, but the one in Patrick was an almost perfect circle. Bartholomew could not imagine what could have made it. He could only assume it was some kind of spike, like an awl, rather than a blade. The injury was clean, and there were no splinters or fragments of dust that Bartholomew could see, so he assumed the weapon must have been made of metal.

Eventually he straightened up, put Patrick back the way he had found him, and made his farewells to the Principal, knowing that he had found nothing that would help uncover the killer of the gossiping friar; he had probably wasted the Principal's time as well as his own. As always when he encountered violent and futile death, he was aware of an odd combination of helplessness and gloomy resignation, and did not feel at all like teaching. Instead, he sat in Michael's room while the monk slept, thinking about what little he had learned from Brother Patrick's death.

In the late afternoon Runham came, wanting to see for himself why two of his Fellows had missed all three meals that day after he had expressly ruled that attendance was no longer optional. He relented when he saw Michael's illness was genuine, but stated that Bartholomew would not be excused the following day. Bartholomew agreed, just to be rid of the man, although he had no intention of leaving Michael's side if the fever became worse.

'My fourpence, please,' said Runham, thrusting out his hand.

Bartholomew gazed blankly at him.

'My fourpence,' repeated Runham impatiently. 'If you recall, I fined you for your unwarranted lateness at church this morning. I told you to pay it after breakfast, but you defied me in that, so I will have it now.'

'Will you fine me, too?' demanded Michael hoarsely from the bed. 'I missed mass totally.'

'You had an excuse,' said Runham, although the tone of his voice suggested that he considered it a poor one. 'But Bartholomew did not. Give me the fourpence now, or I shall be obliged to fine you an additional fourpence for late payment of a forfeit.'

Bartholomew found the correct change. 'Wash it before you handle it too much,' he advised, as he slapped the coins into the Master's upturned palm. 'It came from a patient with a fatal contagion, and I would not like to see the disease strike you, too.'

He was maliciously gratified to see Runham blanch and hastily drop the money into his hat. The new Master scrubbed his fingers vigorously on the side of his tabard as he left, and through the window Bartholomew saw him running to the lavatorium once he reached the yard.

'That must be one of the first times he has ever voluntarily washed his hands,' said Bartholomew, turning to grin at Michael.

'Was it true?' asked Michael. 'Did the coins really come from a patient with a contagion?'

Bartholomew shook his head. 'If I thought a contagion might be carried on them, I would hardly keep them in my purse. I am not keen to have Runham as Master, but I am not ready to kill myself over it.'

Michael gave a weak grin. 'Either you have been practising your lie-telling, or I am more ill than you are letting on. You had me convinced!'

Bartholomew smiled, and gazed across the brown mud of the courtyard below.

In the evening, Gray came to ask Bartholomew to tend a sick stable boy in Agatha's quarters. The lad was afflicted with an ailment that Gray claimed he could not diagnose. The physician sat on the straw mattress and took the boy's hand in his, noting that the pulse was strong and steady and the skin cool and dry, even though he appeared to be insensible. There was a small bruise on one leg, presumably from some childish game of rough and tumble, but nothing else seemed amiss. Bartholomew sat back, and stared thoughtfully at the thin face with its tightly closed eyes.

'It is all right, Roger,' he said kindly. 'You will not be thrown out of Michaelhouse with nowhere to go like the other servants. I will have a word with my brother-in-law and I am sure he will find you something.'

Roger's eyes flickered open. 'Do you promise?'

Bartholomew nodded, and left him to the relieved ministrations of Agatha, who bared her terrifying teeth to indicate pleasure. Where a normal mortal might have quailed at the sight of the fangs honed to a primeval sharpness bearing down on him, Roger just smiled with a child's easy acceptance of the peculiar.

When Agatha had agreed to undergo some beauty treatment at Deynman's hands earlier that summer, she had been lucky that Bartholomew had discovered what was in progress and had prevented matters going further. And Deynman was lucky to be alive, given Agatha's fury when a mirror revealed that the painful scrapings and grindings had not given her the pearly white smile she had been promised, but the uneven fangs of a demon. Deynman had still not been forgiven for his crime, and even his slow wits sensed he needed to avoid unnecessary meetings with the laundress if he wanted to survive to become a physician.

Gray followed Bartholomew into the yard. 'Runham told us Roger would be dead by this evening. He was wrong.'

'Runham is not a physician,' said Bartholomew tartly. 'And neither will you be if you listen to men like him telling you about your own profession. Roger knew that as long as he pretended to be ill, Michaelhouse would not cast him into the streets. It did not take much to work that out.'

'How is Brother Michael? asked Gray, deftly changing the subject away from his misdiagnosis. 'I hope you have managed to keep Runham away from *him*!'

'I certainly have,' said Bartholomew fervently.

'Will he live? Brother Michael, I mean.'

'Yes,' said Bartholomew, surprised by the question. 'He is not that ill.'

'I thought his condition must be serious, because you have spent so long with him today,' said Gray. His eyes grew round with feigned innocence. 'I do not suppose it is providing you with an excuse to miss the misery of meals in the hall under the eagle eyes of Runham, is it?'

Bartholomew wondered whether it was as obvious to Runham himself. 'Michael does have a fever,' he said vaguely. 'And I confess I am surprised by the speed at which the infection has spread.'

'Fat men succumb easier to fevers than thin ones,' said Gray wisely. 'Master Saddler was fat, and look what happened to him. His leg rotted, and even Robin of Grantchester's delicate surgery could not save him.'

Amused by Gray's statement of 'fact', Bartholomew trudged back across the sticky morass of the yard to Michael's room. The two sombre Benedictines who shared the room had moved to the now-vacant servants' quarters, and had prepared a straw mattress so that the physician could sleep next to his patient. Thoughtfully, one of them even left a candle stub, so that Bartholomew would be able to see what he was doing if Michael needed help during the night.

Outside, the sounds of evening gradually faded to sounds of night. The lively chatter of students in the yard was replaced by the soft murmur of scholars in their rooms, and the clank and clatter from the kitchens was eventually stilled to the occasional sharp crack as the fire spat. Bartholomew lit the candle and tried to work on his treatise on fevers, until he fell asleep at the table.

By the following day, Michael was essentially better, but slept most of the time and had lost his appetite. To Bartholomew's surprise, he even declined some of his favourite delicacies from the kitchen. He was not too ill to remind Bartholomew of his promise to visit Simekyn Simeon at Bene't College, however, and insisted that the physician went there that morning. Bartholomew did not want to become embroiled in the insalubrious affairs of another College, recalling that the murdered Wymundham had told him he would be better not knowing what they were, and he took his time readying himself to go out.

At last he could delay no longer, and began to walk slowly across the yard to the gate. He had taken no more than a few steps when he saw a man wearing the distinctive blue tabard of a Bene't scholar striding towards him. From under the tabard protruded a pair of shapely legs clad in striking yellow and green striped hose. Bartholomew knew very well that neither they, nor the bright gold-coloured hat that sat at a jaunty angle on the man's head, were part of the prescribed uniform of Bene't, and was astonished that the Master allowed one of his Fellows to flaunt the rules so flagrantly.

The man greeted him cheerfully. He was younger than Bartholomew, and wore his long dark hair in elaborate ringlets of the kind currently in favour at the King's court. He was rather more plump than a man of his age should have been, indicating that he had not been eating College fare for very long, and he had the kind of glowing complexion that more likely resulted from a carefree existence of hunting and falconry than of a life spent in study.

'My name is Simekyn Simeon, Fellow of Bene't College,' he said, favouring Bartholomew with an impressively courtly bow. 'I know it is an unlikely appellation, but it is the one with which my parents saw fit to encumber me.'

'Matthew Bartholomew,' said Bartholomew, grateful that *he* did not have to go through life with a name better suited to a court jester.

'I have come to see the Senior Proctor about the sad demise of John Wymundham, lately Fellow of Bene't College,' Simeon continued. 'Is he in his room?'

'He is ill, but he asked me to visit you. I was just on my way.'

'I saved you a journey, then,' said Simeon jauntily. 'Tell me, is Brother Michael's illness such that we should avoid him for fear of contamination, or can I loiter at his sickbed with no ill effects?'

'He does not have a contagion,' said Bartholomew curtly, not impressed by the man's brazen self-interest.

'Good,' said Simeon. 'I mean no disrespect, Bartholomew, but I will discuss this matter with him, not you. I am aware of his reputation for solving mysteries in the University, but you I do not know. Is this the way to his room?'

He had ducked past Bartholomew and was up the stairs to Michael's chamber before the physician could do anything to stop him. Irritated at being so summarily dismissed by a man who wore green and yellow hose, Bartholomew followed him, intending to prevent him from disturbing the ailing monk, but Simeon had moved quickly and was through Michael's door before Bartholomew had reached the top of the stairs. Michael regarded the intruder in astonishment, hauling his blanket up under his chin like a maiden caught in bed by a knight intent on mischief.

'Did I waken you?' Simeon asked, not sounding especially contrite. 'I do apologise. However, one of my colleagues died on Saturday night, and I feel that is a matter of sufficient import to raise the Senior Proctor from his slumbers. I expected you to visit us yesterday.'

'I am unwell,' said Michael peevishly. 'I sent Matt to see you in my stead.'

Simeon sat on the chamber's only chair and gave a disarming smile. 'But now I am here, we can speak directly to each other. There is no need to communicate through one of your lackeys.'

'I am ill,' repeated Michael. To make sure Simeon understood the true gravity of his condition he added, 'I have eaten nothing all day!'

That seemed to convince Simeon. He leaned forward and gazed at Michael's pale face and red-rimmed eyes.

'I am sorry, Brother. I see now that you are not malingering; you do have something of the appearance of a corpse three days dead. You must understand, though, that the sudden death of one of our members – two, if you count Raysoun's fall on Thursday – has been a blow, and I wanted to know what you are doing about it. But I appreciate the fact that you are unwell, and so I suppose I shall have to leave you in peace for now.'

'You are here now, so you may as well stay,' said Michael ungraciously. 'You have heard, I take it, that Wymundham was found dead in Mayor Horwoode's garden?'

Simeon nodded. 'Of course. We are not that uninformed. One of your beadles told me that you had the body examined, and the verdict was that someone had smothered him. Are you certain of that? Are you sure he did not drown himself?'

Michael waved a feeble hand, indicating that Bartholomew was to answer.

The physician nodded. 'Wymundham's body was not wet, and, as far as I could tell, there was no water in his lungs to suggest drowning. His blue face and swollen tongue, along with damaged nails and a broken tooth, indicated that he had been smothered, and that he had fought hard against his killer.'

Simeon regarded him sceptically, as if he did not consider such details convincing. 'So, do you have any idea who might have done this?'

'None. Yet,' said Michael. 'I was hoping you might be able to help. Did Wymundham have any enemies in Bene't, or other people who might wish him harm?'

Simeon frowned slightly. 'Not that I can think of. Bene't is a small College and there are only four Fellows now that Wymundham and Raysoun are dead. We all liked each other well enough.'

'That is not what Wymundham said after he had watched Raysoun die,' said Bartholomew bluntly. 'He told me that Raysoun had claimed with his dying breath that he had been pushed.'

Simeon's expression was unreadable. 'Are you suggesting that there have been two murders – not one – in Bene't?'

'Wymundham believed Raysoun was murdered, and then he was murdered himself,' said Bartholomew. 'What does that imply to you?'

Simeon crossed one striped leg over the other and leaned back in his chair. 'I believe someone has made a mistake. Either Wymundham misheard or misunderstood Raysoun's dying words, or someone is guilty of gross fabrication – making up stories about our dead scholars because they are not in a position to confirm or deny them.'

'Wymundham told *me* what Raysoun said,' replied Bartholomew coolly. 'I can assure you that I did not invent it.'

'Then did Wymundham tell you *who* Raysoun said had pushed him?' asked Simeon, raising his eyebrows questioningly.

'No,' said Bartholomew. 'He said it would be better if I did not know.'

'Really,' said Simeon flatly. 'How very inconvenient.'

'Matt has no reason to lie,' said Michael. 'If he says Wymundham claimed Raysoun had been pushed, then Wymundham claimed Raysoun was pushed. So, the question we must now ask is: was Wymundham himself lying or was he speaking the truth? Let us assume first that he was lying: why would he want people to believe Raysoun had been murdered if his death were an accident?'

'Perhaps he was not lying in the true sense of the word,' suggested Simeon. 'Perhaps the shock of Raysoun's accident unhinged him, and he said things he did not mean.'

'It is a possibility,' said Michael. 'But then, two days later, Wymundham is found dead, which makes me inclined to believe there was some truth to his claim.

In which case, we must ask who would kill Raysoun and then murder Wymundham to ensure he told no one what Raysoun murmured with his dying breath?'

Simeon sighed and shook his head. 'Certainly no one at Bene't. The Fellows keep their distance from the students – unlike Michaelhouse, which I hear encourages friendships between masters and their charges – and we would never stoop to fraternising with servants, again unlike Michaelhouse.'

'How dare you make such comparisons,' snapped Michael, offended. 'You have never been to Michael-house!'

'Actually, I have been here on a number of occasions. For my sins, I am acquainted with your Ralph de Langelee, who pursues me relentlessly because of my court connec-tions. Langelee tells me all sorts of scandalous stories about Michaelhouse.'

'Such as what?' demanded Michael, peeved.

'Such as Bartholomew's friendship with his book-bearer,' said Simeon with a grimace of distaste. 'Langelee informs me that Bartholomew treats that dirty little man like a brother. I certainly would not trust my life to a common man!'

'With an attitude like that, you would be wise not to,' retorted Bartholomew, angry that the foppish scholar should insult the loyal Cynric.

'And then there is the Michaelhouse choir,' continued Simeon, ignoring him. 'Those who are not thieves or beg-gars are engaged in lowly trades like ditch-clearing and barging, and yet Brother Michael quite happily spends every Sunday afternoon in their company.'

'They are good people,' said Michael coldly. 'It is not their fault that greedy landowners have forced them into such poverty that they are forced to steal to feed themselves.'

'That sounds seditious,' said Simeon, regarding Michael in amusement. 'You are not one of those modern thinkers who believes peasants should have rights, are you?'

'My personal opinions are none of your affair,' said Michael. 'And they certainly have nothing to do with discovering who killed your colleagues.'

'True,' admitted Simeon. 'My apologies, Brother. Blunt speaking is all the fashion at court these days, and I forget you University men prefer good old-fashioned ambiguity and obtuseness. But, as I was saying, I do not think you will find your killer in Bene't. You will have to look elsewhere for him.'

'Who are the other Fellows?' asked Michael, not liking Simeon's transparent determination to steer the investigation away from his own College. 'And what were you doing when Raysoun fell?'

Simeon shook the luxurious curls that cascaded to his shoulders – locks that Father William would have had shorn had Simeon been a member of Michaelhouse. 'I was not in Cambridge when that happened. I am the Duke of Lancaster's squire when not engaged in College affairs, and I was with him. I have at least a dozen highly respectable witnesses who will vouch for me.'

'And the other Bene't Fellows?' demanded Michael, sounding disappointed that Simeon appeared to have a sound alibi. 'Where were they?'

'Master Heltisle and his good friend Caumpes were buying rat poison from the Franciscans in the Market Square. We have a rodent problem at Bene't, you see.'

Bartholomew was sure they had, and one rat had shoved poor Raysoun to his death, then smothered Wymundham.

Simeon continued. 'And lastly, there is Henry de Walton. I am surprised you do not know him, Bartholomew. I imagined he would be intimate with every physician in Cambridge, given that he is always complaining about some ailment or other.'

'And you still claim that all Bene't fellows liked each other?' Michael pounced.

Simeon gave a rueful smile. 'Yes, generally. I admit I find de Walton's claims of continual poor health a little tiresome, but he is a good enough fellow. He works hard and is patient with our less able students.'

'What were Raysoun and Wymundham like as Fellows?' asked Michael. 'Were they hard-working and patient with inferior students?'

Simeon glanced sharply at him. 'Raysoun was a gentle man, although he did have a penchant for wine. He was worried that the building of Bene't was taking too long, and was afraid that we would run out of funds before it was finished, and so the workmen considered him something of a nuisance because he checked their progress regularly. But the students liked him well enough.'

'And Wymundham?' asked Bartholomew when Simeon paused, wondering whether Simeon's failure to cite Wymundham's virtues without prompting was significant.

'Wymundham was a man who enjoyed life,' said Simeon carefully. 'He had a quick mind, and was sometimes frustrated by the restrictions afforded by College life. I empathise entirely.'

Looking at the way Simeon had adapted his drab College uniform to include a gold hat and striped hose, Bartholomew was sure he did.

'It is difficult to know how to proceed with this,' said Michael. He was beginning to look tired, and Bartholomew stood, intending to ask – or order, if need be – Simeon to leave. 'From what you say, enquiries within Bene't will lead nowhere, so I suppose we must look elsewhere.'

'I wish I could tell you where,' said Simeon. He sounded sincere.

Michael nodded agreement. 'The most obvious solution is that one of the men working on the building gave Raysoun a shove, and then killed Wymundham to keep his identity concealed. One of my beadles, Tom Meadowman—'

'I know him,' interrupted Bartholomew. 'He was steward at David's Hostel before it . . .' He hesitated, not sure how to describe the end of the foundation for Scottish students that had harboured more than scholars under its roof.

'I made him a beadle when he found himself without employment after David's was destroyed,' said Michael. 'His sister is married to Robert de Blaston, one of the carpenters working at Bene't. I will set him to discover what he can.'

'Very well,' said Simeon approvingly. 'That is a good start.'

'And meanwhile, I will instruct my beadles to listen harder in the taverns. The death of a scholar is invariably cause for celebration in the town, and perhaps some reckless boasting might bring this killer to light. My men are already on the alert for rumours about Brother Patrick of Ovyng Hostel, so they can add Raysoun and Wymundham to their list of enquiries.'

Simeon uncoiled his elegant limbs and stood. 'Thank you, Brother. I knew you would not fail us. I can see you will have this killer under lock and key in no time.'

'I will,' vowed Michael in a way that suggested to Bartholomew that he was prepared to follow any clues that came his way, even if they led back to Simeon. 'Matt will visit my office in St Mary's Church, and instruct my beadles accordingly. But I am tired. I will sleep a little before considering further the evidence I have. Good morning, Master Simeon.'

He was dozing almost before Bartholomew had ushered the Bene't man through the door. Simeon walked with Bartholomew to St Mary's Church, where the beadles gathered for their daily instructions. Meadowman smiled warmly at the physician, recalling the peculiar business that had drawn them together in the summer of 1352. He readily agreed to do what Michael had asked, and hurried away immediately to speak to his brother-in-law the carpenter. Meanwhile, the other beadles were delighted that their duties entailed additional business in the taverns, and exchanged eager grins of pleasure.

Simeon seemed satisfied that an adequate investigation was under way, and left Bartholomew to return to his own College. With a feeling of disquiet, Bartholomew walked back to Michaelhouse, nodding absently to people he knew and oblivious to his sister's frown of annoyance when he failed to return her cheerful wave.

He spent the rest of the day in Michael's room, unashamedly using the monk's convalescence as an excuse to avoid the soulless meals in the hall and the repressive atmosphere that prevailed during lectures. Langelee came to visit them and tried to discuss some College matter, but Bartholomew cut him off, not wanting Michaelhouse's bitter politics to intrude on his small, temporary haven of peace.

Michael slept well that night, far better than did Bartholomew on his lumpy straw mattress. When Walter's cockerel announced the beginning of a new day – which was still some hours off, according to the hour candle – Michael turned over and slept again, so Bartholomew used the silence and the Benedictine's candle stub to work uninterrupted on his ever-growing treatise on fevers. When dawn finally broke, he set down his pen, clipped the lid back on the ink bottle and leaned back in his chair, wondering what the next day would bring.

CHAPTER 5

'MATT!' BARTHOLOMEW TURNED AT THE
sound of Michael's peevish voice. He had
been so engrossed in his writing that he
had forgotten where he was sitting. It was mid-morning on
Tuesday, and he was in Michael's chamber, still enjoying
a spell of blissful peace while the monk slept. 'Matt! I feel
terrible! I need a drink.'

Bartholomew filled a cup and held it to the monk's
lips. It was thrust aside indignantly.

'That is water!' Michael cried in dismay. 'You have
given me water! Is there no wine?'

'You have been ill, Brother. Wine would not be good
for you. Drink this first.'

'I will not!' said Michael, turning his head away and
trying to fold his arms. He gave a howl of pain as he
moved his elbow. 'God's blood, Matt! What have you
done to me? I had a mere bee sting, and now I am in
agony! Call yourself a physician?'

'Do you have a complaint to make, Brother?' asked
Runham from the doorway. 'Bartholomew told me at
breakfast that you were feeling better today.'

'I am not feeling better at all!' snapped Michael churl-
ishly. 'There is no wine to be had and I am dying of thirst.
That is what happens when you consult a physician – you
start with a minor complaint and you end up on your
deathbed.'

'You were not on your deathbed, Brother . . .' began
Bartholomew tiredly.

'I will send Bulbeck to you,' said Runham. 'Bartholomew should leave you alone, before he does you any more harm.'

'Hear, hear,' muttered Michael nastily, flexing his arm and plucking at the bandage that covered it. 'I am ravenous. Tell Bulbeck to bring me something nice – a piece of chicken perhaps, or a tender sliver of beef. No vegetables, though. Green things are not good for the sick.'

With Michael well on the road to recovery, and even on the road to gluttony, Bartholomew instructed Bulbeck that on no account should he yield to the monk's demand for wine that day and that the food was confined to a broth, and walked slowly down the stairs into the cool, drizzly grey of a late November morning. Runham followed him.

'Deynman tells me you should have summoned Robin of Grantchester to amputate Brother Michael's arm,' he said.

At first Bartholomew thought he was joking, but the challenging expression on Runham's face suggested otherwise. 'Deynman is scarcely a reliable judge of such matters,' he said, refraining from adding that anyone who listened to the opinions of a boy like Deynman should be locked away for their own safety. 'And, as you can see, Michael has recovered perfectly well without my resorting to chopping parts of him off.'

'That is more due to luck than anything you did,' said Runham unpleasantly. 'I suggest you stay away from Michael until he has fully recovered and is better able to fend off your murderous intentions.'

'What?' asked Bartholomew, shock making him dull-witted.

'You heard,' snapped Runham, striding away across the courtyard to his newly occupied Master's rooms. As he left, he called over his shoulder: 'And I will station

Clippesby by Michael's door to ensure that you do not disobey my orders.'

Bartholomew was too stunned to reply. The spy-turned-philosopher, Ralph de Langelee, came to stand next to him.

'Well, well,' he said, grimly amused. 'Is there any truth in Runham's accusations? Have you really been trying to do away with our favourite Benedictine while pretending to save his life?'

'Do not be ridiculous,' said Bartholomew. 'Everyone is talking as though Michael was at Death's door. He was not: he had a mild fever from an infected arm that put him off his food for two days.'

Langelee raised his eyebrows. 'Two days is a long time for a man of Michael's girth. But are you telling me that it has not been necessary for you to be at his bedside all this time?'

Bartholomew smiled. 'I went out once or twice yesterday, but which would you prefer – the hall with Runham, or Michael's peaceful chamber?'

Langelee smiled back. 'I take your point.'

'I met Simekyn Simeon yesterday, from Bene't,' said Bartholomew conversationally. 'I understand he is an acquaintance of yours.'

'Oh, yes, indeed,' said Langelee proudly. 'Simeon and I are close friends.'

'What is he like?' asked Bartholomew, seizing the opportunity to learn a little about the man who had imposed himself in Michael's sickroom to ensure that the death of a colleague was properly investigated. 'Is he honest?'

'He is a courtier,' replied Langelee matter-of-factly. 'So, no. He is not honest. But he has good connections and is distantly related to the Earl of Suffolk.'

'What has that to do with anything? I want to know

whether he is truthful and whether what he says can be trusted.'

'Sometimes, I imagine,' said Langelee unhelpfully. 'Has he been after Michael to investigate Wymundham's death? He told me he would, because his lord, the Duke of Lancaster, will not want an unsolved murder besmirching the reputation of the College he has chosen to patronise.'

Bartholomew sighed, seeing Langelee was going to be of no use as a source of reliable information. 'Michael has his beadles investigating the deaths of Wymundham and Raysoun.'

'Raysoun, too?' asked Langelee, startled. 'Everyone believes he fell from the scaffolding, because he was a less than limber man who should not have been sipping from his wineskin while scaling the College walls.'

'Perhaps that is true,' said Bartholomew tiredly. 'But his friend Wymundham claimed he was pushed.'

'Wymundham!' spat Langelee in disgust. 'He once tried to put his hand on my knee in St Bene't's Church. I would not believe anything *he* said!'

Bartholomew gazed up at the dripping eaves, not feeling energetic enough to point out that Wymundham's penchant for other men's legs was irrelevant to his honesty. 'At least this rain is keeping the students from making a racket in the yard. I will be able to do some writing this afternoon.'

'Then you should make the most of it,' said Langelee. 'Nowhere will be peaceful after tomorrow, because Master Runham's building work is due to begin then.'

'His what?'

'His building work. I tried to tell you yesterday, but you declined to talk to me. He plans to reface the north wing – where you and Michael live – and to build a new courtyard behind the hall.'

'But where will the money come from?' asked Bartholomew. 'We are always being told how desperate the College finances are.'

'So they were,' said Langelee. 'But all that has changed since you have been closeted with that ungrateful monk. Runham has begged and borrowed – but I hope not stolen – enough cash for the work to start in the morning.'

'Tomorrow?' asked Bartholomew, his tired mind trying to come to grips with what Langelee was telling him. 'But surely there are architects' plans to be drawn up, and estimates of costs to be worked out before any work can begin?'

'All done,' said Langelee. 'Runham is not a man to dally, it seems, and he says he wants his College to look its best. While you have been nursing your fat friend, the rest of the Fellows have had meeting after meeting, and it is all decided.'

'But how could Runham raise the kind of money in two days needed to build a new court?' asked Bartholomew, astounded. 'It is not possible.'

'It is, apparently,' said Langelee. 'He has taken out loans from the guilds of St Mary and Corpus Christi, and he has inveigled donations from a number of wealthy townsmen – including your brother-in-law. Oswald Stanmore gave us five marks.'

'Oswald gave Michaelhouse five marks?' asked Bartholomew, staggered.

Langelee nodded. 'Plus there is the money Runham is saving from the servants' wages now that he has dismissed them all. So, work will commence on two fronts. First, scaffolding will be erected on your building so that the stone can be renewed and a new roof put on. And second, foundations will be dug to the north of the hall for the new courtyard buildings.'

'But—'

'But nothing, Bartholomew,' said Langelee. 'The Master has spoken, and we must jump to obey his commands. Have you made your decision yet, by the way?'

'What decision?'

'Come on, man! You are like my undergraduates today, repeating everything I say like a baby learning its first words. The decision on whether you stay in Michaelhouse or whether you leave us.'

'Runham cannot force me to make that choice,' said Bartholomew, leaning against the door jamb and turning his face to the sky, feeling the rain patter on to it.

'No, but he can make life very difficult for you if you do not,' said Langelee. He gave a vindictive grin, and poked Bartholomew hard in the ribs with one of his powerful elbows. 'I imagine you are already regretting not voting for me as Master, eh?'

'I am regretting not voting for the Devil as Master,' said Bartholomew. 'You should not have brought up that business about Michael being in league with Oxford, you know. He would have made a much better Master than Runham.'

'But not better than me,' replied Langelee. 'And I saw Michael as my main competitor, so I had no choice but to tell the others what I knew about him.'

'You had a choice,' said Bartholomew softly. 'You were once a spy; you know perfectly well that things are not always as they seem. It was unprofessional of you to disclose Michael's dealings with Heytesbury of Merton.'

'Oh, I am well aware that Michael would never allow Oxford to triumph over Cambridge,' said Langelee airily. 'But that is irrelevant. My sole objective was to prevent Michael from pitting himself against me in my bid for the Mastership – and I was successful in that.'

'But at what cost?' asked Bartholomew bitterly. 'You

thwarted a good man and now we have a tyrant. All these dismissals of servants and new buildings that we cannot afford are your fault.'

'Now just a moment,' began Langelee angrily. 'It is *not* my fault that the others voted for Runham. If they had voted for me, everything would have been all right. I am an upright and moral man.'

'How is Julianna, by the way?' asked Bartholomew, recalling this 'upright and moral' man's dalliance with a town merchant's niece.

Langelee gazed at him sharply. 'Why?'

'Because you were once close,' said Bartholomew casually. 'I was almost a witness at your wedding ceremony, if you recall.'

'That was a long time ago,' said Langelee shortly. 'We seldom see each other now.'

'Not even in Grantchester church?' asked Bartholomew wickedly, recalling a rumour Michael had mentioned that summer, that Langelee had wed the lively Julianna in the seclusion of a small parish church a mile or so from the town. Fellows were not permitted to marry, and Langelee had been faced with an agonising choice of his own – wife and family, or a career in Michaelhouse. It seemed he had been unable to make up his mind, and, like a child offered two types of cake, reached out with greedy fingers and grabbed both.

'That is none of your affair,' snapped Langelee. He took Bartholomew's arm in a painful pinch and bundled him into the medicine store, where they would not be overheard. 'What have you heard about this?'

'Nothing recently,' said Bartholomew. He was not inclined to begin an argument with the loutish philosopher – especially since Langelee liked to settle debates with his ham-sized fists – and he regretted his incaution in mentioning Langelee's secret marriage.

Langelee's grip intensified, and the physician winced. Immediately, Langelee released him.

'Sorry,' he said. 'I forget sometimes that I am a strong man, and I occasionally bruise people when I intend no harm.'

'Then you should learn not to go around grabbing them,' said Bartholomew, rubbing his arm. Langelee was right – he was a strong man, and his vicelike grip hurt.

'Can I share a secret with you?' Langelee asked, out of the blue. He closed the door and furtively looked both ways out of the window before fastening the shutters securely.

'No!' said Bartholomew in alarm. 'I do not want to be let into secrets that necessitate locked doors and closed windows. Please keep whatever it is to yourself.'

'I *did* marry Julianna at Grantchester church,' said Langelee, ignoring the physician's appeal. 'But once we had the opportunity to get to know each other, we found we were incompatible.'

'I told you that before you married,' said Bartholomew, recalling the arrogant, thick-skinned Julianna and wondering what had attracted Langelee to her in the first place. Or her to him.

'So you did, but it is not helpful to mention it now, is it? Anyway, there I was with a pregnant wife I did not want on one hand, and a glorious future ahead of me as a University scholar on the other. I could hardly let the likes of Julianna spoil my chances for a successful career, could I?'

'I suppose not,' said Bartholomew, heartily wishing he were somewhere else. 'Look, Langelee, if you are about to confess that you did away with her, I do not want to know.'

'Of course I did not do away with her,' said Langelee indignantly. 'What kind of man do you take me for?'

Bartholomew did not reply.

'The agreement we made was mutual – and it did not involve anyone being done away with. I gave her nearly all the money we had, including a nice little manor up near Peterborough. She is there now, ruling the roost with a rod of iron, I imagine.'

'But you are married,' said Bartholomew. 'So you cannot be a Fellow of Michaelhouse.'

'You sound like Runham the lawyer,' said Langelee distastefully. 'But I am not married actually, because we had the arrangement annulled. It cost a fortune, I can tell you! So, everything is all right; it was not all right for a while, but it is now.'

'I am glad to hear it,' said Bartholomew. 'But why did you tell me? It is the kind of thing you would be better revealing to nobody.'

'It is good to speak to someone about it,' said Langelee. 'Now we share something personal. You can confide something in return, if you like.'

'I am sorry, but I have no secrets that come anywhere close to the magnitude of yours.'

'How very dull,' said Langelee, disappointed. 'Are you sure? Is there nothing you can dredge up? You must have done something interesting in your life. Did you ever deliberately kill a patient you did not like? Or what about your affair with that whore – Matilde? Is there nothing salacious to tell me about that?'

'There is not,' said Bartholomew shortly. 'And I swore an oath to save lives, not help people into their graves, so I have nothing to confess to you along those lines. But why do you want to know such things?'

'Shared confidences make people friends, like you and Brother Michael. If you were my friend, you would vote for me as Master, as you were going to vote for Michael.'

Bartholomew was not too tired to be amused by Langelee's contorted logic. 'But we have a Master,' was all he said. 'His name is John Runham, remember?'

'I know that,' said Langelee testily. 'But what I am saying is that if Runham dies conveniently, I want you to vote for me as his replacement.'

'I see,' said Bartholomew. He rubbed a hand through his hair. 'This has been a sensational week at Michaelhouse: Kenyngham resigns, Runham takes over, I am given an ultimatum to choose between my teaching or my medicine, Cynric is dismissed, and you are already preparing to step into Runham's shoes.'

'I am merely readying myself, in case he has an accident or something.'

Bartholomew gazed at him in the gloom. 'I hope you are not planning to arrange one for him.'

Langelee sighed. 'I would, if I could be sure I would get away with it, but it is too risky. I shall put my faith in God instead.'

'I do not want to hear any more of this,' said Bartholomew, trying to push past Langelee to the door. Langelee blocked his way, and with a resigned sigh, knowing he would never manage to best the philosopher in a shoving contest, Bartholomew retreated and sat on the edge of one of the benches that lined the walls.

'I know what is making you so irritable,' said Langelee, with sudden inspiration. 'It is Matilde! She is angry because you never bother to visit her. But do not worry – she will come round. Take her a bit of ribbon or something. Then she will fly into your arms, and it will be *you* confessing to *me* about an annulled marriage.'

The door snapped open suddenly, making them both jump. Bartholomew had been sitting on the workbench with Langelee standing next to him. At the crash of the door, they leapt apart. Runham stood there, regarding them suspiciously.

'What are you two up to?' he demanded. 'It had better not have been any improper behaviour.'

'What do you mean?' asked Langelee, puzzled.

'I mean lustful behaviour,' elaborated Runham.

'But there are no women in here,' said Langelee, frowning in bemusement. He suddenly realised what Runham was implying and his jaw dropped in shock. Bartholomew looked from the gaping philosopher to the stern, prissy features of the new Master, and began to laugh.

The following day, the College was filled with the sounds of frantic activity. Scaffolding was being erected around the north wing, and foundations were being dug for the buildings that would form the new court. Hammers pounded on wood and nails, saws scratched, metal clinked and rang, and workmen called and yelled in casually jovial voices. It was almost impossible to teach in the hall – not only was the noise distracting, but the students were far more interested in what was happening outside than in their lessons.

Bartholomew persisted until mid-morning, but when Langelee, Kenyngham and Runham gave up, and their students' delighted voices joined the racket outside, he was forced to concede defeat. Even William, whose stentorian tones usually rose energetically to such a challenge, threw up his hands in resignation and allowed his small group of novices to escape with the others. Only Michael's Benedictines persisted, retreating to the abandoned servants' chambers to discuss St Augustine's *Sermones* in low, reverent voices. Although Bartholomew had recommended that his own students study specific sections of Galen's *De Regimine Acutorum*, he knew very well that none of them had the slightest intention of doing so.

Runham had made his presence felt in other aspects of College life, besides disrupting the teaching routine. He had decided that fires in the hall and conclave were a sinful waste of money, and had decreed that scholars could only light them if they were prepared to buy the fuel themselves. Since Runham himself was virtually the only one able to afford such an extravagance, Bartholomew and his colleagues found themselves teaching rows of unhappy faces bundled inside blankets, rugs, and even wall hangings as the students tried to keep themselves warm. Bartholomew's own hands and feet were so cold that he could barely feel them, and he was not looking forward to the rest of the winter, when wet clothes would take days to dry and there would be nowhere to go to escape the chill. He decided he might have to visit his sister and Matilde more often – both were wealthy enough to have a cheerful fire in the hearth.

'How is Michael?' asked William pleasantly, as they watched the activity in the yard together from the window in the conclave.

'Better.'

'But he keeps to his bed,' observed William. 'Is he malingering, then?'

'Of course not,' said Bartholomew, not entirely truthfully, given that there was no reason at all why the monk should still be in bed. But since Bartholomew had also taken advantage of Michael's illness to avoid meals in College, he felt he was not in a position to be critical. 'It is best that he recovers completely before resuming his duties.'

'His duties,' mused William, a predatory gleam in his eye. 'I was planning to discuss those with you.' Bartholomew regarded him warily. 'Now that Brother

Michael is incapacitated, I wondered whether I should act as Senior Proctor in his stead. I—'

'No,' said Bartholomew hastily. 'Michael has beadles doing that.'

'But there are a number of suspicious deaths that need to be investigated,' pressed William. 'There are those deaths at Bene't College – Raysoun and Wymundham. At least one of them was murdered, and the case needs a man like me to get to the bottom of the matter.'

'Michael has already started his own enquiries,' said Bartholomew. 'You should not initiate an investigation of your own, because you might interfere with his.'

'Then I will concentrate on the brutal slaying of that blameless Franciscan novice – Brother Patrick from Ovyng Hostel,' said William. 'It seems no one has the courage to admit to being a witness, and I know Michael has no idea how to begin to solve that crime. I will do it for him.'

Bartholomew sensed that Michael would have to prise himself from his sickbed if he did not want William agitating the uneasy relationship between the Franciscans and the Dominicans. There was nothing Bartholomew could say that would encourage the friar to leave well alone, and he hoped he would not be obliged to accompany William on Michael's behalf, to ensure the friar did not cause too much trouble.

William gestured to the building work in the yard below with a sweep of one of his powerful arms. 'I do not like this,' he boomed in a confidential bellow. 'It is all happening too fast.'

'You must have been at the meetings that have been held over the past couple of days to discuss it,' said Bartholomew. 'You should have made your point then.'

'Meetings!' spat William in disgust. 'That is what Runham calls them, is it? To me, "meetings" implies an exchange of views, where people listen to each other.

These were not meetings: they were sessions where Runham told us what would happen. And it is not good to plunge the College into this kind of disorder so abruptly. In my experience, it is better to go more slowly.'

'It is better to act quickly, while we have the money to hand,' said Runham, suddenly appearing behind them and making them both jump. 'Why wait months for the work to be completed when we can have a splendid new College finished within weeks?'

Bartholomew rubbed a hand through his hair and turned away. Personally, he felt William was right, and that time should be allowed for foundations to settle and for timbers to weather. The speed at which the building work was to be completed seemed an ostentatious and unnecessary display of Runham's new authority.

'This morning I noticed that Justus's body is still in the porch,' he said, partly because the fact that the book-bearer's continued presence in the church was beginning to be a problem, and partly to prevent William from arguing with Runham. 'When do you intend to have his requiem?'

'Justus was a suicide,' replied Runham. 'He will not have a requiem.'

Bartholomew was not surprised that Runham had followed the traditional line of the Church, although he felt the judgement was overly harsh. 'But regardless, he needs to be buried. We cannot keep him in the church indefinitely. It will not be much longer before he poses a threat to the health and well-being of St Michael's parishioners.'

'A threat to health!' spat Runham in disdain. 'The dead cannot harm us. All that nonsense about dangerous miasmas rising from corpses is just an excuse for physicians to demand high fees for remedies and consultations.'

'But Justus *is* beginning to reek,' declared William. 'And I, for one, would rather pray without a festering corpse for company. Is that why you have those powerfully scented flowers on Wilson's grave – to disguise the stench emanating from the dead who cry out to be placed in the ground?'

'It is his kinsmen's responsibility to bury him,' hedged Runham. 'Osmun and Ulfo of Bene't.'

'It is ours,' stated William uncompromisingly. 'He was Michaelhouse's servant, and Michaelhouse is morally bound to deal with his corpse.'

'Brother Michael is asking for you, Bartholomew,' said Runham, unable to keep the disapproval from his voice as he changed a subject that was becoming uncomfortable. 'I cannot imagine why, after you almost killed him with your dangerous ministrations. The man must be weak in his wits.'

'Matthew would never harm another Michaelhouse man,' announced William, not at all truthfully; Bartholomew was feeling very much like harming Runham at that precise moment. 'He takes his oath of allegiance to the College seriously – as do I.'

'Does he now?' asked Runham, regarding Bartholomew through his hooded eyes with an expression that Bartholomew could not fathom. 'We will see about that when he makes his choice whether to continue to grace the College with his unseemly presence, or whether to do the honourable thing and leave us.'

'You cannot force him to resign,' came an unfamiliar voice. They turned in surprise to see that the cheery Suttone had been listening to their conversation from across the room. He came to stand with them at the window. 'I paid attention to the statutes that were read to Clippesby and me the other night. The Master cannot make a Fellow leave, if he does not want to go.'

'He can if that Fellow brings the College into disrepute,' snapped Runham, not pleased to be lectured about the statutes by the College's most recent member. 'And how I deal with my senior Fellows is none of your concern.'

'But Matthew has not brought the College into disrepute,' objected William.

'He has!' snarled Runham. 'He attempted to kill Brother Michael with his poisonous salves.'

'What?' cried Bartholomew, scarcely believing his ears. 'How did you—'

'How did I know?' interrupted Runham furiously. 'Because Michael told me himself. It happened the night of my election, when you defied my wishes and stayed out in the town after I had expressly ordered you to return to the College as soon as you had escorted Father Paul to the Friary.'

'And that was another evil deed,' muttered William. 'Paul's treatment.'

Runham ignored him, his attention still on Bartholomew. 'When you did deign to return to Michaelhouse that night, you immediately slunk off to your bed, but Michael talked to me for a while.'

Runham and Michael had been arguing, Bartholomew recalled, remembering their angry voices in the hall outside his room as he had been undressing for bed. Runham had tried to tell Michael that he could no longer leave the College for his proctorial duties, and Michael had informed Runham exactly what he had thought about such a preposterous suggestion.

'Michael told me then that you had put a salve on his injured arm to prevent itching – not in the comfort of the College, but outside in the street, where no one would see you.'

'Is this true?' asked Suttone, regarding Bartholomew doubtfully. 'Did you treat Brother Michael's arm in the street, rather than in your room?'

'No!' said Bartholomew. 'I mean, yes, but it was not—'

'And this salve contained a poison that all but took the poor man's life,' Runham forged on. 'And *then* Bartholomew tried to kill Michael by refusing to allow Robin of Grantchester to amputate his arm. Deynman told me so.'

'I neither have the time nor the inclination to listen to such nonsense,' said William haughtily. 'You have taken leave of your senses! Matthew is not the type to commit murder. I have a feel for these things.'

He made to leave, considering the conversation over, but Runham caught his arm. Angrily, the friar pulled away. William was a strong man, and righteous indignation made him careless. As he tried to haul his arm from the Master's fingers and the Master suddenly released it, William's hand shot up and caught Runham a blow under the nose.

With a yowl of pain, Runham danced backward, his eyes streaming with tears and blood flowing freely from his nose. His new henchman, the Dominican Clippesby, heard his cry and raced into the conclave to see what was happening. When he saw Runham's blood-splattered face, he stopped dead and glared accusingly at the others.

'What have you done?' he demanded, his wild eyes boring into each of them in turn. 'Which one of you struck the Master of your College?'

'William! And he did it deliberately!' raged Runham.

'It was an accident,' said Bartholomew, rummaging in his bag for a piece of cloth to hold to Runham's nose. 'Sit down and put your head between your knees. William will fetch some water.'

'It was no accident!' stormed Runham, his voice muffled by the cloth Bartholomew pressed against his face to stem the bleeding. 'William deliberately struck me.'

'Easy,' said Bartholomew soothingly, noting the deep

redness that suffused the man's face. 'You will give yourself a seizure if you do not calm down.'

'You will give me a seizure, you mean,' stormed Runham, snatching the cloth from him and flinging it to the floor. 'What is that? A rag infused with poison, so that I will die when it is put to my face?'

'Do not be ridiculous!' snapped William irritably. 'Do you think Matthew carries poisoned cloths around with him, waiting for an opportunity like this? Quite frankly, I do not think you worth the effort.'

'Insolence on top of assault,' screeched Runham, verging on the hysterical. The great veins in his neck and face were thick with tension and rage, and his colour was far from healthy. 'That is it! That is it!'

'That is what?' asked Clippesby, clearly itching to do something to rectify the great wrong that had been inflicted on the Master, but not sure what.

'That is the last straw. William is suspended!'

'Suspended from what?' asked Bartholomew. 'Even the Master of a College cannot prevent a friar from carrying out his religious duties. Only his prior can do that.'

'He is suspended from his Fellowship,' howled Runham, small flecks of spittle flying from his mouth as he spoke. 'Look at me! I am marred for life, because he struck me with murder in his heart. I will not have him loose in my College. Clippesby, Bartholomew, Suttone – I order you to escort him to his room and lock him in.'

'You cannot do that,' said William furiously, fending off Clippesby as the Dominican rashly surged forward to do his Master's bidding. 'The statutes say—'

'You personally signed a new set of statutes two days ago which stipulated that the Master has the final say in disciplinary matters,' shouted Runham. His eyes glittered with smug satisfaction when he saw William blanch. 'Hah! You see? You do remember!'

'I did not sign any new statutes,' said Bartholomew. 'When was this?'

William's mouth was working stupidly, although no sound came out. Suttone regarded Runham nervously, clearly uncomfortable at having witnessed the scene that had been played out in the conclave. But Clippesby, like Runham, wore an expression of grim satisfaction.

'Your signature on these new statutes was not required, Bartholomew,' said Runham, wiping his nose with his hand and leaving a vivid smear of red across one cheek. 'You were trying to dispatch Brother Michael at the time, and declined to attend a meeting of the Fellows. There are eight of us, and I needed five signatures for a majority – me, William, Clippesby, Suttone and Langelee.'

'But what did these statutes say?' asked Bartholomew, looking from Runham to William with the distinct impression that he would not like what he was about to hear.

'For a start, they give me the authority to lock that dangerous fanatic where he will do no harm,' said Runham, eyeing William with naked hatred. 'So, you had better do as I say, or you will be joining him.'

'There is no need for them to accompany me,' said William coldly, sensing defeat and deciding to leave with dignity. 'I will take myself to my room, thank you.'

He turned on his heel and stalked out. Runham nodded to Clippesby, who ran after the friar. With a sense of foreboding, Bartholomew started after them, certain that if anything could rekindle the Franciscan's fiery temper, it would be the thought of a Dominican checking to see if he kept his word. He was not mistaken.

William became aware that he was being followed down the stairs, and that it was Clippesby who dared to question his honour. He gave a roar of anger. Clippesby shrieked in horror as the Franciscan's powerful hands fastened around his throat; the noise quickly became a strangled gurgling as William's fingers began to tighten.

'William! Let him go!' yelled Bartholomew, struggling to pull the friar away from Clippesby. In the confines of the spiral staircase Bartholomew could not find a good position from which to intervene. 'For God's sake, William! You will kill him!'

'He is the Devil's spawn!' howled William in a frenzy, squeezing tighter still. 'He has been doing Runham's dirty work for him ever since he set foot in Michaelhouse. He is not fit to tread the same floors as good and honest men.'

'Then he is not worth hanging for. Let him go.'

Bartholomew managed to insert himself between the struggling men, and used the wall as a brace to lever William away. The Franciscan lost his grip, and Clippesby began to take great rasping breaths as he tottered sideways, holding his bruised neck.

Seeing William's temper was still far from spent, Bartholomew grabbed his arm to prevent him from renewing the attack. With a howl of frustration and anger, William gave Bartholomew a hefty shove. Unprepared for the sudden move, Bartholomew lost his balance and tumbled head over heels down the stairs to land in a helpless sprawl of arms and legs at the feet of Agatha, who happened to be walking through the porch towards the kitchens.

Agatha gazed at him in astonishment, then stood over him, waving her meaty fists protectively. William, whose anger had dissipated the instant Bartholomew had disappeared down the steps, was horrified. But when he dashed after the physician, he found himself faced with an enraged laundress – a sight at which the bravest of men balked. William took several steps backwards.

'I am sorry, Matthew,' he said in an unsteady voice. 'I did not mean . . .'

'It was you who pushed him, was it?' demanded Agatha dangerously. 'You should be ashamed of yourself, Father! Brawling like some ale-sodden apprentice! And do not hover there thinking you will get a second chance. Come near Matthew, and I will tear you limb from limb.'

No one who knew Agatha doubted that she meant every word, and, not wanting William's attack on Clippesby to become Agatha's attack on William, Bartholomew scrambled quickly to his feet, to place himself between them. He heard the furious voice of Runham in the stairs as he tried to squeeze his way past the prostrate Clippesby.

'William, run!' said Bartholomew urgently.

'What?' The Franciscan, his ponderous mind bewildered by the rapid sequence of events, was slow to understand.

'Go to your friary and stay there until all the fuss has died down. I will send you word when the time is right for you to make your peace here.'

'I do not deserve your kindness,' said William, hoarse with emotion. 'I did not mean—'

'He is coming!' said Bartholomew, hearing footsteps as Clippesby was manoeuvred out of the way. 'Go, quickly, before it is too late. Runham will not settle for locking you in your room now – he will have you arrested and charged with assault.'

William gave him a hunted look, edged warily past the angry Agatha, and raced across the courtyard. He had just reached the gate when Runham emerged from the stairwell.

'After him!' the new Master yelled, his face suffused with red fury. 'He is escaping! Do not just stand there, Bartholomew! Give chase!'

Frustrated almost beyond words when he saw his quarry

haul open the gate and escape into the lane, Runham gave Bartholomew a shove to encourage him to pursue the friar, but backed off quickly when Agatha advanced purposefully.

'Call her off!' he screeched in a voice thick with panic. 'She has the look of madness about her.'

'I am not some wild animal to be "called off",' snarled Agatha, although with her fierce teeth and ferocious glare, even Bartholomew was sceptical. 'Do not think you can treat me like dirt, as you have everyone else in the College. I am Agatha, one of God's chosen.'

'What?' whispered Runham, scarcely believing his ears.

'I was chosen by God to survive the Death, because He has plans for me. Only evil men – like your cousin – were taken by the pestilence.'

'That is heresy!' howled Runham, using the bewildered Clippesby as a barrier between him and the laundress. Foolishly imagining that the frail body of a Dominican afforded him protection from Agatha, he became rash. 'I will have you dismissed for saying that!'

'Will you now,' said Agatha in a voice that, although low, dripped with menace. She batted Clippesby out of the way as if he were no more than a fly, and began to advance on Runham with an expression of pure loathing on her face.

'Help me, Bartholomew!' shrieked Runham, realising that Suttone was standing at the foot of the stairs, blocking his escape. He was trapped, and Agatha clearly meant business. 'Tell her I was joking! Of course I would not dismiss her.'

Bartholomew was tempted to stand back and let Agatha have her wicked way with the Master, but he did not want to see Agatha in the proctors' gaol any more than he had William, so he stepped forward and took her gently but firmly by the arm.

'Leave him, Agatha,' he said softly. 'There has been more than enough violence in Michaelhouse for one day.'

'As long as *he* lives to walk in our halls and eat our food, there has not been enough violence,' snapped Agatha, before turning and striding towards the kitchens, her skirts swinging purposefully around her substantial hips.

That evening, the atmosphere in the College was tense. The Fellows gathered in the conclave, where Suttone did his best to keep a conversation going, and the students in the hall were unusually subdued. Runham sat in the conclave's best chair, with his hands folded over his paunch, and regarded Suttone's increasingly desperate attempts to initiate a civilised discussion with an amused disdain.

Eventually, no longer able to bear the sneering presence of the Master or Suttone's painful determination not to sit in morose silence, Bartholomew wished his colleagues goodnight, and escaped with relief into the chill, damp evening air. He stretched and yawned, but it was too early to go to sleep. He wondered what he could do. He had used all his candles, and so could not work on his treatise on fevers or read. He saw Beadle Meadowman walking across the yard, to make his report on the investigation into the Bene't deaths to Michael, but did not like to interrupt them just because he was at a loose end and wanted someone to talk to.

He turned when he sensed someone else emerging from the hall, having also escaped the oppressive atmosphere of the conclave. It was Suttone.

'I found I could not take any more of that,' said the Carmelite friar with a grin. 'Once you left, I realised that no one else was even listening to me. Langelee has drunk so much that he is sound asleep; Kenyngham is praying; Clippesby is having a conversation with himself in a corner; and Runham was doing nothing but enjoying my discomfort.'

'Clippesby was talking to himself?' asked Bartholomew warily.

Suttone nodded. 'He does it a lot. I am surprised you have never noticed. The worrying thing is that he answers himself, too, as if he thinks he is more than one person.'

'Lots of scholars do that,' said Bartholomew. 'It is the best way to make sure you never lose a disputation.'

Suttone laughed. 'Can I interest you in a cup of ale in the kitchen? Agatha told me she would have a pan of it mulling for when Runham drove me away with his unpleasant company. I thought she was being unkind, but it seems to me that Agatha is a very astute woman.'

Bartholomew followed the Carmelite into the College kitchens, where Agatha sat in a great wicker chair near the embers of the fire. The room was warm, and smelled of baking bread, wood-smoke and the old fat that had splattered from roasting meat into the hearth. The College cat was curled in her lap, and she stroked it gently with her rough, thick-fingered hands. She smiled when the two scholars entered, and gestured that they were to help themselves to the ale that simmered over the glowing remains of the fire.

'I knew it would not be long before you joined me,' she said. 'I am only surprised the rest of the Fellows are not here, too, leaving that fat old slug to his own devices.'

'I do hope you are not referring to our noble Master,' said Suttone mildly. He took a deep draught of the ale, and then refilled his cup. 'This is good, Agatha. Did you brew it yourself?'

Agatha favoured him with a coy smile. 'You know how to flatter a woman, Master Suttone. But I buy ale from the Carmelite Friary for us servants; the College brewer provides that cloudy stuff that the scholars drink.'

'The servants drink better ale than we do?' asked Bartholomew, startled.

Agatha cackled. 'You lot down anything I decide to put on the dinner table, but we servants are a little more discriminating. Only the best ale appears for our meals. Since you pay us such miserable wages, we have to reward ourselves in other ways.'

'Clippesby told me that you attended a fatal accident at Bene't last week,' said Suttone to Bartholomew, as he settled himself comfortably on a stool near the hearth. 'Is that true, or is it something he has imagined?'

'It is true,' said Bartholomew. 'I wish I had not, though, because the colleague who sat with Raysoun as he died claimed he had been pushed, while everyone else seems convinced he fell. Then, two days later, this colleague also died – in circumstances that are suspicious, to say the least – and so I do not know what to believe.'

Suttone regarded him gravely. 'You think this colleague may have been murdered because he claimed Raysoun was pushed? Lord, Matthew! That is a nasty business!'

Bartholomew nodded. 'Bene't does seem to have some problems.'

'Clippesby was supposed to take a Fellowship at Bene't,' said Suttone thoughtfully. 'Raysoun, the man who fell – or was pushed – from the scaffolding, had some connection with the Dominicans at Huntingdon, where Clippesby hails from. Clippesby told me that Raysoun arranged him an interview with the Master of Bene't, but said that the meeting did not go well.'

'Why?' asked Bartholomew curiously.

Suttone shrugged. 'It is difficult to say. Clippesby seems to believe that the Master took against him for some undetermined reason. Personally, I suspect that the Master had some reservations regarding Clippesby's suitability, and so recommended he apply to Michaelhouse instead.'

Agatha gave a guffaw of laughter. 'I must tell Brother Michael that one! The subtlety of that move by Bene't against another College will make him smile.'

'I do not think so,' said Bartholomew. 'He would only find it amusing if Michaelhouse had foisted an "unsuitable" student on Bene't, not the other way around.'

'Clippesby told me that he was shocked when he saw Raysoun,' said Suttone. 'Apparently, the man had been a cheerful sort of fellow, given to playing practical jokes on his friends. But when Clippesby met him recently, he said he had changed. He had become gloomy and listless, and drank more than he used to.'

'Perhaps drinking and gloominess are connected,' said Bartholomew. 'It seems wine led poor Justus to take his own life.'

'Ah, yes,' said Suttone. 'Runham's book-bearer who came from Lincoln. It is a pity he died: I would like to have met a man from my own city.'

'Justus had Bene't connections, too,' put in Agatha. 'His cousins are the two Bene't porters, Osmun and Ulfo. Justus wanted to work at Bene't when he first came from Lincoln a year ago, but they had no money to pay an additional porter, so he went to work for Runham instead.'

'Langelee also seems to have an association with Bene't,' said Suttone. 'If I had a penny for every time he told me he was going to visit Simekyn Simeon (the Duke of Lancaster's man) at Bene't, I would be a rich man.'

'And I have Bene't connections, do not forget,' said Agatha. 'I have a cousin who is a cook there, and he has been pressing me to honour Bene't with my services.'

'I hope you do not,' said Bartholomew. He smiled at her. 'Where would Suttone and I go on a cold winter's night for good ale and entertaining company?'

Agatha puffed herself up. 'True. Michaelhouse would not survive long without me here to oversee matters. But Bene't is offering me twice the salary that you pay, and I get a bigger room. It knows how to treat its valued members of staff.'

'I could have a word with Runham, and see whether we can afford to give you more,' said Bartholomew. 'You are right: we should pay you what you deserve.'

Agatha reached out and chucked him under the chin. 'You are a kind man, Matthew. I will miss you most of all if I leave. But I cannot say that I relish the prospect of remaining here with that Runham at the helm. He is like a great fat spider, spinning webs to ensnare anyone unfortunate enough to cross his path. And I will never forgive him for what he did to Father William today.'

'That was an unedifying incident,' agreed Suttone. 'Father William is not an easy man to like, but he is loyal, open and I think generous underneath all his religious bluster.'

'Michaelhouse will not be the same without him,' agreed Bartholomew. 'Still, perhaps it will all blow over in time. Then William can come back and make his apologies to Runham.'

'William can apologise all he likes,' said Suttone. 'But Runham will never allow him to make his peace. I saw the triumph in Runham's eyes when William struck him: he knew at that point that he had the excuse he needs to rid himself of the man.'

'But why would Runham want William to leave?' asked Bartholomew. 'He is a reliable teacher and his students seldom cause us any trouble.'

Suttone and Agatha exchanged a mystified glance.

'I am surprised you need to ask that, Matthew,' said Agatha. 'I have heard you complain often enough that you cannot teach while William rants and raves in the hall.'

'And his fanatical dislike of the Dominicans may prove dangerous for Michaelhouse,' added Suttone. 'It is not good to harbour men who hate another Order within our walls in as uneasy a town as Cambridge. It would not do for Michaelhouse to become the focus of an attack by Dominicans enraged by claims of heresy by our resident Franciscan.'

'But it is irrelevant now, anyway,' said Agatha, staring into the dying embers of the fire. 'William has been driven out. Which of you will be next, I wonder?'

The following day saw the first sunshine they had experienced for days. Bartholomew woke at dawn, heartened to see the streaks of pale blue and gold striping the banks of grey clouds. He walked with the others to mass in St Michael's Church, watching the windows as the first delicate strands of sunshine began to dapple the chancel floor. He was less sanguine when the same sun caught the gilt on Wilson's grotesque effigy and set it glittering and gleaming like some pagan idol, but tried to ignore it and concentrate on the reading from the Old Testament.

When the mass was over, he peeled off from the end of the procession and walked across the courtyard to check on Michael. The monk was sleeping, although a number of empty dishes suggested that Agatha had already brought him his breakfast. He stirred, and muttered something about Yolande de Blaston, the prostitute. Afraid he might hear something he would rather not know, Bartholomew beat a hasty retreat and joined his colleagues in the hall.

The uninspiring meal – watery oatmeal and equally

watery ale – was eaten in silence, while the Bible Scholar
read about the trials and tribulations of King David.
Runham's own meal was supplemented with some raisins
and a bowl of nuts from his personal supplies. Kenyngham
seemed sad and distracted, barely touching his food and
not even listening to the sacred words of the Bible
Scholar, which suggested to Bartholomew that he was
deeply unhappy. Langelee was nursing yet another of his
gargantuan wine-induced headaches, and was irritable
with the harried servant who single-handedly struggled
to attend the Fellows – Runham had dismissed his two
assistants.

Next to Runham was Clippesby, whose eyes darted
around the room as though looking for hidden assassins.
He ate like a bird, in jerky, pecking movements, almost
as if he were afraid that if he devoted too much attention
to his meal, something dreadful might happen to him.
Technically, Clippesby should not have been sitting so
near the Master: as one of Michaelhouse's newest members, he was obliged to sit farthest from the seat of power.
But no one else wanted Runham's company, and when
Clippesby had defiantly selected the seat, no one cared
to wrest it from him.

Suttone looked as grave as his colleagues. His jovial
face was glum, and the merry twinkle in his eyes, which
Bartholomew had so liked at their first meeting, was
gone. As if he sensed he was the object of scrutiny, he
glanced up at Bartholomew. The physician indicated with
a grimace that it was time the meal was brought to an end,
and Suttone gave him a quick grin of agreement. The
genial sunniness returned, and Bartholomew suspected
that Suttone's sombre expression had been cultivated to
suit the timbre of the meal.

Runham read the grace in unnecessarily sepulchral
tones, and the meal was over. The students scraped their

benches on the flagged floor as they made their escape, returning to their rooms to collect pens, parchment and as many blankets as they could carry for a morning of teaching in the chilly hall. The few remaining servants ran to clear away the dishes, and then to dismantle the trestle tables and lean them against the screen at the far end of the room. The benches were left as they were, so that the masters could move them as they were needed.

'My Carmelite brethren warned me that life as a scholar might be grim,' said Suttone, walking across the yard with Bartholomew as they went to collect the books they would need that morning. 'But I told him I was not going to some poor hostel with a dormitory-cum-refectory-cum-lecture-room-cum-laundry. I told them I was going to Michaelhouse, one of the greatest houses of learning in the country, where scholars live a life of respectable comfort, and where education is placed above all else.'

Bartholomew laughed.

'I do not think teaching is among Runham's principal objectives,' Suttone continued. 'I think his main aim is to create a glorious temple, where scholars can sit in neat little rows and shiver together, wishing they were somewhere else.'

'I hope he changes his mind about the fires when it snows,' said Bartholomew. 'Everyone will succumb to fevers and chills if there is nowhere to dry wet clothes and nowhere warm to sit.'

'We will be losing our students to the more congenial atmosphere of the taverns,' agreed Suttone. 'But perhaps Runham will loosen his stranglehold when he learns he does not need to prove his power to us at every turn.'

'Perhaps,' said Bartholomew doubtfully. 'But Michaelhouse still has many advantages over the hostels. We have some faithful servants – Harold, Ned . . .'

'All dismissed,' interrupted Suttone. 'What else?'

'Well, not the food,' said Bartholomew. 'And our wines leave something to be desired.'

'They certainly do,' laughed Suttone. 'I did not think that any respectable establishment would stoop to provide Widow's Wine for its members. When I first tasted it, I thought someone was playing a practical joke on us newcomers. But then I saw the rest of you drinking it, and I felt obliged to follow suit. Nasty stuff, that. My priory in Lincoln keeps it for cleaning the drains.'

'That bad, is it?' asked Bartholomew. 'I thought it was just rough wine.'

'*Very* rough wine,' corrected Suttone.

Bartholomew continued with his list of Michaelhouse's virtues, not wanting the genial Suttone to leave the College and allow Runham to appoint a man of his own choosing in his place. 'We have a fine collection of grammar and rhetoric texts, and there will be plenty of opportunity for academic debate when things have settled down.'

'Who with?'

'Well, there is Langelee,' began Bartholomew. He saw the dubious expression on Suttone's face and hurried on. 'Runham is a clever lawyer who argues brilliantly when the mood takes him; Kenyngham understands the scriptures better than anyone else I know, and will certainly give you cause for contemplation; Father Paul—'

'Paul is dismissed.'

'Right. Michael's logic is flawless, and he is an entertaining sparring partner.'

'And there is you,' said Suttone, smiling again. 'I would like to hear more of the theories that everyone seems to believe are so heretical. In my experience, heretical notions often need only a little tweaking here and there to render them acceptable to the general populace. Perhaps I will stay a while, even if only to learn from you how simple water can cause so many diseases and how horoscopes are irrelevant to a person's well-being.'

Bartholomew smiled back. 'And since Brother Michael often accuses me of having a poor grasp of logic, perhaps I can learn from your lectures on the subject, too.'

Suttone clapped him on the back. 'Once Master Runham sits a little more easily in the saddle of power, Michaelhouse will be a better place to live, and then you and I shall spend many happy hours discussing medicine and logic.'

Bartholomew sincerely hoped Suttone's gentle optimism was not misplaced.

During the morning's teaching, Bartholomew was summoned by a patient with a badly crushed hand; the injury was so severe that it necessitated the removal of two fingers. He was surprised to see the surgeon, Robin of Grantchester, already there, lurking in the shadows with his terrifying array of black-stained implements. Physicians were not supposed to practise surgery, and amputations were Robin's domain, although Bartholomew personally would rather have died before allowing the surgeon anywhere near an injury of his own. Surprisingly, Robin demurred and watched silently while Bartholomew deftly removed the useless digits from the howling man and sutured the stumps. When the patient had been bandaged and dosed with a pain-killing draught, Bartholomew and Robin left the house together.

'Why did *you* not operate?' asked Bartholomew as they walked along the High Street. 'It was a straightforward case. Was it because he could not pay you?'

'I was paid,' said Robin, showing him six pennies. 'That is why they had no money left for you.'

'But you did not treat the man, so why did you take his money?' asked Bartholomew curiously.

'I charge for consultations,' said Robin loftily. 'I asked for sixpence and then advised him to contact you. I am banned from surgery until this wretched Saddler case is resolved, you see.'

'You were arrested because he died after you amputated his leg,' Bartholomew recalled. 'But most people die after you cut off their limbs. Why is this one different?'

'His family are wealthier than most,' said Robin mournfully, not in the slightest offended by Bartholomew's brutal summary of his medical skills. 'I spent three nights in Sheriff Tulyet's prison with criminals for company – including one with that ruffian Osmun, the porter from Bene't College.'

'What was he doing there?'

'He was arrested for fighting in the King's Head. Vile man! I spent the whole time awake clutching my cutting knives in anticipation of being robbed by him.'

Bartholomew glanced at the surgeon's clothes, stiff with ancient blood, and decided that even Osmun would have balked at searching Robin for hidden riches. Politely, he said nothing.

'And he talked all night,' continued Robin. 'He was drunk and was blathering all sorts of nonsense. He told me that he believed one Bene't Fellow named Wymundham had stabbed another called Raysoun with an awl after he had fallen from the scaffolding. Do you know anything about this? I was busy with Saddler at the time, God help me.'

'Wymundham did not kill Raysoun,' said Bartholomew, confused. 'He was kneeling next to Raysoun when he died. I saw him holding the man's hand and exhorting him to stand up.'

'Osmun did not say Wymundham killed Raysoun,' said Robin pedantically. 'He said Wymundham stabbed Raysoun after he had fallen. He claimed that Wymundham was the kind of man to stab a corpse to make an accident look like murder.'

'I do not think so,' said Bartholomew doubtfully. 'Wymundham could not have stabbed Raysoun with half the town watching, and anyway, Raysoun was not a corpse when Master Lynton pulled the awl out of him.'

'Well, the Fellows of Bene't are altogether odd,' said Robin firmly. 'The Master, Heltisle, is too ambitious for his own good; his second-in-command Caumpes likes to play with boats in his spare time, because he comes from the Fens; while de Walton has a fancy for Mayor Horwoode's massive wife. And the last of them, Simekyn Simeon, is the Duke of Lancaster's spy!'

'Did Osmun tell you all this?' asked Bartholomew curiously.

'Lord, no!' said Robin. 'He is too fond of that foul place to utter seditious thoughts about it. What I tell you about the Fellows of Bene't is general town knowledge.'

Bartholomew realised that Osmun was merely trying to shift any suspicion on to Wymundham, who was hardly in a position to defend himself, because he was dead. Perhaps Osmun had been the murderer, climbing the scaffolding to shove Raysoun to his death. And in that case, Osmun must have killed Wymundham, too, to silence him regarding the identity of Raysoun's killer. Bartholomew decided he should pass the gossip to Michael, so that the Senior Proctor could decide what was truth and what was lies in the mess of charge and counter-charge. He was thankful that the affair was not his to solve.

Bartholomew was with his students in the conclave later that morning, in the midst of a long and involved explanation about a diagram of a neck in Mondino dei Liuzzi's illustrated *Anatomy*, when there was a colossal crash.

Anatomy forgotten, students and master rushed to the window to see that a pulley hauling slates to the roof had snapped, littering the yard below with smashed tiles.

For several moments there was a shocked silence, both in the hall and in the courtyard, and then the workmen began shouting in alarm. Afraid that someone might have been crushed, Bartholomew ran outside, pushing through the gathering crowd to see if there was anyone who needed his expertise.

They had been lucky: no one had been standing underneath the pulley when it had broken. With relief, Bartholomew heard the workmen's shouts of alarm give way to laughter and bantering; evidently they considered the fall more of a matter for humour than anger or recrimination, although it seemed to Bartholomew that they were working too fast, and were abandoning safety for speed. He sprinted up the stairs to Michael's room to find the monk standing at the window watching the chaotic scene below in disapproval. He shook his head as Bartholomew entered.

'That could have killed someone. What is the hurry with this building? Why are the workmen so desperate to finish a task they have barely begun? Is it the prospect of being under Runham's direction that makes them so keen to have the job done?'

'If so, then I cannot blame them,' replied Bartholomew. 'Are you feeling better? You look better.'

Michael nodded. 'I feel dizzy if I stand too long and I tire easily, but I am well enough.' He gestured at his table, which was piled high with scrolls and parchments. 'I am making good use of the fact that I am confined to my room, though. I have resumed my dealings with Master Heytesbury of Merton College in Oxford, and I have been sifting through the reports from my beadles about these murders.'

'Have they learned anything?'

Michael shook his head gloomily, and not even the fragments of gossip from Robin of Grantchester and Suttone seemed to lessen his despondency about the slow pace of the investigation. Bartholomew left him sitting at his table, muttering obscenities about the fact that the reports his beadles dictated to the University's scribes in St Mary's Church were so ambiguous that he was obliged to send for most of them anyway, so that they could clarify what they had intended to say.

By the time Bartholomew quit Michael's chamber he had lost his students, who were enjoying the spectacle of the workmen picking through the smashed tiles, and it was almost time for teaching to end anyway. He returned to the hall where he carefully secured the colourfully illustrated anatomy book to its chain in the wall, straightened the benches, and replaced the ink stands, spare parchment and pens in the aumbry in the corner of the conclave. When he had finished, Suttone came to stand next to him at the window, staring into the yard below.

'That is what happens when corners are cut,' he said, looking down at the mess with a resigned sigh. 'Master Runham is forcing the pace of this building work to the point where it is dangerous.'

'Then tell him,' suggested Bartholomew. 'We do not want someone injured because Runham wants a new College instantly.'

'He will not listen. He does not care if a workman is killed, anyway. I reminded him that Master Raysoun of Bene't College died because he fell from unstable scaffolding, but Runham merely thanked me for my advice, and assured me that *he* would take care not to climb on any of ours.'

'He said that?' asked Bartholomew, not sure whether

to be indignant or amused by the Master's brazen self-interest.

Suttone frowned. 'There he is. What is he doing now?'

Runham was staggering under the weight of a small chest. It was one of the College 'hutches' – a box containing money that benefactors had provided so that scholars could borrow from it if they found themselves short of cash. The Master would give the student money, while the student exchanged a *caucio* or pledge of comparable value. So, for example, when Gray had needed two marks to pay for his tuition fees, he had deposited a gold ring in the chest that he would redeem as soon as he had saved enough money. Similarly, Deynman had left his beautiful copy of Galen's *Tegni* in the chest when he wanted money for pens and ink. If Gray or Deynman were unable or unwilling to repay their loan, the College would then be the proud owner of a gold ring and a book for the library. The College's hutches, containing varying amounts of money, were stored in a heavily barred room in a cellar under the hall.

'He must be going to do an inventory of the contents,' said Bartholomew, watching Runham sweating under his load. 'Some of our hutches contain a lot of money – or its equivalent.'

'Are all the hutches for the students' use?' asked Suttone.

'No. Some of our eight or nine hutches are for Fellows, too. They are useful if we need money to pay some fine or other.'

'I owe no fines,' said Suttone. He gave a sudden, wicked grin. 'Although I might well be fined for being insubordinate to Runham before too long. But I do need money to buy the alb I will need to conduct masses in the church. I shall see Runham about it this morning.'

He wandered away, and Bartholomew went to visit a

patient near the river before the bell announced the midday meal. His patient had been bitten by a rat, so Bartholomew cleaned the wound and then rummaged in his bag for the betony plaster that would help prevent festering. It was missing and he suspected it had been borrowed by Gray, who had then forgotten to replace it. He remembered that the last time he used it was when he had treated Michael in the lane the night Runham had been elected. He paid an urchin a penny to fetch some more from the apothecary, and talked with the man's family while he waited.

It was not long before they were joined by the old brothers Dunstan and Aethelbald, who always came to see what was happening if a stranger visited the row of hovels that crouched near the seedy wharves on the river where they had lived all their lives.

'We are going to Bene't College today,' announced Dunstan without preamble. 'Now that Wymundham and Raysoun are dead, their choir is depleted, so we thought we would offer our services.'

'I see,' said Bartholomew, wondering whether Bene't knew what it was letting itself in for if it accepted the rivermen's reedy tenors.

'They will have to give us bread and ale, though,' added Aethelbald. 'We do not sing for nothing.'

'Isnard the bargeman tried to join the Peterhouse choir,' said Dunstan. 'Peterhouse gives its singers wine after each mass, you see. But the music master told Isnard he should take pity on the world and swear a sacred oath that he would never utter another note as long as he lived. Now why should the man say a rude thing like that, Doctor?'

'I cannot imagine,' said Bartholomew, deliberately not looking at the old man, who sounded genuinely surprised.

'Bene't will be glad to have us,' said Aethelbald with conviction. 'And when Michaelhouse hears us singing like angels, it will be sorry that it allowed us to leave.'

'You could be right,' said Bartholomew, sure he was not.

'We heard one of your lot came to a nasty end,' said Dunstan suddenly, with inappropriate salaciousness.

'Who?' asked Bartholomew absently, thinking about Raysoun, Wymundham and Brother Patrick.

'One of your lot – that miserable Justus, Runham's book-bearer. His body is in St Michael's Church porch.'

Bartholomew sighed. It was already a week since the book-bearer's body had been found, and it was clear that Runham had no intention of arranging a burial. Bartholomew saw he would have to do it himself if he did not want the corpse to remain in the church until it decomposed completely.

He was angry: Justus had served Runham for almost a year, and paying a few pennies for a shroud should not have been an insurmountable problem, even to a miser like Runham. Compared to the efforts Runham had made to beautify the tomb of his loathsome cousin, Bartholomew found the new Master's attitude to the dead perplexing and inconsistent. Justus had not been a likeable man, but that was no reason to treat his body with such disrespect.

'It is disgraceful,' added Aethelbald gleefully. 'Still, given what Runham did to our choir, I cannot say I am surprised. And then there was Brother Patrick – another victim of that University.'

'I know,' said Dunstan, shaking his head. 'Stabbed through the heart, I heard.'

'Stabbed in the back,' corrected Aethelbald. 'A coward's blow.'

'Who told you all this?' asked Bartholomew, amazed

at the speed at which gossip seemed to rip through the town.

'Everyone knows,' said Aethelbald dismissively. 'It is no secret. And everyone knows who killed this Brother Patrick, too.'

'They do?' asked Bartholomew hopefully.

Dunstan nodded vehemently. 'Another scholar. It could not have been a townsman because it was on University property.'

'That does not necessarily follow,' said Bartholomew. 'It is not unknown for townsmen to trespass on University land.'

'I would like to trespass on Michaelhouse,' said Aethelbald with feeling. 'No offence, Doctor, but I would like to see it burn to the ground for what it did to our choir. And I would like to see every one of its fat, grasping scholars strung up like the common criminals they are – not you, of course, Doctor, and not that sainted Brother Michael.'

'If I were twenty years younger, I would do it,' announced Dunstan.

'Forty years younger might see you in with a chance,' cackled Aethelbald. 'I tell you, Doctor, that College is destined for a great fall. And when it comes, not a soul in the town will raise a finger to save it.'

For some unaccountable reason, their words unnerved Bartholomew. When the betony plaster arrived, he slapped it on his patient's leg with almost indecent haste, and strode quickly back up the lane, his head bowed in thought, wondering what he could do to prevent the ever-widening rift between his College and the townsfolk.

Since it was a lenten day, fried herring giblets were on the menu at Michaelhouse. Bartholomew thought about William as he toyed with the unappetising mess, because any kind of fish organs were a favourite with the friar. Bartholomew hoped William would be getting his share of them in the Franciscan Friary.

The entrails were served on thick slabs of stale bread made from rye flour, which served as platters. Although scholars were not usually expected to consume their trenchers, Bartholomew ate most of his that day because he was hungry and he did not fancy the oily, fishy guts that were heaped in front of him. Glancing down the table, he saw that none of the other Fellows were devouring them with much enthusiasm, either, and Runham had gone so far as to hire a personal cook to provide *him* with something else.

As well as giblets and stale bread, there was a thick, brown-green paste made from dried peas. It was bland and contained some crunchy parts that Bartholomew imagined it was better not to try to examine too carefully. The last time he had investigated a foreign body in his food it had transpired to be a toenail, although none of the cooks would admit to being its owner. The Bible Scholar droned on, skimming through the text quickly and without any indication that he had the slightest understanding of what he read.

When Runham rose to say grace, Bartholomew escaped with relief from the oppressive atmosphere of the hall and went to his own room. The College was still in a chaos of noise following the collapse of scaffolding, and Runham had announced that the rest of the day's lectures were cancelled. The students were delighted although Bartholomew fretted that so much lost time would mean poor results at the end-of-year disputations.

He was about to go inside when he saw Beadle Meadowman hurrying across the yard towards him, and so escorted him to Michael's room. In tones of barely concealed pride, Meadowman informed the monk that he had persuaded his brother-in-law, Robert de Blaston the carpenter, to hire him to work alongside the men who had been building Bene't College the day Raysoun had died. Meadowman hoped to gain the confidence of his fellow workmen, and see whether he could ascertain if any of them had given Raysoun a timely shove.

Meadowman also reported that the other beadles had been diligent in their enquiries around the taverns, but although the townsmen professed to be delighted by the deaths of scholars of the much-hated University, no one seemed to be taking the credit for killing them. Michael instructed him to ensure the enquiries continued, and then sent him away to begin mixing mortar with his new colleagues.

'This is a bad business,' said Michael gloomily. 'I have all my beadles on the alert for information regarding the deaths of Patrick, Raysoun and Wymundham, but they have heard nothing. It is unusual, because there is nearly always some rumour or accusation passed on over a jug of ale that I can act upon, but in these deaths, there is nothing.'

'You are essentially better, so why do you not leave your room and take control over these investigations?' suggested Bartholomew. 'Meadowman will do his best, but he is not you.'

'I wish it were that easy, Matt. But my talents lie in dealing with scholars, and I suspect our victims were killed by townsfolk. The kind of mean, vicious fellows who would stab a friar in the back, shove an ageing academic from a roof, or smother a man with a cushion and leave his body in the Mayor's garden are unlikely to open their hearts to the Senior Proctor – whether the ale is flowing or not. But they might tell my beadles, who are townsfolk themselves. I may do more harm than good if I interfere.'

Bartholomew left him and went to his own room, where he threw open the window shutters and sat at the table to begin work on his treatise. The section on infection reminded him of the riverman with the rat bite, and from there he thought about the conversation he had had with Dunstan and Aethelbald. Although the old rivermen were a pair of shameless gossips, their stories often carried an element of truth, and he was concerned by their assertion that the town was resentful that Michaelhouse had left the book-bearer's body unattended and forgotten in St Michael's Church for a week.

He considered mentioning the matter to Runham again, but suspected it would be a waste of time. With some reluctance, he laid down his pen, swung his cloak around his shoulders, and left the College to walk to St Michael's Church. Justus's body was still there, shut into the porch and draped carelessly with a dirty sheet. Bartholomew lifted the corner and peered underneath. Justus's face had darkened, and the corpse released an unpleasant, sickly odour: it was not as bad as the stench from the butchers' stalls because the cold weather had slowed putrefaction, but it would not be long before it was providing some impressive competition.

He returned to Michaelhouse, asked Agatha for a sheet to use as a shroud, and then set off with it across the yard. On the way back to the church he met Suttone, and the Lincoln-born friar immediately agreed to conduct a funeral for a man who had hailed from the same city. Together, they wrapped the body in the sheet and then prepared it for burial, lighting candles, anointing it with chrism, and sprinkling scented oil over it to mask the smell as it was brought from the porch to the chancel.

Because Justus was a suicide, the verger would not allow him to be buried in the churchyard, so Bartholomew hired a cart to take the body to the desolate spot near the Barnwell Causeway that had been set aside for people who had taken their own lives. As Suttone said his prayers, Bartholomew stood at the side of the shallow grave and shivered, his cloak billowing around him in the wind. The scrubby bushes that shielded the burial ground from the yellow stone buildings of the nearby Austin priory whispered and hissed when the breeze cut through them, and small, stinging dashes of rain spat at Bartholomew and Suttone as they completed their mournful task.

The grave-diggers, who had decided it was too cold to wait for the Carmelite to finish his benedictions, were nowhere to be found after he and Bartholomew had rolled Justus's floppy remains into the wet hole in the ground. Not liking to leave the grave open, Bartholomew took a spade and filled in the gaping maw himself, while Suttone continued to pray. When they had finished, they stood in silence for a few moments, gazing down at the soggy pile of earth until wind and rain forced them to hurry back along the Causeway and into the town. Suttone returned to St Michael's Church for more prayers, while Bartholomew walked back to the College, feeling cold and dirty. As he went, he grew increasingly angry with Runham, despising the man for having so little concern for others that he had consigned Justus to the paltry ceremony Suttone had just conducted.

He was so engrossed in his thoughts that he almost collided with a horse being ridden down the High Street at a healthy clip, and was only saved from injury by some very skilled horsemanship on the part of its rider. He backed up against a wall in alarm, and watched Adela Tangmer, the vintner's daughter, control her panicky mount.

'You should watch where you are going, Matthew,' she called when the horse had been calmed. He was relieved that she did not seem cross at his carelessness; the tone of her words bore more sisterly concern than censure. She grinned down at him, and he was amused to note that she still wore her comfortable brown dress, set off by a pair of rather manly riding boots and a belt from which hung a no-nonsense dagger.

'Sorry,' he said. 'I was thinking about something else.'

'You should be more careful. You would have been trampled had I not been such an accomplished horse-woman. Worse yet, you might have done Horwoode an injury.'

'Horwoode?' asked Bartholomew in confusion. 'The town Mayor?'

Adela gave a guffaw. 'I call this horse Horwoode, because he is skittish, weak, rather stupid and has overly thin legs.'

'I see,' said Bartholomew, startled by such a bald, if astute, summary of the Mayor's most prominent attributes. 'I have never noticed Mayor Horwoode's legs, personally.'

'Well, you are not a woman, are you?' Adela pointed out. 'But I do not like that man.'

Neither did Bartholomew, but he was not so imprudent as to be bawling his opinions in one of the town's main thoroughfares.

'Horwoode is Master of the Guild of St Mary, you know,' Adela went on. 'His advice to my father's guild, Corpus Christi, to invest in Bene't College was bad. That horrible College is turning out to be a lot more expensive than my father was given leave to expect. And a couple of their scholars have been put down in the last few days, which does not reflect well on my father's guild.'

'Put down?' asked Bartholomew, not sure what she meant.

She waved an impatient hand. 'Killed. Put out of their misery. Or rather, put out of ours. That drunken Raysoun and his friend Wymundham have already gone to meet their maker, and the rest of the rabble are bickering about who was responsible.'

'What are you talking about?' asked Bartholomew, confused by her diatribe.

'Bene't College is a nasty place, Matthew. Its porters are a gang of uncontrollable louts, its students are worse than some of the town's apprentices for wild behaviour, and the Fellows are always fighting and squabbling.'

'It sounds just like any other University institution to me,' said Bartholomew. 'What is it that singles Bene't out as particularly disreputable – other than the fact that you do not approve of your father's money being spent on it?'

She gave him a hard stare, and then broke into one of her toothy smiles. 'You are an astute man, Matthew. I *do* resent the money my father is always ploughing into the place. But Bene't is more than just a waste of gold: it seethes with secrets and plots. One of its patrons is the Duke of Lancaster, and *he* is so worried about what might happen in the College with which he is associated, that he has made one of his squires a Fellow there, just to keep an eye on it.'

'You mean Simekyn Simeon?' he asked. 'He told us he was the Duke's squire.'

'Well, he is, and his task is to watch the place and report its nasty secrets to the Duke.'

To Bartholomew, her assertions sounded the kind of rumours that the townsfolk loved to circulate about the University, and they contrasted sharply with what Simeon had claimed about Bene't being a harmonious College where Fellows enjoyed each other's company. Yet Michael had also detected something strained about the atmosphere at Bene't, and only that morning, Robin of Grantchester had told Bartholomew that the porter Osmun had been making the peculiar claim that Wymundham had stabbed Raysoun himself.

'What kind of thing is the Duke afraid will happen?' he asked.

She shrugged carelessly. 'I have no idea. That feeble Henry de Walton is bleating about foul play, but no one takes any notice of him.'

'Who is Henry de Walton?' Before she could answer, Bartholomew recalled that Robin of Grantchester had mentioned a Henry de Walton who had an inappropriate fondness for the Mayor's wife. Simeon had described him as a sickly soul with a list of ailments.

'One of the Fellows,' replied Adela. 'A snivelling little man who is always complaining about the state of his digestion – not an attractive subject, you must admit.'

Adela was not the person to be criticising others about their choice of suitable conversational gambits, since her own included ending unwanted pregnancies in horses and equine breeding habits.

'Do you know the Bene't Fellows well?' asked Bartholomew, intrigued by the contrast between the picture Adela presented and the one Simeon would have them believe.

'I most certainly do not,' said Adela, offended. 'Scholars are an unsavoury brood, to be avoided at all costs – present company excepted, of course. Caumpes of Bene't is nice, but he is a Fenman, and so is better than all these foreigners from Hertfordshire, Yorkshire and other distant lands. My father and I would never willingly socialise with the Bene't scholars, although we are forced to deal with them when we discuss their College's finances.'

Mayor Horwoode had also been offended by the notion that he hobnobbed with scholars, Bartholomew recalled. He had claimed that he would never invite one to his house.

'That pathetic de Walton is not fit to be called a man,'

Adela continued. 'Raysoun and Wymundham murdered indeed! What arrant nonsense!'

'Why do you say that?' asked Bartholomew curiously.

Adela regarded him with a puzzlement that equalled his own. 'You would not ask that if you knew the man. All he thinks about is his health, and he sees danger at every turn. Would you believe that he refuses to mount a horse in case he falls off and bruises himself?'

Bartholomew, who detested riding, did not consider de Walton's refusal to clamber on to a snorting, prancing animal that was much bigger than himself to be the final word in cowardice. He thought Adela was being overly harsh.

'I cannot imagine how de Walton came to the conclusion that his colleagues were murdered,' Adela went on. 'The workmen at Bene't say that Raysoun fell while he was drunk, while Wymundham is said to have thrown himself from the King's Ditch – remorse for having made Raysoun's last few months on Earth so miserable with his sharp tongue.'

Bartholomew supposed he could tell her what Wymundham had claimed to have heard Raysoun declare with his dying breath, but his gossiping with her would only serve to fan the flames of rumour and untruth. Anyway, it seemed she had already made up her own mind about what she thought had happened, and he did not see why he should convince her otherwise. It would do no one any good, and might even cause harm.

'I should go,' she said. 'If I leave my father for too long, there is always a danger that he will have found me a husband by the time I return. I expect your sister is the same. I know she would like to see you married.'

Bartholomew smiled. 'She is determined to see me with a wife,' he admitted. 'But then I would have to give up my teaching, and I do not want to do that yet.'

'Quite right,' said Adela. 'The country needs as many trained physicians as you can give it. Master Lynton is so overwhelmed by summonses from his human patients these days that he can seldom spare the time to see my horses when I need him. He was never too busy before the Death.'

'Lynton physics your horses?' asked Bartholomew, startled. 'But that is what blacksmiths do.'

'Physicians are better,' said Adela. 'They are more careful, and they consult the stars before suggesting a course of treatment.'

Bartholomew laughed in disbelief. 'So, all these years that Lynton has been berating me for dabbling in surgery, he has been poaching the blacksmiths' trade?'

'Horses are sensitive animals, Matthew,' protested Adela. 'Not to mention expensive. I do not want any grubby old tradesman tampering with them. But, as I just said, Lynton is invariably too busy for me these days.' She regarded Bartholomew speculatively. 'I do not suppose you would be interested in helping on occasion, would you? I pay well.'

'No,' said Bartholomew firmly. 'I know nothing about horses.'

'Pity,' said Adela with genuine regret. 'That will reduce your value as a potential husband.'

'Will it?' asked Bartholomew, bewildered by the peculiar twists and turns the conversation took with the eccentric Adela Tangmer. 'No one has mentioned this before.'

'No woman wants a man who does not look good in his saddle,' declared Adela with conviction. 'It would be like having a mate who does not know how to hunt.'

As a boy, Bartholomew had been given a basic training in such manly skills by his brother-in-law, but suspected that if he ever needed to catch his own food he would quickly starve. He supposed that to Adela, he would be about as poor a catch as she could imagine.

Adela grimaced and continued. 'My father has become quite tedious about the subject of marriage. I do not want a husband chasing me morning, noon and night to demand his conjugal rights. I have better things to do with my time.'

Adela's age and appearance made it unlikely that she would be the object of such desperately amorous attentions, although Bartholomew was too polite to say so.

He shrugged. 'Your father probably wants an heir for his business.'

'He does, but I am not some old nag to be bred to suit *his* needs. When I decide to couple with a man, it will be on *my* terms and in my own time. Do not let your sister grind you down over this, Matthew. You and I should draw strength from each other to fight these match-makers, or you will end up with some empty-headed imbecile and I will be provided with some man who knows nothing about horses and who has skinny legs into the bargain.'

'Heaven forbid,' said Bartholomew.

'Allies, then?' asked Adela, leaning down to extend a powerful, calloused hand for Bartholomew to shake. 'Shall you and I stand together against unsuitable matches?'

'Why not?' said Bartholomew, taking the proffered hand with a smile. He wondered what his sister would say if she ever learned he had formed such an alliance.

CHAPTER 6

MICHAEL CHUCKLED AS HE RECLINED ON his bed the following afternoon. The dirty plates and empty goblets scattered around the room suggested that he had regained his appetite with a vengeance, and Bartholomew suspected that the monk was rather enjoying his convalescence.

'And Agatha threatened to do away with Runham?' asked Michael, eyes gleaming with merriment as he listened to Bartholomew's account of what had happened when William had bloodied Runham's nose and Agatha the laundress had become involved in the fracas.

'Not in so many words, but she does not like him.'

Michael chortled again. 'Foolish man! He will never run a successful College without the acquiescence of Agatha. And if he tries to dismiss her, he is dead for certain.'

'She has been offered a post at Bene't College,' said Bartholomew. 'It provides higher pay and better living accommodation, and she is seriously thinking of taking it.'

The humour faded from Michael's face. 'Bene't is poaching our servants?'

'We do not have many left,' said Bartholomew. 'All the porters have gone – including Walter, which is a blessing – and all but one of the cooks, while poor Cynric was dismissed the day after the feast.'

'We will both miss him,' said Michael sincerely. 'But things are getting out of hand, Matt. I am at Death's door for a few days and I recover to find my College is a different place.'

'You have not been at Death's door, Brother. Did you know that Runham believes I am responsible for your illness?'

Michael regarded him incredulously and then started to laugh. 'You? Not the bee that stung me?'

'He said I used a poisonous salve – secretly in St Michael's Lane – and he claims I refused to allow Robin of Grantchester to amputate your arm because I was afraid it would save your life.'

'My God, Matt! That is venomous stuff! I suppose it was my bantering accusations a couple of days ago that put that notion in his silly head. That man has a nasty mind!'

'It was his accusations that started the row with William,' said Bartholomew. 'Poor William. He might be a fanatic, but he stood up for me. Runham has effectively removed him, Paul has already gone, and he aims to be rid of me tomorrow. I wonder who will be next.'

Michael shifted restlessly. 'This is dreadful. My College is tumbling about my ears even as I lie here – quite literally, at times. A lump of ceiling became detached by the banging of the workmen this morning and narrowly missed my chair.'

'Teaching has all but stopped,' continued Bartholomew. 'It is too noisy, and it is difficult to keep the students' attention when there are workmen tramping through the hall every few moments, whistling and singing. I took my classes in St Michael's Church this morning – until Runham found out and told me to leave.'

'Why did he do that?'

'He said it was sacrilegious to teach medicine in a church. A little later, I saw that he had moved his own class there and was teaching it civil law.'

'Civil law is far more sacrilegious than medicine,' observed Michael. 'One aims to promote health and the other to promote wealth – for the lawyers. But did William make good his escape from Runham's wrath?'

Bartholomew nodded. 'I visited Father Paul last night, to tend his eyes, and he told me the Franciscan brethren have William secreted away somewhere, and will only reveal his whereabouts when they are sure Runham will not persecute him.'

'Now William will know how those poor so-called heretics felt when he chased them all over southern France,' said Michael grimly.

'At least he will not be able to begin the investigation he threatened,' said Bartholomew. 'He was going to look into the death of that Franciscan, Brother Patrick.'

'Was he?' asked Michael coolly. 'On whose authority?'

'Yours. Since you were incapacitated, he decided to act as unofficial Proctor. I think he planned to present you with the killer as a gift to aid your recovery, and then solve your other cases, too – Raysoun and Wymundham.'

'Thank God he did not,' said Michael with a shudder. 'The circumstances surrounding the deaths of Raysoun and Wymundham are complicated – far more so than the likes of William could appreciate; while poor Patrick's case seems hopeless. My beadles are having no luck with their enquiries in the taverns, and I am beginning to fear that none of us will find whoever is responsible for that. Any suspects William produces will almost certainly be innocent.'

'He is rather good at frightening people into making false confessions,' agreed Bartholomew. 'And he will concentrate on the Dominicans.'

'I am told the foundations are already dug for our new kitchen courtyard,' said Michael as an especially violent clatter from outside reminded him of the presence of the builders.

Bartholomew nodded. 'They are not as deep as they should be, and Runham is forcing a pace for the work that is too rapid for safety. Did you know that he has employed forty labourers? I do not know how he raised the money so quickly. I only hope he *does* have it, and we do not find ourselves with forty enraged workmen demanding payment when they have finished. It would be like the choir all over again, only these would be armed with hammers and saws and not a few scraps of music.'

'The choir?' asked Michael, sitting up abruptly. 'What are you talking about?'

Bartholomew stared at him. 'Has no one told you? I thought you would have heard by now.'

'Heard what?' demanded Michael dangerously, his voice hard and cold. 'I do not appreciate being kept in the dark about matters that involve my choir.'

'Runham disbanded it.' Seeing the anger that immediately clouded the monk's face, Bartholomew understood exactly why none of his colleagues had accepted responsibility for breaking that particular piece of news. 'He put the Michaelhouse singers under the control of Clippesby, but he dismissed the rest.'

'He what?' howled Michael, outrage mounting by the moment. 'He disbanded my choir?' He scrambled to his feet, his face white with rage. 'Why did you not tell me this before?'

'I thought someone else would have told you,' said Bartholomew, trying to wrestle him away from the door. 'But do not confront Runham while you are in a rage. Anyway, the damage is already done; it is too late to do anything now.'

'Let me go, Matt!' warned Michael, his green eyes

flashing with a fury that Bartholomew had seldom seen before. 'I am going to kill that miserable snake! And then I am going to teach my choir how to sing his requiem mass – and I hope he hears it from hell!'

'Wait until tomorrow, Brother,' said Bartholomew breathlessly, not surprised to find that the monk was as strong as ever. But just because Michael was fit did not mean that Bartholomew should allow him to storm into Runham's room and choke the life out of him.

'I will not wait!' shouted Michael furiously. 'Do you not realise what that man has done? There are children in my choir who need their free bread and ale; there are adults who take it home where it serves as a meal for a whole family. That Devil-in-a-tabard cannot dismiss them just like that. My choir needs Michaelhouse, and Michaelhouse will need my choir, if the riots ever start again and we do not want to be ransacked and pillaged.'

'What happened to the subtle revenge you promised when Paul was dismissed?' gasped Bartholomew, struggling in vain to prevent the monk from reaching the stairs. 'What happened to the plan that would strike at Runham's reputation and leave yours intact?'

Michael stopped his relentless advance. 'You are right. Two black eyes to go with his bleeding nose would be no kind of punishment for the likes of him. I must consider something else – something more permanent.'

'Good,' said Bartholomew wearily, leaning against the wall and wiping his forehead with his sleeve. 'Just be discreet about it.'

Michael frowned. 'You seem very frail these days, Matt. First you allow Father William to push you down the stairs, and now you are unable to prevent a sick man rising from his bed.'

'You are not sick,' said Bartholomew. 'You are fitter

than I am. All this rest and good food has made you one of the healthiest men in Cambridge.'

'I do feel well,' admitted Michael. 'And it has been pleasant to be the centre of so much loving attention over the past few days. Still, I suppose all good things must come to an end. But what about you? Are you ill?'

'Just tired,' said Bartholomew. 'And I think the effects of that powerful wine we had at the feast still linger on.'

Michael's frown deepened. 'Really? Bulbeck and Gray claimed the same thing. Agatha sent me some of it yesterday – left over from Saturday's débâcle – and Bulbeck advised me not to drink it.'

Bartholomew smiled. 'Langelee is in charge of laying in the College wine. For all his pretensions to being courtly and well-connected, he does not know a decent vintage from a bad one.'

Michael shook his head slowly. 'I have been thinking about that feast. Most members of the College – including me – are used to sampling the nectar of the gods in considerable quantities, and yet virtually everyone I have spoken to claims to have been the worse for drink that night. Even you – abstemious to the point of being tedious – were reeling and lurching like a drunkard.'

'But it was Widow's Wine. You told me the stuff is deliberately brewed to be strong and nasty.'

'But not *this* strong and nasty,' said Michael. 'I wonder whether someone tampered with it.'

'I do not think so, Brother. It was probably just a bad brew.'

'You are wrong, Matt,' said Michael. 'Think back to other College feasts. They sometimes continue until morning, and no one – *no one* – would consider leaving while there was still wine to be had. But there was wine left from this feast, because Agatha sent me some only yesterday.'

'But there was no great cause for celebration, if you recall,' said Bartholomew dryly. 'We had just elected our new Master.'

'The students would drink anyway,' said Michael. 'Yet when we returned from Matilde's house, the whole College was silent and still, and everyone was sleeping.'

'It was late.'

'Not too late for student carousing, Matt. I think someone did something unspeakable to the Widow's Wine – or gave us an especially powerful batch – so that we would all have a comparatively early night. And, of course, with Widow's Wine, no one would notice: the flavour is so damned unpleasant that you could add the most noxious substances known to man and they would do nothing but improve the taste.'

'But why would anyone do such a thing? And anyway, at least two scholars were not sleeping – the pair who pushed me over in St Michael's Lane.'

'Precisely,' said Michael. 'They were not drunk, and I told you at the time that they were no mere students sneaking out for a night in the taverns. I think that Michaelhouse was provided with extra-strong or doctored wine so that this pair could complete whatever it was that they were doing.'

'That seems a little far-fetched,' said Bartholomew doubtfully. 'Perhaps not everyone drank as much as we did. They are not all gluttons.'

'They are students, Matt. Wine pigs. Of course they are all gluttons! I am certain that something odd was going on in Michaelhouse that night – and you and I almost stumbled on it.'

'I think you are reading too much into this, but I agree that the wine was unusually strong. Most of our colleagues looked awful the next morning, even Kenyngham. He was also uncharacteristically tearful.'

'Tearful?' asked Michael in surprise.

Bartholomew told him about Kenyngham's remorse because he had not intervened when the choir had almost attacked him after they had been dismissed.

'Runham again,' said Michael harshly. 'It seems to me that he was one of the few people who did *not* fall victim to this powerful wine. Was he one of the two who pushed you over in the lane, do you think?'

'Impossible. He was lurking in our staircase when we got back to our rooms, remember? He could not have run off down the lane with a beadle in hot pursuit and been hiding on the stairs at the same time.'

'True,' admitted Michael. 'But someone was up to no good in the College that night. I will do a little investigating here this afternoon, while you can assist me with the Bene't deaths. My beadles are doing all they can, but I have decided I need your assistance in the matter of Wymundham and his claim that Raysoun was pushed.'

'But surely the Junior Proctor is looking into that? He must be back from Ely by now.'

Michael shook his head. 'He is still away. Will you go to St Bene't's Church and have another look at the bodies of Raysoun and Wymundham, as you promised? Go to Bene't College first, and ask permission from Master Heltisle, just to be polite.'

'But I have teaching to do . . .'

'You have just been complaining that teaching is impossible. From what Gray tells me, you and Runham – who has bagged himself the comfort of the church – are the only two Fellows still trying to teach in all this racket anyway.'

'But—'

'You promised you would do it,' pressed Michael. 'And Agatha heard you. Shall we summon her and have her repeat what she heard you agree to do?'

'That will not be necessary,' said Bartholomew hastily. 'I will do it.'

'Good.'

'I might not be teaching much longer at Michaelhouse in any case,' said Bartholomew, thinking that running Michael's nasty errands was not something he would miss if he were forced to resign his Fellowship. 'Runham is expecting me to choose between Michaelhouse and medicine tomorrow.'

'Then we have a day to prove Runham doctored the Widow's Wine and had two cronies illicitly in the College that night,' said Michael, rubbing his hands together. 'Because I, for one, do not want you to make that choice.'

Bartholomew did not feel at all inclined to inspect bodies that afternoon, but the banging and crashing had reached such a crescendo that he could barely hear himself think, let alone write his treatise. He unlocked the chained medical books from the hall – books were a valuable commodity, and most libraries kept their tomes under lock and key – and distributed them among the students with strict instructions as to what they should read. They were resentful, aware that most of the others had been given leave to watch the building progress, but Bartholomew was grimly determined that Runham's ambition to make Michaelhouse one of the grandest edifices in the town would not interfere with the College's academic responsibilities.

At the gate, Bartholomew paused and looked back across the courtyard. The north wing was swathed in a complicated mess of planking, most of it old and crumbling, and he assumed it comprised timbers from condemned houses that could not be used for anything else. Workmen swarmed over it, hammering and sawing furiously, some adding yet more levels to the already precarious structure, while others were repointing the stonework on the windows or replacing broken tiles on the roof.

The yard was a chaos of activity, with men running here and there, carrying timber on their shoulders or staggering under the weight of blocks of Barnack stone. Apprentices wearing the distinctive liveries of their masters darted this way and that, ferrying tools, or performing tasks that were beneath the dignity of the qualified tradesman – sawing wood, sanding the rough edges of stones, counting nails, and mixing mortar of lime and sand. The area of the planned new court was equally frenetic. Shallow foundations had been dug, and the first beams that would form the skeleton of the wattle-and-daub kitchen and stables were already in place.

'It is impressive, is it not?' Bartholomew jumped at the closeness of Clippesby's voice behind him. The scholar's eyes were soft and dreamy, and he looked almost sane. 'Master Runham is amazing to have organised all this so quickly. I am glad I came to Michaelhouse and not Bene't.'

'You would have had an opportunity to reside in a building site had you gone to Bene't, too,' said Bartholomew. 'It is also having a new wing raised.'

'But ours will be better,' said Clippesby. 'Raysoun was always complaining that the progress was too slow; he thought the masons would still be labouring on it in a hundred years' time. Master Runham is not permitting such sluggishness.'

'I did not know we had so many builders in Cambridge,' said Bartholomew, regarding the milling workmen in awe. 'I always understood labour was short after the plague.'

'Not if you know where to get it,' said Clippesby smugly.

'And the terms Runham offered are very enticing – these men will be paid double if they can complete all this within a month. Instead of the usual three and a half pence per day, masters will earn a total of eighteen shillings for a mere four weeks' labour.'

Bartholomew raised his eyebrows. 'No wonder they are working so hard! And what happens if they do not finish within a month?'

'That will not be an issue,' said Clippesby confidently.

Bartholomew was not so sure, knowing very well that builders often encountered unexpected problems that delayed matters. He hoped the scramble to complete on time would not result in roofs that leaked, walls that needed buttressing, and windows that did not fit their frames.

'Are you sure Runham has the funds to pay them?' he asked doubtfully. 'If they have been promised double pay, there will be a riot if they do not get it.'

'I am sure,' said Clippesby, indignation on Runham's behalf making his voice suddenly loud. 'He has a great chest of gold in his room – I have seen it myself.'

'A great chest of gold in his room?' asked one of the builders cheerily as he staggered past them bearing a heavy pole. Several of his colleagues heard him, and exchanged acquisitive grins. 'Now that is reassuring to hear. We were worried the old fox might not be able to pay up.'

'There is no question of that, Blaston,' said Clippesby superiorly. 'But you should get back to work if you want to see any of it.'

The master carpenter winked at Bartholomew and continued on his way, whistling merrily as he went. He wore no shoes, Bartholomew noticed, which was unusual for a man of his status. But Robert de Blaston was married to Yolande, the prostitute-friend of Matilde; they had nine children and doubtless no funds to spare on luxuries like footwear. Yolande's own shoes were so ill-fitting that they had caused her feet to swell, he recalled.

'I hope this gold is securely locked away,' said Bartholomew, turning back to Clippesby and thinking it was not wise to advertise the fact that Michaelhouse was swimming in ready cash. Desperately poor people often resorted to desperate measures, and Michaelhouse would not be difficult to burgle now that Runham had dismissed the porters who had guarded its gates.

Clippesby shrugged. 'I expect it is. Runham is no fool. He is a great man who will transform this College from a cluster of shabby hovels into the grandest institution in Cambridge.'

'Our hall is not shabby,' objected Bartholomew, who personally thought the main building with its oriel window and handsome porch one of the finest in East Anglia.

Clippesby gave it a disparaging glance. 'It is haunted by tortured souls. I hear them howling to each other sometimes.'

Bartholomew regarded him uncertainly, wondering whether he was jesting. 'You do?' he asked cautiously.

Clippesby nodded casually. 'It is not a pleasant sound. It keeps me awake at night. Have you never heard it?' He turned eyes that were not quite focused on the physician.

Bartholomew shook his head. 'I cannot say that I have.'

'Then how about the voices of the dead stable boys that mutter in the south wing?' Clippesby gave a sigh. 'But you live in the north wing, so I suppose you would not know about them.'

Bartholomew nodded noncommittally, and escaped from the unstable Dominican with some relief. While *religieux* regularly claimed to hear voices, the context of their messages was usually saintly, not the gabble of dead groomsmen. He wondered whether he should take Clippesby to the Hospital of St John, where the Prior knew a good deal more about the various forms of insanity than did Bartholomew. But, he supposed, as long as Clippesby did not pose a risk to himself or others, there was not much to be done. He was sure at least half the masters of the Cambridge colleges were more lunatic than sane anyway, and Clippesby was no odder than many of them.

His encounter with Clippesby, and the nagging worry that Michaelhouse might have demanded more than it could pay for, meant that he was not in the right frame of mind for visiting St Bene't Church to inspect the bodies of Raysoun and Wymundham. He knew he should do it sooner rather than later, but doubted that a second examination would reveal more than he knew already. He appreciated Michael's desire to leave no stone unturned but he was weary of the University and its scheming, plotting scholars.

In the High Street he hesitated, wondering whether Edith might be in town. Ignoring the fact that if he were not inspecting corpses for Michael he should be supervising his students' reading, working on his treatise on fevers or revisiting the riverman with the rat bite, he strode towards Milne Street, suddenly yearning for the uncomplicated and spontaneous cheerfulness of his sister's company.

A light drizzle fell as Bartholomew walked the short distance to the row of grand houses and storerooms on Milne Street, where the town's richest and most successful merchants resided. As always, the road was full of apprentices in brightly coloured liveries bustling here and there, and ponies and carts delivered and collected loads of every size and shape. The air rang with shouts, curses and the impatient stamp and whinny of horses in their traces, and was thick with the odour of manure, the yeasty smell of grain, the filth of the gutters and the brighter tang of spices.

Oswald Stanmore's property, one of the largest and most impressive, boasted a cobbled yard and several sheds piled high with bales of cloth. Multicoloured strands of wool were caught in the rough wood of doors and windows, pasted into the mud on the ground and entangled in the thatching of the roof.

Stanmore's own apprentices were busy unloading a cart carrying silk and wool that had just arrived from London. The guards, who had protected the precious cargo from the outlaws who plagued the roads between the two cities, were pulling off leather helmets and hauberks, and Cynric was pouring them cups of mulled ale to wash away the dust of the journey. When the ex-book-bearer had finished, he came to stand next to Bartholomew.

'How is life at the College from Hell?' he asked conversationally, watching the mercenaries with proprietary eyes.

'Growing worse by the hour,' replied Bartholomew. 'How is life as a merchant's man?'

Cynric rubbed his chin thoughtfully. 'It has its moments, but I admit I miss my friends – you, Brother Michael, Agatha and even Walter. And I miss our night forays to catch killers, thieves and other ne'er-do-wells.'

'I have not done that for months, thank God,' said Bartholomew fervently. 'Not since we were in Suffolk.'

'What about when you went to find the body of Wymundham?' asked Cynric. 'That was at night. I was still your book-bearer, but I was tucked up in bed with my wife. You should have asked me to go with you.'

'I missed you,' said Bartholomew. 'We had one of Michael's beadles, but it was not the same.'

Cynric grinned and slapped him on the shoulder. 'We had some good times, you and me. Visit me some evening, and we will reminisce over a jug of good wine. I can afford good wines on the salary Master Stanmore pays me – not like what I had to drink at Michaelhouse.'

He wandered away to stand with his soldiers, refilling their cups and listening to their reports about the journey. Just as Bartholomew was about to climb the stairs to Stanmore's office, the merchant emerged with Edith close on his heels.

'Matt!' Edith cried in delight. 'You have come to visit us!'

Stanmore's smile of welcome faded suddenly. 'You are not in trouble, are you?' he asked anxiously. 'You only come to see us these days if there is something wrong.'

'There is nothing wrong,' said Bartholomew guiltily, knowing that Stanmore had a point. 'I had some free time and I felt like spending it with my family.'

Edith gave such a beam of pleasure that Bartholomew's guilt increased tenfold. 'How is Brother Michael?' she asked. 'We heard he has been ill.'

'He is well,' said Bartholomew, 'and eating enough to plunge the College into debt with all the grocers and bakers in Cambridge.'

Edith laughed. 'Poor Michael. You should not tease him about his appetite, Matt. He is happy when he is eating, and unhappy when he is hungry. Which of the two conditions do you think is better for his health?'

'True. But I did not come to talk about Michael, I came to see you.'

'Do you want to come in?' asked Stanmore, gesturing to the door. 'We were about to visit Mayor Horwoode, but it will not matter if we are a little late.'

'I will walk with you,' said Bartholomew, taking Edith's arm and escorting her across the courtyard. 'Is this meeting with Horwoode business or pleasure?'

'Business,' said Edith promptly, casting a disapproving glance at her husband.

'Pleasure,' said Stanmore at the same time.

'I see,' said Bartholomew. 'He has invited you both to his house to spend a pleasant evening with him, but will probably mention some matter of town politics at the same time?'

'Not politics, exactly,' said Stanmore. 'I suspect he wants me to join his guild. Corpus Christi is one of the two organisations that founded Bene't College, and rumour has it that the venture is turning out to be expensive. The old members are weary of the continual drain on their purses, and are busy recruiting new ones.'

'Will you join?' asked Bartholomew.

Stanmore smiled. 'I shall eat Horwoode's food, drink his wine and listen to what he has to say. But I can think of worthier places to squander my finances than Bene't.'

'It is a dreadful place, by all accounts,' agreed Edith. 'Its Fellows are always squabbling, and its students constantly try to goad our apprentices into fights.'

'So what makes it different from any other College?' asked Bartholomew. He did not intend the question to be humorous, but Stanmore and Edith laughed.

'Nothing, really,' said Stanmore. 'But Michaelhouse does not let outsiders know about its internal rows and unseemly behaviour. Michaelhouse men take their oaths of loyalty seriously; Bene't men do not seem to care who knows about their nasty quarrels.'

'It is more than that,' said Edith. 'Bene't has those dreadful porters – the rudest and most vicious I have ever encountered. One of them – Osmun – bumped into me as I was walking down the High Street the other day.

I dropped my basket and spilled apples all over the road, but he just sneered and declined to apologise or even to help me pick them up.'

'Perhaps I should join the Guild of Corpus Christi after all,' mused Stanmore. 'Then I could use my influence to have the man dismissed from his post. That will teach him to learn some manners.'

'There is Adela Tangmer,' said Edith urgently, pointing to the robust daughter of the town's vintner who was riding towards them. 'Quick! Duck in here before she sees us.'

Before her brother or husband could react, they found themselves bundled inside the workshop of Jonas the Poisoner. The apothecary glanced up from his work in surprise as three people suddenly exploded into his domain.

'What?' he demanded of Bartholomew nervously. 'Has the Death returned? Is there fever in the city? Is Robin of Grantchester amputating limbs again?'

'No, no,' said Bartholomew hurriedly, embarrassed at having burst into Jonas's property uninvited. 'But I need more of your plaster of betony. I seem to have lost mine.'

'I do deliver, you know,' said Jonas, standing to select the salve from the shelf. 'There is no need for you to come in person, or to drag your family here with you.'

'We made it,' breathed Edith, her eye to the gap in the door. 'She did not see us.'

'And what is wrong with meeting Adela Tangmer?' asked Stanmore, watching as the untidily confident figure rode past. 'If it were her father you were seeking to avoid, I would understand – the man is a disreputable villain who waters the wine he sells.'

'Does he?' asked Jonas, handing Bartholomew the jar.

'I thought the last cask I bought from him tasted weaker than usual. Crafty old dog!'

'She is a dreadful woman,' said Edith, her eye still fastened to the crack. 'She came bustling up to me in the Market Square yesterday, when I was in the middle of a conversation with the Prioress of St Radegund's, and, without any kind of preamble, demanded to know which pardoner sells absolutions for the sin of lust.'

Bartholomew started to laugh, amused by Adela's question, the fact that she had chosen Edith as someone who might be able to answer it, and Edith's indignation that Adela had asked such a thing in the august presence of the Prioress of St Radegund's Convent.

Edith regarded him coolly. 'It is not funny, Matt. It left me completely speechless. She has all the social graces of a carthorse, and she looks like one, too!'

'Well, she has gone now, and we should leave poor Jonas in peace,' said Stanmore, opening the door and stepping outside. He glanced back and gave a long-suffering sigh. 'Are you sure you have enough money to pay for that salve, Matt?'

Bartholomew had emptied the contents of his purse on to one of Jonas's workbenches, and the apothecary was helping him to count out the mass of small change.

'Penny and a half short,' said Jonas eventually, looking hopefully at Stanmore.

'I do not carry pennies,' said Stanmore loftily. 'I am not a peasant. Here is a shilling. Give Matt back his farthings, Jonas. From what I hear, he needs a regular supply of base coins to pay fines every time he is late for church.'

'Who told you that?' asked Bartholomew.

Stanmore tapped his nose and assumed a smug expression. 'I have a very good network of informants in Cambridge, Matt.'

'Did Runham tell you?' asked Bartholomew. 'When did you meet him?'

'He paid me a visit,' said Stanmore vaguely. He made a moue of disapproval. 'I do not like that man, and I certainly do not want to be seen having scholars calling on me. What would my neighbours say?'

'I take it that does not apply to me,' said Bartholomew.

Stanmore clicked his tongue impatiently. 'You are different – family. But I do not appreciate scholars like Runham visiting me in broad daylight, when anyone might see him.'

'What did he want?'

'Five marks for his new buildings,' said Stanmore. 'But here we are, at Horwoode's house.'

Mayor Horwoode answered his door to Stanmore's knock before Bartholomew could ask why his brother-in-law had parted with his money to a man like Runham. Five marks was a fortune – more than a year's salary for Bartholomew.

The Mayor did not look pleased to see Bartholomew. He gazed coolly at the physician's muddy cloak and patched tabard, and then glanced quickly up and down the street to see whether anyone had observed that a man as important as the Mayor of Cambridge should be visited by such a low fellow.

'Have you resolved that matter of Wymundham's death?' he asked frostily, having apparently decided that no one was looking and that he could afford to indulge his curiosity. He did not, however, invite Bartholomew inside his home.

'Not yet,' said Bartholomew. 'But Brother Michael's investigation is continuing.'

'He will discover nothing amiss,' said Horwoode with great conviction. 'Whatever you may have thought when you poked at the corpse the other night. I am certain the poor man flung himself to his death in despair after witnessing Raysoun's fall.'

'I am on my way to look at his body again,' said Bartholomew.

'Then you might like to know that St Bene't's Church lies in the south of the town, and you seem to be walking north. Is Michaelhouse still in its cups, celebrating the election of Runham as Master?'

'It certainly is not,' said Bartholomew, with more feeling than he intended to show.

'Then I shall not detain you,' said Horwoode. 'Go and inspect your corpses. You will find that I am right, and that Wymundham committed suicide.'

'I will bear it in mind,' said Bartholomew noncommittally, wondering why so many people were determined to have poor Wymundham condemned to a suicide's grave. Could Horwoode be involved in his murder? Bartholomew could not see how, although the Mayor's insistence that his findings were wrong had the effect of making Bartholomew more determined than ever to uncover the truth behind the Bene't man's death.

'Good,' said Horwoode flatly. 'In that case, I will bid you good afternoon.'

'He came with—' began Edith, indignant that the Mayor should dismiss her brother so rudely.

'There is Matilde,' said Bartholomew quickly, not wanting Edith to inveigle an invitation from a man who clearly did not want to extend his hospitality to scholars. 'I must pay my respects.'

'A whore?' asked Horwoode disapprovingly. 'Is the University in league with harlots these days?'

'Not on Fridays,' retorted Bartholomew, recalling Matilde's friend telling him about her weekly visits to the Mayor's house. 'The prostitutes have civic engagements on Friday nights.'

Leaving Horwoode scarlet with mortification and outrage, Bartholomew bowed to Edith and Stanmore and took his leave.

Matilde was inspecting some brightly coloured ribbons on a pedlar's cart, stretching long, elegant fingers to touch each one and assess its quality. Bartholomew remembered Langelee telling him that he should buy her some ribbons, although he could not imagine that the loutish philosopher had any advice about women that was worth following; after all, he had just extricated himself from a disastrous marriage.

'Matthew,' said Matilde, turning to smile at him as he approached. 'What are you doing here? Surely Mayor Horwoode would not admit a mere scholar into his home? Or is someone ill?'

'I did not know there was such a strong dislike of scholars among the great and the good of the town,' said Bartholomew, still bemused.

'Then you must be blind,' said Matilde bluntly. 'Important men like the Mayor, the burgesses and the merchants no more want poor scholars in their homes than they do the sisters. To both of us, their doors are only open when they think no one else will see.'

'I am sure it never used to be this bad. Sheriff Tulyet is important, but he is never hostile to me or Michael.'

'Dick Tulyet is a good man, and your role as physician and your family connections make you less objectionable than most. But you are right – relations between town and University are less friendly since Michaelhouse disbanded the choir. It was an ill-considered act on Runham's part.'

'I know.'

Matilde smiled at him. 'But let us not talk about such things. Which of these ribbons do you prefer? The green or the blue?'

'Green,' he said, barely glancing at them. Even in the dull light of a grey November afternoon, Matilde was lovely. Her hair shone with health, and her skin was clean and unblemished. In her cloak of dark blue wool she looked as respectable and affluent as any of the wealthy merchants.

'Green it is, then,' she said, holding the ribbon out to the pedlar to fold. She smiled when Bartholomew paid the threepence. 'Thank you. I seldom carry pennies – they are always so dirty, not to mention heavy. Where are you going now? Home to Michaelhouse?'

'To Bene't College, to ask the Master if he will allow me to inspect the bodies of those two scholars again.'

'I know Raysoun fell from the scaffolding,' said Matilde, 'and the word is that Wymundham flung himself from the bank of the King's Ditch in sorrow at losing his only friend.'

'That is what Mayor Horwoode thinks, certainly.'

'Mayor Horwoode,' mused Matilde. 'You said it was his garden in which the body was found, so I suppose he *would* want a verdict of suicide.'

'Would he?' asked Bartholomew. 'Why?'

'Well, no one wants their home to be the scene of a gruesome crime,' said Matilde. 'And no one wants their home to be open to the interested scrutiny of the Senior Proctor, whose task it is to investigate the murders of scholars. Also, if it were proven that a scholar was killed on his property, Horwoode might have enraged students storming his house, seeking revenge.'

'That is true,' said Bartholomew. 'But all this suggests that Horwoode suspected that Wymundham was murdered – or even that he had a hand in it – and that he deliberately set out to make Michael believe the death was not suspicious.'

'It does indeed,' said Matilde. 'Although I think you

will find that Horwoode is more likely to be guilty of concealing a crime than of committing one. If he had killed Wymundham himself, he would have removed the body from his own property. But what did you think when you examined the corpse that night? Did it look as though Wymundham had killed himself in a fit of grief?'

'No,' said Bartholomew. 'I was a little drunk at the time . . .'

Matilde laughed. 'A little? You were reeling like an apprentice with his first wine!'

'. . . but it looked to me as though he had been suffocated in some way. There was no injury to his head and I do not think his neck was broken, but the blueness of the face and the damaged fingers suggested that he was prevented from breathing.'

Matilde shuddered, her amusement fading. 'What nasty business this is, Matt. You should be careful. If Horwoode did try to make Wymundham's murder appear suicide – perhaps even by calling you in the depths of the night, so that it would be too dark for you to see properly – then he will not take kindly to you investigating it too closely.'

'I know,' said Bartholomew. 'And the Mayor is a powerful man in Cambridge. If ever I need to apply for a licence to practise medicine in the town, I would need his good favour.'

'Are you thinking of leaving Michaelhouse, then?' asked Matilde in astonishment. 'But you cannot, Matthew! You love your teaching too much! You would be unhappy!'

Would he? Bartholomew wondered. If he were no longer affiliated with Michaelhouse, then there would be nothing to stop him from pursuing Matilde in any way he pleased. And, he thought, spending long winter evenings in the presence of so lively and intelligent a mind, not to mention a lovely body, was infinitely more appealing than shivering over candle stubs in the rising damp of his Michaelhouse cell.

'What about Ovyng Hostel's Brother Patrick?' asked Matilde, changing the subject quickly, as if embarrassed by her outburst. 'Did you learn anything about him? I told you one of the sisters had denounced him as an inveterate gossip. Did you check that? Was she right?'

'His Principal certainly thought so,' said Bartholomew. 'But he also said that Patrick was not privy to the kind of secrets that would warrant someone killing him.'

'It is quite astonishing what some people object to, and the trouble they take to conceal things,' said Matilde. 'You should not dismiss Patrick's gossiping too lightly as a motive for his murder. But I have a present for you. It has been ready for some days now, but you have not visited me, and so I have been unable to give it to you.'

Bartholomew experienced a resurgence of the guilt he had felt when Edith had accused him of being lax in his brotherly attentions. 'You should not give—' he began.

Matilde brushed his objections aside. 'Actually, it is not really *for* you, and it is not really *from* me. But it is waiting to be collected from the blacksmith's forge.'

'The blacksmith?' asked Bartholomew nervously, sincerely hoping it was not a horse.

Matilde smiled mysteriously and slipped her arm through his. They walked briskly to the smelly, filthy, fiery hole in which the blacksmith and his two soot-blackened assistants laboured in the hiss and roar of flames and the deafening clang of metal against metal. The smith glanced up as Matilde entered, then went to fetch something.

Rifling through an assortment of weapons, horse shoes, and pieces of armour, he found what he was looking for and presented Matilde with a bundle of greasy black sacking. She declined to sully her hands with it, and indicated that it was for Bartholomew.

Curiously, the physician peeled away the material to reveal a pair of shiny forceps, equipped with a pair of jaws that opened to the size of a small head. Bewildered, he gazed at them and then at her.

'They are the tool that midwives use for drawing forth babies from their mothers,' she explained.

'I know what they are,' said Bartholomew, as he turned them over in his hands. They were beautifully crafted, with wide ends that would allow the pressure to be spread across a wider area of the skull and so lessen the chance of damage to the baby's brain, and the metal had been polished smooth, so that rough edges would not harm the mother. 'But why are you giving them to me?'

'Rosa Layne,' said Matilde in a soft voice. 'Do you remember her?'

'Yes, of course. She died in childbirth last week. Her family had hired a charlatan midwife, who killed the poor woman. A real midwife, armed with a pair of these forceps, would have saved her.'

'She was a sister,' said Matilde quietly. 'A prostitute. In fact, she was the sister who told me that your murdered Brother Patrick was such a gossip.'

'A friend of yours, then,' said Bartholomew sympathetically. 'I am sorry, Matilde. I was called too late, and there was nothing I could do to save her.'

'I know that,' said Matilde. 'But a group of us were discussing the problem penniless women now face in securing qualified midwives for difficult births. We know you occasionally attend such women, so we decided you should be properly equipped for the task. The gift is to be used to honour the memory of Rosa Layne.'

Bartholomew did not know what to say. 'There are good midwives in Cambridge—'

'Two. But they are expensive to hire, and they do not deign to attend whores when they could be hovering at the scented bedsides of merchants' wives. We need someone who does not condemn us, and who knows what he is doing. We would prefer a woman, of course, but you are the next-best thing.'

'Thank you,' said Bartholomew, supposing it was meant to be a compliment.

'We did quite a bit of investigating before we settled on this design,' Matilde continued, looking down at the instrument in Bartholomew's hands. 'The person who helped us most was Adela Tangmer. She told us all about a pair she had devised for assisting the birth of foals, and so we modelled ours on hers, although smaller, of course.'

'They are perfect,' he said, performing a few trial grabs with them, and making the blacksmith and his assistants wince. 'They could well save a woman's life.'

'Good,' said Matilde warmly. 'That is what we hoped. And we are friends again now – I was angry with you but it is impossible to be cross with you for long. But I should go. Poor Yolande de Blaston had just learned that she is to bear her tenth child, and she is all but overwhelmed with the first nine. She is in sore need of a little cheerful company and a lot of practical advice about managing household expenses.'

'You might do better telling her how to avoid unwanted pregnancies in the first place,' said Bartholomew, before he could stop himself.

'Really, Matthew!' exclaimed Matilde, and Bartholomew could see that not all her shock at his blunt suggestion was feigned. 'What a dreadful thing to say to a respectable woman!'

'Sorry,' muttered Bartholomew, mortified.

'I should think so,' she said. 'You should not believe all you hear, you know.'

And with that enigmatic statement, she was gone,

weaving in and out of the late afternoon crowds and clutching a piece of bright green ribbon in her slender fingers.

When Bartholomew felt he had outstayed his welcome at the forge, brandishing and snapping his new forceps, he carefully wrapped them in some clean cloth and slipped them inside his medicine bag, where they all but doubled its weight. He supposed he should leave them in his storeroom, to be collected whenever he was summoned to a childbirth, but was too pleased to abandon them just yet. Somewhat guiltily, he began to make a list in his mind of all the pregnant women he knew, in anticipation of putting his latest acquisition to practical use.

He realised that he had delayed his visit to St Bene't's Church for far too long, and left the forge to set off down the High Street. But he needed the permission of the Master of Bene't College to examine the bodies: he did not want to be caught tampering with the corpses of another College's scholars without first obtaining the blessing of their Master. Physicians in Italian universities had a sinister reputation for using dead human bodies to teach anatomy, and Bartholomew did not want to be accused of prospecting for potential subjects.

When he reached the part of Bene't College that faced the High Street, he saw that his medical colleague, Master Lynton, must have done as he had threatened and complained to the Sheriff about the unsafe state of the scaffolding. Parts of it had been dismantled, and the incessant clatter that had driven Bartholomew to distraction at Michaelhouse was refreshingly absent.

Like all the Cambridge Colleges, Bene't was being built to repel invaders. There was a substantial gatehouse, which comprised a stocky tower with an entrance large enough to allow a cart through it, some chambers on the upper floors, and a dim little hole in which the porters lurked. Since the door was usually kept closed, anyone wanting to enter or leave the College was obliged to pass the porters first.

Bartholomew tapped on the gate and waited to be admitted. He knew the porters were in their lodge, because he could hear the click of bone against bone as dice were rolled and the muted sniggers of one player as he won a game. He knocked again, a little louder.

'Go away,' came an irritable voice from within. Bartholomew recognised it as that of Osmun. 'Bene't College is closed to visitors.'

'I have come to see Master Heltisle,' called Bartholomew. 'I have business with him on behalf of the Senior Proctor.'

'That is too bad,' came the reply. 'Shove off.'

Although Bartholomew knew of the Bene't College porters' reputation for rudeness, he had never experienced it first hand. He considered doing as they suggested, unwilling to become embroiled in a physical confrontation. But he was a doctor of the University and one of its most senior Fellows, and he did not see why he should be sent away by a mere porter, especially given that his purpose for entering the College was to try to solve the murders of Bene't's own scholars.

'Tell Master Heltisle I am here to see him,' he snapped. 'At once.'

'He is busy,' growled Osmun, and a clatter from within suggested that the dice were being rolled again. 'Shove off, or I will break your arms.'

Bartholomew gazed at the closed door for a moment, debating what to do. He stepped forward and put his hand to the wicket door. It was unlocked, so he pushed it open, stepped across the threshold and started to walk across the courtyard towards the hall, hoping to find a student who would tell him where the Master's rooms were located.

'Hey, you!' bellowed Osmun in disbelief, tearing open the door to the porters' lodge and pounding after him. 'I told you the College was closed. Now get out, before you regret it.'

'You cannot just close a College,' said Bartholomew. 'And I am on University business.'

'I do not care what you want or who you are,' snarled Osmun, grabbing a handful of Bartholomew's cloak and beginning to haul him towards the gate. 'You cannot come in.'

Before he could be throttled, Bartholomew quickly undid the clasp and slipped out of his cloak, leaving the startled porter with a handful of cloth. More determinedly than ever, he began to walk towards the hall again, aware that several students had emerged from their rooms and were watching the scene in the courtyard with nervous interest.

'I have come to see Master Heltisle,' he shouted to them. 'Please fetch him.'

Osmun lunged, and Bartholomew deftly side-stepped him, so that the burly porter staggered and all but lost his balance. Seeing his comrade in difficulties, a second porter emerged from the lodge. Like Osmun, he was thickset and heavy featured, and wore the ugly striped hose and ridiculous blue cap that were the uniform of the Bene't servants. Osmun had supplemented his with the peculiarly patterned tunic in which his cousin Justus had died, while at his waist hung Justus's blunt dagger – although even that could cause a serious injury. The physician began to have second thoughts about his moral stand as the pair of them began to advance on him.

'The Senior Proctor will not be pleased to hear that you laid hands on his agent,' he blustered, backing away.

'You are on Bene't property,' snarled Osmun, snatching at Bartholomew and missing again. 'What I do to you here is none of the Senior Proctor's business.'

'And this is how you represent your College, is it?' demanded Bartholomew. 'By attacking Fellows of the University and disregarding the authority of the Senior Proctor?'

'The Senior Proctor is not here, is he?' said Osmun with a cold smile. 'And the authority in Bene't is me. What I say goes, and those who do not believe me must learn the hard way.'

'Like the Fellow you fought last Saturday?' asked Bartholomew, recalling Michael's beadle telling of Osmun's arrest for riotous behaviour. 'Is that what you were doing? Teaching him a lesson?'

'Maybe,' said Osmun. 'I spent a night in the proctors' prison, but that miserable Henry de Walton learned something of College rules, so it was worthwhile.'

Bartholomew recalled that it was Henry de Walton whom Adela had described as a 'snivelling little man' who complained about the state of his health. The foppish Simeon had not liked him much either.

None of the students who ringed the courtyard had gone to fetch Heltisle, and Bartholomew realised he had been foolish to enter Bene't College alone, when it was apparent that at least two of their number had met ends that were far from natural.

'De Walton now does what he is told,' said the second porter, circling Bartholomew like a dog with a cornered rat. 'We do not tolerate Fellows who are critical, and who do not put their loyalty to the College above all else.'

The notion that Fellows at Bene't were not permitted to express themselves freely sounded sinister to Bartholomew. Was that how Michaelhouse would be under Runham? Would Clippesby be the equivalent of

Osmun, listening at doors to see whether his colleagues were voicing discontent, and meting out physical punishment to those who spoke out against him?

His thoughts had distracted him, and he did not move quickly enough to avoid Osmun's sudden lunge. With an expression of intense satisfaction, the porter found himself in possession of a handful of the physician's tabard. Bartholomew tried to struggle free, but Osmun was not about to let him go a second time.

'I have him, Ulfo!' he shouted, as the second porter darted to his assistance. 'It does not take two Bene't porters to rid the College of a worm like this.'

'Osmun! What is all this unseemly skirmishing in our courtyard?'

With relief, Bartholomew glanced behind him to see the Master of Bene't College standing there. Heltisle was a tall, handsome scholar with the easy confidence of a man born to power and wealth. He had been a clerk on the King's Bench before he had forsaken law for academia, and was apparently a man destined for great things in the University, and perhaps beyond. One of his Fellows, a small, sharp-eyed man with stained teeth and a blotched complexion, hovered at his side, watching the spectacle in front of him with disapproval.

'This man was trying to break into our College,' said Osmun sullenly, before Bartholomew could reply. 'Me and Ulfo were just throwing him out.'

'His tabard suggests he is a Fellow from Michaelhouse,' said the Fellow who stood with Heltisle. His voice had the soft burr of a local man. 'You are right, Osmun: we want none of that filth in Bene't. Get rid of him.'

With malicious vindictiveness, Osmun and Ulfo began hauling Bartholomew towards the gate. Bartholomew was not aware of particular ill-feeling between the two Colleges – other than the usual suspicion and rivalry that characterised any relationship between most academic institutions – and did not understand why the mention of Michaelhouse should evoke such a hostile reaction.

'Wait,' commanded Heltisle, striding forward to inspect Bartholomew as though he were a pig in a market. 'Do you not recognise this man, Caumpes? He is Matthew Bartholomew, one of the two physicians who attended Raysoun when he fell from the scaffolding . . .'

'Yes,' said Bartholomew, trying to pull free of the porters. 'Osmun summoned me on the advice of Master Lynton. I am sorry I was unable to do anything to save Raysoun.'

Heltisle regarded him curiously. 'I am sure you did your best on that score. But you did not allow me to finish what I was going to say. After Raysoun died, both you physicians registered complaints with the Sheriff about the state of our scaffolding. You told him it was dangerous.'

Lynton had said he would do just that, Bartholomew recalled, and the fact that some of the scaffolding had already been dismantled suggested that Sheriff Tulyet had acted on it. If Heltisle had been informed that two physicians had voiced objections, then Lynton must have added Bartholomew's name to strengthen his cause.

'At the time, we thought the complaint was made out of concern for us and for public safety,' Heltisle went on coldly. 'But now we know the truth, and it has nothing to do with the well-being of anyone except the scholars of Michaelhouse.'

'What do you mean?' asked Bartholomew.

'The only reason you complained to the Sheriff was so that you could poach our builders to work for you instead,' answered Caumpes bitterly.

'What?' exclaimed Bartholomew, horrified. 'I have poached no builders . . .'

But Runham might well have done, he realised suddenly. With a shock, he guessed exactly where some of the dismantled scaffolding had been re-erected, and why Michaelhouse's had such a used look about it. It also explained why Runham was able to recruit so many workmen in such a short period of time – he had simply gone to an existing building site and offered the men wages that they could not afford to decline.

With a sinking heart, Bartholomew saw he should have guessed how Michaelhouse's army of builders had been raised. There was Robert de Blaston, the carpenter, for a start. Bartholomew had known he was working for Bene't, because at Matilde's house Yolande had related how her husband said Raysoun was a drunk, given to clambering on the Bene't scaffolding to seek out shirkers. And then Bartholomew had seen Robert de Blaston at Michaelhouse: it was he who had overheard Clippesby mention the big chest of gold Runham had gathered to pay the workmen's wages. Blaston had been working at Bene't, and Michaelhouse had poached him, just as Heltisle and Caumpes were claiming.

'You have no answer, do you?' asked Heltisle softly, as he hesitated. 'You know you have done Bene't a grave disservice, and you have no excuse to make.'

'It was clever of you,' added Caumpes. 'First you urge the Sheriff to impose new safety measures on our workforce, hampering the speed of their progress, and irritating and frustrating them so that they are ripe for rebellion; and then you offer them new jobs at higher wages.'

'But I did not speak to the Sheriff about your scaffolding,' protested Bartholomew. 'It *was* dangerous, but I did not mention it to the Sheriff.'

'But you went to his house the very next day,' said Caumpes. 'You were not man enough to visit him openly in the Castle, so you sneaked to his home. I saw you myself, shaking the man's hand on his doorstep.'

'I had been summoned to physick his son,' said Bartholomew, not liking the way his movements had been watched. 'Not that it is any business of yours.'

'So, what do you want here?' asked Heltisle icily. 'Have you come to offer us compensation for what your College has done to mine?'

'The Senior Proctor asked me to come,' he said, wishing he had never agreed to become Michael's menial. 'He wants me to examine the bodies of Wymundham and Raysoun, to ascertain the precise causes of their deaths.'

'I am sure he does,' said Caumpes nastily. 'The Senior Proctor – a Michaelhouse man to the core – is trying to use the deaths of those two unfortunates to bring our College to the brink of ruin.'

'Quite,' agreed Heltisle. 'He wants to start rumours that their accidental deaths were actually murders, so that he can bring Bene't into disrepute.'

'I can assure you that is not true,' protested Bartholomew, hoping sincerely that it was not. Michael loved University politics, and would be quite happy to see another College fall from grace if it promoted his own.

He was wondering how he could extricate himself without acknowledging that Michaelhouse had acted somewhat shabbily – despite his personal opinion of Runham, he did not want to be openly disloyal to his own College – when the sound of horses' hooves clattering on the cobbles drew attention away from him.

He was released abruptly, and Bartholomew saw that porters, Fellows and students were all busy bowing so deeply and obsequiously that a good many blue uniforms trailed in the mud. He glanced at the new arrivals, and immediately recognised the portly figure of the Duke of Lancaster.

The Duke was one of Bene't College's most noteworthy benefactors, and was often seen in the town, inspecting progress on the foundation that was costing him a small fortune. Riding with him was his squire, the elegant Simekyn Simeon, who sported hose and tunic of scarlet and a cloak of an impractical corn yellow. His shoes were made of an exquisite soft calfskin that would not last a day in Cambridge's filthy streets.

The Duke himself cut a dowdy figure. He wore a mud-brown cloak trimmed with fur that was spiky and stained with rain, and his hose and tunic were a dull moss green. Bartholomew looked from his dour, uncompromising features to the sardonic, amused face of Simeon, and suspected that their arrival would not make his awkward position any easier.

'My lord,' said Heltisle, and Bartholomew was impressed to see him bow so low that he was bent almost double. 'It is an honour to have you within our walls once more. May I offer you wine?'

'You may,' said Lancaster coolly. 'But I am not here to exchange pleasantries, Heltisle. Simeon informs me that Wymundham and Raysoun are dead. Is this true? And why are there no builders at work and the scaffolding dismantled? My coffers are not bottomless, you know; if Bene't's new hall is not completed soon, you will have to look elsewhere for a gullible benefactor.'

'It is not our fault,' protested Heltisle in alarm. 'It was all going excellently: the upper floor was almost completed and Raysoun spent most of his time supervising the workers and making sure no one shirked. Then he fell and was killed, and Michaelhouse stole all our labourers. If you want someone to blame for this setback, look to Michaelhouse.'

As one, every Bene't scholar's gaze went from the Duke to Bartholomew, who suspected he cut a sorry figure with his darned and patched tabard and clothes dishevelled from his tussle with the porters.

'This is one of them,' explained Caumpes to the Duke. 'He complained to the Sheriff that our scaffolding posed a danger to the public, and then enticed away our labourers while the matter was rectified.'

'Well?' demanded the Duke, regarding Bartholomew coldly. 'Have you come to demand money before our craftsmen are reinstated? Speak up!'

'Of course not,' said Bartholomew. 'I did not even know the men working on Michaelhouse were from Bene't. I am a physician and I came here at the request of the University's Senior Proctor to examine the bodies of the two Fellows who died.'

'Well, you are far too late for that,' said Heltisle with grim satisfaction. 'They were buried days ago.'

chapter 7

T HE DUKE OF LANCASTER HAD NO INTENTION OF standing in Bene't's chilly yard in the gathering gloom of dusk to discuss whether or not Michaelhouse had wronged the College into which he had ploughed a good deal of his own money. He tossed his riding gloves to Osmun, ordered Ulfo to stable his horse, and strode to the hall, where more servants flitted around him like moths around a candle.

Bartholomew, flanked by Heltisle and Caumpes, watched the Duke being made comfortable and thought about the last time he had been in Bene't's hall. Although only eight days before, it felt longer. He had been attending Wymundham, fetching him wine from behind the serving screen to calm him after the death of his friend Raysoun.

Had Wymundham been telling the truth about Raysoun's last words? And had Wymundham then been killed to prevent him from telling Michael? Adela Tangmer, Matilde and the Stanmores had all told Bartholomew that Bene't seethed with dissension. Was that why Heltisle had ordered the bodies buried before the Proctors' office had given permission for them to be released, to prevent Bartholomew from learning the truth about the way they had died? Or was it simply because Michael's illness had delayed matters too long, and, quite naturally, Bene't College was reluctant to keep decomposing corpses in the church it used for its daily prayers? They would certainly be within their rights.

But if Wymundham *had* been murdered, then how did Mayor Horwoode fit into the plot? Was he an innocent bystander, whose garden was selected at random as a place to dump the body? Or did he and his Guild of St Mary, which had co-founded Bene't, have something to hide? And was the Duke of Lancaster aware of or involved in the murder? Since the Duke had made his squire a Fellow of Bene't for the express purpose of keeping an eye on the place, he clearly sensed the College was not all it should be. With a sinking heart, Bartholomew suspected he was about to be drawn into something he would rather avoid.

'Michaelhouse must have been planning this for weeks!' Caumpes burst out, evidently unable to restrain himself any longer. 'It is a coincidence, is it not, that all this happens the instant Runham is elected as their new Master?'

Bartholomew wondered if that were true. It usually took many months for the concept of a building to become reality, and yet Runham had arranged for plans to be drawn up, materials to be delivered, a workforce hired and money to pay for it all within a few days. On reflection, Bartholomew decided that Caumpes's accusation was undoubtedly true. And if that were the case, then Runham must have been anticipating Kenyngham's resignation, too, and had been ready to spring into action the moment he, Runham, was elected.

'It would not surprise me to learn that Michaelhouse was responsible for Raysoun's death,' Caumpes continued hotly. 'It certainly seems to have benefited Michaelhouse.'

'No,' said Bartholomew firmly. 'That is not true. Michaelhouse has always striven for peaceful relations with its neighbours, whether townsmen or other Colleges.'

'That is a lie!' Heltisle pounced immediately. 'Michaelhouse cares nothing for peaceful relations. As a case in point, Runham recently dismissed his College choir, and almost caused a riot by refusing to pay them the bread and ale they were owed.'

Bartholomew was silent, cursing Runham for his short-sighted actions.

'And worse, we have been subjected to an almost continual stream of unemployed singers hoping to be allowed to join the Bene't choir,' Heltisle went on. 'That none of them has the slightest iota of musical talent seems irrelevant to them. They are not interested in singing, only in whether we can feed them after the Sunday mass.'

'Why did you want to examine the bodies of our scholars?' the Duke asked of Bartholomew curiously.

Simekyn Simeon rested his elegantly clad feet on the table, and observed the spectacle that was being played out in front of him, with half-closed eyes. That Simeon declined to acknowledge that it was he who had insisted Michael should conduct a more rigorous enquiry indicated to Bartholomew that his errand had not been on the command of his Master. Simeon, it seemed, had acted independently. Bartholomew wondered whether that was significant.

He hesitated before he replied to the Duke's question, not sure that it was wise to mention his suspicions that the two Bene't Fellows might have been murdered when their killer could be standing in the hall at that very moment. While Simeon might be certain that the killer was not a Bene't man, Bartholomew wanted to reserve judgement until he knew more about the College that Michaelhouse had wronged.

'He is reluctant to answer you, my lord,' said Caumpes, when Bartholomew did not respond immediately. 'Could that be because I am right, and Michaelhouse had them killed, and now it wants to hide any evidence of it?'

'Michaelhouse is more cunning than that,' said Heltisle. 'I do not think it had a hand in killing Raysoun or Wymundham, but I do think it might be trying to start rumours that a Bene't scholar had a hand in their deaths. That is the kind of subtle damage the likes of Michaelhouse men would inflict on us. Rumours are easy to start, but less easy to stop.'

The Duke of Lancaster made an impatient sound at the back of his throat. 'Enough of this! You scholars are obsessed with petty details. If Michaelhouse had wanted Raysoun and Wymundham dead, there would be clear evidence that they had been murdered. Was there?'

'No, my lord,' said Heltisle immediately. 'Raysoun fell from the scaffolding and Wymundham flung himself over the bank of the King's Ditch in his grief.'

Bartholomew said nothing. Neither did Simeon, who had been told that Wymundham's body showed signs of a struggle. Bartholomew wondered why the courtier kept his peace. Was it simply because he did not believe a body could yield that sort of information? Or was there another reason for his silence?

'Well, there you are, then,' said the Duke. 'No one was murdered, and if no one was murdered, then no one can accuse Bene't of anything. And that is the end of the matter, except for one thing.'

'And what is that, my lord?' asked Heltisle, a little nervously.

'The fact that you did not tell me that work on my College has stopped, and yet money continues to be drawn from the funds I left for you.'

'We were going to tell you,' protested Heltisle, swallowing hard. 'The money was drawn to pay a carpenter to make the scaffolding safe after the workmen looted it to take to Michaelhouse.'

'Well, I am far from pleased,' said the Duke. 'I am

a busy man, and have better things to do than visit Cambridge every week to rescue Bene't from its latest disaster.'

'It is not a disaster,' said Caumpes stiffly. 'It is a minor setback.'

'You call the deaths of two Fellows a minor setback?' asked Simeon coolly.

'That is not what I meant,' said Caumpes. 'I was referring to the building. But since you mention it, I am not sorry Raysoun and Wymundham have gone. Raysoun was a drunkard who would have brought the College into disrepute at some point, while Wymundham was a malicious tale-teller. We will appoint more Fellows. There are plenty of good clerks who would be willing to accept positions at Bene't.'

'There will be no more clerks' stipends until the buildings are finished,' growled the Duke. 'How many Fellows are there, now that you have buried two of them?'

'Four,' answered Heltisle, white-faced with anger. 'Me, Caumpes, Henry de Walton, and your man – Simekyn Simeon.'

'Simeon is a Fellow only to ensure that my money is not squandered,' said the Duke. 'But, in the light of recent events, I plan to leave him here until the building is finished.'

Simeon's jaw dropped in horror, and he seemed about to object vigorously when the Duke forestalled him with a raised hand.

'It will be an incentive for you to see that Bene't College is completed, Simeon. The sooner it is ready, the sooner I will allow you to resign your Fellowship and return to court with me.'

'But—' Simeon's handsome face was dark with outrage.

'No buts. I want you to stay in Cambridge to see my

College finished, so that when I die there will be a body of men to say prayers for my soul. A man cannot live for ever, and I must make some preparation for the next world.'

The Duke and the scholars continued to argue, their voices becoming louder and more acrimonious. Heltisle claimed that he, too, had not liked Raysoun and Wymundham, while Caumpes railed that there was a plot afoot to damage Bene't, masterminded by Michaelhouse. Simekyn Simeon, his sardonic smile gone now that he was obliged to remain at Bene't, glared at everyone with open hostility. The students, a scruffy, disreputable crowd, shuffled restlessly, some of them shoving and pushing at each other like a group of bored children.

The man who Bartholomew assumed was the last of the four Fellows, Henry de Walton, said nothing. He stood near the wall, a pallid, fox-faced man who looked unwell. On one cheek was a dark bruise, and Bartholomew remembered Michael's beadle telling him that Osmun had been arrested for brawling with one of the Bene't Fellows. The skinny little man, whose nervousness was apparent in every flutter of his hands and twitch of his face, would have been no match for the brawny porter, and Bartholomew suspected it was not de Walton who had started the fight.

So, had one of these four Fellows pressed something over Wymundham's face to silence him before he could pass what he knew to the Senior Proctor? Had Wymundham actually been fleeing from the murderer when Bartholomew had seen him slipping so furtively into Holy Trinity Church the afternoon Raysoun had died? And had the same murdering Fellow also stabbed Raysoun and then pushed him from the scaffolding?

'I am sure you have found our discussion most entertaining,' said the Duke, becoming aware that Bartholomew was a witness to the unseemly quarrel. 'You now know that there is more to life at Bene't than squandering my money.'

'What shall we do with him?' asked Caumpes. 'We cannot let him return to Michaelhouse to tell lies about us.'

'He says he is here on the instructions of the Senior Proctor,' said the Duke. 'The poor man is only trying to do his job, and even you must admit that the deaths of two scholars within a couple of days might appear a little peculiar to outsiders.'

'I disagree,' said Heltisle. 'Things like that happen all the time in the University.'

'You should watch your back, then, Simeon,' said the Duke wryly. 'I want my College completed under your watchful eye, but I would like you alive at the end of it.'

'I am touched by your concern,' said Simeon sullenly.

Heltisle fixed Bartholomew with a cold stare. 'I do not want to confide in you, but I see I have little choice. What I am about to tell you is for the Senior Proctor's ears only. I do not want this to become an amusing story for Michaelhouse's high table.'

'Do not tell him!' exclaimed Caumpes in horror. 'He will make us a laughing stock in the University.'

'I see nothing amusing about it,' said Heltisle. 'You see, physician, Wymundham preferred the company of men to women.'

'Really,' said Bartholomew flatly, recalling Wymundham's brazenly effeminate manners, and the way the man had rested his hand on Bartholomew's leg.

Heltisle glanced at him sharply, but then went on. 'Raysoun and Wymundham were more than friends. So, you see, there is nothing odd in the fact that Raysoun died in Wymundham's arms, or that Wymundham subsequently killed himself from grief.'

Bartholomew gazed down at the floor. Grief-stricken

though he might have been, Wymundham had certainly not asphyxiated himself. Suicide by smothering was not easy to achieve, and anyway, there had been nothing at the scene of his death for him to have suffocated himself with. The nature of Wymundham's relationship with Raysoun did not alter the fact that he had been murdered.

'Did you know about Wymundham's preferences?' asked the Duke of Simeon, surprised.

Simeon tried hard not to regard the Duke in disbelief, and only partly succeeded. 'It was very obvious, my lord.'

Heltisle agreed. 'It is not unusual in places like this, where women are forbidden and scholars spend hours in each other's company. I imagine Michaelhouse is no different.'

'Is that true?' asked the Duke salaciously.

'I have never thought about it,' said Bartholomew vaguely, unwilling to satisfy the Duke's odd fascination with the subject. 'I do not like to pry into my colleagues' personal affairs.'

'Then I cannot see that anything more can be gained from this discussion,' said the Duke, sounding disappointed. 'You are free to go, physician. Make your report to the Senior Proctor, and we will lay these two sad souls to rest for ever.'

'What report?' asked Bartholomew. 'I have nothing to tell him now that Raysoun and Wymundham are buried.'

'I doubt there was more to be learned from their bodies anyway,' said Simeon, pulling himself, with some reluctance, from his fit of pique. 'The Senior Proctor has his beadles making enquiries in the taverns, to see if any townsmen are bragging about the murders. That is far more likely to be successful than poking about with corpses.'

'There *are* no murders,' said Heltisle in exasperation. 'How many more times do I have to repeat myself?'

Simeon said nothing.

'Heltisle is right,' said the Duke. 'There is no evidence that either of these men were murdered, but a good deal to suggest that one had an accident and the other killed himself with grief. That is what you can report to the Senior Proctor, physician. Meanwhile, you can tell your Master Runham that I am not pleased he has poached my workmen to build his own College, but I suppose as long as they do not work, I will not have to pay. How long do you plan to keep them?'

'A month, apparently.'

'A month?' exclaimed Caumpes in disbelief. 'But that is impossible! The workmen will never reface the whole of the north wing *and* raise a whole new courtyard in that time.'

'They might,' said Simeon. 'But I would not be impressed by the quality of the completed item.'

'A month it is, then,' said the Duke. 'And then they will return to Bene't.'

'Now just a moment,' said Caumpes indignantly. 'I am not prepared to stand by as Michaelhouse steals our servants and accuses us of murdering our colleagues.'

'You will do nothing,' said the Duke angrily. 'I have made my decision, and I will not have squabbling scholars giving Bene't a bad reputation in the town.'

'It is not I who—' began Caumpes furiously.

'I said enough!' roared the Duke. 'You must learn some decent manners, Caumpes. No wonder the wealthy towns-folk are loath to associate themselves with scholars. You are all a band of bickering pedants who are more inter-ested in rivalries with other Colleges than in learning.'

Caumpes reddened with rage. 'Bene't is my College. I will do anything to protect it against—'

'Go,' said the Duke wearily. 'All of you. I have had more than enough of you for one day. Bring me more wine, Simeon. And Heltisle can fetch me the College accounts to inspect. Other than that, you are all dismissed from my presence.'

Bartholomew was grateful to escape from the tense atmosphere of the hall. He almost ran across the yard, slowing only when he saw a familiar pair of hips swinging vigorously as their owner bent over a steaming vat of laundry.

He went past the porters' lodge without a word, ignoring their transparent attempts to provoke him into a confrontation. Runham might have commandeered Bene't's builders, but Bene't had poached a far greater prize than that from Michaelhouse – they had Agatha the laundress.

It was almost dark when Bartholomew left Bene't. The streets were still busy with people trying to complete their business and return home before the light faded completely. He was tired and dispirited, and did not feel at all like going back to the College where Runham lurked liked a spider in his web waiting for innocent flies.

He saw Matilde, bundled up against the chill of early evening in a fine green cloak, and yet still managing to look slim and elegant among the burlier figures of the people who surged around her. He caught her eye and waved, intending to offer to escort her home. As she gazed back, an expression of such intense hurt crossed her face that he recoiled in shock. Bewildered, he ran after her and caught her hand, but she pulled away from him, and would not answer his repeated questions as to what was wrong.

'Is he bothering you?' asked a rough voice. Bartholomew recognised the familiar dirty apron of the carpenter,

Robert de Blaston, whose wife Yolande was a friend of Matilde's. 'Tell me if he is, and I will see to him.'

'He is just leaving,' said Matilde shortly. 'Thank you, Robert.'

'But, Matilde,' protested Bartholomew. 'What is the matter? Is it one of the sisters? Is someone ill? Can I help?'

'Nothing you do or say will help,' she said in a voice that was simultaneously cold and unsteady. 'Just leave me alone. And you can take this, too!'

Before he could reply, she had turned and fled up the High Street, and Blaston's hefty hand was on Bartholomew's shoulder. On the ground at his feet was a fluttering green ribbon, already smeared with mud from the road. Slowly, he bent to pick it up, wondering what he could have done to distress her in the short time since they had last spoken. But, he thought, perhaps it was not him at all; perhaps something else had happened. Cambridge was a small town, and if something dire had befallen the prostitutes, he would hear about it sooner or later.

'Lovers' tiff?' asked Blaston with rough sympathy.

'Not on my part,' said Bartholomew. He closed his eyes, disgusted at himself for virtually admitting that he, a scholar of the University, was engaged in a romantic relationship with a prostitute. Blaston patted his arm.

'Never mind,' he said consolingly. 'She will come round; women always do. Just make her a gift of a bit of ribbon, and she will love you dearly until the next time you do something wrong.'

'Perhaps it was the ribbon that did it,' said Bartholomew, looking at the green material in his hand and thinking that he would never again take Langelee's advice about women. 'Maybe I should have chosen the blue one instead.'

Blaston took it from him. 'This is a fine thing,' he said,

rubbing it between his rough fingers and ingraining filth so deeply into it that Bartholomew wondered whether it would ever be clean again. 'Yolande would love something like this, but with nine children and a tenth on its way, such foolishness is out of the question.'

'Take it,' said Bartholomew. 'I do not want it.'

Blaston gazed at him. 'No,' he said with clear reluctance. 'I could not take something so fine from you – you are almost as poor as we are.'

Bartholomew tried not to show he was amused. If impecunious men like Robert de Blaston thought him impoverished, then it was small wonder that influential dignitaries like Mayor Horwoode did not want to be seen with him. 'Please take the thing. Matilde told me that Yolande was not overjoyed to learn about this tenth child. A ribbon might cheer her.'

'It would!' agreed Blaston. 'And a nice bit of ribbon like this might enable her to attract a better class of customer until she becomes too incapacitated to work.'

Bartholomew could not but help wonder how many of Yolande de Blaston's expanding brood were the result of her occupation. He brushed aside the carpenter's effusive thanks and walked briskly back to the College. Michael was sitting at the table in his room, writing a letter by candlelight. He professed himself disheartened by his lack of progress in discovering the identities of the cloaked intruders they had encountered leaving Michaelhouse the night Runham was elected. He grew even more dispirited when he had heard what had transpired at Bene't, although his eyes narrowed in suspicion when he learned that the Bene't Fellows were determined to dismiss Wymundham's death as accidental.

'I thought we told Simeon about your findings from the corpse,' he said.

'We did, but perhaps he did not believe us. He certainly appeared to be sceptical.'

'Or perhaps he has his own reasons for dismissing them.' Michael sighed. 'My only hope is that Beadle Meadowman will learn something from the workmen. The one good thing to come out of Runham's disgraceful "borrowing" of Bene't labourers is that Meadowman is now here, in Michaelhouse, and so better able to keep me informed of his progress.'

'What about the other beadles?' asked Bartholomew. 'Have they learned anything yet?'

Michael shook his head. 'Not so much as a whisper. It is very frustrating. I would dearly love to go myself, but, as I said before, the men likely to yield the information we need are not the sort I would be able to intimidate, bribe or cajole. We will just have to be patient, and hope that sooner or later the killer finds he is unable to resist boasting about what he has done, and then I will have him.'

Bartholomew left him listening to Meadowman apologising for having nothing to report, and went to check that his students had completed the reading he had set them. He was surprised to learn that the senior undergraduates had obeyed his instructions to the letter, and that one of them had even donated a candle, because they had not finished their task when dusk fell.

They were frowning in concentration as Bulbeck ploughed his way through Averroës' *Colliget*, a difficult text that Bartholomew insisted they understand completely before they began their fourth year of study. Bartholomew stayed with them for a while, answering questions and enjoying the atmosphere of enthusiasm and scholarship that Bulbeck had managed to generate, despite the noise of the builders and the bitter chill of the chamber.

The junior students were in the room Sam Gray shared

with Rob Deynman. Deynman was wealthy and could afford to buy fuel for the fire in his room, so that flames cast a welcoming orange glow on the whitewashed ceiling and walls. But despite the pleasantly warm chamber, any pretence at debate and learning was absent. Deynman glanced around guiltily when Bartholomew entered, and something fell from his hand.

'What in God's name are you doing?' whispered Bartholomew, gazing at the chipped plaster and stained walls in horror. 'Runham will be furious when he sees this, Rob!'

'Runham has dismissed him,' said Gray bitterly. The other students muttered resentfully. There was a strong smell of wine in the room, and Bartholomew knew that the students had been drinking.

'What are you talking about?' he asked impatiently. 'And get rid of that wine. You know you are not supposed to drink during lessons.'

'Runham dismissed Rob,' repeated Gray. 'He said that Rob "is not of the intellectual calibre that Michaelhouse requires".'

His imitation of the pompous stuffiness of Runham's voice was rather good, and Bartholomew might have laughed under other circumstances. It was true Deynman was no Aristotle, but it was Bartholomew's understanding that Michaelhouse needed the unusually high fees it charged Deynman's wealthy father, and that Deynman's position was probably more secure than anyone else's for that reason alone. Bartholomew was astonished that Runham would relinquish such an easy source of cash so casually.

'Is that why you are merrily destroying your room?' he asked of Deynman, nodding to the knife that lay at the lad's feet, and the wine that had been splashed across the walls.

'It serves Runham right,' said Deynman in a muffled voice, not looking at Bartholomew.

'But Gray will have to live here after you have gone,' Bartholomew pointed out. 'It is not just Runham you are punishing with this wanton act of loutishness.'

'He will not be here long enough to care,' mumbled Deynman.

Bartholomew regarded Gray warily. 'Why? Did Runham catch you dicing again?'

'Stealing ink,' supplied Deynman. 'We all do it – masters and students alike. But Runham said if Sam does not copy out the entire first part of *Corpus Juris Civilis* by this time tomorrow, then he will be dismissed, too.'

'*Corpus Juris Civilis* is a legal text,' said Bartholomew thoughtfully. 'Is he using you as a scribe to improve his personal library, then?'

'No,' said Gray bitterly. 'Because I cannot do it. It is so long that even if I worked all night, I would never be able to finish it. Runham set me a task that he knows is impossible, and he did it because he wants me gone – like Father Paul, Rob and Master Kenyngham.'

'Kenyngham?' asked Bartholomew. 'He has not gone anywhere.'

'He will soon, though,' said Gray. 'Runham suggested that Kenyngham might find it difficult to see his College under a new Master after managing it so long himself. Kenyngham, like a meek little lamb, agreed. He leaves on Sunday.'

Bartholomew's thoughts began to whirl. It was clear that Runham intended to dismiss anyone he thought he might not be able to manipulate, and that he intended to fill his College with scholars who would not oppose anything he tried to do. He stared at the resentful students who sat in huddles in front of him. Deynman, filled anew with anger and grief, snatched up the knife and raked a deep gouge down the wall.

'Stop that,' said Bartholomew sharply. 'And clear all these wine cups away. You have some writing to do.'

'What do you mean?' asked Gray suspiciously.

'You might not be able to copy out the whole text yourself, but there are fifteen of you here. Start with a page each – and remember to use a similar style of handwriting.'

'What is the point?' asked Gray sullenly. 'He will only find another excuse to be rid of me.'

'Just start scribing,' said Bartholomew. 'And we will face the next problem when it comes.'

'What about me?' asked Deynman hopefully. 'Will you tell Runham that he was mistaken, and that I am all that Michaelhouse could ask for in a scholar?'

There were limits, Bartholomew thought. 'I will see what I can do. Hang a rug over that mess on the wall before anyone sees it.'

He left the students hunting around for parchment and ink and made his way to the hall. Runham's actions seemed to be methodical and premeditated – a neat pruning of unwanted parts like a gardener hoeing weeds – and Bartholomew guessed that the pompous lawyer had been planning exactly how he wanted his College for a long while. He felt unwarranted anger at Kenyngham for resigning and leaving them in this mess, but it had only been a matter of time before Kenyngham had become too old to continue, and then Runham would have made his move anyway.

He ran up the stairs to the hall, hoping to find some of his colleagues with whom he could discuss the issue of Deynman. The room was deserted, and a draught from the open door had scattered parchments across the floor, so that it had a desolate, abandoned feel to it. It was also cold with no fire, and Bartholomew's breath plumed in front of him as he looked around. There was something different about it, and at first he could not pinpoint what. Then he noticed that some of the best wall-hangings, which had lent the hall its cosy feel, had been removed, leaving the bare stone exposed. Because the tapestries would go well with the cream walls in Runham's new quarters, Bartholomew guessed exactly where they had gone.

Kenyngham was sitting in the fireless conclave with Langelee and Suttone. The gentle Gilbertine was pale, but his face wore a serene expression, as though he had accepted Runham's curt dismissal of a Fellowship spanning almost thirty years, and was already thinking of other matters.

'We were just talking about you, Bartholomew,' said Langelee. His voice lacked its usual ebullient quality. Like Kenyngham, he was wan; his heavy jowls were dark with stubble and there was a pink sheen to the whites of his eyes. Bartholomew suspected that Deynman and Gray were not the only ones who had spent the afternoon drowning their sorrows. 'You will have no students left if Runham sends down any more.'

Bartholomew sat next to the empty hearth, prodding at the dead white ashes with a stick and sending a scattering of dust across the flagstones. 'I am surprised he dismissed Deynman. I always thought we needed his money.'

'So did I,' said Kenyngham. 'I would never have accepted him had we not – no offence, Matthew, but that boy has no place in a University.'

'He certainly does not now,' agreed Langelee gloomily.

'So why is it that we do not need Deynman's money all of a sudden?' asked Suttone. 'Is there a new benefactor so that we can afford to discount our old sources of income? I do not understand. These new buildings must be costing Michaelhouse a fortune, and it seems we should be conserving our regular income, not doing away with it.'

'Especially given that Runham has offered to double the builders' wages if the work is completed within a month,' said Bartholomew.

Suttone and Langelee gaped at him in astonishment.

'Really?' asked Langelee. He blew out his red-veined cheeks in a sigh of surprise. 'That will mean a lot of ready money.'

Kenyngham nodded. 'But he has it – I saw it in a chest in his room. He is overly trusting to keep it in such an insecure place. Anyone could wander in and help themselves.'

'You mean it is in an open box?' asked Langelee, startled. 'Just lying there?'

Kenyngham nodded again. 'I asked him where it came from, but he would not tell me.'

'I do not like the sound of this at all,' said Suttone uneasily. 'I am a law-abiding man – a friar from a respectable Order. I do not want to be associated with anything illegal.'

'And we will be,' said Langelee glumly. 'If Runham has obtained this wealth by underhand means, we will be considered as guilty as he is, because we are Fellows of the same College.'

'But what can we do?' asked Suttone, alarmed. 'We cannot just sit idly by and let him do things that may be dishonest.'

'We have no proof that he has been breaking the law,' said Kenyngham reasonably. 'Just because he will not reveal the source of his wealth does not mean that he acquired it by criminal means.'

'Does it not?' said Suttone, clearly unconvinced. 'Well,

I do not feel comfortable with his secrecy. What are we going to do about it?'

'There is nothing we can do,' said Kenyngham wearily. 'We can hardly approach the man and ask him where he stole his money from.'

'Really?' said Langelee harshly, standing with sudden purpose. 'Well, I was once an agent for the Archbishop of York, and I have dealt with all manner of criminals and traitors in my time. I have no intention of allowing my career to be cut short by the activities of a common thief. We shall confront him with our suspicions like men, not skulk here in the dark because we are afraid of him.'

'Ah, my loyal colleagues,' said Runham smoothly, as he walked into the conclave with Clippesby at his heels. Bartholomew noticed that the door to the hall had not been properly closed, and assumed that the pair had been listening outside.

'I want a word with you, Runham,' began Langelee bluntly.

Bartholomew cringed. Runham was a clever man, and was not likely to yield any of his secrets or render himself amenable to reason if Langelee went at him with all the subtlety of a bull in heat.

'And I want a word with you, Langelee,' countered Runham immediately. 'It has come to my notice that you are not all you should be.'

'Am I not?' asked Langelee, aggression evaporating as puzzlement took over. 'In what way?'

'You are married,' said Runham, in a tone of voice that suggested wedlock was more akin to a contagious disease than a union made holy by the blessing of God. 'And because you are married, you have rendered yourself ineligible for a Fellowship at Michaelhouse. You will remove yourself and all your belongings by morning. Your deceit is reprehensible.'

'But I am not married,' protested Langelee. 'I was, but I am not now.'

'Did you or did you not hold your Fellowship while you were wed to a woman called Julianna Deschalers?' asked Runham coldly.

'Well, yes, but I—'

'Then you have broken one of the fundamental rules of our College, which is grounds for dismissal. And, since you also claimed your Fellow's stipend when you had no right to do so, I demand that you repay the entire amount by the end of next week – a total of two marks.'

'But I cannot pay so large a sum that soon!' cried Langelee, aghast. 'I spent all my money on obtaining the annulment and in buying off Julianna.'

'Your domestic arrangements are not my concern,' said Runham distastefully. 'But I will have every penny of the money you drew fraudulently from Michaelhouse, or I shall ask the proctors to arrest you.'

'Who told you about my marriage?' asked Langelee in a whisper, his face white. 'Was it Bartholomew?'

'It was not,' said Bartholomew, offended that the philosopher would believe he had betrayed a trust to a man like Runham – even when that trust had been foisted upon him without his consent.

'It *was* you,' said Langelee, anger slowly replacing the dull shock in his face. 'It must have been, because you were the only one I told. I will kill you for this!'

Bartholomew leapt backward as the enraged Langelee dived at him with murder in his eyes. He edged behind a heavy bench, but Langelee kicked it to one side as though it were parchment, oblivious to the horrified cries of Kenyngham. Langelee snatched up a poker from the hearth, and only missed Bartholomew with his sweeping blow because blind fury made him clumsy.

Kenyngham seized Langelee's sleeve in a feeble attempt to pull him away, but Langelee shook him off impatiently. Kenyngham stumbled and fell to the floor, where Suttone quickly dragged him out of the path of Langelee's feet. Bartholomew glanced at Runham, expecting him to berate Langelee for his unprovoked display of violence or dart forward to prevent a brawl in his College. But Runham remained where he was, a smug smile on his face and his hands tucked in his wide sleeves. Clippesby stood next to him, grinning and apparently enjoying the unedifying scene as much as was Runham.

Bartholomew tore his gaze away from the Master just in time to see Langelee bring the poker down in a savage arc that was aimed at his head. He scrambled away, hearing the crunch of smashed wood as the blow destroyed one of the carved benches.

'Stop!' cried Kenyngham in dismay, trying to shake off Suttone. Wisely, Suttone maintained his restraining grip, knowing that a gentle old man like Kenyngham would be no match for the pugnacious Langelee. 'You will hurt someone.'

'Hurt? I am going to *kill* someone,' Langelee howled furiously.

Bartholomew grabbed a stool and raised it to parry the next blow. The poker crashed down, iron meeting wood. His arms hurt from the force of the impact, and then the stool fell to pieces in his hands. He gazed at it in horror, then glanced up to see the hot hatred in Langelee's eyes as the philosopher's muscles bunched for another strike.

'Langelee! Put that down!' Michael's imperious tones turned every head in the room, and Langelee faltered just long enough to allow Bartholomew to snatch the poker from him.

'*You* are up and about again, are you?' asked Runham coolly, sounding none too pleased.

Michael shoved Clippesby to one side, and gazed around him with cold green eyes. 'This is a discreditable little tableau,' he said, his voice conveying disgust. 'Is this how you plan to run Michaelhouse, Master Runham? Will you allow your Fellows to brawl and threaten each other with lethal weapons, while you stand and watch like a blood-lusting peasant at a cockfight?'

Runham's face hardened. 'You forget who you are talking to, Brother. I am the Master of your College, and not a man to be insulted. And what did you expect me to do? You saw Langelee: he was out of control. There was nothing I could do to stop him.'

'*I* stopped him,' snapped Michael. 'And if you were any kind of man, you would have done so, too. Even frail Master Kenyngham tried – you just stood there and laughed.'

'Well, it is over now,' said Runham carelessly. 'Langelee is dismissed from Michaelhouse for being a married man – although I could equally well dismiss him for riotous behaviour – and Bartholomew is fined two shillings for brawling in the conclave.'

'I do not think so,' said Michael icily. 'Matt was not brawling. He was scrambling to escape Langelee's murderous onslaught. Any fool could see that.'

'Bartholomew betrayed my trust,' whispered Langelee, his voice soft with disbelief and hurt now that the fury had drained away. 'How could he?'

'It was not Matthew,' said Kenyngham quietly. 'It was me. I am afraid it just slipped out. It was that wretched wine that made me loose-tongued; I shall never drink the stuff again.'

'You told Runham I was married?' repeated Langelee slowly. '*You?*'

Kenyngham nodded sadly. 'At the feast. Master Runham wanted to know about the Fellows who would soon be under his fatherly eye, and he asked about your dalliance with Julianna. I told him that you had married her in Grantchester church, but that within a few weeks you had sought an annulment. I helped you to arrange it, if you recall.'

Langelee's shoulders slumped and he left the conclave without a word. Runham regarded the remaining scholars with cool disdain.

'I will not tolerate disobedience among my Fellows. You four – Bartholomew, Clippesby, Michael and Suttone – will be all who are left once Kenyngham goes. I shall expect total loyalty to me and the College, and if I find you lacking, I shall dismiss you, too. The new statutes that you signed yourselves give me the right to rid myself of anyone committing acts of dissension.'

Michael glowered, but said nothing, knowing there was no point. Bartholomew also remained silent, feeling too drained of emotion to argue. Kenyngham's eyes brimmed with tears when he saw the sorry way his College was going, while Clippesby stood behind Runham and grinned and nodded like a half-wit.

'But Langelee was loyal to you,' Suttone pointed out reasonably. 'He was doing his best to support you in what you wanted. It is unjust of you to send him away.'

'The man is a lout,' said Runham in distaste. 'And do not preach to me about injustice, Suttone. I know all about you – about the missing gold from your friary in Lincoln, and who everyone believed stole it.'

Suttone gaped at him. 'How in God's name did you learn about that?'

'Your name was cleared only because no one could prove you were guilty,' said Runham. 'And I know about Clippesby's strange ailments, too – hearing voices in empty rooms and imagining himself to be an angel.'

'What is this?' asked Michael, startled.

'No!' cried Clippesby, his grin evaporating like rain on hot metal.

'I had words with your Prior before you came here,' said Runham spitefully, watching Clippesby's face fall with dismay. 'You have a vivid imagination, it seems, and spent some time being treated for madness.'

'But not recently,' said Clippesby in a small voice, shooting agitated glances at the other Fellows. 'I am well now. Ask Master Raysoun of Bene't. He knows.'

'But Raysoun is dead, Clippesby,' said Runham softly. 'We do not possess your abilities to commune with those in the next world.'

'That is not what I meant,' cried Clippesby in agitation. 'I forgot Raysoun was dead. It had slipped my mind. I am not a lunatic!'

'Of course you are not,' said Suttone kindly, shooting Runham a warning glance. Clippesby seemed to be on the verge of tears. 'Come and sit next to the fire. It is all right.'

'I am well now,' said Clippesby again, sounding pathetically bewildered.

'So you are,' said Runham, patting his shoulder paternally, his abrupt change of behaviour leading Bartholomew to wonder whether Clippesby was the only one who had been assessed for the state of his wits. Runham beamed suddenly. 'Well, the day is wearing on, and I have many things to do if I want to make Michaelhouse a College to be proud of. I shall be in my chambers.'

With that, he turned abruptly, and strode out.

Michael had been alerted to the trouble by Bulbeck, who had heard Langelee yelling in the conclave, and although Michael was keen to discuss the matter in the privacy of their rooms, Bartholomew was too disillusioned and dismayed. He felt sick with Runham's machinations and spiteful revelations, and knew he would be unable to concentrate on his treatise on fevers if he tried to work. With nothing else to do in Michaelhouse, he strode across the yard and hauled open the gate, intending to escape the College for a while. He walked briskly up the High Street, slipped through the Trumpington Gate while the guards were busy with a family of tinkers who wanted access to the town, and started to stride along the road that led to the village where his sister lived. He wanted only to be away from the town and the tense, accusing atmosphere of his College.

It was only just evening, but darkness fell early in November. The trackway stretched ahead of him as he walked, black as ink, so that once or twice he felt the soft wetness of dew-laden grass under his feet rather than the stony mud of the path. He knew very well it was not wise to be out alone on one of the main roads, but he was angry and despondent enough not to care. He had a small knife in his medicine bag, which he pulled out and carried in his hand, and there were always the heavy childbirth forceps that Matilde had given him – a well-placed blow from those would make most would-be robbers think again.

He rubbed a hand through his hair as he walked, wondering how long Runham had harboured such deep hatred towards his colleagues. He could not imagine what the man had against the mild and gentle Kenyngham, although he understood his dislike of Langelee well enough. And it had been a cheap trick to use some ancient accusation against Suttone and make a weapon of Clippesby's past illness to ensure their co-operation. Runham was despicable, he thought, kicking viciously at a weed by the roadside.

His mind returned to the disturbing deaths of the scholars that Michael had charged him to investigate.

Of Brother Patrick's murder, Bartholomew had learned nothing: the man had been stabbed and no one had seen what had happened. He hoped Michael was right, and that someone would start to brag about the crime he had committed, and patience would bring the killer to justice.

Of the Bene't deaths, Bartholomew had discovered little that he and Michael did not already know or had not already guessed: it seemed Raysoun and his intimate Wymundham were disliked by their colleagues, and there was an undeniable atmosphere of unpleasantness in the small community. Had the Master or his henchman Caumpes killed them? Was that why they were so determined that no investigation should take place? And what of the courtly Simeon? Why had he visited Michael to encourage a more rigorous investigation without the knowledge of his Master? Did he suspect his colleagues were involved in the killings? He had intimated to Michael that he suspected a workman, and had urged Michael to look in that direction. But was that to divert attention from himself?

Bartholomew found himself unable to concentrate on the Bene't murders, when his own College played on his mind. Where had Runham's sudden wealth come from? Had he acquired it dishonestly, as Suttone feared? Was Michael right, and Runham had somehow tampered with the Widow's Wine so that the whole College would be either drunk or incapacitated, thus allowing him to do something unseen? Bartholomew frowned. Runham had been waiting for them when he and Michael had arrived back at Michaelhouse after seeing Wymundham's body. If Runham had not been one of the pair of intruders, was that evidence that he knew them and their secret business?

And there was another thing. The morning after the

feast, Runham had arrived very early at the church to complete Bartholomew's chores before he arrived. Had he been up all night doing something connected to the sudden influx of money? Bartholomew racked his brains to recall whether Runham had also drunk the Widow's Wine, but could not remember. Runham had certainly not been drunk when he had loomed out of the shadows to accuse Bartholomew and Michael of being late.

The wind blew keenly, and Bartholomew shivered in the damp chill, sensing there would be rain before too long. He pulled his cloak tighter around him and fumbled in his bag for his gloves, groaning when he realised he had lost one. A new pair would cost sixpence, and he did not have sixpence to spare because Runham kept fining him. And that reminded him of another problem. The following day, he would have to tell Runham whether he was to resign his Fellowship. At that precise moment he wanted to tell Runham exactly where to put it, but knew that was just what the lawyer wanted. Bartholomew had no intention of doing anything that would please Runham.

At the same time, he did not relish the notion of life at College with Runham at the helm. Michael's connections with Bishop and Chancellor seemed to give him a certain influence over Runham, and he perhaps would be able to control some of the smug Master's wilder schemes, but would Michael be able to bring about a reconciliation between William and Runham? And what of Paul and Kenyngham? Was there any hope that they might be reinstated? Michaelhouse would be a poorer place without their gentleness and patience.

So engrossed was Bartholomew in his thoughts that he was surprised to find he had walked far enough to see the warm twinkle of the lights of Trumpington beckoning to him through the darkness. He continued towards them, and stopped outside the house where his sister and her husband had their country home. The great gates that led to the cobbled yard were closed for the night, but he could see candles burning in the house itself when he peered through a crack in the wood. He thought he could hear the sound of a lute being played very softly, accompanied by a woman singing. He smiled to himself, recalling many nights when he had been a child, listening to Stanmore playing and Edith singing the latest romantic ballads or the more ancient poems of the troubadours.

He hesitated, not wanting to walk any further, but reluctant to foist himself on Edith and Oswald when they were enjoying an evening in each other's company. And he did not much feel like companionship, preferring to wrap himself in the dark with his own thoughts.

He strolled to the village church. It was locked and no lights shone from the priest's house, suggesting that the man had retired to his bed once darkness had fallen. Bartholomew found a spot on the west wall that was out of the wind and sat in the grass, pulling his cloak around him for warmth. He thought about Michaelhouse, and the people he had considered friends as well as colleagues, and about his students. Could he really abandon the teaching to which he had committed himself? He supposed he could take one or two of the more senior undergraduates and train them as he worked; other practising physicians did so.

He thought long and hard about his decision, carefully weighing up the advantages and disadvantages of each option – to his students and patients as well as to himself. And then he made up his mind. He would leave Cambridge and travel to Paris, where the Arab physician who had taught him his medicine still lived. Ibn Ibrahim would be delighted to see him, and would undoubtedly be able to secure him a teaching post at the University. With the exception of Edith, who was happily married and scarcely required any financial support from him, he had no family, while Michael was a resourceful man who would be able to find himself another tame physician to assist him in his enquiries. Cynric had already gone, and there was no one else who needed him. He was a free agent – alone.

He sat for so long amid the waving grass of the church-yard, careless of the light drizzle that began to fall, that by the time he dragged his mind away from his thoughts he was soaking wet and chilled to the bone. He had no idea what the time might be, although no lights burned in any of the village houses, so it must be very late. He wondered if it were too late to call on his sister.

He walked briskly to where the gates of Stanmore's manor house abutted on to the road. Peering through the split timber, he saw that a light still gleamed in the upper window he knew was Edith's. Not wanting to rouse the whole household, he skirted the retaining wall to an old tree that leaned its crusty branches against the stone. Bartholomew had spent his childhood with Edith and Oswald Stanmore, and knew very well how to slip undetected in and out of their house at night.

The tree was older and more brittle, and Bartholomew was heavier and less lithe than thirty years before, so it took some scrambling before he had eased himself over the uneven wall. He landed with a bone-jarring thump in some rhubarb, and heard something rip on his tabard. Brushing the tree bark from his hands, he walked across the vegetable plots towards the light that still glowed in Edith's bedchamber. He picked up a small clod of moss and hurled it upward, hoping to attract her attention. Nothing happened, so after a moment he tried again with a larger piece.

There was a sharp splinter of cracked glass and several dogs started barking. Lamps began to gleam all over the house and within a few moments, the front door opened and Stanmore's steward came out, carrying a bow with an arrow already nocked. Bartholomew called out to him, uncomfortably aware of a black dog snarling and slavering around his knees.

Stanmore poked a cautious head out of the door. 'Matt?' he called suspiciously. 'Is that you? Come out where I can see you.'

Bartholomew walked into the halo of light cast by the lamp one of the servants held, hands above his head in the hope that the wary steward would not shoot him.

'What are you doing?' demanded Stanmore, once he had recognised his brother-in-law. 'How did you get in? The gates have been locked since dusk.' His faced hardened. 'The apple tree by the rhubarb patch! I thought you had grown out of that sort of thing years ago.'

'Sorry,' said Bartholomew, moving forward slowly and wishing Stanmore would call off the dog. 'Is Edith in?'

'Is Edith in?' echoed Stanmore in disbelief. 'Of course she is in! It is almost midnight, man! Where did you think she would be?'

Bartholomew advanced a little further, and felt the dog's teeth suddenly take hold of the hem of his cloak and pull furiously.

'Are you alone?' asked Stanmore, trying to see him in the dim light and the haze of drizzle. 'Is Michael with you? Or your woman, perhaps?'

'Woman? Why would a woman be here with me at this time of night?' asked Bartholomew, startled by the peculiar question. With annoyance, he heard a sharp rip as the dog won the encounter with his cloak. 'And which woman do you mean?'

'You tell me,' said Stanmore, putting his hands on his hips and regarding Bartholomew as if he had just dropped from the sky. 'You are a changed man these days, Matt. Full of secrets and nasty surprises. So, is she with you, or are you skulking in my garden in the dead of night and distressing my dog all by yourself?'

'I am alone,' said Bartholomew, wondering who was the mysterious 'she' that Stanmore seemed to think might be lurking nearby. The chance would be a fine thing, he thought wryly; he could not imagine any woman being prepared to accept an impoverished physician who was about to forsake Cambridge for the dubious delights of Paris.

'Well come in, then,' snapped Stanmore. 'It is cold with the door open, and it is raining, too. And put your arms down, man. You know perfectly well that Hugh will not shoot you.'

Noting the gleam of suspicion that lit the steward's eyes, Bartholomew was not so sure. Hugh made no move to step aside for him, and he was obliged to edge around the man more closely than was comfortable. He considered giving the steward a shove as he passed, but Hugh was armed with a bow and wore a wicked-looking dagger at his belt, and Bartholomew knew when prudence was more sensible than futile displays of manly pride.

Inside, he was immediately aware of the familiar smells of Edith's home – wood-smoke scented with pine needles, baking bread and the herbs she hung to dry in the rafters of the kitchen. It was an aroma that whisked him back many years, to a time when life had been happy and far less complicated.

The house was a simple hall-type structure, with a large ground-floor chamber, and several smaller rooms above. It was timber-framed and cosy, with rich woollen tapestries hanging from the walls and dark polished wooden floors. The embers of the hearth that stood in the centre of the hall still glowed red, and Bartholomew moved towards them, stretching his chilled hands to their feeble warmth. Stanmore dismissed the curious servants and the disapproving Hugh, and bustled about lighting candles and throwing an extra log on the fire. When the room was flooded with a pleasant amber glow, he turned to face his brother-in-law.

'What have you been doing?' he asked in amazement, seeing for the first time Bartholomew's bedraggled state. 'You are soaking wet, filthy with grass stains and slime from the tree, and your clothes are ripped. Really, Matt! You are supposed to be a respectable citizen, but you arrive at my house in the middle of the night looking like a vagrant and offer me no explanation.'

'You have not given me the chance,' objected Bartholomew. 'And I did not realise it was so late, or I would not have disturbed you. I saw a light and assumed you were still awake.'

'We were talking,' said Stanmore vaguely. 'About you, as it happened. But what were you doing, roaming the dark countryside so that you do not even know what time it is?'

'I was thinking,' began Bartholomew.

'I imagined academics thought all the time,' said Stanmore, regarding him more curiously than ever. 'And most of them do not end up looking like you do! You have been doing more than thinking, my lad!'

'I am going to Paris,' said Bartholomew. 'On Sunday, probably.'

Stanmore gazed at him in stupefaction. 'What for? Paris is full of Frenchmen.'

'I have no choice – no real choice. Can I speak to Edith?'

'I do not think so,' said Stanmore. 'You have done more than enough to distress her for one night. You can see her tomorrow.'

It was Bartholomew's turn to gaze. 'What are you

talking about? What have I done? Why can I not see her? She is awake – you told me you were talking before I arrived.'

Stanmore sighed. 'You really are obtuse, Matt. But very well. Since you insist, I will ask her to leave her warm bed and come downstairs so that you can pay her a visit at a time when all honest men are sleeping. Wait here a moment, and I will see whether she wants to see you.'

Bartholomew caught his arm as he made to leave. 'I do not understand. What am I supposed to have done?'

'How can you even ask such a thing?' said Stanmore reproachfully. 'Edith was very upset by what you did. In fact, her dismay over you is the reason we were still awake – we were trying to think about what we might do to rectify matters.'

Bartholomew frowned in confusion, racking his brains to think of something he might have said or done to provoke such a strong reaction from the sister who was generally tolerant of his occasionally eccentric behaviour.

Stanmore sighed. 'You are incorrigible, Matt. Which of your various actions do you think would be the one to upset your only sister? It is your betrothal to that dreadful Adela Tangmer.'

Wearing a dry shirt and hose of Stanmore's, and with a cup of warm ale in his hands, Bartholomew began to feel comfortably drowsy. Edith was curled up on the cushioned bench next to him, a thick blanket around her shoulders, while Stanmore leaned towards the hearth and poked with an ornate iron poker at the merry flames that blazed there. Except for the cosy snap and crackle of burning wood, the room was silent, and the ceiling and walls flickered orange. Bartholomew realised it was the first time he had been really warm since Runham had become Master of Michaelhouse and had banned the unseemly wastage of fuel in the hall and conclave.

'So, you are not really betrothed to Adela?' said Edith yet again. 'She is mistaken?'

'I am not, and she is,' said Bartholomew. 'I cannot imagine how she managed to interpret any of our conversations as a proposal of marriage. We did discuss Mayor Horwoode's legs, but that was about as intimate as it got.'

'His legs are very thin,' said Edith distastefully. 'Most women prefer a calf with a little more shape to it.'

'But Mayor Horwoode's disappointing physique apart, are you sure you did not offer yourself to this woman?' asked Stanmore. 'She seemed very certain about the arrangement when we met her this evening, and her father is even talking about how my business will benefit his once we are related: he wants the offcuts from my cloth as padding to protect his wine barrels when they are transported by cart.'

'We did discuss marriage,' admitted Bartholomew. 'But only to acknowledge that we were both under some pressure to take spouses, and so were in similar positions. She told me we were allies against unwanted unions.'

'What else did she say?' asked Edith anxiously. 'Did she mention children? Heirs?'

'She did, yes, but not in a way that led me to believe she expected me to provide them. She told me she was opposed to marriage to anyone, and that she would sooner remain single.'

'I was horrified when I heard the news,' said Stanmore. 'Such an arrangement would have been no good to me at all. What could a clothier gain from an alliance to a vintner? And Henry Tangmer is master of the Guild of Corpus Christi – a band of greedy misers, if ever there were one!'

'I was not horrified, but hurt,' said Edith. 'Since you and I had discussed marriage only last week, I was upset that you should have selected a wife without bothering to talk to me about it first.'

'You should know me better than that,' said Bartholomew. 'And I thought you did not like Adela, anyway.'

'I do not!' said Edith vehemently. 'She is a terrible woman – all teeth and hips, and her idea of genteel conversation revolves around breeding horses. Did you know that she challenged that knife-thrower we watched in the Market Square to a competition? Her behaviour is wholly inappropriate for a merchant's daughter.'

'Who won?' asked Bartholomew mildly.

Edith pursed her lips. 'She did, actually. But being able to hurl a knife better than an entertainer is not something that would endear her to a prospective husband – or a prospective sister-in-law.'

Bartholomew laughed, and reached out to touch her hand affectionately. 'I promise you, if I ever decide to marry Adela, you will be the first to know.'

'Good,' muttered Stanmore with great feeling. 'Then we can lock you up until you regain your wits, and save you from yourself.'

'After our discussion last week, I have been to considerable trouble to line up some suitable candidates for you,' said Edith. 'Then I heard about your betrothal, and was obliged to cancel them all. It was dreadfully embarrassing.'

'How many did you arrange?' asked Bartholomew nervously. 'I can only marry one.'

'Oh, about six,' said Edith carelessly. 'And Matilde is furious with you, of course. She heard it this evening from Yolande de Blaston, who was told by Mayor Horwoode, and Horwoode had it from Adela's delighted father.'

So that explained Matilde's curious behaviour, thought

Bartholomew. She must have learned the news while he was at Bene't College.

'What was Yolande doing with Mayor Horwoode?' he asked, puzzled by the curious chain of informants who had provided Matilde with the piece of gossip in the first place.

Edith and her husband exchanged an amused glance. 'Well, she is a prostitute, Matt,' said Stanmore dryly. 'So, I expect they were talking about needlework.'

'Ah, yes,' said Bartholomew, slightly embarrassed by his slowness, and recalling that Friday was the day when Yolande claimed to have a long-standing arrangement with the Mayor. 'I can visit Matilde and tell her it was all a misunderstanding. Then we can go back to being friends again.'

'Not if you plan to leave for Paris,' said Edith. 'What brought you to this decision?'

Bartholomew took a deep breath and told them all that had happened since Runham had come to power. And for good measure, he talked about the deaths at Bene't and Ovyng, too.

Bartholomew stopped speaking when he saw that Stanmore was white-faced with anger. 'Now what?' he asked, sensing he had committed another inadvertent misdemeanour.

'Runham,' said Stanmore tightly. 'I gave him five marks.'

'Five marks?' echoed Edith. 'But that is a fortune, Oswald! Why would you give that kind of money to the wretched man, especially given what he has done to Matt?'

'But that is precisely why I *did* give it to him,' said Stanmore. 'Runham intimated that life would be more pleasant for Matt if I made a donation to the College's building fund. He chose his words carefully, but I have had enough dealings with artful men to understand his meaning perfectly.'

'What are you saying?' asked Bartholomew. 'That Runham threatened you into making a donation to Michaelhouse?'

'He threatened *you*,' said Stanmore. 'He was as circumspect as it is possible to be, and nothing he said could be construed as directly intimidating, but the upshot of the discussion was that if I did not make a donation to Michaelhouse, your days there would be numbered. And now I hear he has forced you into a position where you feel obliged to resign – and if you resign, I am powerless to accuse him of dismissing you. Damn the man for his cunning!'

'Ask for the five marks back,' said Edith. 'Runham reneged on the deal you made.'

Stanmore poked the fire with unnecessary force. 'It was a gentlemen's agreement: I gave him five marks, and he agreed to leave you alone. Nothing was written down, and I will never be able to prove that I gave him the money only to protect Matt. That snake!'

'You really gave Runham five marks for my benefit?' asked Bartholomew, touched.

Stanmore nodded. 'Of course, this was before I learned about your betrothal to Adela Tangmer. I am not sure I would have been so generous had I known who you were about to inflict on me as a sister-in-law.'

'Especially since such a marriage would have meant me leaving Michaelhouse anyway,' said Bartholomew. 'Fellows cannot marry.'

'I do not like the sound of this business at Bene't,' said Edith, bored with Michaelhouse and its machinations. 'Their scholars are always at each other's throats. It would not be wise to become embroiled in their evil quarrels.'

'That is good advice, Matt,' said Stanmore. 'You should

take it. The Bene't men are an unwholesome crowd. Heltisle is a power-monger, who cares only for his own ambition. Caumpes is fiercely loyal to Bene't, but he has a liking for boats, which is odd for a scholar, and he dabbles in the black market.'

'In what way?' asked Bartholomew curiously. 'The black market, I mean.'

'He often has things to sell,' said Stanmore. 'There is no evidence that the items he peddles are stolen, it is true, but most scholars keep away from the buying and selling business – thankfully.'

'And the Duke of Lancaster's man, Simekyn Simeon, is no more a scholar than I am,' said Edith in disdain. 'He is a court popinjay who knows more about clothes than he does about learning.'

'Really?' asked Stanmore, suddenly interested. 'I wonder if I might persuade him to look at a bale of silk I have just imported . . .'

'Well, what would you expect from a man with a name like Simekyn Simeon?' asked Edith, not to be side-tracked into a discussion about cloth. 'Meanwhile, Henry de Walton is pathetic and spends all his time worrying about his health. Agatha the laundress told me that there is not a scholar in Bene't who does not despise him for his weak and selfish ways. And the two who died – Wymundham and Raysoun – were no better.'

'Lovers,' said Stanmore with grim satisfaction. 'And Wymundham was especially reprehensible, according to my informant. He deliberately started rumours that would lead to strife among the others, and collected items of gossip like children collect berries on a summer's day.'

'Unlike you,' said Bartholomew, seeing no difference between Wymundham's alleged love of stories and Stanmore's network of informants who were paid to do the same thing.

Stanmore fixed him with an unpleasant look. 'It is entirely different, Matt. I collect information because I need to know what is happening in the town to help my trade. Wymundham loved rumours for their own sake, and if there were none that suited him, he was not averse to inventing a few. I would not be surprised if someone did away with him.'

'The Bene't Fellows are a horrible crowd,' reiterated Edith. 'You should not allow Michael to involve you with them, Matt, especially now you have no Cynric to protect you.'

'It was good of you to take him after Runham dismissed so many of our staff,' said Bartholomew. 'Of course, it would have been nicer if you had discussed the matter with me first.'

'Why?' asked Stanmore with a shrug. 'Cynric is perfectly capable of making up his own mind about what he wants. It is high time he was released from all that creeping about in the night that you seem to demand of him. I have given him and Rachel Atkin a pleasant room in my property in Milne Street, where they are very happy.'

'He does seem happy,' admitted Bartholomew. 'You have always been kind to me – and are even prepared to make anonymous donations on my behalf – but I am afraid I have yet one more favour to ask of you.'

'You are thinking about young Roger, the stable boy dismissed from Michaelhouse.'

Bartholomew gazed at him in astonishment and Stanmore smiled, gratified to see his brother-in-law so impressed by the scope of his knowledge.

'That was taken care of days ago,' Stanmore continued loftily. 'Agatha brought him to me, and said that you thought I might find a place for him. He is currently employed in the kitchen, with the promise of an apprenticeship if he proves himself to be a diligent worker.'

Bartholomew smiled. 'Thank you, Oswald. You are a good man.'

'I am, but do not spread it around the town, or I will have all manner of people striving to take advantage of me – like that damned Runham.'

They continued to talk until the first streaks of dawn appeared in the sky. The more he thought about his decision to make a new life in Paris, the more Bartholomew felt the choice was the right one. Edith, however, was determined to persuade him to remain in Cambridge as a physician and take one of her six hopeful ladies as a wife. Stanmore fell asleep, lulled by their voices, and only woke when a heavy-eyed servant came to rake over the cooling ashes and build a new fire.

Bartholomew was enjoying a breakfast of coddled eggs and fresh bread with honey when there was a clatter of horse's hooves in the courtyard. Intrigued by the urgency of the voices that rang out as the rider dismounted, he followed Stanmore outside and was startled to see Cynric holding the reins of a panting, sweating horse.

'There you are, boy,' said the Welshman breathlessly. 'I thought I might find you here.'

'Why?' asked Bartholomew, as a sense of unease began to uncoil in the pit of his stomach. 'What has happened? Is it Michael? Is he ill again? Or is it Matilde?'

Cynric shook his head, resting his hands on his knees to try to bring his ragged breathing under control. 'I went to collect the last of my belongings from Michaelhouse at dawn – Runham said he would sell them if I had not claimed them by then – and I found the College in a terrible commotion.'

'Why?' asked Bartholomew again, feeling the unease turn into outright anxiety.

'Runham,' gasped Cynric, still doubled over. 'I thought I should warn you as soon as I could. He was found dead in his room this morning. And Michael says if it was not murder, then it should have been!'

CHAPTER 8

IT WAS SATURDAY, AND THE ROAD THAT LED INTO Cambridge was already busy with traffic heading for the town market. Huge, lumbering carts pulled by plodding oxen and laden with firewood, bundles of reed for thatching and faggots of peat cut from the Fens clogged the middle of the path, while impatient horsemen and pedestrians jostled for space at the sides. There were chapmen with their packs filled with ribbons, buttons, needles and toys; there were pardoners wearing wide-brimmed black hats and carrying scrolls that gave the buyer absolution of all manner of sins; there were shepherds and drovers and geese boys, all driving their livestock to the market in squawking, braying, lowing, bleating herds; and there were soldiers, weary from a night of patrolling, with the mud of their travels splattered on their cloaks and boots.

The faster Bartholomew tried to ride, the slower was his progress. Although it was only just past dawn, the crowds heading for the market did not want to waste a precious moment of the winter daylight, and Bartholomew was not the only one in a hurry. A man with several braces of pheasants slung over his shoulder gave Bartholomew a venomous glower when the physician's horse bumped him, but backed away when he saw Cynric's hand resting lightly on his short Welsh sword.

By the time Bartholomew reached the Trumpington Gate, the bells were ringing for prime, and the streets were filled with dark-garbed scholars heading for the churches. Friars, monks and students bustled along the muddy roads, some sporting the distinctive uniforms of their College or hostel, and others wearing the habits of their Order. Bells rang all over the town. The tinny clatter of St Botolph's, the flat clank of St Edward's and the shrill ding of St John Zachary's vied for attention above the great bass toll of St Mary's.

He saw the scholars of Bene't heading for their church in an orderly line. Heltisle and Caumpes seemed to be discussing their partly completed building, and gazed up at its abandoned scaffolding as they walked, their thoughts clearly on temporal matters rather than on mass. Simekyn Simeon, his colourful clothes exchanged for the sober blue of his College, slouched after them, rubbing the sleep from his eyes and making it evident that he was unused to being woken at such an ungodly hour.

Behind him, and moving in a way that Bartholomew could only describe as a slink, was the fourth Fellow – Henry de Walton – the man whom no one seemed to like because of his obsession with the state of his health.

Osmun the porter brought up the rear of the procession, wielding a hefty stick that he seemed prepared to use if any students broke ranks or moved too slowly. He saw Bartholomew, and his face creased into an ugly snarl. Bartholomew was surprised to see Walter, the dismissed night porter from Michaelhouse, walking next to him, and assumed that Walter had inveigled himself a post at Bene't. When Walter spotted Bartholomew, he gave what almost passed for a smile. Bartholomew could only suppose that it had been Walter's legendary surliness that had enticed Bene't to give him a position.

Scholars and traders were not the only ones awake that morning. Sitting astride a splendid grey was Adela Tangmer, riding briskly down the centre of the High Street, showing off her equestrian skills by weaving expertly between the carts and academic processions that jammed the road.

'I think you and I need to have a chat, Matthew,' she said when they drew level. He saw that she at least had the grace to appear sheepish.

'We most certainly do,' agreed Bartholomew. 'But not now. I must get to Michaelhouse.'

He tried to ride on, but his way was blocked by a baker who was selling sticky cakes from a greasy tray that he carried on his head. Adela watched Bartholomew critically as he tried unsuccessfully to direct his horse around the obstruction.

'You ride like a peasant,' she said bluntly. 'Sit straight. And do not wave your hands in front of you like a magician. Keep them still and low.'

'I do not have time for this,' he said, digging his heels in his horse's flanks. It snickered at him and twisted its head around to favour him with a look of pure malevolence. 'Runham is dead, and I need to return to College as soon as possible.'

'Then perhaps you will allow me to help you,' she said, leaning down and snatching the reins from his hands. 'It is the least I can do.'

She turned her horse, and then they were off along the High Street, moving more quickly than Bartholomew felt was safe. But they reached Michaelhouse without mishap, and he slid off the horse and handed the reins to Cynric.

'Thank you,' he said, addressing both Cynric and Adela.

'Send for me if you want me, boy,' said Cynric, still hovering anxiously. 'I know I no longer have a post at Michaelhouse, but I will come if you need me.'

'Thank you, Cynric. But you have a wife to think about now. You should not be offering to embroil yourself in University troubles.'

'I am not offering because I feel the urge to dabble in scholarly politics,' said Cynric, a little impatiently. 'I am offering because I am worried you may come to harm in this den of thieves and murderers without me to protect you.'

'This is my home,' said Bartholomew. 'I will be fine.'

Cynric gave Michaelhouse's sturdy gates a disparaging glance. 'The University was home to Wymundham, Brother Patrick and Raysoun, too, and look what happened to them. You would be safer with me here to watch your back. Remember that, boy.'

Leading Bartholomew's horse, he began to ride back to Stanmore's premises. As Bartholomew turned to squeeze through the wicket gate, Adela leaned down and gripped his shoulder with a surprisingly firm hand.

'We do need to talk, Matthew,' she said. 'Meet me this afternoon, just before sunset, in Holy Trinity Church.'

'If I can,' said Bartholomew noncommittally, wriggling free of her and ducking through the door. He was uncertain what the day would hold for him, and did not want to commit to assignations with Adela until he had ascertained what was happening at Michaelhouse.

Aware that Adela was still watching, he closed the gate and looked around Michaelhouse's courtyard. Students stood in small groups, looking up at the shuttered windows of Runham's room and talking in low voices. Near the hall, the three remaining servants – who now cooked and cleaned as well as dealing with the horses, the laundry and the extensive vegetable gardens – stood wiping their hands on their grimy aprons. They appeared exhausted, and Bartholomew imagined they had probably been threatened with dismissal if they found themselves unable to carry out the workload normally shared by eight or nine people.

All along the north wing the refacing project was

continuing apace, and the hammering, thumping and scraping was not in the least muted by the presence of sudden and unexpected death. Apprentices still whistled and sang as they mixed mortar and sawed planks, and their masters still called in cheerfully jaunty voices. It was not their concern that a scholar had died, and they certainly were not prepared to stop their work and risk losing their bonus if they did not complete the project in the allotted time. Bartholomew hoped their confidence that they would still be paid now that Runham was dead was not misplaced.

He walked past the builders to the groups of watching students. The atmosphere among them was more akin to eager anticipation than grieved silence, and Deynman gave him an inappropriately delighted grin as Bartholomew went to stand with his own undergraduates.

'Runham is dead,' Deynman announced with great satisfaction, as if he imagined Bartholomew might not know. The physician sensed that the other students were on the verge of giving a heartfelt cheer. 'He was found in his chamber this morning.'

'So Cynric told me,' said Bartholomew. 'Do you know what happened?'

Deynman shook his head. 'I expect this means I can stay,' he said gleefully, thumping Gray and Bulbeck on the shoulders in unrestrained delight. 'It was only Runham who wanted me to leave. Everyone else wants me to stay and become a physician.'

One would not necessarily lead to the other, Bartholomew thought, as he gazed at the happy smile of his student. While he was sure that Michaelhouse would be relieved to accept Deynman's fees back into the fold, he knew the lad could study until he was as old as Methuselah, but still would not pass his examinations.

'We should wait a while before we think about the future,' said Bartholomew, reluctant to begin discussing which of Runham's many unpopular decisions would be rescinded now that the tyrant was dead.

'The rumour is that someone killed him,' said Gray, as ecstatic at the turn of events as was Deynman. 'And not before time, I say!'

'Enough, Sam!' said Bartholomew sharply. 'Keep those sorts of thoughts to yourself. If these rumours are true, then the proctors and their beadles will be listening very carefully to people who profess themselves pleased by Runham's death.'

'Then they will be doing a lot of listening,' said Gray, unruffled by his teacher's reprimand. 'Not a single person in this College – you included, Doctor – liked the man.'

'Clippesby,' said Bartholomew, after a moment's thought. 'Clippesby liked him. And so, probably, did the late Master Wilson.'

'Wilson is dead,' said Gray dismissively. 'And anyway, I happen to know that Wilson did not like his cousin any better than the rest of us did. Father Paul, who knew their family's house priest, says that Wilson detested Runham, and that Runham was always using Wilson as a means to better himself, because of his own mediocre ability.'

'Father Paul would never say such things,' said Bartholomew disbelievingly.

'I have paraphrased Paul's words,' said Gray, waving a hand to indicate that Bartholomew's objection was a mere quibble. 'But the meaning is the same.'

'It is true,' said Bulbeck quietly. 'Father Paul did tell us that he failed to understand why Runham built his cousin such a handsome tomb, when they had hated each other in life.'

'Grief afflicts people in different ways,' said Bartholomew.

'Perhaps Runham did not realise how much he loved Wilson, until after Wilson had died.'

'More likely he was building a fabulous tomb to prove to Wilson that he was alive and Wilson was dead,' said Deynman.

The others stared at him uncomprehendingly.

'Most people do not feel the need to prove such things to the dead, Rob,' said Bulbeck. 'Whatever we might think of him, he was not insane.'

Gray addressed Bartholomew. 'But you are also wrong when you say Clippesby liked Runham. He did not. I heard him weeping in his room last night. Naturally, I listened outside his window to learn what the problem was, and I heard him cursing Runham, and wailing something about his no longer being considered mad.'

'Sam!' warned Bartholomew sternly. 'This kind of talk could cause an innocent man a lot of trouble. Be careful what you say.'

'There is Brother Michael,' said Bulbeck, pointing to the fat monk, who was leaning out of Runham's window. 'He is beckoning to you.'

Bartholomew acknowledged Michael's wave and strode across the yard to the north wing. He ducked under some coarse matting that had been draped across the doorway to protect its delicate tracery from falling masonry, squeezed past a huge bucket of mortar that had been left in the porch, and clattered up the wooden staircase to Runham's room. The door was closed, so he pushed it open and stepped inside.

Michael stood with his back to the window, leaning his bulk against the sill, while he looked at the men who had gathered in the Master's room. He appeared fit and healthy, and any weight he might have lost during his brief illness had been regained with a vengeance. To his left was Langelee, who seemed tired and dishevelled, as though he had slept badly and had only just woken. Next to him Kenyngham wrung his hands in dismay as he gazed down at the body of Runham, his lips moving quickly as he prayed for the Master's soul. Clippesby and Suttone stood together near the fireplace, Suttone resting a hand on Clippesby's shoulder, as though offering comfort. Finally, Father Paul was sitting at the table, turning his head this way and that to try to ascertain by sound who had just entered.

'It is Matthew,' said the blind friar, smiling. 'Only you make so much noise on the stairs, running up them as though the Devil were on your tail.'

'Except that the Devil is in here,' muttered Langelee, turning his eyes from Bartholomew to the body on the floor.

Runham was lying on his back, with the smooth arch of his ample stomach rising towards the ceiling. His eyes were half open and his lips were apart, revealing a tongue that was bluish and swollen. To Bartholomew, the body had a stiff look about it, suggesting that Runham had been dead for several hours or more. What really caught his eye, however, was that the corpse lay on a handsome woollen rug that had been purloined from the hall.

Bartholomew turned his attention to the rest of the room. Although Runham had only recently taken it from Kenyngham, his unmistakable touch was already obvious. The walls were hung with tapestries – at least two of them from the conclave – while the wooden floor was completely covered with the best of the rugs from the hall. The pair of finely carved chairs that stood next to the table had belonged to a recently deceased scholar called Roger Alcote, and had been placed in storage to await collection by his next of kin. Runham had apparently been into the attics, and had removed the furniture for his personal use.

Bartholomew also noticed that the overstuffed cushions that lined one of the chairs were from Agatha's old wicker throne in the kitchen.

Besides the rugs, tapestries and chairs that Runham had so skilfully looted from the College, there were the chests. Under the window – perilously close to where an enterprising workman could reach in and touch it – was the large strongbox from which Runham had intended to pay for his new building. A number of small coins and pieces of cheap jewellery lay in the bottom, but it had clearly been ransacked and the most valuable items removed.

Next to the strongbox were Michaelhouse's loan chests – the College 'hutches' – that allowed payments to be made to needy scholars. Even from the door, Bartholomew could see that all were empty. He turned a horrified gaze on Michael. The monk nodded to his unspoken question.

'I think you can see where Runham obtained at least some of the money for his building work, Matt. Every single one of our nine hutches is empty. There will be no loans for desperate students from Michaelhouse from now on.'

'Runham raided the hutches for his building work?' asked Father Paul in horror, gazing around him with his opaque eyes. 'But the hutches are sacrosanct; they were given to us by benefactors who left money for the purpose of loans, and loans only. No one – not even a Master – has the authority to take money from the hutches for things like buildings.'

'Nevertheless, that seems to be what Runham did,' said Michael. 'I even saw him carrying some of them to his room. In my ridiculous innocence, I merely assumed he was taking an inventory of their contents. It did not occur to me that he would empty them of cash for his wretched buildings.'

'We do not know Runham took the money,' said Kenyngham reproachfully. 'Perhaps whoever stole from the building chest also emptied the hutches.'

Michael shook his head as he reached into Runham's strongbox to retrieve a metal bracelet that lay at the bottom. 'It is decent of you to be charitable, but I know this piece of jewellery was in the Illegh Hutch. As you saw, I just retrieved it from Runham's building chest, where it had no business to be.'

'Runham denied me a loan,' said Suttone thoughtfully. 'I asked him yesterday if I could have two groats from the Fellows' hutch to buy a new alb, but he told me that the tradition of borrowing from the hutches was over, and that I should go elsewhere. I wondered what was behind all that, and now I understand.'

'It seems there is no doubt,' said Michael. 'Runham found himself short of the funds he needed for his building, and so took out a loan himself – a loan that comprised all the remaining money in every one of the College hutches.'

'We should not be concerned about money when one of our colleagues lies dead at our feet,' said Kenyngham softly. 'We should be praying for him. All the Fellows are present except Father William. When will he return, Paul? Does he know the news?'

'He does, but he will not come,' said Paul. 'He says he has no wish to be accused of murder, given that he quarrelled so bitterly with Runham the other day.'

'What makes you say that Runham was murdered?' asked Suttone curiously. He nodded to the body on the floor. 'I am no expert, but he looks to have had a fatal seizure to me.'

Everyone stared at Bartholomew, who gazed at the body in distaste. He wondered why it never seemed to occur to anyone that he did not like inspecting the bodies of people he knew, looking for clues regarding their causes of death. It was partly because their bodies reminded him uncomfortably of his own mortality, but also because he was a physician: his business was with the living, not the dead.

'Well, Matt?' asked Michael, when Bartholomew did not move towards Runham's corpse. 'Are William's fears justified, or did Runham simply have a fatal seizure as he fondled his ill-gotten gains in the middle of the night?'

With a distinct lack of enthusiasm, Bartholomew knelt next to Runham and began a careful inspection, although he had known the answer to Michael's question the instant he set eyes on the body. He noticed that the dead Master's hands were slightly bloody and that the nails were ripped: Runham had struggled and fought against something. Another peculiarity was the fact that there was a small feather protruding from Runham's mouth. Ignoring his colleagues' exclamations of disgust, he felt under the tongue and in the cheeks to retrieve two more feathers and a ball of fluff.

'William is right to be cautious,' he said, sitting back and gazing down at the lifeless features of his Master. 'Someone smothered him: Runham was murdered.'

Once Runham's body had been removed to St Michael's Church, and two student friars of his own Order had been commandeered into keeping a vigil over it, the Fellows met in the conclave. Kenyngham, who they unanimously agreed should resume the Mastership until another election could be organised, had gathered the students in the hall and informed them that Runham had fallen prey to a fatal attack. The ambiguous wording was Michael's idea: he said it would not be wise to declare that Runham had been murdered until they had some idea who might be the culprit. Kenyngham concluded his brief announcement by suggesting that the scholars might like to use the remainder of what was now a free day to pray for Runham. None of them did, and Bartholomew's students were among the noisy throng that disappeared with alacrity though the gates to enjoy themselves in the town.

'Is that wise?' asked Kenyngham anxiously, watching them leave from the conclave window. 'Despite my obtuse announcement, it will not be long before word seeps out that Master Runham was murdered, and our students may start a fight over it.'

Michael shook his head as he settled himself in one of the best chairs. 'None of them is going to fight to defend Runham's good name, Master Kenyngham. Let them go. At least they will not be under the feet of the workmen. And all the Fellows should be here, discussing what we should do, not trying to supervise a lot of restless lads.'

'As a mark of respect, I think the building work should stop,' said Kenyngham, as Clippesby and Suttone, with unspoken agreement, began to light the conclave fire. 'It is only right that we interrupt our normal affairs to show our sorrow over this tragic death.'

'I have already tried to send the workmen away,' said Michael, ignoring the fact that there would not be much sorrowing. 'But thanks to Runham himself, they see any attempt by us to prevent them from working as an excuse not to pay them their bonus. They would not hear of going home, and I dare not force the issue. I have no wish to see us go up in flames for antagonising them.'

'And that would be easy with all the scaffolding everywhere,' said Langelee, watching Clippesby blowing on the smouldering wood in the hearth. 'A torch touched to all that cheap timber will see the College ignite like a bonfire.'

'Please!' said Kenyngham with a shudder. 'Dwelling

on riots and arson is not helping us discover the killer of poor Master Runham. Are you certain someone took his life, Matthew? Are you sure you are not mistaken?'

'I am not mistaken,' said Bartholomew. 'I showed you the feathers and fluff he had inhaled when the cushion was placed over his mouth, and I showed you the damage he did to his hands as he tried to claw his killer away from him.'

'And we found the guilty cushion,' added Michael. 'It was that lovely one which Agatha made for her fireside chair. It was stuffed with goose feathers that matched those Matt found in Runham's mouth, and stained with drool where it had been forced over his face.'

'Perhaps even more incriminating,' said Bartholomew, 'is the fact that it lay on the opposite side of the room from the body. After the killer had used it to smother Runham, he set it down on the bench under the window. Even if Runham had suffocated himself – which I am certain he did not – he could not have placed the cushion on the bench after he had died.'

'This is dreadful,' said Kenyngham in a whisper. 'Who would do such a terrible thing?'

'Who said it was terrible?' muttered Langelee.

'We have an impressive collection of suspects,' Michael went on. 'First, there is Langelee.'

Bartholomew could not but help wonder whether Langelee was top of Michael's list because Langelee had thwarted the monk's ambition to be Master by raising the issue of his dealings with Oxford. Bartholomew knew that it was only a matter of time before Michael had his revenge, and suspected that the first step had just been taken.

'Me?' asked Langelee in astonishment. 'Why should I kill Runham?'

Michael sighed. 'Do not treat us like imbeciles. Runham

dismissed you because of your marriage to Julianna. Now that he is dead, you are likely to be reinstated by a more lenient Master, not to mention the fact that the repayment of your stipend will not be forced. You have a very good reason for killing him.'

Especially if Langelee expected to be the next Master, thought Bartholomew. He recalled Langelee confiding details of his marriage so that Bartholomew would support him if Runham ever 'conveniently died', to use Langelee's own words.

'So do a lot of people,' said Langelee angrily. 'Father William also lost his Fellowship because of Runham – perhaps *he* crept out of his friary last night and shoved a cushion over Runham's face. Why else would he refuse to join us?'

'Because he fears exactly the accusation you have just made,' said Michael. 'As Paul has already told us.'

'And what about *him*?' snapped Langelee, pointing an accusing finger at Paul. 'He lost *his* Fellowship because of Runham, too. And do not even think of claiming that his blindness means that he could not commit murder. It is dark at night – Paul was probably at an advantage.'

'An interesting conjecture,' said Michael blandly, although Bartholomew had no idea whether he had taken the suggestion seriously or was just humouring the belligerent philosopher.

'And him.' Langelee swung his accusing finger around to point at Kenyngham. 'He lost a Fellowship of almost thirty years' duration to Runham. You cannot tell me that *he* did not have good cause for wanting the man dead.'

'Are you referring to me?' asked Kenyngham, genuinely startled. 'But I have never killed anyone in my life!'

'Every murderer has to start somewhere,' said Michael drolly.

Bartholomew shook his head, not liking the way the scholars were already turning on each other in the search for a culprit. He hoped their meeting would not turn into a witch hunt. But regardless, of all the Michaelhouse scholars, Bartholomew thought Kenyngham the one least likely to murder someone – especially in such a cold and deliberate a way. Suffocation required that the killer press hard against his victim, forced to hear the gasps and entreaties for mercy, and obliged to watch the helpless drumming of heels on the floor and the scrabbling of ever-weakening hands. It was not like a swift knife under the ribs, which might happen in the heat of the moment; suffocation took longer and there was less chance that it could be accidental.

'And Paul, Kenyngham and William are not alone in having reasons to strike Runham dead,' continued Langelee. 'What about Clippesby and Suttone? They fell victim to Runham's charming temperament, too.'

'That is unfair,' said Suttone quietly. 'We have only just arrived in Cambridge, and have not had time to make an enemy of Runham.'

'But he has had time to make an enemy of you,' Langelee pressed on relentlessly. 'I recall quite clearly Runham telling us that you had been accused of theft at your friary in Lincoln.'

'Why would that be cause for me to kill him?' asked Suttone. 'He had already announced to the entire Fellowship that a long time ago I was accused of a theft of which I was later found to be innocent. What would be the point of killing him when the "secret" was already out?'

'Then what about him?' snarled Langelee, casting a venomous glower at Clippesby. 'Runham accused him of being insane, and so *he* had motive enough to silence his tormentor once and for all. He has worked hard to ingratiate himself with Runham by spying for him on the other Fellows, but Runham turned on him after all his labours.'

Clippesby's face was like wax, and his eyes were hollow and haunted. 'I did not spy,' he whispered.

'You did,' said Suttone tiredly. 'Do not lie, Clippesby. It is better to be honest. I saw you on a number of occasions hovering near the rooms of other scholars, hoping to hear something seditious that you could pass to Runham.'

'I heard you loitering outside doors, too,' said Paul quietly. 'And I overheard you with Runham, plotting to trick Matthew into making incriminating remarks about his teaching that could be used to bring about his resignation.'

'What?' asked Bartholomew, horrified. 'When was this?'

'In the church the day after Runham was elected,' said Clippesby miserably. His chin came up in a feeble gesture of defiance. 'But Master Runham was right in his concerns: you *did* confess to him that you used the Devil's wiles to heal your patients.'

'I can assure you that I did not,' said Bartholomew in disgust. 'If you want to be a spy, you should at least make sure you listen carefully and that your memory of conversations is accurate.'

'And what about *you* as a suspect for Runham's murder?' demanded Langelee, rounding on Bartholomew. 'You would have lost your Fellowship today, because Runham had driven you into a corner. You have as good a motive for killing Runham as anyone.'

'He would not have lost his Fellowship,' said Michael confidently. 'Matt would rather give up practising medicine than forsake his teaching.'

'Actually, I—' began Bartholomew.

'Even so, Runham would have made life so uncomfortable that you would not have stayed long,' Langelee continued, cutting across Bartholomew's words. He turned to Michael. 'And that goes for you, too. Were you aware that he had plans to ration the food? That would have driven *you* out pretty quickly.'

'When was this?' asked Michael in surprise. 'I have not heard about such a harsh measure.'

'It happened at one of the meetings held when the only Fellows present were those not strong enough to object,' said Suttone bitterly. 'Runham was cunning – he passed all manner of statutes and ordinances when the more senior of you were absent.'

'So,' said Michael, 'we are left with two unpleasant facts: first, we have a dead Master; and second, every one of his Fellows had a reason to wish him harm. And there are students and servants, too, who had run foul of him and were dismissed – like Rob Deynman, Sam Gray, Cynric, Walter and Agatha.'

'Especially Agatha,' said Langelee. 'After all, her cushion was the murder weapon.'

'I am sure she sewed every stitch with Runham's demise in mind,' said Bartholomew facetiously, unable to see Agatha as a smotherer, and disliking the way unfounded suspicions were being bandied about. Langelee gazed at him uncertainly.

'How awful this is,' said Kenyngham in a small voice. 'So much hatred and bitterness.'

'So, what we must do is consider our oath of loyalty to the College,' said Michael. 'There is only one way we can fulfil that: we must find a way out of this unfortunate affair without compromising Michaelhouse.'

Bartholomew almost laughed when the full import of the monk's words sank in. 'You mean we should hatch a plot that will cover up Runham's murder, and pass it off as suicide or death by natural causes?'

'Suicide would be better,' said Langelee reflectively. 'Then we will not have his vile corpse cluttering up our cemetery.'

'Then he can lie next to his poor book-bearer, Justus,' said Suttone. 'Runham consigned Justus to a grave in that desolate spot – although I understand he had not planned to consign him to a grave at all, if it would cost him money – and so it is fitting that Runham's own body suffer a similar fate.'

'I am not suggesting we "hatch a plot",' said Michael, fixing Bartholomew with offended ,eyes. 'I am merely pointing out that nothing will be gained from rumours running around the town that one of us murdered his unpopular Master. The students have already been told that Runham died of a fatal seizure and we do not need to worry about the servants, because there are virtually none left.'

'We must not overlook the fact that Runham's murder might have been a case of opportunism,' said Paul. 'You say this chest of money was next to the window. Perhaps one of the workmen saw it and decided to help himself. Then, when Runham caught him, he thrust the pillow over Runham's face to quieten his accusations, and, once he had started, he realised that he would have to finish.'

'Perhaps we can eliminate some of the suspects by looking at *when* Runham died,' said Suttone practically. 'I last saw him when he left the conclave after dismissing Langelee – just before dusk last night.'

'I did not see him after that, either,' said Langelee quickly.

'Did anyone see him later?' asked Michael. He looked around: all shook their heads. 'He announced to us all that he was going to his chamber to work, so I imagine we can assume he went there. That means he was killed some time between sunset and . . . when, Matt?'

Bartholomew shrugged. 'The body is a little stiff, but the room is cold. It is almost impossible to tell. All I can say for certain is that he died some time between sunset when he was last seen alive, and at dawn when he was found.'

'Are you sure you cannot be more specific?' asked Michael, a little irritably. 'You see, the University's Chancellor came to see me just after sunset, and he stayed very late – until ten or so. He may provide my alibi.'

'Were you discussing the affair with your Oxford collaborators?' asked Langelee unpleasantly. 'Does the Chancellor know you correspond regularly with William Heytesbury of Merton College?'

Michael gave him a venomous glare. 'That is none of your affair, Langelee. But, since you seem to be so obsessed by my private activities, I can tell you that the Chancellor knows exactly what I am doing and that I have his blessing.'

'I do not believe you,' said Langelee immediately. 'Why would the Chancellor allow you to squander valuable University property just to get scraps of worthless information from Oxford men?'

'For reasons that are too complex for you to understand,' snapped Michael. 'But we are not here to chat about my duties as Senior Proctor; we are here to discuss Runham's murder. And as I was saying, if he died before ten o'clock last night, the Chancellor is my alibi.'

'I cannot help you, Brother,' said Bartholomew. 'There is no way for me to tell what time Runham died. Perhaps he was killed at sunset, while it was still light enough for the workmen to be around. Or perhaps it happened later – perhaps a few moments before he was found dead. I really cannot say.'

'I was stalking around Cambridge in a rage,' said Langelee. 'But no one saw me.'

'I went to Trumpington and sat near the church, thinking about whether to leave Michaelhouse,' said Bartholomew.

'I was also alone part of the evening,' said Suttone. 'I was in St Michael's Church, praying for the patience to deal with Runham. Several people were in and out – including Clippesby and Kenyngham – but no one can vouch for me the whole time. I attended compline, at seven o'clock, and I stayed later to pray – probably until ten.'

'I do not even recall where I was myself, let alone expect anyone else to do it,' said Kenyngham, to no one's surprise.

'You were at compline,' Suttone reminded him. 'And after, we both lingered. You were at the high altar and I was at the prie-dieu near Wilson's tomb.'

'Ah, yes,' said Kenyngham, frowning. 'After that, I think I returned here.'

'I was at the friary,' said Paul. 'After compline, I went to sleep in my cell. Since we do not share cells at the Franciscan Friary, I have no one to vouch for me, and neither will William.'

'I was in my room,' said Clippesby in a hushed voice. 'I share it with three students, but they were all in Sam Gray's chamber engaged in some kind of scribing exercise. So, I spent the night on my own.'

'What a mess!' said Michael gloomily. He scratched a flabby cheek with a dirty fingernail. 'I confess, I do not know how to proceed with this, but I do know we should all agree to say that Runham had a fatal seizure. Now, I tire easily after my recent brush with death, and so will consider this matter in more detail after I have rested. Do nothing. Act normally – well, as normally as you usually do – and I will try to think of the best way to deal with it. Any questions?'

There were none. One by one, the Fellows of Michaelhouse filed from the conclave, wondering which of them, if any, was the murderer.

*   *   *

'I thought you said you were tired, Brother,' said Bartholomew, watching as Michael paced back and forth in the chamber he shared with his fellow Benedictines. It was mid-morning, and Bartholomew had just returned from seeing a patient who lived near the Castle. Since he was nearby, he had knocked at Matilde's door, to tell her that Adela Tangmer had made some unwarranted assumptions, but either Matilde was out or she did not want to see him, because there was no answer.

He went to the nearby church of All Saints, and borrowed a pen and a scrap of parchment from a scribe to write her a note. It took him a long time to compose a message that did not sound as though he was trying to exonerate himself at Adela's expense, but in the end he felt he had achieved the right flavour. He tapped on Matilde's door a second time, then slid the parchment underneath it when there was still no reply. He returned to Michaelhouse feeling more cheerful. At the back of his mind was the thought that Langelee had been right, and that now that Runham was dead, Bartholomew would not have to leave Cambridge for Paris after all.

He reclined on the bed in Michael's room, feeling the thick-headed lethargy of a night without sleep creep over him, and wondered whether life at Michaelhouse would ever return to its hectic but predictable routine of teaching and learning. He hoped with all his heart that Kenyngham would agree to resume his duties as Master until Suttone and Clippesby had settled in, so that they would know for certain which candidate would make the best Master instead of being obliged to vote for people they barely knew. Bartholomew had reservations about the peculiar Clippesby, but he liked Suttone, who seemed a kind-hearted man. Bartholomew was grateful for his assistance in burying Justus, and appreciated the fact that the Carmelite had not just muttered a few prayers, but had helped with the preparation of the body and had tried to imbue the mean little ceremony with some dignity.

'I am not tired at all,' said Michael, continuing to pace. The wooden floor creaked and groaned under his weight, and Bartholomew was grateful he was not in his own chamber below, trying to concentrate on his treatise. 'Unlike you, it seems – you look as though you are about to fall asleep. When I claimed fatigue in the conclave earlier, I was merely bringing that uncomfortable session to a close. In fact, the little puzzle surrounding Runham's demise is most invigorating, and I am beginning to feel much more like my old self.'

'I am sure Runham would be delighted to hear that he is the cause of your miraculous recovery,' said Bartholomew dryly.

'He would,' agreed Michael comfortably. 'Because then he could rest happily in Hell knowing that I will track down his killer and bring him to justice. You are *sure* there is a killer, are you? Only I would hate to expend my energy, time and talent on this, only to learn later that no crime has been committed after all. I am relying wholly on your say-so that Runham was murdered.'

'Runham was definitely murdered,' said Bartholomew drowsily, linking his hands behind his head. 'But I do not see how you will solve this, Brother. You have more suspects than you know what to do with – and those are just the ones you know about. I am sure Runham had enemies in all sorts of places, about whom we know nothing.'

'Meaning?' asked Michael.

'Meaning that there are the Fellows of Bene't, for a start. None of them were exactly delighted to learn that their labourers had been poached by Runham to work for Michaelhouse. To pay us back, they even went as far as enticing Agatha from us. They may regret doing that. Fond though I am of her, she is not exactly what you would call a pliant and dutiful servant.'

'Very true,' said Michael complacently. 'And that is why I encouraged her to accept the Bene't post. I do not like that superior Heltisle, or his conniving henchman Caumpes. Having Agatha in their fold will serve them right. She will put Osmun in his place, too: he will not be bullying the students with her around.'

'Is there anything connected to the University that is beyond your influence?' asked Bartholomew in disbelief.

'No,' said Michael, pleased by the recognition of his meddling skills. 'But my talent for managing University affairs is not what we should be talking about. We need to wrap our minds around the few facts we have regarding the saintly Master Runham's exit from this world.'

'Must we?' asked Bartholomew. 'I am sure we will not like what we discover.'

'Ignorance is bliss, eh?' asked Michael. He gave his friend a wicked grin. 'Runham did not leave you a purse of gold to build him a fine tomb, as did his cousin, did he?'

'If he had, then we would need it to pay all these workmen,' said Bartholomew. 'How are we going to do that now? Michaelhouse is virtually penniless.'

'We will face that problem when it arises,' said Michael. 'We should not waste time by fretting over it now.'

'It may arise sooner than you think,' said Bartholomew worriedly.

'Not for another twenty-six days. The builders agreed to work for a month, and they have only been going since Wednesday.'

'I made the decision to leave for Paris tomorrow,' said Bartholomew, almost absently. 'If the killer had struck at

Runham then instead of last night, I would not have been caught up in this.'

'Paris?' asked Michael. His jaw dropped. 'No, Matt! I do not believe you! You were going to yield to Runham and leave Michaelhouse, just as he wanted you to do?'

'I was,' said Bartholomew. 'I still might.'

'I was certain the fact that Runham wanted you to leave would be sufficient to make you want to stay,' said Michael, astonished. 'It goes to show that you should never take for granted the people you think you know, and that they can still give you the odd surprise. We would be as well to remember that as we investigate this murder, Matt.'

'We?' asked Bartholomew weakly.

'I need you,' said Michael in the kind of tone that made it final. 'And you cannot slink off to Paris now, anyway. It would look as if *you* killed Runham.' He gave Bartholomew a sidelong glance. 'You did not, did you?'

'No. And you know me better than to ask that,' said Bartholomew, irritably.

Michael smiled. 'Yes, I do. But it does no harm to ask. You had the motive: he threatened everything you hold dear – your teaching and your medicine. And you had the opportunity, given that you have no one to vouch for your whereabouts at the salient time.'

'Neither does anyone else. Including you.'

'True.'

Bartholomew sighed. 'I know *you* did not kill him, Brother. You are more likely to create some colossal scandal to bring him down, not murder him by stealth in the middle of the night. You are no cushion-over-the-face man.'

'Nicely put,' said Michael. 'Lord, I am hungry! Will you walk with me to the Brazen George?'

'Not now,' said Bartholomew, closing his eyes. 'Fetch something from the kitchen.'

Michael pulled a face of disgust. 'There is nothing in the kitchen! Runham decided not to pay the grocer, and so there is not a scrap to eat. Of course, there is always that plum cake you were given by the Saddler family, which has been sitting alone and forgotten on your windowsill.'

'Not forgotten, it seems,' said Bartholomew, astonished by the things the monk seemed to notice.

Within moments, Michael had collected the cake and was back in his room, cutting generous slices with the slim knife he used for sharpening his pens. He handed Bartholomew a piece that was about half the size of the one he took for himself, and then settled himself in a chair.

'I have never before encountered a case like this, Matt,' he said conversationally as he ate. 'Usually, once you have a man with a motive, it is only a case of establishing that he had the means and the opportunity. Given that Runham died some time between sunset and dawn, then virtually all our suspects – Fellows, students, servants and workmen – had the *opportunity*, and the *means* was nothing more sinister than a pretty cushion. And most of Cambridge had a *motive* to kill the man.'

'I cannot imagine how you will proceed.'

'It certainly poses a challenge! And I need a challenge like this to put me on the road to recovery.'

'There is nothing wrong with you, Brother,' said Bartholomew tiredly. 'You are quite well enough to outwit the killer of Runham.'

Michael sighed. 'I know. But I must admit I have enjoyed the last few days. I should be ill more often: people have been kind, I have been provided with better food than the slop I am normally expected to live on, and everyone keeps telling me how much I am missed. My week away from the University has proven to everyone what I have always known: that I am indispensable.'

Bartholomew had reached an interesting part in his treatise on fevers, and was able to distance himself from the clatter of the workmen outside. He worked until the bell should have sounded for the midday meal, but was told by the cook that the scholars had not been summoned because Michaelhouse had no food. Langelee had been correct when he had claimed Runham had declined to pay the College's bills, and an infuriated grocer had arrived that morning to claim any unused stock he could lay hands on. There were some flat, hard loaves baked with flour and water, but the absence of fat or salt made them unpalatable on their own – like chewing on parchment.

As far as Bartholomew could tell, virtually every other scholar was out – either in the church praying for Runham, like Kenyngham, or celebrating their unexpected release from tyranny, like everyone else. Bartholomew was unable to concentrate on writing when his stomach was growling for food, and so he decided to walk to the Market Square to buy something from one of the bakers.

He wandered down Shoemaker Row, his mind still on the relationship between the nearby marshes and the sweating sicknesses that sometimes crippled the town, absently nodding greetings to people he knew. He met Isnard the bargeman, who demanded to know whether Michaelhouse had plans to reinstate the choir now that Runham was dead. Bartholomew promised to mention it to Master Kenyngham, and Isnard suggested he made sure he did.

Next, he was hailed by Agatha, who was striding

through the Market Square with a string of dead rabbits swinging from one hand.

'Would you like one?' she asked generously, waving the little corpses uncomfortably close to Bartholomew's face. 'Cynric gave them to me. He has been practising his archery in the water meadows near Newnham. I do not see why those Bene't scoundrels should benefit from his skills and enjoy rabbit stew tonight while you eat nothing but dry bread.'

'Why did you leave us?' Bartholomew asked. 'Did Runham put pressure on you to go?'

Agatha regarded him as if he were insane. 'Do you think I would have gone if he had? God's chosen do not pander to the whims of men like him.'

'Oh, yes. I forgot about that,' said Bartholomew weakly.

'I went to Bene't because Master Caumpes offered to pay me a respectable wage. And, of course, because Brother Michael suggested I could do God's work better at Bene't than at Michaelhouse for the moment. He has instructed me to watch those nasty Bene't Fellows to see whether I can learn which of them killed Raysoun and Wymundham. Those of us who were spared the Death by God to make the Earth a better place do not approve of murder.'

'None of us do.'

'Wrong,' declared Agatha. 'Some people approve of it very much, and are skilled at it. But they will not best the likes of me and Brother Michael. And when I have brought this killer to justice, I shall return to Michaelhouse. The better pay at Bene't is very nice, but I do not like working with that Osmun. I can see I will have to box his ears before too long, to teach him the lesson he is always trying to inflict on others.'

She stalked away, leaving Bartholomew the reluctant

owner of a dead rabbit. He thought Michael must be growing desperate indeed, to use the unsubtle Agatha to spy on Bene't.

'I did not take you for a hunting man, Matthew,' came Suttone's amused voice at his side, as he gestured to the rabbit. 'Or is that how your patients pay you these days?'

Bartholomew smiled. 'Agatha gave it to me.'

'I miss her,' said Suttone. He saw Bartholomew's doubtful expression and gave a grin. 'I do. Your University is full of intriguers and liars, and her blunt honesty is a refreshing change.'

'Well, perhaps she will return now that Runham has gone,' said Bartholomew vaguely.

'Are you really certain that Runham was murdered?' asked Suttone, suddenly earnest. 'So many people wanted him dead that it seems inevitable that one of them should have succeeded in killing him. But that logic worries me. Are you certain you are not jumping to conclusions? Perhaps he died naturally. He almost gave himself a seizure the other day when he became so enraged with William. Maybe he did the same again.'

Bartholomew shook his head. 'There is no doubt.'

Suttone sighed. 'What a pity. But we must set about rectifying some of the wrongs he perpetrated over the last week – it may help his soul escape from Purgatory that much sooner. We should set about reinstating the choir as soon as possible. Brother Michael tells me that the bread and ale are important to those folk.'

'We must see whether we can pay for it first. And we must ensure we have enough for the workmen.'

'There were some coins and a few scraps of jewellery left in the chest. Use that.'

'We cannot give away our resources while we have debts,' said Bartholomew reasonably. While he sympathised with Suttone's point of view, he did not think the builders would be happy to see Michaelhouse feeding the poor while refusing to pay their wages. They would have the townsfolk up in arms in an instant, and Michaelhouse would be attacked. And that would do no one any good.

'I suppose you are right,' said Suttone reluctantly. 'What a vile mess that man has left us to sort out!'

After Suttone had returned to Michaelhouse, Bartholomew wandered around the Market Square, thinking about the disbanded choir and the death of Runham. As he was buying a pie from a baker with some of the blackest and most rotten teeth Bartholomew had ever seen – which the physician hoped had not resulted from consuming his own wares – he spotted Caumpes. The Fellow of Bene't College was striding briskly towards the goldsmith's premises, which stood in an alleyway behind St Mary's Church. Bartholomew watched him stop outside the home of Harold of Haslingfield, glance around in a way that made it perfectly clear he did not want anyone to see him, and slip inside. Bartholomew sat on the low wall that marked the boundary of St Mary's churchyard and ate his pie, his attention half on Michaelhouse's financial travails and half on Caumpes's suspicious behaviour.

He was just brushing the crumbs from his hands when Caumpes emerged from the goldsmith's shop, first poking his head around the door to peer up and down the alleyway to see whether anyone was watching. Bartholomew pretended to be looking up at the church tower, and Caumpes, apparently satisfied that he was unobserved, walked quickly across the Market Square in the direction of Bene't College.

Harold of Haslingfield was one of Bartholomew's patients, treated regularly for a wheeziness in the lungs that the physician thought might be caused by years of inhaling the fine dust that tended to accompany working with hot metals. Bartholomew had recently acquired some myrrh from a pedlar, and had developed a balsam with Jonas the Poisoner that they hoped would ease shortness of breath in people with Harold's complaint. He decided to visit Harold, to tell him about the new medicine and to see whether he could ascertain what Caumpes had been doing so furtively.

He pushed open the sturdy wooden door and stepped into the dim, acrid-smelling shop. Harold was stoking up a small furnace that produced waves of heat so intense that Bartholomew's eyes watered, and was busy setting up the equipment he used for melting gold. Lying on the bench next to him were two bracelets of a heavy Celtic design.

'Those are pretty,' said Bartholomew, wondering whether Caumpes's visit and the bracelets were connected. He recalled Stanmore mentioning that Caumpes dabbled in the black market, and that he often sold things to the town's merchants. 'May I see them?'

Carelessly, Harold picked up one of the pieces and tossed it to him. 'Actually, they are rather ugly. There is not much call for Celtic work these days, and I will never be able to sell them as they are. I am about to melt them down and use the metal to make something more appealing.'

Other merchants might have seen Bartholomew as a potential customer, but Harold had known him for a long time and was aware that the physician did not have the resources to buy gold bracelets.

'Did Thomas Caumpes sell them to you?' asked Bartholomew, deciding to take a blunt approach.

Harold regarded him warily. 'Yes, why? I hope you are not going to tell me they are stolen. I bought them from

Master Caumpes in good faith, and he has never sold me anything illegal before.'

'He sells items like this to you regularly?'

'Yes,' said Harold. 'Why do you ask?'

'No reason,' said Bartholomew. 'I just saw him coming out of your shop a few moments ago, and I wondered what scholar could afford to buy jewellery from the best goldsmith in the town.'

Harold smiled. 'You would be surprised, Doctor. Not all your colleagues are as penniless as you. But Caumpes brings me items to sell or to melt down occasionally, and has done for years. I admit I was wary at first – we gold merchants are often offered pilfered goods, and I would lose my licence if my Guild thought I was doing anything illicit. I took what he had offered me to Sheriff Tulyet and to other members of the Guild, but nothing was identifiable as stolen.'

'Does that mean they are not?'

Harold smiled again at Bartholomew's forthright question. 'No, but I told Caumpes exactly what I was going to do, and he was quite happy for me to check them before making my purchase. Had they been dishonestly obtained, he would have demanded them back and approached another merchant.'

'How much gold has he offered you?'

'I do not think I should tell you Caumpes's secrets, Doctor,' said Harold. 'But I have been doing business with him for years – since he decided to abandon his own career as a merchant and become a scholar instead. You know that the University does not pay well, and its scholars need something more than their stipends to keep body and soul together. Caumpes comes to me when and if he has items he thinks I might want. He trades spices to Master Mortimer the baker, too.'

'Spices?'

Harold shrugged. 'Pepper, cinnamon, saffron and so on. But over the last few days, it has been gold and pieces of jewellery that he has had to sell.'

Bartholomew was puzzled. How did Caumpes have access to such items? Had they belonged to Wymundham or Raysoun, and Bene't was selling them and keeping the profits, rather than passing the dead scholars' possessions to their next of kin? Unlike Harold, Bartholomew was certain Caumpes's business could not be entirely honest, because of the furtive way he had approached and left the shop. Bartholomew decided he would pass the information to Michael, and then they could discuss how it fitted in with the Bene't scholars' deaths – if indeed it did.

He told Harold about the new medicine for his lungs, left him to his gold fumes, and started to walk back to Michaelhouse to resume work on his treatise on fevers. On the way, he met Matilde, who smiled shyly at him.

'Did you read my message?' he asked anxiously. 'For some reason known only to herself, Adela Tangmer has announced that we are to marry, even though she did not see fit to ask me first.'

'And I take it you would not have accepted her offer, if she had?' asked Matilde.

Bartholomew laughed. 'I do not think so! And I suspect she would not take me anyway. I do not know enough about horses to interest her.'

'Well, I am glad. I confess I was shocked when I heard the news.' She hesitated. 'I do not suppose you still have my green ribbon, do you? It was extremely rude of me to hurl it at you after you had given it to me. I am sorry, and I would like it back.'

'I gave it to Robert de Blaston for Yolande,' said Bartholomew apologetically. 'He said it would cheer her.'

'It would,' agreed Matilde, although disappointment was clear in her face. 'Never mind. How are your various investigations proceeding: Brother Patrick of Ovyng Hostel, Wymundham and Raysoun of Bene't College, and now Runham of Michaelhouse?'

'Put like that, they form quite a list,' he said. 'And they are Brother Michael's cases, not mine.'

'But you always help him in such matters. He would not be nearly so successful without your help, despite the high opinion he holds of his own abilities.'

'You have heard about Runham's death, then?' he asked.

She nodded. 'How did he die? There are rumours that he died by his own hand, that he was so delighted with his ever-growing coffers that he had a fatal seizure, and that one of the scholars did away with him. Which is true?'

'We do not know,' he said, looking down at his feet so that she would not see he was lying.

'Murdered, then,' she said immediately.

'We think so,' he admitted reluctantly. 'But please do not feed that into your information network just yet – at least not until we can narrow our list of suspects from virtually every man, woman and child in Cambridge.'

'Runham was just as unpopular as his nasty cousin, Master Wilson,' observed Matilde. 'Did you know that during the Death, Wilson used to sneak out of Michaelhouse every night to visit his mistress, the Prioress of St Radegund's Convent?'

'I did know,' said Bartholomew. 'It was how he came to catch the plague in the first place. During the day he stayed in his room and refused to see anyone, but at night he must have believed the sickness lost some of its potency, because he visited the Prioress regularly.'

'He was a strange man,' said Matilde. 'One night, I remember coming back very late from sitting with one of the sisters who was ill, and I saw him gliding through the streets like the Grim Reaper. Someone cried out to him, begging him to give last rites – Wilson was an ordained priest and he was wearing his priest's habit.'

'But he ignored the plea and continued on his way to his lover?' asked Bartholomew, knowing Wilson to have been a man devoid of compassion, particularly where it posed a risk to himself.

To his surprise, Matilde shook her head. 'The dying man was a rich merchant, who had been abandoned by his terrified family. He said Wilson could have all he could carry from the house, if he would grant absolution.'

'And Wilson agreed?' asked Bartholomew in astonishment. 'After skulking in his room all day to avoid contamination, he then went into the house of a sick man who offered him money?'

Matilde nodded. 'I was intrigued, and so I hid in the shadows to watch. Moments later – Wilson must have furnished a very fast absolution – he came out, so loaded down with silver plates and gold cups that he could barely walk. Then he staggered off in the direction of Michaelhouse.'

Bartholomew shook his head in disbelief. 'I have always wondered how Wilson managed to contract the disease. I assumed he would have run through the streets to reach the convent, and declined contact with anyone. So now I know.'

'According to the sisters, that was not the only time. You know what it was like – people were terrified of dying unabsolved, and were prepared to give a willing priest all they owned in this world to help them safely into the next. By all accounts, Wilson made a tidy profit from the sick, because he helped people like Adela Tangmer's mother, Sheriff Tulyet's sisters, and Mayor Horwoode's first wife, who were all wealthy citizens.'

'And Wilson then gave it to me to pay for his own tomb,' mused Bartholomew. 'How ironic!'

'But enough of Wilson,' said Matilde with a shudder. 'Even now I find him a repellent character. What about these more recent deaths?'

'Wymundham and Raysoun are buried, and although I know Wymundham's death was no accident, I have no idea whether the same was true of Raysoun's. Michael's beadles have been visiting taverns every night to see what they might learn – about Patrick as well as the Bene't men – but they have heard nothing.'

'But I told you Patrick was a shameless gossip. You should investigate the people he gossiped about,' suggested Matilde.

'I tried doing that at his hostel,' said Bartholomew. 'But it led nowhere. Perhaps the beadles will have better luck.'

'Are these dead scholars associated in any way?' asked Matilde. 'Both Wymundham and Patrick were men who loved to tell tales and peddle information. Perhaps they were killed to ensure their silence regarding the same rumour.'

'No,' said Bartholomew. 'The only connection, as far as I can see, is that they were University men. There is doubtless a link between the murder of Wymundham and the death of Raysoun – who were at the same College – but not with Patrick.'

'Are you certain?' pressed Matilde.

Bartholomew regarded her curiously. 'As certain as I can be, given that we have very little information about them. Why? Do you know differently?'

'No,' said Matilde. 'I have had the sisters asking questions in all sorts of places to see what they might discover for you, but they have revealed nothing useful, other than what I have already passed on.'

'It is good of you to be going to so much effort,' said Bartholomew sincerely.

She smiled and touched his cheek affectionately. 'It is because I am concerned for you. I do not like the way Brother Michael drags you into these affairs.'

'Neither do I,' said Bartholomew vehemently. 'I would rather concentrate on my teaching and visiting my patients.'

'And seeing your friends?' asked Matilde softly. 'Is that important to you, too?'

'You know it is,' said Bartholomew, a little confused by her question.

She stood on tiptoe, quickly kissed his cheek and then was gone, stepping lightly over the muddy ruts of the High Street as she walked towards her home. He smiled suddenly, and thought that Michaelhouse, Bene't and their various troubles were not so important after all. Briskly he walked back to the College, where he wrote an inspired description of the symptoms of quartan fever before falling asleep on the table.

The dull ache of cold feet woke him two hours later. He glanced out of the window to see that it was late afternoon, and that candles already burned in some scholars' rooms. He straightened, wincing at his stiff shoulders and back, and rubbed his face, trying to dispel the peculiar light-headed sensation that he always experienced when woken from a deep sleep in the middle of the day. He was about to walk to the conclave to see whether anyone had lit the fire so that he could doze in front of it, when he recalled that he had an assignation with his self-proclaimed fiancée at sunset.

He seriously considered not going to meet Adela in the Church of the Holy Trinity, but suspected that it would be wiser to thrust his head into the lion's mouth and address the issue of her rumour-spreading directly.

In the back of his mind was the uneasy suspicion that unless he confronted her soon about her decision to marry him, she might very well assume his compliance and take matters a stage further by inviting people to their nuptial celebrations.

Still fastening his cloak, he set off up St Michael's Lane, crossed the High Street and walked down Shoemaker Row to the church Adela had selected for their rendezvous. The sun was low in the sky, huddled behind a band of clouds, and the market people were beginning to pack away their wares as the shadows lengthened and the afternoon dulled. The air rang with the increasingly strident yells of vendors wanting to sell the last of their perishable goods, while horses and carts cluttered the streets as the others began to make their way home. Bartholomew bought an apple pie from a baker at a ridiculously low price. It was surprisingly good, so he bought one for Michael, too.

The Church of the Holy Trinity on the edge of the Market Square was a honey-coloured stone building with fine traceried windows. Bartholomew pushed open the great wooden door and stepped inside, feeling the temperature immediately drop and the air become chill and damp. It was also gloomy. The sun was too low to provide much light, and there were no candles lit except for the one on the altar, which was kept burning day and night as a symbol of the perpetual presence of God.

Three Cluniac monks knelt in the chancel, and their low voices whispered through the darkness as they recited their offices. At the back of the nave, a scruffy clerk yawned as he packed away his pens and parchment, while in one of the aisles a vagrant snored and snuffled on a wall bench as he slept off an afternoon of drinking. The church smelled rather strongly of cat, which all but masked the perfume of cheap incense, and Bartholomew saw at least six amber eyes gleaming at him from the shadows.

The effects of a night without sleep were beginning to tell, and as soon as he sat on one of the benches near the wall, his eyes began to close. From nowhere, a voice hissed at his elbow.

'Want to buy some wine?'

'I beg your pardon?' asked Bartholomew. The man who had spoken was a scruffy individual with a heavily whiskered face and the kind of purple nose that suggested he liked a drop to drink himself. He sighed impatiently. 'Are you here for wine?'

'No, of course not,' said Bartholomew, puzzled. 'Why would I come to a church for wine?'

The man looked hurt. 'Because it is known all over town that I sell the cheapest wine in Cambridge, and that I can usually be found here late of an afternoon. I thought all scholars were aware of that.'

The selling of smuggled goods was not uncommon in Cambridge. Its location on the edge of the Fens meant it was easy to spirit contraband down the myriad of ditches and waterways without paying the heavy taxes imposed by the King to finance his wars with France. But Bartholomew had not been aware that Holy Trinity Church was the place to come for wines. He assured the man that he wanted nothing to drink, and watched him melt away into the shadows.

Adela was late, and Bartholomew gazed without much interest at the poorly executed wall paintings and at some graffiti that claimed in a bold hand that the Death would come again to claim all those who did not renounce their evil lives immediately. The sun set, and dusk settled in deeply, so that the shadows became impenetrably dark and Bartholomew could barely see the ground at his feet. He was about to give up and leave when the door crashed open, and Adela arrived. She slammed the door behind her, causing enough of a draught to douse the eternal flame.

'I am glad you came, Matthew,' she announced without preamble, grinning at Bartholomew with her long teeth. She either did not notice or did not care about the outraged scowls of the three Cluniacs who hastened to relight the altar candle. 'I have something to tell you.'

'Is it anything to do with the fact that you have determined upon plans for my future?' he asked, raising his eyebrows but not smiling back at her.

She waved a dismissive hand. 'Oh, forget that silly nonsense. I have something much more interesting to tell you than stupid marriage stories.' She put her hands on her hips and took a deep breath. 'I am quite winded, Matthew! Do you have any idea how difficult it is to find somewhere to tether a horse in Cambridge? I swear the streets are growing more crowded in this town. Soon it will be impossible to move at all, and we shall be stuck nose to tail in a solid line from dawn to nightfall.'

'Then perhaps you should forgo horses and travel on foot,' he suggested.

She regarded him as though he were insane. 'The rumours are right about you – you *do* have peculiar opinions! A decent woman cannot be seen without a horse, and neither should a decent man. You should invest in a mount, Matthew. It would improve your standing as a physician in the town. I am sure your patients would be reassured to see you arrive at their sickbeds on a splendid filly, rather than crawling along the gutters in filthy boots.'

'And I am sure they do not care one way or the other. Anyway, if they are in their sickbeds, they will not see me arrive at all.'

'Do not quibble. The point remains the same: it is not fitting for a man of your station to be walking.'

'But I do not like horses,' he objected. 'They smell of manure and rotten straw. And I am not keen on the way they slobber on your hands when you try to feed them.'

She gazed at him before releasing a raucous peal of laughter. The monks' indignation increased, and they marched down the nave towards the west door. The vagrant snored on, and the clerk finished packing away the meagre tools of his trade and followed the monks, smiling at the unrestrained guffaws that echoed around the church. Bartholomew was not sure what Adela found so amusing.

'They do smell,' she said, when she had finally brought her mirth under control. 'But so do people. And as for slobbering, all I can say is that you must have met some damned strange nags in your time. But I did not come to talk to you about horses, pleasant though that would be. I came to tell you about the dead friar at Ovyng Hostel. Matilde told me you were looking into it.'

'Matilde?' asked Bartholomew curiously. 'How do you know her?'

'Irrelevant,' said Adela. 'But the day Brother Patrick died—'

'You are not one of the sisters, are you?' he asked, unable to see many men wanting to romp with the energetic, mannish Adela, but knowing there was no accounting for taste.

She laughed again, hard and long, wiping the tears from her eyes as she did so. Bartholomew had not meant to be so outspoken, and was glad she had not taken offence at his blunt and impertinent question. He was tired, and knew he needed to pull himself together if he did not want inadvertently to insult someone else.

'Really, Matthew!' she gasped when she could speak.

'Do you really think my father would allow me to run with the women of the night? He is a town burgess and the Master of the Guild of Corpus Christi – a respectable and influential man. I know he is more lenient with me than most parents would be, but there are limits.'

'So how do you know Matilde, then?'

'You do her an injustice if you think the "sisters" are her only interest.'

'The birthing forceps,' said Bartholomew, aware of their reassuring weight in his medical bag. 'She said you helped her to design them.'

'I did,' said Adela. 'I showed her the pair I use to ease foals from their mothers on occasion. But I also know her because she distributes food to the poor every Thursday afternoon, and I sometimes help with the odd donation of bread or meat.'

'I did not know she did that,' said Bartholomew.

'There is a lot you do not know about her,' replied Adela. 'But unless you shut up and listen, you will not know what I have to tell you, either.'

'Very well. Go on, then.'

'It is about the death of that Franciscan – Brother Patrick. What I have to tell you occurred on the same day that I met you and Edith in the Market Square, when your sister told me she liked my favourite brown dress. Do you remember?'

'Yes,' said Bartholomew warily, recalling that he had been concerned that Adela would know that a compliment was not what Edith had intended.

'I waited for a while – the friars always drop the price of their rat poison at sunset – and then I went to collect my horse, which I had tethered outside this church. I had to leave him here, because there was absolutely nowhere else. I told you finding somewhere to leave a horse is such a problem in Cambridge—'

'Brother Patrick?' prompted Bartholomew.

'Well, I was just walking through the churchyard to collect the nag – it was Horwoode, if you remember him, the beast with the thin legs? – when I saw a Franciscan friar come racing from the church all white-faced and shocked-looking. He was running so blindly that he collided with me, and all but took a tumble in the mud.'

Bartholomew found it amusing and not entirely surprising that Adela seemed to have weathered the impact far better than had the friar: it had been he who had almost fallen, not her.

She put her hands on her hips and looked disgusted. 'He ran off up Shoemaker Lane without uttering the most basic of apologies, as if the Devil himself were on his heels. Naturally, I was curious to know what had provoked such a reaction.'

'Naturally,' said Bartholomew. 'So, what did you do?'

'I came in here, to see what had frightened him. Men can be a bit feeble at times, and so I was anticipating that he had seen a spider or a mouse or some such thing, and had taken flight. But instead I saw a group of scholars standing at the high altar.'

She seized his arm in a grip that had tamed the wildest of horses, and hauled him to the spot where the gathering of scholars had allegedly taken place. Bartholomew was not sure where her involved tale was leading.

'Some people would claim that insects and small rodents have a lot in common with scholars,' he said, rubbing his arm where her fingers had pinched.

'Very true,' she agreed with a wheezy chuckle, positioning him at the low rail that separated the sanctuary from the main body of the church. 'These scholars stood in a line along this bar, as you and I are standing now.'

'But why should this friar – whom I assume you think was Patrick – find a group of scholars so terrifying?' asked

Bartholomew. 'He was a scholar himself. He would not feel the need to flee from them.'

'When I entered the church – in none too good a temper, I can tell you – they immediately started all that Latin muttering that they think passes for praying. And they quickly closed ranks, standing so that I would be unable to see past them.'

'Is that it?' asked Bartholomew, not sure why she considered that her tale would be of interest to him. 'And how do you know this friar was Patrick anyway, and not someone else?'

'Because I went and had a look at his body after he died,' said Adela promptly. 'He was laid out in St Mary's Church, as though his colleagues at Ovyng Hostel grieved for him, although I am sure they do not.'

'Why do you say that?'

'Matilde has already told you that he had a reputation as a gossip. No one likes a tale-teller.'

'But what induced you to go inspecting corpses in the first place?'

She sighed. 'I wanted to make sure Ovyng's murdered friar and the man who collided with me were one and the same before I passed along my intelligence to you.'

'Well, thank you,' said Bartholomew politely.

She gave him a vigorous slap on the shoulder that made him wince. 'But I have not finished my story yet. I am saving the best part for last.'

'Then what is it?' asked Bartholomew, massaging his shoulder, and wondering how many more thumps and pinches he would have to endure before her tale was told.

'These scholars all closed ranks at the rail, thinking that they would obscure my view of the altar. There were five of them, and they were all from that Devil's den – Bene't College.'

'So, Bene't scholars frightened Brother Patrick the day he died?' asked Bartholomew.

'Yes they did, but I still have not told you the best bit. You will keep interrupting, Matthew! They closed ranks, as I said, but I am a tall woman, and I was able to see over them. What I saw was a leg – the leg of a man who lay on the ground. Perhaps a dead man's leg.'

CHAPTER 9

BARTHOLOMEW GAZED AT ADELA IN THE DARK church, and tried to match the story she had told him to the details he had already learned about the death of Brother Patrick. He wondered whether she was trying to side-track him, to distract his attention from the fact that she had claimed an intimacy with him that did not exist. If so, it was a desperate measure.

'So, what did you do when you saw this leg – possibly that of a corpse – that the Bene't Fellows were evidently trying to hide from you?' he asked.

'What do you think I did?' she demanded, incredulous that he should even enquire. 'I left and rode home as fast as Horwoode could carry me. Why? What would you have done?'

'I do not know,' said Bartholomew with a shrug. 'Probably tried to see whether the leg belonged to someone who might need my help.'

'If it had been a fetlock, I might have done the same,' said Adela. 'But since it was a human leg, and it occurred to me that they were concealing the corpse of a person, I did what any sane woman would do – I beat a prudent and hasty retreat, and did not linger to meddle in affairs I wanted nothing to do with.'

'And these five men were definitely from Bene't College?'

'Oh, yes,' said Adela. 'I know them all, because my father is Master of one of the two guilds that founded Bene't, remember? I recognised that haughty Heltisle, that snivelling de Walton, that gaudy Simekyn Simeon who dresses like a woman, and those two revolting porters.'

'Osmun and Ulfo?'

'The very same. They are an unsavoury pair. I wonder that Heltisle keeps them on. They cannot be good for his College's reputation.'

'And Heltisle's henchman, Thomas Caumpes? Was he there, too?'

'No. Caumpes tends to keep his distance from the rest of that crowd. Who can blame him?'

'He did not keep his distance when I was rash enough to pay Bene't a visit yesterday. He seemed very much a part of their unpleasant little community.'

'Doubtless he strives to give the appearance of unity to outsiders. He is an intensely loyal man, and cares very much about what other people think of his College.'

'Then *he* should persuade Heltisle to rid Bene't of Ulfo and Osmun.'

'Perhaps he has tried. My father says he is the most reasonable of the Bene't men and that he makes fewer outrageous demands on the Guild of St Mary and the Guild of Corpus Christi than do the others. As scholars go, he is the least offensive one that I know – other than you, I suppose.'

'And it was definitely a leg you saw poking from behind this crowd who had gathered at the altar rail?'

'As opposed to what?' demanded Adela archly. 'I may be a spinster, Matthew, but I know a leg when I see one. It was thin and scrawny with pale goldish hairs on it. Not particularly attractive. I prefer legs with a bit more meat on them.'

'You would approve of Brother Michael's, then.'

'Not that much meat, thank you. I like something with muscle, as well as fat.'

'Why wait until now to tell me this?' asked Bartholomew, hastily changing the subject before they became too bogged down in anatomical details. 'You have seen me several times since the day that happened, and you must have known the proctors are making enquiries into Brother Patrick's death.'

'It did not occur to me to tell you until Matilde mentioned that you were helping Brother Michael to investigate the matter when I met her this afternoon,' said Adela. 'I always thought you were more concerned with the living than the dead, Matthew. You are not interested in Patrick because you want his corpse to dissect for your students, are you?'

'It is already buried,' said Bartholomew. 'But Brother Michael occasionally asks me to examine bodies for him.'

'I see,' said Adela, regarding him doubtfully. 'Well, each to his own, I suppose. Matilde mentioned that you sometimes delve into the unsavoury world of murder. Most distasteful, I thought. You should develop an interest in horses instead. It would be much healthier.'

'You seem to have had quite a lengthy discussion with Matilde about this. Did you also admit to her that you and I do not have an arrangement?'

Adela's laughter echoed around the church again. 'An "arrangement"! What a quaint way of putting it, Matthew! You mean did I tell her that you are free to pursue her, should she desire it?'

Bartholomew was not quite sure how to reply, seeing pitfalls in every direction.

Adela sighed. 'She already knew I have no binding claim on you, although she did ask me to confirm it. I assumed that because Edith is so busy assessing all the available spinsters and widows in the town on your behalf, you were free of such attachments. I had no idea there were women who have a hankering for you.'

'Are there?'

She smiled at him. 'You seem more interested in my discussion with Matilde than in my leg story. Typical man! I risk my life telling you about something I was not meant to see, and all you can do is fix your lustful sights on a lady.'

'Do you think the Bene't scholars might harm you because you saw this leg?' asked Bartholomew, concerned.

Adela's smile remained, although it became wistful. 'So, you do harbour a little feeling for me after all. You are worried lest they try to silence me, as I suspect they silenced Brother Patrick. I imagine he saw the body they were trying to hide, and now he is dead.'

'Have you told anyone else about this?'

'Not a soul. When it first happened, I assumed I had walked in on one of those silly fights you scholars so love. My instincts told me to forget what I had seen, and hope the Bene't men would assume they had been successful in concealing the body from me. Then I discovered that the murdered friar and the man who had fled from the church were one and the same, and I realised the matter was a little more serious. I saw I should remain silent no longer.'

'Why? You did not need to put yourself in danger.'

'You know why,' she said, looking down the nave and refusing to meet his eyes. 'I felt I ought to make amends for the trouble I have caused you by claiming we were betrothed. But I am sure you will be careful with my information. I do not see you as the kind of man to go straight to that band of lunatics at Bene't proclaiming that I saw them hiding a corpse in one of the town's churches.'

'I will be careful,' he promised. 'But why did you make

up the story about our "betrothal" in the first place?'

'Exasperation and desperation,' she said with another sigh. 'My father will not stop talking about marriage. I have horses to tend to, and have no time to listen to him prattling about heirs and childbirth and other equally unappealing topics. So, I said I was betrothed just to shut him up. Of course, then he wanted to know who to.'

'Why pick me?'

'I am sorry to disillusion you, Matthew, but you were the first appropriate mate who sprang to mind. I almost said Master Lynton from Peterhouse, because he had been helping me with a sick colt that afternoon, and I only just recalled in time that he is one of those chastity-bound fellows. Then I remembered you. It worked better than I could have hoped. My father kept quiet about weddings for a good four days. But then I heard that he had been spreading the news.'

'He certainly had,' agreed Bartholomew. 'Edith was furious with me.'

Adela gave an apologetic grin. 'But you and I *did* agree to become allies against marriage. I thought you would not mind if we put our understanding to some practical use, and was hoping we would have a long betrothal with no wedding day to mar our lives, which would leave us both free to do what we liked.'

'Well, I suppose there is no harm done,' said Bartholomew. He had been leaning against a pillar, and he straightened in anticipation of leaving.

'It was blissful for a while,' said Adela dreamily. 'My father even bought me a new saddle, so delighted was he that he would soon have a brood of grandchildren galloping around his feet. And he was pleased to think he would have a contact with your brother-in-law, too. Good for business, he said.'

'I must go,' said Bartholomew, stretching. He wanted

to return to the College to see whether Michael had made any headway in uncovering the killer of Runham.

'It has been a pleasure talking with you,' said Adela, holding out a rough, calloused hand to him. 'I hope we will be able to do business again some day.'

'Right,' said Bartholomew carefully, trying not to wince at what was one of the firmest grips he had ever encountered, and recalling that the last time he had shaken her hand, he had almost ended up accepting it in marriage, too.

The following day, life at Michaelhouse seemed almost back to normal. It was Sunday, so there were no workmen hammering and crashing, although a number of them had disobeyed the rule that no work was to be done on the Sabbath, and were surreptitiously performing small, unobtrusive tasks to ensure that they did not fall behind schedule.

On the way back from the church Bartholomew saw Mayor Horwoode, dressed in his finery as he walked to morning mass. The Mayor declined to acknowledge Bartholomew, although the youngest of his three step-daughters gave the physician a friendly wave. He hoped the chubby ten-year-old was not someone Edith had approached as a prospective wife.

In the High Street, a pedlar risked a heavy fine by selling his wares on the Sabbath. Bartholomew risked the same by purchasing a piece of green ribbon and arranging to have it delivered to Matilde's home that morning.

Almost as soon as breakfast was over, he received a summons from the itinerants who lived in skin tents near the Castle, and was delighted to be presented with an opportunity to use his new birthing forceps. While the patient's man looked on with a white face, Bartholomew successfully extracted a healthy baby before its mother laboured so long that she bled to death. Nevertheless, he spent the rest of the day in the chilly camp, to ensure that there were no complications. By the time he returned to Michaelhouse it was dark, and cooking fires were lit all over the town, so that the air was thick with a haze of smoke and smelled of burning wood and food. He coughed as the particles suspended in the night mist tickled the back of his throat, and wondered how the damp, foggy evenings affected those of his patients with lung diseases. He was certain the thick atmosphere at this time of night was not good for them.

He knocked at Michaelhouse's gate, and waited for some moments before he remembered that Runham had dismissed the porters and that no one would answer his hammering. Assuming that someone would have locked the gate as dusk fell, he was wondering whether he might have to scale the walls, when it occurred to him to try the handle before attempting anything so energetic. He was surprised and not very impressed to discover that not only was the wicket gate unlocked, but that the great wooden door was not barred either. Cambridge was an uneasy town, and leaving the gates open after dark was tantamount to inviting an attack. Disgusted, he made a mental note to remind Kenyngham that students would have to act as guards until more porters could be hired.

He picked up one of the heavy bars and was manoeuvring it into place when he saw two scholars walking towards him, their hoods pulled over their heads to combat the evening chill. The hoods rendered them unrecognisable, and he assumed they were students intending to spend the night on the town. Well, they could give up that notion, he decided. While Runham might have been content to allow Michaelhouse students to frequent taverns

– where they would inevitably fight with the townsfolk – by not employing porters to keep them in, Bartholomew was not prepared to risk it. As one of them reached out to open the wicket gate, Bartholomew grabbed his arm.

'You can help me bar the gate, and then you will return to your rooms,' he said curtly. 'You know you are not supposed to leave the College at night.'

The pair exchanged a glance, and then one of them bent to pick up one end of the heavy wooden bar, indicating that Bartholomew should lift the other.

'Who are you?' asked Bartholomew, struggling with the timber. 'I cannot see you in the dark. You had better not be Gray and Deynman.'

The bar went crashing to the ground so abruptly that Bartholomew lost his balance. Then the wicket gate was wrenched open, and the pair were away. With sudden clarity, the physician recalled another time when two scholars had emerged from Michaelhouse and disappeared into the darkness – when they had shoved him into the mud the night Runham became Master. Determined that they should not elude him a second time, he dived full length and managed to grab the cloak of the second of them. The scholar was jerked to a dead stop in his tracks as the garment tightened around his throat, and then began frantically tugging to try to free it.

Bartholomew yelled at the top of his voice, aiming to attract the attention of the other Michaelhouse Fellows. Distantly, he heard his colleagues, irritably demanding to know why someone was making such an ungodly row in the courtyard. Among them was Michael's voice, although that stopped the instant the monk became aware that some kind of tussle was in progress, and Bartholomew could hear his footsteps thundering down the wooden stairs that led from his room.

Just when Bartholomew was confident he could main-
tain his precarious hold on the student's cloak long
enough to allow the others to reach him, there was a
deep groan that seemed to shudder through the very
ground on which he lay. The voices of his colleagues
faltered and then fell silent. The scholar Bartholomew
held hauled at his cloak with increasing desperation.

And then there was an almighty crash, louder than
anything Bartholomew had ever heard before, and the
ground shivered and shook. A great cloud of dust billowed over him the same instant that the cloaked scholar
finally freed the hem of his cloak. The physician glimpsed
the soles of his shoes as the student fled, and the wicket
door slammed closed behind him as he made good his
escape. Meanwhile, small pieces of timber and plaster
began pattering down like rain, and Bartholomew instinctively covered his head with his arms.

He clambered to his feet, coughing and staggering in
the swirling dust. For several moments he was completely
disorientated, but then the dust began to clear and he
could see that the entire mass of scaffolding which had
been erected over the north wing had collapsed, tearing
with it part of the roof and all the gutters.

Had it been chance that two mysterious strangers were
in Michaelhouse just as the scaffolding had fallen? Were
they the same pair that he had encountered the night
that Runham had been elected Master? Bartholomew felt
certain that they were.

'Where is Michael?' came Kenyngham's worried voice
from the crowd of scholars who milled about excitedly in
the yard. 'He was in his room when I last saw him.'

With growing horror, Bartholomew saw that the eastern
end of the north wing – where Michael's room was located
– had been seriously damaged by the collapsing timber.
And Bartholomew had quite clearly heard Michael's

distinctive footsteps on the stairs moments before the whole thing had fallen!

Bartholomew gazed aghast at the rubble of Michael's room, his stomach churning as his disbelieving mind tried to make sense out of what had happened. Dust still swirled in hazy clouds, and somewhere there was a second crash as yet more staves and supports tumbled to the ground. Scholars raced from their chambers, the hall and the conclave and stood in the yard in shock. A few workmen, still illicitly working as the Sabbath light faded, joined them, and stood next to the scholars, white-faced at the damage and the delay it would cause.

'What has happened?' cried Clippesby, as he dashed into the College from the lane. 'I heard that terrible noise all the way from the High Street! I have been visiting Master Raysoun at Bene't.'

Suttone shot him an anxious glance. 'Raysoun is dead,' he said warily.

'Yes,' replied Clippesby, as if it were obvious. 'But the dead like to be visited, and to be asked their opinions about this and that. It helps pass the time of Eternity for them, and I often stop at Raysoun's tomb to hear what he has to say.'

'Perhaps you should go and lie down,' began Suttone nervously, evidently deciding that the College could do without a madman on the loose at that precise moment.

Clippesby waved a dismissive hand. 'Later. What happened here? Has the whole north wing collapsed?'

'Michael!' whispered Bartholomew, who was still staring at the crushed shell that had been the monk's chamber. 'He was in the building. I heard him on the stairs.'

'Then we need to fetch him out,' shouted Langelee,

darting forward and beginning to scramble through the wreckage.

The carpenter Robert de Blaston tried to haul him back. 'No, not yet! It is not safe. Wait until it has settled.'

Langelee shook him off, and, oblivious to the danger to himself, continued to clamber across the dusty rubble to where the door to Michael's staircase had been located. Finally recovering his wits, Bartholomew followed his example, grazing hands and knees in his desperation to reach the monk.

'No!' cried Blaston, advancing a few steps to snatch at Bartholomew's tabard. 'Your weight might bring more of it down. Wait until we are able to assess it properly.'

He watched helplessly as Bartholomew tugged himself free, and he and Langelee picked their way through broken spars, smashed tiles and endless tangles of rope.

'I said you were working too fast,' yelled Langelee furiously, casting an accusing glower over his shoulder at the carpenter. 'And now look what has happened.'

Bartholomew stepped on a timber that was poorly balanced and it collapsed, sending him sliding down in another explosion of dust. Choking and gagging, Langelee proffered a meaty hand to haul him up.

He was not the only one coughing. From somewhere deep inside the wreckage, Bartholomew could hear Michael.

'Brother? Where are you?' he yelled.

'Sitting on the stairs in the hallway,' the monk shouted back. 'Has the scaffolding fallen? It is pitch black in here and I cannot see a thing.'

'Thank God!' breathed Suttone, coming to join them. 'For a moment, I feared the worst.'

'Are you hurt?' called Bartholomew.

'No,' said Michael. 'I was just coming to help you with that pair of ruffians when there was a crash and everything went dark. The exit is blocked, so I will wait in my room for you to excavate it.'

'You do not have a room, Brother,' said Langelee. 'The roof was smashed when the scaffolding fell. Stay where you are and wait for us to reach you.'

'Well, just how long will that be?' came Michael's peeved tones. 'I have better things to do than to sit around on dark staircases, you know.'

Bartholomew exchanged a grin of relief with Langelee and Suttone. There was nothing wrong with the monk if he was able to complain. The physician yielded to Blaston's persistent tugs and moved away from the wreckage, allowing him and his workmate Adam de Newenham to decide the best way to untangle the mess and free Michael. While the two carpenters stood together arguing and planning in loud, important voices, Bartholomew sat on the steps to the hall and rested his arms on his knees. Across the courtyard, he could hear Kenyngham taking a roll-call, ensuring that no one but Michael was unfortunate enough to have been caught in the collapse.

He looked around the College, as if seeing it for the first time, gazing up at the black silhouettes against the sky, and at the faint golden gleams of candles and firelight that filtered through badly fitting window shutters. Langelee came to sit next to him, regarding the wreckage with a shake of his head.

'I think your room and medical store survived, but anything you left on the windowsill will be destroyed, and there will be dust everywhere – although I see you left the shutters closed, which will help. Poor Michael's chamber is a lost cause, though. Did he own anything valuable?'

'Probably,' said Bartholomew tiredly. 'I do not know. We did not discuss that kind of thing.'

'You sound like Father William,' said Langelee disapprovingly. 'There is nothing wrong with possessing a few worldly goods to render life a little more tolerable, you know.'

'It was good of you to risk yourself to help Michael,' said Bartholomew, recalling the philosopher's wild scramble through the wreckage. He wondered whether Michael would have done the same for Langelee, and quickly concluded that the answer was definitely no.

'Guilt,' said Langelee.

Bartholomew stared at him uncomprehendingly.

Langelee sighed. 'You were right: I should not have mentioned the Oxford business to prevent Michael from standing as Master. Unsavoury though it is to have dealings with that place, it was unfair of me to have used it against him.'

'I studied at Oxford,' said Bartholomew. 'I do not understand why everyone has taken against it so. It is bigger than Cambridge, so there are more fights, but it has an undeniable atmosphere of learning and scholarship. Some of the best minds in Christendom are there.'

It was Langelee's turn to gaze. 'You are an Oxford man? Well, that explains a lot about you,' he said rudely. 'I thought you learned your leeching in Paris.'

'That was later. You realise that Michael will not readily forgive you for destroying his chance of becoming Master? He cannot stand even now that Runham is dead, because your accusations still hang over him.'

'But I just saved his life,' Langelee pointed out. 'We are even again.'

Bartholomew was certain Michael would not agree, and was equally certain that at some point in the future, Langelee would pay dearly for his error of judgement in thwarting Michael's ambitions.

'So, what were you yelling about just before this happened?' asked Langelee, changing the subject. 'Did you see the scaffolding about to fall? I heard you howling at the top of your voice when the whole lot crumbled.'

'There were two men in the College whom I did not recognise,' said Bartholomew, not sure what else he could say about the mysterious cloaked figures who had fled when he challenged them.

Langelee regarded him askance. 'It is not a crime for people to visit us, Bartholomew. I had a couple of guests myself, as it happened. They left just before the scaffolding collapsed, so it was probably them you hollered at.'

'Really?' asked Bartholomew, his mind whirling. 'Who were they?'

'Simekyn Simeon from Bene't and one of his College's porters – a man called Osmun. Simeon and I have known each other for years; he is in the service of the Duke of Lancaster and I met him often when I worked for the Archbishop of York. It was he who invited me to Bene't last week, so that I could meet the Duke.'

Bartholomew stared at him. Could it be possible that the two Bene't men had done something to make the scaffolding collapse, perhaps to spite Michaelhouse for poaching its labourers? Was it Simeon and Osmun who Bartholomew had grabbed as they tried to leave? It could have been – as far as he could tell in the dark, they were about the right size and shape.

But surely it would have been somewhat brazen, not to mention risky, for the two Bene't men to sabotage Michaelhouse while visiting Langelee? Bartholomew rubbed his head. There was Clippesby, too: he had entered the College just after the two intruders had left, claiming to be returning from Raysoun's grave. Had he merely thrown off his cloaked disguise and re-entered the College as himself, pretending to be as shocked by the incident as everyone else?

Or was the collapse merely an accident? Langelee was not the first to observe that the scaffolding had been thrown up in too great a hurry, while the carpenters Blaston and Newenham did not seem surprised that the whole thing had come tumbling down around their ears. Embarrassed and annoyed, but not surprised.

Bartholomew closed his eyes tiredly. At least now that Runham was dead the College should settle back into the routine of its everyday affairs, especially if Kenyngham were to be Master again, to heal with kindness and understanding the rifts and squabbles engendered by Runham.

'Come on!' shouted Blaston, turning to the watching scholars. 'We can have that fat monk out in a few moments, if there are willing hands to help.'

Bartholomew and Langelee moved forward with the others, while the carpenters carefully directed the removal of each timber, so that the whole operation was conducted safely and efficiently and none of the scholars suffered so much as a splinter. Lights flickered like great fireflies as Kenyngham, Clippesby and Suttone held lamps and the only sounds were the detailed orders of the two carpenters. It was not long before the mess of wreckage was sufficiently untangled to allow Michael to climb out. Brushing dust from his habit, he stepped daintily across broken timbers and smashed tiles to the safety of the courtyard beyond.

'I thought you were in your room when that lot came down,' said Langelee, as he offered the monk a cup of wine to wash the dust from his throat. 'Kenyngham told me you had gone to rest.'

'I had,' said Michael, drinking deeply and holding out the cup to be refilled. Langelee grimaced but did as he was bidden. 'I was fast asleep when Matt woke me with all that yelling. I was on my way down the stairs to see what the fuss was about when the scaffolding fell.' He gazed up at the ruins of his room and shuddered. 'I see I would have slept all too well had I been lying in my bed when that happened.'

'I said it was all going ahead too quickly,' reiterated Langelee, snatching the cup from Michael before he could demand yet more wine. 'I know about buildings – the Archbishop of York likes to raise them when he can get the money – and I told Runham this was all moving forward far too fast.'

'I need a drink,' said Michael with a sigh, as though the two cups provided by Langelee had never existed. 'I cannot bear to watch my lovely College in such a state. Come on, Matt. The Brazen George awaits.'

'We cannot go to a tavern and leave the others to do all the work,' said Bartholomew, looking across to where students and Fellows alike still laboured over the fallen scaffolding.

'They are stopping,' said Michael, watching Blaston clap his hands and announce it was too late and too dark to manage anything more that night.

'Good,' said Langelee. 'I will arrange some refreshment for everyone in the hall – assuming Michaelhouse has bothered to invest in optional extras, like food and wine, of course. There is still some Widow's Wine left, but no one but William and I seem to like that.' He strode away, hailing the cooks as he went.

'Are you sure you are unharmed, Brother?' asked Suttone anxiously, looking Michael up and down. 'You are covered in dust.'

'It will brush off,' replied Michael. 'And I am perfectly unharmed, thank you.'

'Then I will go and ensure that Langelee does not turn his evening of refreshment into something that might be construed as a celebration of Runham's death,' said Suttone. 'The students have been itching to do exactly that all day, and such an occasion would do Michaelhouse's reputation no good at all.'

'Oh, Lord!' said Michael wearily. 'I had not thought of that.'

'I will enlist the help of Father William, if I can persuade him to leave his friary,' said Suttone with a somewhat wicked grin. 'He will not allow any unseemly debauchery.'

'He still has not returned?' asked Bartholomew.

Suttone shook his head. 'According to Paul, he remains afraid of being accused of Runham's murder. Still, perhaps the notion of students enjoying some refreshment without the benefit of his censuring eye will entice him out. I will send Deynman with a message urging him to come back.'

'Good idea,' said Michael.

Suttone looked concerned. 'But you should rest, Brother, to ensure you do not suffer another bout of your recent illness. Your room is ruined, but you are welcome to use mine.'

'You are most kind,' said Michael, touched. 'But the empty servants' quarters will serve me for tonight.' He watched Suttone hurry across the yard, calling for Deynman. 'He is a good man, Matt. I wish there were more like him in Michaelhouse.'

'Perhaps Paul will come back now that Runham is dead,' suggested Bartholomew. 'And at least Kenyngham will not leave for a while yet.'

'I do not like that Clippesby,' said Michael, turning to look at the Dominican, who seemed to be having a discussion with a bucket of mortar. 'I am not sure he is sane. With scholars, it is sometimes difficult to tell, since academic eccentricity is often very close to plain old lunacy. But I need time to think, away from this place. How do I look? Am I too dusty to be seen in public?'

'It is dark, Brother,' said Bartholomew. 'No one will notice.'

Michael brushed himself down. 'Lend me one of your cloaks – the good one, not that tatty thing with the moth-holes in it. And let us go forth to see what fare is on offer at the Brazen George tonight.'

As usual, the Brazen George offered a good many things that a man of Michael's ample girth would have been wise to avoid. There was chicken baked in goose fat, sweet pastries swimming in a sickly sauce and saffron bread served with plenty of butter. Ignoring Bartholomew's warning that such rich food would not be good for a man so soon out of his sickbed, Michael ordered it all, and settled down comfortably to enjoy it with his knife and horn spoon held like weapons and his face wearing a beam of pure contentment.

'All we need to make the evening complete are a couple of ladies to keep us company,' he said, smiling at Bartholomew, who was regarding the repast with the trepidation of a man too used to plain College food. 'Perhaps we could send for Matilde.'

'We are breaking the University's rules just by being in a tavern after dark,' Bartholomew pointed out. 'It would probably be prudent not to make matters worse by fraternising with prostitutes.'

'I am the Senior Proctor,' said Michael, taking a healthy mouthful of chicken. 'I can fraternise with whomever I like – on University business, of course.'

They were sitting in a small chamber at the back of the tavern, which the innkeeper reserved for people who did not want to drink – or be seen drinking – with the rabble. It was a pleasant room, with its own fire. Its walls were colourfully and tastefully decorated with paintings, and there were clean, sweet-smelling rushes on the floor. Michael and Bartholomew had used it many times, and the monk did sufficient business in the Brazen George to ensure that it was his any time he requested it.

'Well, Matt, that was an unpleasant accident,' said Michael, taking another large mouthful of chicken and following it with a huge slurp of wine. He began to choke.

'Eat slowly, Brother,' said Bartholomew automatically, slapping the fat monk on the back. 'If it was an accident. I am not so sure about that.'

'What?' gasped Michael, eyes watering. 'Of course it was an accident. You heard what Langelee said. We all knew that Runham was forcing the pace of the building work too hard, and that corners were being cut. It all boils down to cheap materials, careless work and bad luck.'

Bartholomew shook his head. 'Those two scholars I almost caught sneaking out of Michaelhouse just before the collapse might have been the same two we saw the night Runham was elected. Remember what we considered then? That the Widow's Wine may have been specially provided, so that those two could enter the College to do something while everyone was too intoxicated to notice?'

'But we did not know what that "something" could be,' Michael pointed out.

'That is irrelevant,' said Bartholomew. 'The point is that they could be the same pair as the ones I encountered tonight. I think it is too much of a coincidence that the scaffolding collapsed the instant they were making their way out of College.'

'Coincidences do occur, you know.'

'But if their intentions were innocent, why did they

run when I tried to speak to them?' asked Bartholomew. 'If they had nothing to hide, it would not have been necessary to make an escape.'

'It depends on who they were,' said Michael. 'I occasionally have meetings with people who would rather their identities were not made known to the world at large. Why do you think I am so efficient at solving crimes?'

'But you are a proctor,' said Bartholomew. 'People have good reason to be telling you secrets. None of the other Fellows should need to have furtive guests in their quarters. Perhaps it was Simeon and Osmun from Bene't that I saw; Langelee said they had been to visit him shortly before the building collapsed.'

'If they were visiting Langelee innocently – and the fact that he mentioned them to you suggests they were – they would have no reason to hide their identities from you as they walked out.' Michael had almost finished the chicken, and all that remained was a growing heap of gnawed bones. He turned his attention to the bread and pastries.

'I suppose so,' said Bartholomew. 'But I am still certain that it was no accident that the scaffolding fell.'

'If you are right, Matt, that means one of two things. Either someone – the scholars of Bene't, for example – wants the building work at Michaelhouse to suffer a serious setback for some reason. Or someone intended another person harm.'

'Who would induce that kind of dislike?' asked Bartholomew.

Michael chewed his bread thoughtfully. 'Well, since it was my room that was demolished, I think we must suppose that I was the intended victim.'

'You? But why?'

'I imagine because I have a fabulous reputation for solving murders, and someone is worried that I might uncover who did away with our much-beloved Master Runham.'

'A Michaelhouse scholar?' asked Bartholomew, after a moment. He closed his eyes. 'Not again, Brother! It is bad enough that someone murdered Runham, but that the killer is also prepared to strike at you so that his crime goes undetected is much worse – it is premeditated and deliberate.'

'Do not be so ready to jump to conclusions,' said Michael. 'Personally, I think you are wrong about the scaffolding. I think it was coincidence that it fell just as you were wrestling a couple of visitors to the ground, and I think it was chance that my room happened to be the one that was worst affected. But I do think that the two hooded men you attacked tonight were probably up to no good, and I suspect it was somehow connected to the other pair you challenged last week.'

'Something to do with Runham?'

'Possibly,' said Michael.

Bartholomew sighed. 'Another coincidence in all this, if I am right about the scaffolding and the whole thing was an attempt on your life, is that it is odd that the last time the mysterious pair were seen emerging from the College was the night you became ill.'

Michael raised sardonic eyebrows. 'But you said it was the insect bite that made me unwell. Are you now suggesting someone hired a bee to act as an agent to kill me? How was it paid? In honey?'

'I am merely mentioning that I think it is odd that those two appear both times your life has been in danger recently.'

Michael selected a pastry and deigned to humour him. 'So are you certain it was the bee sting that made me ill, and not something else – something slipped into my food or drink, perhaps?'

'No, the infection in your arm caused the problem. It . . .'

With sudden clarity, Bartholomew remembered the salve he had used to relieve the intense itching in Michael's arm – the salve that was missing from his bag by the time he needed it to heal the rat bite in the riverman's leg a couple of days later. Had someone tampered with it, replacing the healing balm with something sinister? Was that why Michael's wound had festered? It was too ludicrous to imagine. How could anyone know which salve Bartholomew would use on Michael? But the answer to that was clear: it was a standard cure and instructions for its use were written on the jar.

Bartholomew told Michael what he had reasoned, but the monk shook his head impatiently. 'No, Matt. You have let Runham's accusations about me being poisoned unsettle you. The fact is that you told me not to scratch that sting, and I did not listen. My resulting illness was my own fault – although I will never admit that to anyone else.'

He reached out and selected one of the sweet pastries, swallowing half of it in a single bite. Bartholomew was still uncertain. 'Then what happened to the salve afterwards? Who took it?'

'No one took it, Matt. You probably lost it – or Gray or Bulbeck borrowed it and forgot to replace it.' He shoved the second half of the cake in his mouth. 'This is good. You should try some.'

Absently, Bartholomew took a pastry and ate it, while he tried to think of a reason why two men might enter the College – at least twice now – and decline to allow their identities to be made known. Nothing came to mind, and he turned his thoughts to his conversation with Adela. He outlined what she had told him, adding that Matilde remained insistent there was some link between the gossiping Patrick and the equally loose-tongued Wymundham, while Michael ate the last of the food.

'That is very interesting, Matt. It was good of Adela to put self-preservation second to seeing justice done. Her information helps me a good deal.'

'It does?' asked Bartholomew, sipping the mulled ale that he had allowed to grow cold.

'It tells me that the Bene't scholars know more than they have revealed about Wymundham's death – it seems reasonable to assume that the leg was his – and it might even tell me who killed Brother Patrick. I feared that case might prove impossible to solve, but now I have a clue.'

'You think Heltisle and his colleagues killed Wymundham in Holy Trinity Church? And that Brother Patrick saw the murder, and that he was stabbed to ensure his silence?' asked Bartholomew, thinking Michael's deductions from Adela's revelations sounded just as far-fetched as his own musings about Michaelhouse's two intruders.

'That is about the size of it. It fits what we already know. Shortly after Raysoun's death, you saw Wymundham slip into Holy Trinity Church. You said he was moving furtively, as though he did not want to be seen. I suspect one of his colleagues had lured him to that meeting, perhaps claiming to be me wanting to know what Raysoun had whispered with his dying breath.'

'And then, when he arrived, he found a deputation from Bene't awaiting him, and they smothered him in the church?' asked Bartholomew uncertainly. 'I do not know, Brother. It was a weekday, and Holy Trinity stands on the Market Square. It is scarcely a secluded spot for a murder.'

'But Wymundham would not have gone to a secluded spot,' argued Michael. 'The man was not a fool, and he was already burdened with anxiety about the secrets he wanted to tell you, but did not. Holy Trinity would have been perfect – public enough to make him feel safe, but far enough from Bene't so that he would not associate a summons there with his murdered colleague.'

'But it was a poor choice as far as the killer was concerned,' Bartholomew pointed out. 'Both Brother Patrick and Adela probably saw what happened.'

'The door should have been barred,' agreed Michael. 'But I doubt there was time to arrange a murder too carefully. Raysoun was already dead, possibly stabbed then pushed, and Wymundham was on the verge of exposing his College's misdemeanours. You cannot expect any plan developed in so short a time to be perfect.'

'But then what happened?' asked Bartholomew. 'Wymundham was killed in the church, and then what? How did his body end up in Horwoode's garden?'

'Holy Trinity is not far from the King's Ditch,' said Michael. 'In fact, all that separates the two is a patch of scrub that would be easy to traverse with a small, light body like Wymundham's. I imagine it was then loaded on to a boat and dumped off at a conveniently isolated place.'

'Do you think the choice of Horwoode's garden was random, then?' asked Bartholomew.

Michael shrugged. 'I have no idea. It *is* a desolate spot – despite the fact that Horwoode said he likes to stroll there – and so would suit our killer's purpose very well. No murderer wants to travel far with the body of his victim in a boat.'

'But why kill Patrick and not Adela?' asked Bartholomew, still not understanding all the twists and turns. 'It seems to me that they saw the same thing.'

'Perhaps Patrick caught him actually suffocating Wymundham – heard gasps and saw someone holding a pillow,' Michael said. 'Adela saw nothing but a leg, and the scholars probably thought that she did not even see that. Besides, it would have been easy to murder Patrick. Friars are always killing each other, especially the Franciscans and Dominicans, and the unwitnessed death of yet another in the grounds of his own hostel would not raise – has not raised – too many eyebrows.'

'But the murder of a merchant's daughter would attract a lot more attention.'

'Quite. And anyway, Adela kept silent about what she had seen, so they probably assumed – wrongly as it happened – that she had witnessed nothing incriminating.'

'And it probably *was* Wymundham's body she glimpsed,' said Bartholomew. 'I never saw his legs, but he was a slim man with fair hair. The leg Adela says she spotted was thin and covered in goldish hairs.'

Michael raised his eyebrows. 'That is uncommonly observant of her.'

'She seems to like looking at legs,' said Bartholomew. 'A conversation with her seldom passes without a comment on some man's limbs.'

'Our path is clear,' said Michael, wiping his greasy fingers on the hem of Bartholomew's cloak. 'Tomorrow *I* will visit our friends in Bene't and see whether I can frighten them into telling me more about Wymundham's death. And perhaps I will also ask them if they have been creeping around Michaelhouse recently wearing hooded cloaks, just to please you. But there is something I want to do first.'

'What?' asked Bartholomew, picking up the shabbier of his two cloaks, and swinging it round his shoulders. Something dropped from it to the floor.

'An apple pie!' exclaimed Michael, pouncing on it.

'I bought it for you yesterday,' said Bartholomew, taking the broken pastry from him. 'But you will not be wanting it now that you have eaten. It will be stale, anyway.'

'Nonsense,' said Michael, taking it back and secreting it in his scrip for later. 'It was a very kind thought, and I would never offend you by declining such a gift. There will be too many people around tonight, after the collapse of that scaffolding, but tomorrow, after everyone has gone to bed, I would like you to come with me to Master Runham's room.'

'Why?' asked Bartholomew nervously.

'Because that is where he died, and that is where we will find any clues to help us discover who killed him. If the murderer left a single thread of evidence, you and I must find it.'

The window shutters were closed in Runham's room, and nothing had been damaged when the scaffolding had fallen the previous evening. The sill lay under a thick layer of dust, and there was a fine smattering of powder all across the room where it had billowed through the gaps in the wood, but apart from that, the room was exactly as it had been when Runham's body had been discovered.

Runham himself lay in a fine coffin in St Michael's Church, where students had been bribed, threatened and cajoled into taking turns to keep a vigil. He was due to be buried in three days, and his will had stipulated that the occasion should be a suitably grand one. When Kenyngham had read Runham's demands for his own requiem at dinner that evening, even he had been unable to silence the amused catcalls and derisive hoots of the students as the full glory of the ceremonies that were to take place were unveiled.

Michael had chuckled unpleasantly, remarking several times that Runham would go to the next world as he had lived in this one – full of sham grandeur and without a soul who genuinely liked him. Bartholomew was aston-ished that the dead Master had the money to pay for such an event, and could only suppose that handsome funerals and tombs were something for which his family had a penchant. He was relieved that he had not been given the responsibility for arranging matters, as he had with Wilson, but was dismayed to learn that Runham had selected himself a spot in the chancel of St Michael's Church where his own monstrous mausoleum would outshine even that of his cousin.

Teaching had finished early because of the workmen's noise, and Bartholomew had spent the rest of the day with various patients. He was even able to find a few moments to stop off at Stanmore's business premises in Milne Street and eat one of his sister's excellent cakes. Edith assured him that the hunt for a suitable wife was proceeding apace, and that he should keep the following Sunday free for socialising. She brushed aside his anxious objections, and merely informed him that it would be safer to leave Michaelhouse as soon as he could, given the number of murders that occurred in University circles.

On his way home he had met Matilde, who told him that the case against Robin of Grantchester had been dismissed, because it could not be proven that the surgeon had deliberately tried to kill the man whose leg he had amputated. Bartholomew was relieved, not liking the notion that every unsuccessful outcome should end in the courts. He walked back to Michaelhouse feeling more cheerful, particularly since he had noticed that Matilde wore a green ribbon in her hair.

He worked on his treatise until the daylight faded, then sat with the other Fellows in the conclave, enjoying the cosy warmth of the fire. Suttone had a copy of Homer's *Iliad*, which he read aloud to entertain the others, although the story about the Trojan horse sparked some telling opinions. Michael thought the disaster was the Trojans' own fault for not being properly suspicious of a gift from nowhere; Suttone considered the Greeks' trick unconscionable, and wondered how they ever assuaged their guilt; Langelee was unable to move past the question of how the Trojans managed to exit from the horse to mount a surprise attack when it would have taken them some time to descend the ladders; Clippesby suggested the Trojans should have sent someone to talk to the horse before allowing it in their city; Kenyngham was distressed by the notion of a massacre; and Bartholomew was concerned that the tale would give the gentle Gilbertine nightmares.

Eventually, as the embers in the fire died and the room began to chill, the other Fellows drifted away to their beds.

Michael and Bartholomew lingered in the conclave, preparing for their nocturnal foray to the murdered Runham's chamber. While they waited for the College to sleep, the monk described the visit he had made to Bene't College earlier that day. Fellows and students alike had claimed to know nothing about the death of Wymundham, even the foppish Simeon, who had been sufficiently concerned about the matter to invade Michael's sickroom the previous week. The Bene't men used the Duke of Lancaster's pronouncement that there had been nothing untoward in the two deaths to declare Michael's investigation closed. Knowing that to reveal what Adela had seen might put her in danger, Michael had been unable to confront them about the incident that took place in Holy Trinity, and so left Bene't none the wiser but very much angrier.

Meadowman, the beadle who had infiltrated the body of builders working on Bene't when Raysoun had died, also had nothing to report. None of the craftsmen or their apprentices seemed to know anything about the University deaths. Meadowman was heavy-eyed and weary after nights of carousing with his new-found friends, and the other beadles were in a similar state. Some had even gone so far as to ask to do something else, bored and frustrated with endless evenings in wood-smoke-filled taverns drinking cloudy ale that turned their stomachs.

When the College was still and silent, and the last of the students' candles had been doused, Michael led the way across the courtyard to the room in which Master Runham had been murdered. Not surprisingly, Kenyngham had been reluctant to move back into it, and had insisted on remaining in the chamber he shared with Clippesby until a permanent successor to Runham could be appointed.

As always, when Bartholomew entered the Master's quarters, he was reminded unpleasantly of Master Wilson's death in them, some four years previously. When Wilson had realised that he had been infected with the plague, he had spent his dying hours burning documents and scrolls. After his death, it had been discovered that his affairs were ruthlessly in order, which suggested to Bartholomew that Wilson had given a good deal more attention to his earthly life than he had spent preparing for the one to come. As Wilson had consigned certain parchments to the flames, he had knocked over a lamp and it had set his clothes alight. Bartholomew would never forget the deathbed scene that followed.

The Master's chamber was a large room by College standards. At one end was a bed piled with furs and blankets, and next to it a substantial chest contained Runham's impressive collection of robes, shoes and shirts. His cloaks and tabards hung on a row of hooks fastened to the wall above it. Under the window were a table and a chair, while the shelves to either side of them contained inks, pens, spare parchment and several blocks of a powerful-smelling soap that Bartholomew was certain Runham had never used. Nearby was the strongbox, its lid still dangling open, and the empty hutches.

'It was Clippesby who found Runham's corpse,' said Michael conversationally, setting a candle in a holder. 'His dismayed screeches woke the whole College.'

'What time?' asked Bartholomew.

'An hour or so before first light. Cynric arrived shortly after and decided you were probably at Trumpington, so rode off to fetch you. I miss that man, Matt. Is there any way we could persuade him to come back?'

'I think he is happier with Rachel than he ever was here. She does not ask him to go out at night chasing villains and scoundrels.'

'I thought he enjoyed that – a lot more than you do. Anyway, Clippesby woke us with his unholy racket, and we all arrived to see Runham just as you saw him later, with his great paunch facing the ceiling and his smug face blue and lifeless.'

Michael was not a man who had cause to comment on the great paunches of others, and Bartholomew smothered a smile. He looked around him, not sure what the monk hoped to achieve by rummaging through the Master's chamber when their colleagues were in bed.

'What was Clippesby doing here so early?' he asked, sitting on a bench near the hearth. It was a handsome piece of furniture, and Bartholomew recognised it as a gift from Kenyngham for the conclave. Yet again, he was astounded by Runham's selfish audacity.

'Clippesby said he and Runham usually met at dawn to discuss business,' said Michael. 'And I think that is true. Gray, Deynman and Suttone all saw Clippesby coming here on a number of occasions to plan their evil deeds for the forthcoming day. He was Runham's lickspittle.'

'To smother a man, the killer would need to come relatively close without alarming his victim,' said Bartholomew slowly. 'Runham would be unlikely to let a stranger that near.'

'So, you conclude Runham's killer was someone he knew?' asked Michael. 'That is not a great help, Matt. We know that – we have a splendid list of suspects, remember?'

'Smothering is an unusual way to kill,' Bartholomew went on. 'It requires premeditation: you need a convenient implement and you need to be prepared to hold your victim for several minutes until he dies. It is odd, do you not think, that both Runham and Wymundham died from smothering?'

'What are you saying?' asked Michael. 'That they were both killed by the same person?'

'It is possible. I have seldom come across cases of suffocation like this, and now there are two within a few days of each other.'

'But that would mean Runham's killer was one of the Bene't men,' objected Michael, 'since we already have evidence to suggest that a Bene't Fellow killed Wymundham. And I do not think so, Matt. It is just another of those coincidences that happen in real life, but that you are always trying to read something into.'

'I suppose you are right,' said Bartholomew reluctantly. 'But there is something else that has been nagging at the back of my mind – Justus.'

'Justus? Runham's book-bearer, who killed himself by shoving his head in a wineskin?'

'What if he did not suffocate in the wineskin? What if he were smothered, and the wineskin tied over his head later?'

'You did not say Justus had been smothered at the time. You said he had suffocated himself.'

'I made a series of assumptions. First, I assumed that because the wineskin was tied over Justus's head, that was how he died. Second, I assumed that he had tied it there himself. Third, I assumed he drank himself into a state of depression, and became suicidal.'

'Yes,' said Michael impatiently. 'All that sounds reasonable.'

'But the other servants said Justus was in an unusually good mood the night he died, because he had found some money on the High Street. That evening, of all evenings, he was not unhappy.'

'But he used that money to buy wine, Matt. Men often start drinking merrily enough, but then end weeping for their mothers. His mood earlier that day tells us nothing.'

'But I think he was suffocated,' pressed Bartholomew. 'And so were Runham and Wymundham.'

Michael sighed. 'Very well. Let us consider this rationally. You think Justus's death might be connected to Runham's – that perhaps Justus knew something about Runham's affairs that someone wanted kept quiet?'

'I do not know,' said Bartholomew. 'I am only saying it is possible that the instrument of Justus's death was not the wineskin, as I assumed, but a cushion. And if that is the case, then we have three deaths where the killer used the same, rather unusual, method: Justus, Wymundham and now Runham.'

'I am not sure about this, Matt,' warned Michael. 'Apart from the fact that all three died because they could not breathe, I do not see the connection.'

'Runham fought like the Devil before he died. Remember the torn fingernails? We should check your "splendid list of suspects" for scratches – and that includes the Bene't men.'

'I have already examined our own scholars, but have seen no inexplicable marks,' said Michael. 'I have earned myself a reputation as an ogler around the latrines and the lavatorium, eyeing up our colleagues as they wash themselves. And then I had a good look at the Bene't men when I went there today. None of them is marred by scratches. But I suspect that all my efforts have been for nothing anyway: sit at the table, and I will show you something.'

'Show me what?' asked Bartholomew nervously, not liking the gleam of intent in the monk's eyes.

'I have given Runham's death a good deal of thought, and I know how the murderer prevented him from screaming for help. Sit at the table, like Runham used to do when he counted his gold.'

Bartholomew sat, glancing uneasily over his shoulder as Michael moved about behind him.

'Do not cheat,' said Michael, taking up a cushion. 'You are Runham, engrossed in the business of transferring silver from the College hutches to your building chest, and I am a colleague – a man you know well and whom you have no cause to fear.'

'Runham was not stupid, Brother,' said Bartholomew, turning to face him. 'He knew he had alienated his colleagues, and I do not think it likely that he would have turned his back on the likes of William or Langelee. He knew they both have vile tempers.'

'But Runham did not anticipate that someone would murder him,' said Michael impatiently. 'If he had, he would have taken precautions: he would have hired a bodyguard or kept his door locked – which he did not.'

'All right,' Bartholomew sighed, turning around and placing both hands on the table. 'So, Runham is sitting like this when his killer comes in. Then what?'

'The killer makes gentle conversation,' said Michael. 'He moves around, looking at the plunder Runham has stolen from the College's common rooms for his own use, including Agatha's cushion. He picks it up, pretending to admire the embroidery, and then . . .'

With a single step, Michael bounded across the room and had the cushion slapped across the physician's face before he could utter a sound. Then he wrapped both arms around cushion and head together, holding them in a firm embrace. Startled, Bartholomew began to struggle, but found he was able to move very little, and the lower half of his body was trapped between the chair and the table. When the pressure of Michael's grip increased, Bartholomew felt a surge of panic. He reached backward with his hands but could not reach the monk's face; he could only claw ineffectually at the thick arms that held him.

Deprived of air, he felt his senses begin to reel. He struggled more violently, but the monk's grip was too secure to be shaken or prised away. He tried to call out, to tell Michael to stop, but he could not draw the air into his lungs and the only sound he made was a muffled gasp. He attempted to twist to one side, to break the grip, but Michael merely moved with him. When he leaned down, to jab an elbow or a hand into Michael's stomach or ribs to startle him into loosening his hold, he found the chair was in the way.

Just when he thought his lungs were about to explode and felt on the verge of fainting, the pressure was released, and Michael stood back. Bartholomew staggered out of the chair and backed quickly away from the monk, gasping for breath and leaning on the wall for support.

'Simple,' said Michael, raising his hands, palms up. 'That was how it was done. And afterwards, Runham was laid on the floor, exactly how we found him. Are you all right, Matt?'

The physician shook his head, eyeing Michael in disbelief. 'God's teeth, Brother! I thought we were on the same side. You nearly killed me!'

'I did not,' said Michael dismissively. 'I held you only

for a few moments. If I had let you loose too soon, I would not have proved to you that Runham's broken fingernails need not necessarily have resulted in his killer being scratched. You clawed at the table, the chair and at me, but I am not marked in the slightest.'

He raised the loose sleeves of his habit to reveal a pair of flabby white arms, one still bandaged from his encounter with the bee, but otherwise unscathed.

'You could just touch my arms and hands, but you could not reach my face,' Michael amplified. 'And you were in such an awkward position that you were unable to put any force into your attempts to harm me. Runham must have been killed in the way I have just demonstrated, otherwise it would mean him meekly lying on the floor, while allowing his murderer to place the cushion over his head.'

'Look under the table,' said Bartholomew, still breathless. 'See if you can tell whether Runham kicked it in his death throes.'

Michael knelt. 'Yes! Here! I should have thought of this sooner. There are a couple of sizeable dents and some scratches. Come and look.'

Bartholomew shook his head. 'I am never going to turn my back on you again. From now on, I will stay where I can see you.'

Michael made an impatient sound. 'I barely touched you. I did not squeeze nearly as hard as I could have done. Do not be so feeble, Matt!'

'Let me try it on you,' said Bartholomew, snatching up the cushion and advancing on the monk. Michael stood quickly and moved away.

'Why? So you can smother me to within an inch of my life and claim tit-for-tat? Really, Matt. I had not understood you to be a vindictive man.'

'Because I want to test what you just said,' replied

Bartholomew. 'You said you did not exert as much pressure as you could have done, and yet you still could have killed me. What I want to know is how strong do you have to be to smother someone like that?'

'Are you sure you know what you are doing?' asked Michael, regarding him doubtfully.

'I am a physician,' said Bartholomew. 'Of course I know what I am doing.'

He placed the cushion over the monk's face and wrapped his arms around Michael's head, just as the monk had done. Unlike Michael, however, he did not deprive his subject of air, and instead experimented with various different grips. He discovered that by pulling upward, he could make it even more difficult for his victim to struggle. He was just concluding his investigations by leaning forward, so that Michael was trapped between him and the desk, when the door opened.

'Matthew!' came the shocked, hushed tones of Father William. 'So it was *you* all along!'

With the door firmly closed against curious ears, and William ordered to keep his voice down on pain of death, the three Fellows stood in the centre of Master Runham's room and looked around them.

'I am sorry for accusing you of so vile a crime, Matthew,' said William, yet again. 'I really thought you were smothering Michael. It was clever of you to experiment like that. I wish I had thought to do it myself.'

'We need to go through everything in this room to see whether we can find any clue that will help us discover the identity of Runham's killer,' said Michael, trying to bring the friar's mind back to the task in hand. 'All of us are potential suspects, so our very lives may depend on being thorough – even though we are all innocent.'

'Why are you so sure of my innocence?' asked William

curiously. 'I am innocent, of course, but in this den of suspicion and intrigue, I am surprised you believe me. I was so afraid I would be blamed for Runham's murder that I have been loath to abandon the safety of the friary walls.'

'So, why choose now to leave?' asked Bartholomew.

'It is dark. And I came to look for clues that might help me prove it was not I who did the world this great favour. But I do not have to convince you, it seems.'

'Any man is capable of murder, and so my belief in your innocence does not stem from trust in your innate morality,' said Michael pompously. 'But although you are certainly strong enough to have overpowered Runham, you are not the kind of man to use smothering as a means to an end. Fists, certainly; a blunt instrument, yes; a dagger, very possibly. But I cannot see you slowly and deliberately squeezing the life out of anyone.'

'Then you know me less well than you think,' said William bluntly. 'I think I would have gained a great deal of pleasure from squeezing the life out of Runham.'

'You should learn to take a compliment, Father,' said Michael dryly. 'But, very well, if you must know the truth, several of your brethren told me that the snores emanating from your cell kept them awake half the night. They are prepared to swear that you are accounted for from sunset, when you attended compline, until the morning, when the news came that Runham was no more.'

'You asked my fellow friars about me?' asked William indignantly.

'Yes,' said Michael. 'But it worked to your advantage. You are virtually the only one of us with a sound alibi, and who definitely did not commit this crime.'

William puffed himself up. 'My money is on the culprit being that Dominican – Clippesby. I have never liked him. He is treacherous and duplicitous.'

'Let us not jump to conclusions before we have the evidence,' said Michael. 'But we should start if we do not want to be here all night. You take the table and the aumbry, William; Matt can search under the benches, rugs and chairs; and I will see what we have left in the chests.'

'Our poor hutches,' said William, shaking his head as he began to rifle through the contents of Runham's wall cupboard. 'How will the College survive with no loan chests?'

They were silent, each concentrating on his work. Bartholomew found a list of payments and dates hidden in the lining of a rug, and passed it to Michael, understanding nothing of the figures that were scrawled there, but suspecting they were significant. William discovered an hour candle that had fallen underneath the desk.

'Can I have this?' he asked, secreting it in his grimy habit. 'Runham will not be needing it again.'

'Wait,' said Bartholomew, reaching for it. 'Why did we not think of this before? Now we know when Runham was murdered – exactly!'

'The hour candle fell over during the struggle!' exclaimed Michael. 'So, when was he killed?'

'About eight o'clock,' said Bartholomew, studying the stump. 'That would be four hours or so after sunset, and about two hours after dinner.'

'Well, that excludes Kenyngham, then,' said Michael. 'And Suttone. Both of them were at compline at that time, and I know they lingered at the church afterwards. And it vindicates me, too, because the Chancellor was visiting me on University business from sunset until almost ten.'

'I have no idea where I was,' said Bartholomew gloomily. 'Somewhere on the Trumpington road, alone and in the dark.'

'I can vouch for Paul being with me at compline

between seven and nine, but we still have Clippesby unaccounted for,' said William with relish.

'And Langelee,' added Michael. 'All the workmen had gone by then – they do not work as late as eight, so that eliminates opportunistic robbery as a motive. And there are the servants – Cynric, Agatha, Walter and so on.'

'Not Cynric,' said Bartholomew immediately. 'Rachel Atkin will not let him out after dark. He would not have been at liberty at eight o'clock.'

'I will talk to your students – Gray and Deynman – who fell foul of Runham the afternoon he died, and see if they can tell me where they were at eight o'clock,' said William importantly. 'I have considerable experience of investigating murders, and now I have been absolved of suspicion, I will devote myself to the task in hand.'

'And I will have discreet words with Langelee and Clippesby, to see what they can tell me about eight o'clock on that fateful day,' said Michael.

'I will help,' offered William eagerly. 'I would love to interrogate that Clippesby.'

'I said discreet,' said Michael. 'If the killer is a scholar, then he is not going to be stupid – unless it is Langelee – and I do not want to frighten him into caution. I want him to be relaxed and to make a fatal slip.'

They were silent again, completing their methodical search of Runham's room. The only sounds were occasional footsteps in the courtyard, and the increasingly frequent exclamations of understanding and indignation as Michael came to grips with the documents in Runham's chests.

'This is really outrageous,' he said, waving the piece of parchment Bartholomew had discovered under the rug. 'I am horrified!'

'What is it?' asked William, crawling on his hands and knees to inspect the area behind the table.

'It is a list showing how Runham raised the money for his new building work,' said Michael. 'He estimated that he would need ninety pounds for raising a new court and for refacing the north wing, using the cheapest materials available. He raised thirty pounds in donations, including five marks from your brother-in-law, Matt. That was generous.'

'I know,' said Bartholomew. 'But he regrets parting with it.'

'He is a true merchant,' said Michael. 'But despite his best efforts, Runham was still sixty pounds short. He arranged to borrow thirty pounds from the guilds of Corpus Christi and St Mary – to be repaid with interest within the year. God's blood! Thirty pounds plus interest! That is going to be a millstone around our necks.'

'If he had thirty from donations and thirty from loans, where did he find the remaining twenty?' asked William, proving that he had not paid attention during his arithmetic lessons.

'It seems he raided the College hutches,' said Michael. 'It is all written down here. He took all the available money – which amounted to a total of ten pounds and two shillings – and he sold unredeemed pledges worth another three pounds and eight shillings. Foolish man – he sold that Aristotle of Deynman's for two shillings, and it was worth at least twice that.'

'So that explains why he went about dismissing his Fellows,' said William. 'He did not want us to notice that he was raiding the hutches.'

'You are right,' said Michael. 'He had rid himself of you, Paul, Kenyngham and Langelee, and was working on Matt. And he was also interfering with the cooks, so that I would leave, too. Thus he would have disposed of anyone who knew how much was in the hutches.

With us gone, the hutch money was his to use as he pleased.'

'And he sent down Gray and Deynman,' added Bartholomew. 'They regularly used the hutches when they were short of money – far more frequently than any of the other students – and so would know what was in them.'

'Of course,' said Michael. 'I begin to understand. Runham was not indulging himself in a series of personal vendettas, but had a carefully formulated plan to make Michaelhouse's money disappear with no questions asked.'

'But even with the loans, the funds from the merchants and the contents of the hutches, Runham was still short of sixteen pounds and ten shillings to make up his ninety,' said Bartholomew.

'I know,' said Michael, frustrated. 'He has been selling something, but this list does not specify what. He sold five items for which he received about ten pounds in total. I imagine the rest came from the fact that he did not pay the grocer and that he saved money on the choir's bread and ale allowance.'

'And by dismissing the servants,' said Bartholomew. 'So, how much of this ninety pounds do we have left? How much of it was stolen?'

'We still have about half of it,' said Michael promptly. 'I counted it all with Kenyngham when we found Runham dead. Because of the piecemeal way in which Runham raised his funds, it came in all sorts of ways – gold and silver coins, jewels valued at specific amounts, promissory notes. A lot of it would have been too heavy to carry unnoticed from the College, while the promissory notes would obviously be worthless to a thief. Oswald Stanmore is not going to pay a thief five marks for presenting this piece of paper to him.'

'But someone has the other half of our ninety pounds even as we speak,' said William angrily. 'We must search the College immediately, and see who has his room stuffed with stolen money.'

'Already done,' said Michael. 'Kenyngham and Suttone undertook that unpleasant task, and found nothing. I told them to pretend to be looking for a missing book. If the builders discover that we do not have the cash to pay them, they might riot.'

'But they will have to know at some point,' said Bartholomew. 'We should tell them now, pay them for the work they have already done, and send them all back to Bene't.'

'Never,' declared William vehemently. 'It would not surprise me to learn that Bene't stole our money just to put us in a compromising position.'

'Killing a Master just to embarrass another College is a little extreme, Father,' said Bartholomew. 'Even for Bene't.'

'I disagree,' said William. 'The Bene't men were furious that Runham poached the workmen. I would not put it past them to have stolen the money, just to spite us.'

'We seem to be talking about two different things here,' said Bartholomew wearily. 'On the one hand, we have the theft of money, and on the other we have the murder of Runham. I was assuming they were committed at the same time by the same person or people. Did the killer come to Runham's room to kill him or to take the money? We have already decided Runham knew his killer. Did he know the Bene't scholars?'

'He did,' said William. 'I saw Langelee introducing them a few weeks ago. Langelee likes to latch on to Simekyn Simeon of Bene't, because Simeon knows the Duke of Lancaster. I nonchalantly passed by as Langelee presented Runham to Simeon, but Langelee did not deign to introduce *me* to his fine friends – a mere friar is not important enough, I suppose.'

The possibility that Langelee did not want to inflict the 'mere friar's' belligerent fanaticism on his fine friends had not occurred to William. Looking at the Franciscan's filthy habit and hair so dirty it stood up in a grimy halo around his tonsure, Bartholomew was not so sure he would leap at the opportunity to present such an unsavoury specimen to his own acquaintances, either.

'Well, we need to keep an open mind about Runham's death,' said Michael ambiguously. 'But, since this missing money is not in the College, I think we should assume that it has gone for good.'

'In that case, we *must* tell the craftsmen tomorrow that we cannot pay them,' said Bartholomew. 'You say we have about half of the ninety pounds left, which is not enough to complete the buildings. We will pay them what we owe and that will be that.'

'But of the forty-five pounds remaining, thirty has been loaned from the two guilds and is not ours anyway,' said Michael gloomily. 'And if we do not complete the buildings, we will need to repay the donations that Runham collected.'

'Why?' demanded Father William. 'Those people gave their money to Michaelhouse. The thirty pounds of donations is ours now.'

'Hardly,' said Michael. 'It is not ethical to raise money for a new courtyard, and then decide not to build it and keep the money instead. I think lawyers would be after us for breaching a contract if we tried that – and they would be quite right to do so. But if we repay the loans *and* the donations, it means that we are fifteen pounds in debt – with no workmen's wages paid – not forty-five pounds in credit.'

'Damn that Runham!' exclaimed William, striding back and forth furiously. 'He has left us in a fearful mess.'

'Yes, fancy him allowing himself to be murdered just when we need him,' said Michael.

'I still do not understand how he thought he could manage this,' said Bartholomew, rubbing a hand through his hair. 'Had he lived to see his empire completed, he would have had massive debts. How could he have hoped not to have creditors knocking at our gates at all hours? How did he imagine Michaelhouse could raise a sum like thirty pounds to pay back these guilds? It is a fortune!'

'I have no idea,' said Michael, frowning as he bent over the documents again. 'But I do not like the sound of these mysterious five items that brought Runham ten pounds. Since the buyers of the other items in the hutches paid him a mere fraction of what the goods were worth, I have a feeling Runham sold something quite valuable.'

'Such as what?' asked Bartholomew. 'I did not know Michaelhouse had anything valuable.'

'Whatever it was, it is better gone,' said William sanctimoniously. 'Riches and worldly goods encourage avarice and envy. I want none of them in Michaelhouse.'

'I hope he did not sell the church silver,' said Bartholomew.

'The church silver?' boomed William, outraged. 'But those chalices left to us by our founder are generally regarded to be the finest this side of Ely! They are priceless!'

'They are only worldly goods, Father,' pointed out Michael innocently. 'But I think you are right, Matt. The church silver is usually kept in the Stanton Chest, and that is empty, like the others.'

'Our silver chalices!' cried William in abject dismay. 'All gone, just so that Runham could raise some horrible cheap building to glorify himself!'

'Hush, William,' said Bartholomew urgently. 'You will have the whole College awake.'

'Even so, the Stanton silver was not worth ten pounds,' said Michael. 'It might account for one of these "items" but not all five. Four of them have the initials TW next to them.'

'Thomas Wilson,' said Bartholomew immediately. 'Runham's equally unscrupulous cousin. Perhaps it was something of Wilson's that Runham sold – something that belonged to him, and not to Michaelhouse at all.'

'Perhaps,' said Michael worriedly. 'But I think you are being far too charitable. I think Runham sold something he had no business to sell. And I also think that when we discover what it was, Michaelhouse will find itself in a lot of trouble – and us with it.'

There was little more Bartholomew, Michael and William could do that night, so they put Runham's room back the way they had found it and went to bed. Michael's chamber was still uninhabitable, and Bartholomew was not certain whether his own quarters, directly underneath Michael's, were safe, so they used the tiny, closet-like space in the servants' quarters that Cynric had shared with Walter the porter. William, secure in the knowledge that his innocence of the murder of Runham had been proved beyond the shadow of a doubt, made a triumphant return to the room he shared with three student Franciscans, and his stentorian tones condemning Runham's wicked life and his killer in equal measure could be heard all over the College.

Michael chuckled softly in the darkness. 'I do like William. He is an old bigot and a fanatic, and he has a deep distrust of anything his narrow mind cannot grasp, but he is usually honest, always predictable and entirely without guile.'

'Guilelessness is a rare quality in this place,' said Bartholomew, trying to find a comfortable position on the thin straw mattress. It was lumpy, stank of urine, and the thriving community of insects that inhabited it caused it to rustle and crackle of its own accord. After the third time his drowsing was rudely interrupted by the painful nip of invisible jaws, Bartholomew kicked it away in disgust, rolled himself up in a blanket, and slept on the floor.

He was awoken what felt like moments later by the tolling of a bell. It sounded different than it did in his own room, and he sat up in confusion, not knowing where he was. Michael was at the window, throwing open the shutters to let in the dim light of early morning.

'You are late,' he said. 'It is Tuesday and your turn to help with the mass.'

Bartholomew struggled to his feet, feeling stiff, cold and tired. Michael picked strands of straw from his hair, while Bartholomew tugged on his boots, grabbed his cloak and ran across the yard as he was – unwashed, unshaven and still rubbing the sleep from his eyes. He raced up the lane to the church, cloak flying behind him, and shot across the grassy graveyard to the small porch in the north wall. From inside, he could hear the thundering tones of Father William praying, sounding more as though he were giving God an ultimatum than offering penitent supplications.

Bartholomew was fumbling with the latch on the door when he was aware of a presence behind him. Before he could turn, something was thrown over his head and he found his arms pinioned to his sides. He felt a heavy tug at the back of his neck, and then he was pushed forward – not roughly, but enough to make him stagger into the wall, reaching out blindly with his hands to steady himself.

Alarmed, he struggled free of the sacking that covered his head and looked around, anticipating a mob of townspeople ready to lynch a lone Michaelhouse scholar for its treatment of the choir, or because news had leaked out that the workmen would not be paid. But there was no one in the churchyard except him. Heart thumping, he walked the few steps back to the High Street, looking up and down it to see if he could spot his attacker, but it was deserted, too. It was not a market day, and no carts or traders crammed the roads on their way to the Square. The only person he could see was Bosel the beggar, who often worked in the High Street and sat hunched in the lee of a buttress, out of the wind.

'Bosel!' he called. 'Did someone just come running past?'

Bosel gave a crafty grin and held out his only hand. 'Maybe.'

'I do not have any money,' said Bartholomew, who had left his purse behind in his haste to arrive at the church.

'Then you will not have the answer to your question,' said Bosel, shrugging.

'Please,' said Bartholomew, feeling his scanty patience begin to evaporate. 'It is important.'

'Oh, it is always important,' sneered Bosel. 'Everything is important these days – except the likes of me, left to starve in the gutter after I served the King so loyally in his wars in France. I lose my arm defending England from the French devils, and the only reward I get is kicks and curses and wealthy people like you pretending to have no money.'

'You lost your hand for stealing, not fighting in France,' retorted Bartholomew. 'For breaking into the Guildhall of St Mary and relieving them of their silver, if I recall correctly. Now, will you tell me or not?'

'I will tell you for a penny,' said Bosel stubbornly. 'Give.'

'I do not *have* a penny,' said Bartholomew. 'But you can have breakfast at Michaelhouse after the mass.'

Bosel tipped his head back and regarded Bartholomew down his long, filthy nose, as if calculating the chances of the physician cheating him. 'All right, then.'

'Well? Did someone run from the churchyard just now?'

'No,' said Bosel.

Bartholomew gazed at him. 'Is that it?'

'That is the truth,' said Bosel. 'I will lie for you, to make a more interesting story, if you like. But the truth is that no one came from the churchyard except you.'

Bartholomew slumped in defeat. Because of Bosel's negotiations for payment, it was too late to give chase anyway.

'I saw you run in and then run out moments later,' Bosel clarified. 'And Father William has been yelling his head off inside the church since before first light. But I did hear someone moving about in the churchyard – other than you, that is.'

'Who?' asked Bartholomew.

Bosel made an impatient sound. 'I do not know! I did not see the person, I only heard him. And the reason I did not see him come from the churchyard was because I heard him scramble over the wall at the back and head off down those alleys instead. You will never catch him now. Did he rob you of your purse, then? Is that why you cannot give me a penny?'

'No,' said Bartholomew shortly. 'He just gave me a nasty fright.'

'I will see you after mass, then,' called Bosel, as he left.

Still holding the sacking that had been tossed over his

head, Bartholomew opened the door to the church and walked inside. William had already laid out the sacred vessels, lit the candles and opened the great bible to the correct reading of the day. Bartholomew was suddenly horribly reminded of the week before, when Runham had come to the church to do the physician's duties and fine him for being late.

'Well, I do not have a shilling to pay any fine,' he said irritably to William, as he walked towards the altar. 'I did not even have a penny to give to Bosel.'

'Do you want to borrow one?' asked William, puzzled by the hostile greeting. He rummaged in his scrip. 'I have a couple in here somewhere that I can lend you. As a friar, I have little need for worldly wealth. When can you pay me back?'

Bartholomew tossed the sacking on to a bench, thinking that Bosel had probably been right, and that the attack had been an attempt by a thief to make off with the heavy purses all scholars were thought to possess. It had been a perfect opportunity: Bartholomew had been alone and the churchyard was free of possible witnesses. The only thing wrong with the plan was that they had picked a scholar who had forgotten his purse, and there would have been very little in it anyway.

As the sacking hit the wooden bench, there was a heavy thump. Bartholomew gave it an angry glare, recalling that something had tugged at the back of his neck – probably a weighted rope that would hold the sacking in place long enough to allow the robber to make his escape. The physician had been lucky. In the desperate days following the plague, when food was scarce and people starved in the streets, many hungry people considered a knife under the ribs the best way to rob a victim and leave no witnesses to identify them later.

'Do not leave those rags there,' said William peevishly.

'I came here early this morning to give the church a good clean, and I do not want bits of sacking lying all over the place.'

'It looks nice,' said Bartholomew, glancing around him and noticing that the floor had been swept, the spilled wax from the candles scraped away and the holders polished, and the desiccated flies and spiders brushed from the windowsills.

William smiled, pleased by the compliment. The complacent grin faded when his gaze came to rest on the shrouded corpse that reclined near Wilson's glittering tomb. 'I only wish I could have swept that rubbish from our holy church, too.'

'That is not a very friarly attitude,' said Bartholomew. 'But did you hear that Master Kenyngham thinks we should not have a second grisly tomb in our chancel, as Runham stipulated in his will? He says a tomb like the one Runham wants will not leave enough space for us to pray, and instead he proposes to place Runham in Wilson's tomb – on top of his cousin.'

William chuckled nastily. 'I have heard that Wilson did not like Runham at all, so they will make uneasy bedfellows. Or should I say grave-fellows? That tomb is hideous – it is only right that Runham should spend eternity in the thing.'

'The requiem is to be on Thursday,' said Bartholomew. 'At dawn.'

'I hope you will not be assisting the celebrant,' said William. 'You will be late, and Runham will spend more time above ground than is his right.'

'I am sorry about that,' said Bartholomew. 'It was the combination of our activities in Runham's chambers and sleeping on the floor in Cynric's old room.'

William gave a reluctant smile. 'Well, I guessed you would be late this morning anyway, because Walter took his cockerel with him when he was dismissed.'

'That thing is more unreliable than I am. It is just as likely to oversleep as I am.'

'And even more likely to crow half the night just for the fun of it,' agreed William. 'I am surprised it has not ended up in the pot before now. But I have done your chores for you already. All you need to do, Matthew, is kneel with me and pray that we catch the killer of Runham without too much inconvenience to the College. But first, you can fold up that sacking that is cluttering my clean church. What is it anyway? Where did it come from?'

Bartholomew told him what had happened, and then spent some time persuading the friar that there was no point in waking every household in the wretched runnels and alleyways behind the church until a culprit confessed to his ignoble act.

'It is good-quality stuff,' said William, reaching out a hand to touch the cloth. 'That poor robber did worse than leave empty-handed; he abandoned a decent piece of sacking. It would make a nice short cloak, Matthew – the kind of cloak a poor Franciscan friar might wear in the summer months to ward off evening chills.'

'Would you like it?'

'Me?' asked William, as though the notion had never crossed his mind. 'What a kind thought! I will ask Agatha to sew me . . .' He faltered. Agatha had gone from Michaelhouse. 'Well, it will make a good cloak anyway.'

He shook the material out and something fell to the floor – a rough, shapeless bundle tied with the loop of rope that had been dropped over Bartholomew's head. Bartholomew leaned down to retrieve it and was startled to hear the clink of metal. Curious, he untied the thin rope that held the neck of the bag and gazed in surprise at the coins that gleamed inside.

William snatched the bundle from him and strode

across to Wilson's tomb, where the small altar provided a flat surface. He upended the bag, and he and Bartholomew gaped in astonishment at the heap of gold that glittered on the white cloth.

CHAPTER 10

'TWELVE POUNDS, TWO SHILLINGS AND FOURPENCE,' said Michael, sitting back at last, the coins set in neat piles in front of him. 'And it is definitely part of the money stolen from Michaelhouse, because I was very familiar with the coins in the Illegh Hutch – I was its manager – and I recognise the distinctive way that several of the pieces have been clipped.'

The Fellows – Michael, Bartholomew, William, Kenyngham, Langelee, Clippesby and Suttone – were in the conclave, sitting in the thin winter sun that streamed in through the glass windows. Ignoring some of his colleagues' anxieties that belts would need to be tightened and economies made if Michaelhouse wanted to repay its debts, Kenyngham had ordered that fires must continue to be lit in the hall and conclave, and had given the cooks leave to buy their regular supplies. Bartholomew agreed wholeheartedly, thinking that a cold College with no food was not going to present itself as something worth fighting for. So, a small fire flickered gaily in the conclave, while the furniture, rugs and cushions pillaged by Runham for his personal use were back in their rightful places.

'And someone just gave this to you?' asked Clippesby again, disbelief etched into every line of his face. 'Someone handed it over, just like that?'

'Basically,' said Bartholomew.

Clippesby continued to regard Bartholomew with such rank suspicion that the physician began to wonder whether the man considered him responsible for the theft from

Runham's room. Bartholomew thought Clippesby himself seemed ill at ease and anxious that morning: his hair stood up in peculiar clumps all over his head, as though he had been tearing at it, and his wild eyes were redrimmed and more glassy than usual. Bartholomew could not decide whether the Dominican's odd appearance was the result of grief over Runham, guilt because he was the murderer, or merely the incipient madness that evidently clawed at the edges of his consciousness.

'Recovering this money is very fortunate,' said Langelee cheerfully. 'Perhaps we should send Bartholomew to mass every morning, to see how much more we can retrieve.'

'I do not like it,' said Kenyngham. 'I do not like the notion that the killer of poor Master Runham approached Matthew so brazenly and handed him this gold.'

'How do you know it was the killer?' asked Langelee, taking a gulp from a goblet of wine he had somehow contrived to have with him. He did not sound unduly concerned that a murderer was at large, no doubt because he was confident he could best any would-be attacker, unlike his weaker and less able colleagues.

'Because it is obvious that whoever stole the money also murdered Runham,' said William, regarding the philosopher and his wine with a glower that was partly disapproval and partly envy.

'It is not obvious at all,' said Suttone with quiet reason. 'It is likely, but it is also possible that someone smothered Runham and fled, and then a second person took the gold when he saw it had been left unguarded.'

William said nothing, but stared ahead of him with the stony expression on his face that he always wore when he knew someone else was right and he was not prepared to admit it.

Kenyngham sighed. 'This is all very distasteful, but we must review where we were precisely at eight o'clock on

Friday night. William and Paul were at compline at the Franciscan Friary, while Master Suttone and I were doing the same at St Michael's Church.'

'I was with the Chancellor,' said Michael. 'Which leaves only Matt, Langelee and Clippesby.'

'I was at Trumpington,' said Bartholomew. 'I went to visit my sister.'

'But it was raining on Friday,' pounced Langelee. 'Why did you walk so far in the wet?'

'The guards on the town gate confirm that Matt left around sunset and that he did not return until the following day,' said Michael. 'He was not in Cambridge when Runham was murdered.'

Bartholomew gazed at him uncertainly, fairly sure that the guards had not observed him leaving – their attention had been on a family of tinkers who had been trying to enter the city. But Michael spoke with such authority that no one asked why he had not mentioned such an important fact before.

'What about you, Ralph?' asked Kenyngham of Langelee. 'Tell us again what happened to you that night.'

'I walked,' said Langelee with a careless shrug. 'I went to the wharves, where I stood on Dame Nichol's Hythe for a long time and watched the river flow past.'

'In the rain?' asked Michael, using the same point that Langelee had raised against Bartholomew.

'I was in the watchman's shelter,' said Langelee. 'He was not there because there were no barges to guard that night. And when I grew restless, I went into the town.' He glared defiantly at William. 'I visited a whore.'

'Which one?' asked Michael before William could respond. 'And what time?'

'I have no idea of the time,' said Langelee. 'But the whore's name was Yolande de Blaston.'

'Yolande de Blaston?' echoed Kenyngham, deeply

shocked. 'But she is the wife of one of the carpenters! Are you saying that you compounded the sin of lust with that of adultery?'

'I am one of her regulars,' said Langelee, in the tone of a man who did not know what the fuss was about. 'And Blaston is more than happy to see her earnings support their ever growing brood. They have at least nine children.'

'You seduced the mother of nine children?' whispered Kenyngham, his faced flushed with dismay. He crossed himself vigorously, clasped his hands, and began to pray.

'I hate it when he does that,' muttered Langelee, finally discomfited by Kenyngham's horror. 'Yolande is always more than happy with what I pay her and, being a prostitute, she is fair game for a lonely man. But Kenyngham always makes me feel as though I have done something sordid and dirty.'

'Perhaps he is right,' boomed William. 'And what do you mean by "always"? Is this kind of thing a regular occurrence?'

'What time did you leave Yolande?' asked Michael quickly. 'Was it later than midnight?'

'We fell asleep,' said Langelee. 'I was tired – drained by my unpleasant confrontation with Runham – and we both slept until dawn, after we had—'

'And you, Clippesby?' asked Michael hurriedly, seeing Kenyngham's eyes snap open in alarm at the prospect of more lustful revelations. 'Tell us what you did.'

'I went to vespers,' said Clippesby. 'That was around sunset. Then I wandered around the Market Square, watching the traders pack away their goods.'

'So that is what Dominicans do for a good time, is it?' asked William, coolly judgemental. 'They watch merchants pore over their worldly goods and their filthy gold.'

'And then?' asked Michael, ignoring William.

'And then I heard the bell ring for compline, but I did not feel like attending another office.'

'You "did not feel like" worshipping God?' exploded William in outrage.

Clippesby fixed him with a glower of his own, and the full brunt of a gaze from his mad eyes was sufficient to silence the Franciscan. 'No, I did not. I lingered near the Market Square, watching the mystery plays by candlelight outside St Mary's Guildhall. I was there for hours, and I do not think I was in the College before nine. So, it could not have been me who killed Master Runham,' he concluded triumphantly.

'Which mystery play did you see?' asked Michael.

Clippesby shrugged. 'I do not recall.'

'Did you speak to anyone there who might be able to corroborate your story?'

Clippesby thought for a moment and then shook his head. 'Not that I remember.'

'No one?' pressed Michael.

Clippesby frowned. 'I spoke to a woman – that merchant's daughter who looks like a horse. She was there, I think.'

'This is taking us nowhere,' said Kenyngham, rising from his seat near the fire. 'All you are doing is raising accusations against your fellow scholars – accusations that are based on suspicion and assumptions. This meeting is closed. I will take the money that God has seen fit to restore to us, and put it in a secure place. The rest of you should go to the church and pray for forgiveness for harbouring such uncharitable thoughts against each other.'

The Fellows began to drift out of the conclave to the yard below. As he returned from his room with a bible, and prepared to inflict himself on the students who had gathered in the hall, William announced in a loud, hoarse whisper to Michael that he would enquire after Gray and Deynman's whereabouts on the night of Runham's murder.

'Is that wise?' asked Suttone doubtfully, watching the Franciscan stride purposefully towards the hall, scattering students reckless enough to be in his path. 'Only the good Father is not very subtle, and Gray seems a clever sort of lad. I do not know that William has the necessary skills for cunning interrogation.'

'Gray and Deynman could not have killed Runham,' said Bartholomew. 'They were up all night scribing a copy of *Corpus Juris Civilis* for Runham, and the fifteen students who were helping them are prepared to vouch for their whereabouts the whole time.'

'I think I had better accompany William,' said Suttone, clearly believing that innocence or guilt had nothing to do with the ethics of allowing the Franciscan fanatic loose on the students.

He hurried away, and Michael took Bartholomew's arm to lead him across the yard towards the gate. 'Deynman would have let something slip by now, had he had anything to do with the crime. He does not have the guile to keep his guilt hidden.'

'That is certainly true,' said Bartholomew. 'Tell me, Brother, did the guards really see me leave the town the night Runham was killed?'

Michael grinned. 'Of course not. They are so notoriously unobservant that I did not even bother to ask. But we know you are not the killer, and I did not want to waste time by having the others muse that most innocent men do not walk along outlaw-infested highways on dark, rainy nights and then sit thinking in graveyards until they rouse their sister's households at the witching hour.'

Bartholomew glanced up at the hall, where William

could be heard shouting for Gray and Deynman. 'I do not like the thought of letting him question my students. He will have some of the younger ones confessing to all sorts of things they did not do.'

'Questioning them will keep him busy today,' said Michael, opening the gate and ushering Bartholomew into the lane. 'And better busy than trying to "help" by launching some enquiry of his own that may damage our chances of catching the killer. Suttone is there, anyway. He will not let William harm anyone.'

'True. If everyone were as rational and compassionate as Suttone, Michaelhouse would be a much nicer place to live in.'

'But also a much more dull one,' said Michael, pulling on Bartholomew's arm. 'Being Master of the College of saintly friars will be no fun for me at all.'

'You intend to stand, then, when Kenyngham resigns again?'

'Of course,' replied Michael, opening the gate. 'As I am sure you know I am the best Michaelhouse has to offer. It would be remiss of me not to do my moral duty.'

'Where are we going?' asked Bartholomew, not liking the way he was being steered in the direction Michael wanted him to go.

'To catch our killer,' said Michael cheerfully. 'And we will not do it by lurking in Michaelhouse all day. We have people to see.'

The first person on Michael's list was Cynric, dismissed so callously from Michaelhouse after many years of faithful service. While Bartholomew knew the Welshman well enough to be sure he would not stoop to smothering Runham, there was no denying that he had the skills to enter the College undetected, commit the crime and leave again with no one the wiser, not to mention the fact that his life as a soldier – before he had become Bartholomew's book-bearer – meant he had killed more men than the physician liked to contemplate.

Cynric was just returning from the market, arm in arm with his new wife Rachel. He beamed with pleasure when he saw Bartholomew, although Rachel did not seem quite so delighted.

'Have you come to ask him to help you tackle all these University deaths?' she demanded immediately. 'Because if so, I would rather you invited someone else. I do not want my husband chasing killers on your behalf.'

Cynric looked disappointed. 'But they need me—'

'No,' said Rachel firmly. 'You are too old for the fighting and subterfuge Doctor Bartholomew likes. He is much younger than you, and he has no wife at home, grieving and worrying.'

'I do not like fighting and subterfuge,' objected Bartholomew. 'Quite the contrary; I would far rather live a quiet and uneventful life.'

'Then I hope you have not come to accuse my Cynric of Runham's murder,' said Rachel bluntly, her hand tightening possessively on her husband's arm. 'If so, you are wasting your time. Cynric has finished with all that creeping around in the dark; he stays in with me at nights now, by the fire.'

'We do not know that anyone killed Runham,' said Michael smoothly.

Cynric regarded the monk with patent disbelief. 'He just had a fatal seizure, then, did he?' he asked with a knowing wink.

Michael's lips compressed in a tight line, displeased that people had seen through the ambiguous story he had instructed Kenyngham to tell the students.

'Which of the Fellows did it?' asked Rachel baldly. 'Langelee seems a violent kind of man, while Suttone has a history of theft, and that Kenyngham seems too saintly to be true.'

'It might not have been a Fellow,' temporised Michael.

Rachel glared. 'I hope you are not implying that it was one of the servants.'

'They would never accuse *me* of killing Runham,' said Cynric, patting her arm comfortably. 'Mind you, I have to say that the old devil deserved what was coming to him.'

'So, what did you want, if not to ask for Cynric's help?' asked Rachel.

'Why should we want anything?' asked Michael glibly, conveniently forgetting that he had sought Cynric out with the express purpose of learning whether he had an alibi for the night of Runham's death. 'As a matter of fact, we came to give, not take. We thought you might like this, to adorn the new room Oswald Stanmore says he has given you.'

He rummaged in his scrip and produced a tiny crystal bowl of the kind that would hold lavender to scent a room. It was a pretty thing, intricately carved so that it glittered like diamonds.

'It is lovely,' said Rachel, taking it and inspecting it with pleasure. 'So delicate and fine.'

'You are welcome,' said Michael. 'And now we must be on our way, if you will excuse us.'

Leaving Cynric and Rachel admiring their new possession, Michael led the way up the High Street towards Bene't, deciding that another proctorial visit to the scholars who had probably murdered Wymundham in Holy Trinity Church and then dumped the body in Mayor Horwoode's garden would not go amiss. And this time, he also intended to ask where they had been at eight o'clock on Friday evening.

'That little bowl belonged to Runham,' said Bartholomew. 'I saw it in his room when we were searching it.'

'Actually, it was mine,' said Michael. 'Or at least, it had been. I mislaid it some years ago, and had given up all hope of seeing it again.'

'If you have not seen it for years, then it may not have been yours at all,' reasoned Bartholomew. 'It might be another that looks similar. I do not think it is wise to remove Runham's possessions without the permission of his executors. You might find yourself accused of stealing the College's lost gold – or even of killing Runham for it.'

'That was my bowl,' said Michael firmly. 'My grand-mother gave it to me, and she engraved a message on the bottom. That message was still there. To be honest, I always suspected Wilson of stealing it from me during the Death – I noticed his covetous eyes on it several times – but then he died, and there was no way to confront him about it.'

'Wilson stole from you?' asked Bartholomew, shocked. 'But he was the Master of our College.'

'So was Runham,' said Michael, 'and it did not make him a saint. Wilson stole my bowl and Runham must have inherited it from him. I was quite startled last night to see it boldly displayed on the windowsill, as if Runham had a legal right to it.'

'If he inherited it, he probably thought he did.'

'What he thought does not matter to me. The bowl was mine, and I do not want Runham's heirs to have it. However, I do not want it for myself, because it is tainted by Wilson's thieving hands. I gave it to Cynric because it will go some way to compensate him for the shabby way he was treated by Runham. It is quite valuable, and he will be able to sell it if he ever finds himself in need.'

Bartholomew regarded him affectionately. 'You are a strange man, Brother; you have a peculiar sense of justice.'

'No more peculiar than yours,' said Michael. 'I heard about you offering your own purse to my choir to try to make up for Runham's wickedness. But, look! Here comes your bride-to-be!'

Bartholomew glanced up from where he was negotiating his way around one of the High Street's more crater-like potholes, to see the cheerfully formidable bulk of Adela Tangmer, mounted on a spirited bay and riding at the side of her father.

'Matthew!' she cried in her friendly way. 'There you are again, ploughing your way through the filth of the streets when a horse would raise you above it all.'

'All you ever think about is horses,' muttered her father resentfully. 'You should be thinking about children and marriage before it is too late.'

'Have you tried any of the scholars at Bene't College? Some of them might appreciate a wealthy wife,' suggested Michael.

'The scholars at Bene't are a gaggle of argumentative bores with scrawny legs – like chickens,' muttered Adela. 'I will have none of them!'

'Speaking of scrawny legs, do you know Master Clippesby of Michaelhouse?' asked Michael, seeing an opportunity to test the Dominican's feeble alibi for the night of Runham's death. 'He says he spoke to you on Friday evening, while you were watching the mystery plays outside St Mary's Guildhall.'

'She did not go to the mystery plays,' said Tangmer, giving his daughter a nasty look. 'I suggested she should, but she was busy with some horse or other and was in the stables all night. Why? Is this Clippesby looking for a wife?'

'Friday,' repeated Michael, looking hard at Adela. 'Are you sure you did not meet Clippesby on Friday evening?'

'Positive,' said Adela. 'My father is right: I was with a horse about to foal from sunset on Friday until dawn on Saturday. I have told you that already, Matthew. When your sister asked whether I was planning to attend the mystery plays a week or more ago – the day I challenged that knife-thrower in the Market Square – I informed her that I had a horse to see to, and would have no time to waste on such foolery.

'I saw him on *Thursday* evening, though, wandering around the Market Square,' Adela continued thoughtfully. 'He was talking to himself and gesticulating wildly. He was frightening some of the traders' children, so I told him to return to Michaelhouse and see Matthew – although I do not know whether madness is curable. Of course, horses can be wild and unpredictable, but they do not lose their wits like people.'

Bartholomew and Michael exchanged a glance. So, Clippesby's alibi could be dismissed, and Bartholomew *did* recall that Adela had told Edith she would not be going to the plays. He had been remiss not to have remembered that when Clippesby had made his claim.

'Well then, Clippesby was lying,' said Michael as they walked away. 'I have never trusted him, Matt. He is unstable enough to commit murder and then forget all about it. Or is he clever enough to use his madness to conceal the fact that he is a ruthless killer with a grudge to settle?'

'I thought Clippesby liked Runham. He was certainly prepared to spy for him, and he would probably have done very well at Michaelhouse as Runham's henchman.'

'But Runham revealed details about the illness Clippesby wanted to conceal,' said Michael impatiently. 'And who knows what may have passed between the pair of them during these secret meetings they had at dawn? Who

found the body, Matt? It was Clippesby – and in my
experience, the person who "discovers" a corpse is often
the person who has created it.'

He stopped suddenly, glaring ahead of him. Bartholomew
glanced up from the muck of the High Street and saw
that Michael's gaze was fixed on two people who stood
outside Bene't College, examining the partly demolished
scaffolding. They were the carpenter, Robert de Blaston,
and his wife Yolande. Blaston turned his head this way and
that as he assessed the spars and planks, while Yolande
sighed and fidgeted with boredom.

'What is he doing there?' muttered Michael. 'He is
supposed to be working on Michaelhouse. I hope the
story of the theft from Runham's room is not out.'

'We have already discussed this,' said Bartholomew. 'I
thought we had decided to be honest and send them all
back to Bene't. It is better to have Bene't men gloating
over us, than to see Michaelhouse torn apart by workmen
who want the wages we cannot pay. Blaston cannot blame
us because a thief stole the money Runham had raised.'

'There is no place for reason between a man and his
money,' said Michael. 'You should know that, Matt. If
the workmen learn that we cannot pay the fabulous
wages Runham promised, they will not shrug and happily accept that it is just one of those things. They
will riot.'

Yolande spotted them, and came to bid them good
morning, swinging her hips provocatively as she revealed
her poor teeth in what would have passed for an allur-
ing smile in the dark. She wore a rather grimy green
ribbon in her lustreless hair, which she fingered shyly to
acknowledge Bartholomew's generosity.

'Would you mind if I asked you an impertinent question?' asked Michael, in the tone of voice that suggested
he would ask it whether she minded or not. He gave her a

smile that was more flirtatious than monastic. 'It concerns last Friday evening.'

'I was working,' she said immediately. 'I always work Fridays, if I can.'

'Why Fridays?' asked Bartholomew curiously.

'It is a fish day,' she explained. 'If men cannot have their meat at dinner, they like to have it another way after dark. Trade is always good on Fridays.'

Leaving Bartholomew speculating with interest on whether there was an anatomical explanation for her discovery, Michael continued to question the prostitute about her customers the night Runham had been killed.

'You may consider my question indelicate, but did you see Ralph de Langelee then? He claims he was with you at that time.'

'No,' she said sharply. 'He was not. Ralph who?'

'It is all right, Yolande,' said Michael gently. 'I am not asking to make trouble for him, but I need to know the truth.'

She sighed and then grinned, reaching out to chuck the monk under the chin. Bartholomew looked both ways in alarm, lest anyone should have seen the intimate gesture, while Michael favoured the prostitute with a wicked leer.

'Since it is you, Brother, I will tell the truth. Ralph de Langelee often pays me a visit on a Friday night – it is he who claims fish makes him more desirous of a woman.' The fact that it was a theory of Langelee's that had prompted Yolande's intriguing claim meant that Bartholomew's medical speculations ceased abruptly. 'He came about an hour after sunset. Rob!'

Her husband tore his gaze from the Bene't scaffolding and came towards them. 'What?' he asked, a little irritably. 'I am busy.'

'Busy doing what?' asked Michael suspiciously.

'Busy looking to see how the remaining scaffolding is holding up,' replied Blaston. 'We will have to work on that at some point, and I want to ensure it is not falling to pieces.'

'Not until you have finished your work at Michaelhouse,' said Michael.

'Right,' said Blaston vaguely. 'A word of warning, though. We plan to ask for a week's wages tomorrow. Runham said he would pay the whole amount after we had finished everything, but now that he is dead we would like a bit up front, just so that we all know where we stand.'

They know, thought Bartholomew, trying not to cast an anxious glance at Michael. They have heard rumours that Runham's chest was robbed, and they are worried that they will not be paid.

'Fair enough,' said Michael airily. 'Bring Newenham with you to see me tomorrow and we will see what we can do. But I was discussing another matter with your lady wife.'

'My wife,' corrected Blaston. 'Yes?'

'What time did Ralph de Langelee arrive, Rob?' asked Yolande. 'It was some time after sunset, but I cannot recall exactly when.'

Blaston rubbed his bristly chin. 'Now, let me think. It was still just light, because little Yolande lost a shoe in the garden, and I had to go out and look for it. I was just able to see without a candle – which was a blessing, because we do not have any.'

'That is right,' said Yolande, remembering. 'So, Ralph and I went upstairs, while you saw to the children. Did you find that shoe, by the way? We cannot afford to buy her another.'

'Under the cabbages,' replied Blaston. 'Ralph de

Langelee stayed an unusually long time that night, I recall. In fact, he stayed with you right through until dawn. I remember, because he and I walked to Michaelhouse together – me to work and him to go to mass in the church.'

It seemed a curious arrangement for a married couple, but Bartholomew was not in the habit of judging the lives of his fellow men, particularly after the plague when times were hard and people would do anything to put food on the table and a roof over their heads. Blaston should have been earning a decent wage as a carpenter, but with nine children to support, his income would not go far. The fact that he was willing to work under the dangerous conditions imposed by Runham told its own story, although if he ever had an accident, the Blaston family would be in serious trouble.

Thanking them for their help, Michael steered Bartholomew towards Bene't College's front gate. The physician wondered how the family would manage when Yolande was unable to work on Friday nights. He glanced back at them. They were good people – hard-working and honest – and he hoped they would not find life too difficult.

'They are telling the truth, Matt,' said Michael. 'Langelee is lucky: he believed he was out on the wharves thinking a lot longer than he really was – which just goes to show that a lengthy thinking session means something very different to Langelee than it does to us! He was probably out for no more than an hour, and he arrived at the Blaston house at twilight. That means he arrived some time between five and six, and that at eight o'clock, when Runham was being cushioned to death, Langelee was merrily bouncing between the sheets with the mother of nine children.'

'That means there are only two Michaelhouse Fellows unaccounted for that night,' said Bartholomew. 'Clippesby and me.'

'So, assuming that none of the students or servants killed Runham, we are left with Clippesby,' said Michael thoughtfully.

Bartholomew smiled. 'You have no doubts about my innocence at all?'

'None,' said Michael firmly. 'You strike me as more of a poisons man than a smotherer. But let us see what these Bene't Fellows have to say for themselves. Let me do the talking, Matt. From what they told me yesterday, you did a poor job of interviewing them the last time you were there.'

Their knock at the gate was answered immediately by Osmun, the ill-tempered porter. His brother Ulfo lounged near a crackling fire in the lodge, picking his teeth with a knife that looked sharp enough to sever his tongue if he made a false move. Sitting apart in a corner, sporting a blackened eye and looking very sorry for himself, was Walter, lately night porter at Michaelhouse. Osmun followed Bartholomew's startled gaze.

'Caught him sleeping on duty,' said Osmun with a sour smile. 'We do not pay people to sleep, do we, Walter?'

Walter shook his head, looking more miserable than Bartholomew had ever seen him, which was a considerable feat. Despite the fact that Bartholomew considered Walter a lazy good-for-nothing, he felt sorry for the man in his blood-splattered shirt and bruised face. Walter saw his sympathetic expression and tried to stand. Ulfo kicked out viciously, and Walter sank back to the floor and hid his face in his hands, a picture of despair.

The Bene't Fellows were in their conclave, a chamber off

the hall that was larger than the one at Michaelhouse, but not nearly so pleasant. The rushes that covered the floor were stale and needed changing, while the tapestries on the walls were of an inferior quality and the dyes in the wools had faded in the sun. It was quite a contrast to the carved oak panelling and rich rugs that adorned the hall, and Bartholomew supposed that the conclave had not been deemed worthy of similar attention, because meetings with important benefactors – like the Duke of Lancaster and the guildsmen of St Mary and Corpus Christi – took place in the hall.

The hall itself housed the students, who sat in attitudes of boredom as they listened to the droning tones of their Bible Scholar reading some dense tract from Leviticus. A fire roared in the hearth, burning logs at a rate that even the absent-minded Kenyngham would have balked at. It was hot to the point of being uncomfortable, and Bartholomew was not surprised that several of the scholars had fallen asleep, lulled by the heat and the dry tones of the reader.

There was a palpable atmosphere of unease and unhappiness in the College, both among those students who were still awake in the hall and the Fellows in the conclave. Michaelhouse had its problems, but Bartholomew had never known it to simmer with the same sense of despair and gloom that seemed to grip Bene't. Yet again, he realised that Wymundham and others had been right when they had claimed Bene't was not a happy College.

'I see you buried my cousin Justus at last,' said Osmun as he followed Bartholomew through the hall. 'Not before time, if you ask me. Bene't does not leave its members' corpses to fester in the church for days past the time when it is decent.'

'No; Bene't buries its scholars with unseemly haste,'

retorted Michael. 'Wymundham and Raysoun were under-
ground before my appointed representative had had the
opportunity to inspect them properly.'

'We did not think their deaths were any of your business,' said Osmun, nettled. 'An accident and a suicide
are not matters for the Senior Proctor to poke into.'

'The Senior Proctor can poke into anything he likes,'
said Michael sharply.

'You are like that Ralph de Langelee,' said Osmun in
disdain. 'He is always hanging around Bene't, trying to
ingratiate himself with members of a good College. He
thinks he is Simekyn Simeon's friend, and Simeon is too
much a gentleman to send the man packing.'

'But Bene't willingly takes our servants – Agatha and
Walter,' snapped Michael, beginning to be angered by
the man's insolence. 'And you should watch yourself:
Agatha will not tolerate your rough manners. She will
soon put you in your place.'

'It is the Michaelhouse men again,' announced Osmun
disapprovingly to the Bene't Fellows, as he ushered
Michael and Bartholomew into the conclave. 'I do not
know what they want, but it will be something that will
do us no good, you mark my words.'

He left, slamming the door behind him and making the
fire in the hearth gutter and roar. Bartholomew looked
at the assembled Fellows. Simekyn Simeon sat near the
fire and had apparently been dozing. Under the sober
blue of his tabard, he wore his startling striped hose and
a bright red shirt, apparently to announce to the world
that he was a courtier not a scholar, and that he wore his
Fellow's uniform on sufferance.

Caumpes was reading, folded into a windowseat, where
the light was better. When he set the book down,
Bartholomew saw it was a text by Plato. Heltisle sat at
a table that was covered by scrolls and parchments, and

had been writing. Of the last of the four Fellows, Henry de Walton, there was no sign.

'You come again, Brother,' said Heltisle coolly to Michael. 'However, honoured though we are, we would appreciate it if you state your business and then be on your way; we are busy men.'

'So I see,' said Michael, glancing meaningfully towards the hall, where it was the Bible Scholar, not the Fellows, who was doing the teaching.

'What do you want from us?' snapped Caumpes, nettled.

'A cup of wine would be pleasant,' said Michael, sitting uninvited in a chair near the fire. 'Does Bene't keep a decent cellar, or will I have to return to Michaelhouse for that?'

Why the Fellows of other Colleges always yielded to Michael's none-too-subtle ploys to be served their finest victuals, Bartholomew could not imagine. He assumed pride always made them rise to meet the challenge, to prove that their College could afford the best wines, serve the best food, or had the best students. Heltisle glowered, but then nodded to Simeon, who uncoiled himself from his chair to order a servant to fetch Michael his wine.

Moments later it arrived, a light white in which the grapes of southern France could still be tasted. It was served in handsome crystal goblets, which, Bartholomew had to admit, were more pleasant to drink from than Michaelhouse's pewter.

'Very good,' said Michael approvingly, lifting his glass to the light so that the sun caught the pale gold liquid and made it gleam. 'Almost as good as the brew I was served in the Hall of Valence Marie the other day. Now Master Thorpe of Valence Marie is a man who knows his wines.'

'Why did you come today, Brother?' asked Caumpes icily. 'Other than to insult our cellars, that is?'

'I have come, as Senior Proctor, to assure you that I will do all I can to protect Bene't College's reputation from the vicious rumours that are rife in the town,' said Michael silkily.

Caumpes stiffened. 'What rumours? What have people been saying about Bene't?'

'Have you not heard?' asked Michael innocently. 'You surprise me, Master Caumpes. I am referring to the tales that Raysoun and Wymundham were murdered. We have discussed the issue at length on more than one occasion.'

'So you have come to interrogate us again,' said Heltisle flatly. 'I thought we had answered all your questions about the deaths of our unfortunate colleagues.'

'It is a Michaelhouse plot to discredit us,' said Caumpes bitterly. He pointed accusingly at Bartholomew. 'His feeble attempt to pretend that Michaelhouse means Bene't no harm may have convinced the Duke of Lancaster, but it did not fool us. We know Michaelhouse is jealous of the patronage of the Guilds of St Mary and Corpus Christi and wants to steal it away.'

'I can assure you that is not true,' said Michael, genuinely offended. 'Michaelhouse wants no town money, thank you very much.'

'Did Runham know that?' demanded Heltisle. 'Your tone suggests that there is something unwholesome about town money, but Runham held no such scruples when he was making a nuisance of himself among all the town's merchants, demanding money for his new courtyard.'

'Master Runham is no longer with us,' said Michael smoothly, 'as I am sure you are aware. And Bene't and Michaelhouse have always coexisted peacefully in the past, so I do not see why our relationship should not continue as it was before.'

'Very well, then,' said Heltisle. 'Prove your good intentions by sending us back our workmen.'

'I will discuss the matter with Master Kenyngham,' said Michael. 'He is very keen for us to resolve our differences, and I am sure he will agree to your request.'

Bartholomew was as startled as Heltisle. Then it occurred to him that if the workmen could be discharged the following day on the grounds that Bene't had demanded their return, Michael would have scored a double victory: first, Michaelhouse would not be obliged to pay the workmen the wages Runham had promised; and second, he would ensure that they would hold Bene't – not Michaelhouse – responsible for losing them their bonus. It was a clever, if somewhat shabby, move, and given Blaston's warning, it was also well timed.

'That is very kind of you, Brother,' said Caumpes quickly, sensing perhaps that Heltisle's astonishment at Michael's unexpected capitulation might lead him to say something to disturb the fragile truce. 'We appreciate – and áccept – your gesture of reconciliation.'

'But that does not mean that we will consider impertinent questions about the unfortunate accidents that killed Raysoun and Wymundham,' said Heltisle. 'They are buried in St Bene't's churchyard, and I want them to rest in peace.'

Michael inclined his head. 'Very well. But I have a favour to ask in return for my generosity in returning your workmen to you. There was a theft at Michaelhouse on Friday. We have the culprit under lock and key, and we are certain of his guilt. He is a pathetic fellow, who is spinning all manner of lies to wriggle off the hook he has impaled himself upon. He even accused Matt of giving him medicine that made him do things he did not want to do.'

'Do you have any of it left?' asked Caumpes of

Bartholomew dryly. 'There are one or two students I would not mind dosing with such a substance.'

Bartholomew smiled nervously, wondering where the fat monk's untruths were leading.

'This thief has had the audacity to claim that he was with a Fellow of Bene't on Friday night.' Michael raised his hand to quell the indignant objections that arose. 'We do not believe him for an instant, of course. But I would like to be able to return to him and say that each one of you has accounted for his movements, and that our thief was not included in them.'

'I do not see why we should play this game . . .' began Heltisle.

'Where lies the harm, Master Heltisle?' asked Simeon with a shrug. 'Brother Michael is not accusing us of anything: he is merely asking us to help him trap a thief. What was stolen, Brother?'

'Some rings and gold coins,' said Michael vaguely. 'I appreciate your help in this matter, because I would not like this villain to go free and prey on some other unsuspecting College.' He gazed around him meaning-fully.

Michael really was clever, Bartholomew thought ad-miringly. He would learn the whereabouts of the Bene't scholars without an unpleasant confrontation – unless one of them was the killer of Runham, of course, in which case the culprit would know exactly why Michael wanted to know where they were at eight o'clock on Friday evening. The monk was also cunning in appealing to their instincts for self-preservation, intimating that if his fictitious criminal were to go free, Bene't might be the next victim.

'I attended compline in St Botolph's Church,' said Heltisle. 'I always insist that the students come with me on Fridays – Friday is usually the night that students attempt to slip their leashes and escape to the town to romp with the prostitutes.'

Bartholomew realised that Heltisle's alibi was not a good one. Compline at St Botolph's was earlier than at St Michael's, and a fleet-footed man could have attended St Botolph's and still run to Michaelhouse to kill Runham at eight o'clock. And bearing in mind that hour candles were often not accurate – especially the cheap ones favoured by Runham – the killer might have even had a few additional moments to complete his grisly task. Of course, Bartholomew thought, if Runham's candle had burned faster than normal, Heltisle would be in the clear.

'After we returned from compline, I retired to my room and studied the College accounts,' Heltisle continued. 'I was alone, but you can hardly expect me to have kept company with a thief. Anyway, you can check with Osmun the porter; he will tell you that no visitors came for me that evening. And now, if you will excuse me, I am busy, and have no time to waste sorting out the problems of other Colleges.' He gathered up his parchments and swept from the room.

'I have a confession to make,' said Caumpes, giving a wan smile that revealed his bad teeth. Bartholomew saw Michael look interested. 'I am a simple man and I do not like arguments. Life at Bene't is not always as tranquil as I would like, and there was an altercation on Friday afternoon. I felt I could not attend compline in such an angry atmosphere, and so I went to the one in St Michael's Church instead.'

'Is that it?' asked Michael, acutely disappointed.

Caumpes nodded. 'I know it is unusual to patronise the church of another College, but I hope you will forgive me. I asked Master Kenyngham if I might join him and your new man – Suttone, I believe he is called – and he readily agreed. If you speak to them, they will confirm my story. But I encountered no thief, as far as I know.'

So, that discounted Caumpes as a potential killer, thought Bartholomew. If Bartholomew could choose anyone to give him an alibi, he would select Kenyngham, because the gentle Gilbertine was more honest than any man he had ever encountered. Kenyngham would never lie. And the fact that Suttone had been present, too, meant that Caumpes's alibi was unshakeable. Kenyngham could be a little vague when he was praying, but Suttone was a sensible and practical man, and would remember whom he had met and when.

'I cannot help you, I am afraid,' said the foppish Simeon, looking as though he cared little one way or the other. 'I spent an hour or two in the King's Head – fine me, if you will, Senior Proctor, I offer no defence – and then I went looking for women. I did not see any that took my fancy. Ralph de Langelee had already engaged the only one worth romping with, while the lovely Matilde bestows her favours on no man these days, so I returned here and went to bed alone.'

'Where is the fourth Fellow – Henry de Walton?' asked Michael. 'Could the thief have met him?'

'I sincerely doubt it, Brother,' said Simeon laconically. 'No sensible thief would keep company with our Master de Walton.'

'Why not?' asked Michael. 'What is wrong with him?'

'Leprosy,' replied Simeon, amused by the shock on Michael's face. 'It was diagnosed by Master Lynton of Peterhouse two days ago, and de Walton is on his way to a lazar house even as we speak.'

'Which one?' asked Bartholomew, with the interest of a professional.

'Since I have no intention of paying him a comradely visit, I did not think to find out,' said Simeon with a shrug.

'Somewhere to the north. But it is time for a walk before I take another nap. Good morning, gentlemen.'

He wandered out, leaving Caumpes to see them across the courtyard to the gate.

'Simeon is lying,' said Caumpes as they walked, shaking his head in puzzlement. 'He knows which lazar hospital de Walton will be in, because it was he who arranged it – St Giles in Norwich.'

'When did de Walton leave?' asked Bartholomew.

'Yesterday,' said Caumpes. 'I cannot imagine why Simeon did not tell you. It is not a secret, and there is nothing shameful in sending a sick colleague somewhere he will be properly cared for. All the Fellows came to see the poor man on his way yesterday, and I at least have promised to travel to Norwich to see him soon.'

'You will not be allowed in,' said Michael. 'Lazar hospitals do not encourage visitors.'

'De Walton is my friend,' said Caumpes simply. 'So I will try.' He stopped at the gate and waited for Osmun to open it. 'Goodbye, Brother, Doctor. I hope you convict your thief.'

'So do I,' said Michael fervently.

He and Bartholomew had barely started the walk back to Michaelhouse, when they heard a yell. It was Walter, the lazy ex-Michaelhouse porter, racing down the street after them as though he were being pursued by the hounds of hell. Agatha the laundress was not far behind. Walter grabbed Michael's arm and began demanding back his old job in piteous, wheedling tones.

'Please take me home to Michaelhouse. I promise I will never sleep on duty again.'

'We will see,' said Michael, firmly disengaging his arm and attempting to walk on.

'I am returning to Michaelhouse myself,' announced

Agatha, with every confidence that she would be welcomed back, and that any laundress appointed in her absence would be summarily dismissed. 'I will move into my old quarters immediately. I do not know who killed Raysoun and Wymundham, Brother, but these Bene't men are trying my patience to the limits.'

'Have you learned anything at all?' asked Michael, although the flatness of his voice suggested that he predicted that she had not.

She sighed, and Bartholomew saw that her own lack of success was as disheartening to her as it was to Michael. 'Nothing. And you should not have asked me to go there, Brother. Those Bene't scoundrels are followers of the Devil.'

'Really?' asked Michael with quickened interest. 'What makes you say that?'

'Because, as God's chosen, I should have been able to recognise the guilty man immediately, but they called on the Devil to hide him from me. Still, I did my best. And now I am going home to Michaelhouse. Good wages and a big room are no compensation for bad company and lazy underlings.'

She began to move majestically along the High Street, tossing a bundle of belongings to Walter, who was obliged to carry it for her.

'If she is being reinstated, you can take me, too,' Walter whined, oblivious to the fact that a porter who slept on duty was not in the same league as a laundress who ran the domestic side of the College with ruthless efficiency. 'Please! That Osmun is a brute. He will kill me if I stay at Bene't!'

'Osmun is an animal,' agreed Agatha, walking next to Bartholomew. 'He and Simeon dreamed up such a vile story about poor de Walton. And Caumpes and Heltisle believed every word of it.'

'What are you talking about?' asked Michael. 'De Walton has leprosy, and is currently on his way to a lazar hospital in Norwich.'

'Well, maybe he does have leprosy,' said Agatha. 'I thought he looked a bit peaky. But he is no more travelling to Norwich than you are. That is a story fabricated by the Duke of Lancaster's henchman, so that Heltisle and Caumpes will not be able to see him any more.'

'So, where is de Walton?' asked Michael, trying not to show his bewilderment at Agatha's annoyingly piecemeal story. 'And why should Simeon want to keep him from the others?'

'Simeon wants de Walton away from the others, because Bene't is full of bitterness and rivalry,' said Agatha knowledgeably. 'It is really no different from Michaelhouse. And he has the poor man imprisoned in one of the outbuildings down by the King's Ditch. I saw Simeon taking him there yesterday, *after* de Walton was supposed to have gone to Norwich.'

'Will you tell us how to find it?' asked Michael.

'Now?' asked Agatha calmly, preparing to make her mighty bulk change direction.

'We will go when it is dark,' said Michael. 'Tonight.'

It was only noon, and there was a long time to go before Michael's midnight raid on the shed in Bene't College's grounds. Michael went to question his beadles yet again about their nightly intelligence-gathering in the taverns. Meanwhile, Bartholomew was anxious about the amount of time that had been squandered by the building work and Runham's death, and was keen to remedy the matter by organising a debate for his undergraduates. But none of his students were anywhere to be found in Michaelhouse, and with no Cynric to round them up, Bartholomew was obliged to hunt them down himself.

With ill grace, feeling that trawling the taverns for his truants was a waste of an afternoon, he set out.

His first port of call was the King's Head, a busy establishment near the Ditch with a reputation for brawls. The deafening roar of drunken voices stopped the instant he entered, and he realised that he had forgotten to remove the tabard that marked him as a scholar. While scholars regularly patronised the King's Head, they never did so wearing uniforms that proclaimed their academic calling. Eyes that glittered in the firelight regarded him with such hostile intent that he backed out quickly; to linger would mean an attack for certain.

As the door closed behind him, the bellow of conversation resumed, and he berated himself for being so careless. He took off his tabard, shoved it into the medicine bag he always wore looped over his shoulder, and began to walk towards the next inn on his list. He smiled to himself as he went: even the short spell he had spent inside the King's Head told him that his students were not there, and that the reason they were not enjoying its dubious hospitality was probably because Ralph de Langelee was there. The burly philosopher had been sitting at a table at the far end of the tavern, drinking a jug of ale with a slim, neat man who looked as if he wished he were elsewhere.

Bartholomew turned from the High Street to Luthburne Lane, a dark, muddy street that ran along the back of Bene't College, where a sign that dangled on a single hinge told that the run-down building to which it was attached was the Lilypot, an insalubrious inn with a reputation as a haunt for criminals and practising lawyers. Bartholomew was about to enter, when he saw a familiar figure drop lightly from the wall that ran along the rear of Bene't, brush himself down and then walk jauntily in the direction of the King's Ditch. It was Simekyn Simeon, and the Bene't Fellow had not noticed Bartholomew standing in the gloomy portals of the Lilypot.

Curious as to what should induce the elegant courtier to jump over walls instead of using the front gate, like most law-abiding men, Bartholomew started to follow him, taking care to keep some distance between him and his quarry as Cynric had taught him to do. Simeon moved quickly and stealthily, casting quick, furtive glances behind him as he went. Bartholomew began to wonder whether any Fellow at Bene't was able to walk around the town in a normal manner, given that he had personally observed Wymundham, Caumpes and now Simeon stealing about the streets.

Between Luthburne Lane and the King's Ditch was a small area of pasture that the townsfolk used for grazing their cattle during the summer months. During the winter, it was a weed-infested wilderness lined with mature trees on one side, and the sturdy grey walls of the Hall of Valence Marie on the other. Simeon hurried to a small coppice of hawthorn trees, lifting his tabard so that it would not trail in the long grass. Bartholomew hoped the courtier had not worn his exquisite calfskin shoes, since generations of cows had browsed the area. An eloquent string of expletives and a slackening of pace as Simeon inspected his foot indicated that he had.

When he reached the prickly haven of the hawthorns, the Bene't man glanced around him and, apparently satisfied that he had not been observed, lowered himself carefully on to a fallen tree-trunk and began to scrape at his shoe with a stick. Since Bartholomew was sure the fashionable Simeon had not forged his way through the foliage for some pleasurable exercise and that he was likely to be meeting someone, he skirted the thicket and climbed up the steep bank of the Ditch behind. Lying on his stomach, he found he could look down on Simeon but Simeon was unlikely to see Bartholomew unless he happened to glance up. He slipped his medicine bag off his shoulder, laid it on the grass next to him, and settled down to see what would happen.

Fortunately, he did not have long to wait, which was a blessing. Not only was it cold lying in wet grass under a dark sky that promised rain, but the noxious stench of the Ditch was making him feel sick. Another person was moving across the scrub, looking every bit as furtive as had Simeon. At first, Bartholomew assumed Simeon's liaison was no more sinister than a clandestine meeting with a woman, for the figure that inched its way across the pasture was elfin, protected from the weather by a thick cloak that hid everything except some brown shoes. But then the newcomer reached up to push back the hood, and Bartholomew saw that it was no woman whom Simeon greeted in the manner of an old friend.

'I was waylaid,' the newcomer explained, perching on the tree trunk and pulling his cloak more tightly around him. 'That dreadful Ralph de Langelee spotted me, and I was obliged to pass the time of day with him in a place called the King's Head. Are Cambridge scholars allowed the freedom to carouse in the town's inns? We certainly do not permit that sort of thing at Oxford.'

'Langelee allowed himself to be seen in a tavern with an Oxford man?' asked Simeon, amused. 'He is a confident fellow! Rumour has it that he plans to be Master of Michaelhouse now that the old one is dead. He will not win the votes of that gaggle of old women and bigots by fraternising with William Heytesbury of Merton College in an establishment like the King's Head!'

Heytesbury! thought Bartholomew, suddenly recognising from his own days at Oxford the delicate features of the famed nominalist. It was the discovery of Michael's letters to him that had destroyed the monk's ambitions to succeed Kenyngham as Master of Michaelhouse. And now it appeared that Michael was not the only one with Oxford connections: it seemed Langelee had his own association with the Merton man. Bartholomew had seen them himself in the King's Head together only a few moments earlier.

'The tavern was full of townsmen,' Heytesbury went on with a shudder. 'At one point, a University doctor had the temerity to enter wearing his tabard, and, judging from the hostile reaction of the inn's patrons, I suspect he was lucky to leave alive.'

'It is good to see you, Heytesbury,' said Simeon warmly. 'You are a bright spark of culture and decency in this den of louts. Would you believe that I am obliged to remain here until Bene't is completed? It might take months, at which point I shall be too ancient to be of use to anyone.'

'You will never be too old for fun,' said Heytesbury, smiling and clapping his friend on the back. 'But it is a pity your Duke chose this godforsaken hole into which to plough his money. He should have given it to Oxford.'

'I did my best to tell him that,' said Simeon. 'He declined to listen to a mere squire. But what did Langelee want with you? I am also acquainted with him, for my sins. I have been obliged to waste several evenings in his company, because I am too polite to tell him to go to the Devil.'

Heytesbury sighed. 'He wanted to know about my dealings with Brother Michael. The stupid man apparently used Michael's association with me to prevent the monk from becoming Master of Michaelhouse. From my personal impression of that good Brother, I imagine that Langelee is headed for a serious fall.'

Simeon raised his eyebrows. 'Are you serious? You

think that fat glutton can best a man like Langelee, with his years of experience as the Archbishop's spy?'

'Should I trust Michael then?' asked Heytesbury thoughtfully. 'Should I go ahead with this arrangement that will make Oxford richer by two churches and a farm in exchange for some information that is neither here nor there to us?'

'Why not?' asked Simeon. 'It sounds to me as if you cannot lose.'

'That is what worries me,' said Heytesbury, frowning. 'It seems like an offer made in Heaven, where we gain and Cambridge loses. That is why I came in person to see Michael, and that is why I asked you to meet me, so that you can give me your impressions of the man. He claims he plans to use the information only to secure himself the Chancellorship next year, but I remain sceptical.'

'I think you credit him with too much cunning,' said Simeon dismissively. 'Brother Michael is a bumbling Benedictine who cannot even explain the deaths that have occurred in Bene't College. I doubt he will raise his eyes from the dinner table long enough to be a threat to you.'

That Simeon had so badly misread Michael suggested that Langelee was not the only one in line for a hard fall. Bartholomew knew Michael well enough to be convinced that if Heytesbury and the monk struck some kind of deal, then Heytesbury would not be the one to leave with the better half of the bargain. He shifted slightly in his hiding place, growing chilled and stiff from lying still. He bumped against his medicine bag, which clinked softly as the birthing forceps inside it knocked against a glass phial. Fortunately, the two men below did not hear.

'Now,' said Simeon, shivering slightly as a gust of wind brought the first spots of rain. 'I have fulfilled my part of our arrangement by informing you that you need not fear Brother Michael. What do you have for me?'

Heytesbury rummaged under his cloak and produced a leather bag. 'New shoes, cut in the latest court fashion with toes that curl; a ham from the Duke's kitchen; and a silk sheet, so that you will not have to endure Bene't's rough blankets.'

Simeon grinned, and took the bag from him. 'Excellent. I will—'

When Bartholomew had bumped into his medicine bag, it had been nudged towards the edge of the bank, where it very slowly began to slide. Before he could stop it, it had gathered momentum on the slick grass, assisted by the weight of the heavy birthing forceps inside, and tumbled away down the bank to land with a heavy thud at Simeon's feet. For one horror-stricken moment, Bartholomew was not sure whether to run away or to confront the two men. Although the rational part of his mind told him that he had done nothing to warrant flight, there was always the possibility that the mincing courtier was a murderer, who had already killed two of his colleagues and who would be quite happy to dispatch Bartholomew, too.

But the matter was decided for him. Without waiting to establish the identity of the bag's owner, Heytesbury was away, bounding through the long grass towards the High Street at an impressive pace. Meanwhile, Simeon raced off in the direction of Luthburne Lane and the rear of his College. Bartholomew leapt to his feet, a vague notion of pursuing Simeon forming in his mind, although he was not sure to what purpose. The sudden movement was ill-advised, and his leather-soled boots skidded on the slick grass. He lost his balance, and fell flat on his back in a patch of grey-green slime just above the Ditch's waterline.

Appalled by the notion that he might slide further and end up in the fetid black waters that slunk by in a foul, glassy-smooth curl, Bartholomew twisted on to his stomach and snatched at some weeds. Moments later, he was on firm ground again, although to his dismay he found he was heavily coated in the repulsive ooze from the Ditch's muddy banks. Revolted by the sulphurous stench that already emanated from his clothes, he retrieved his bag and returned to Michaelhouse, earning some curious glances from passers-by as he went.

To his chagrin, one of the people he met was Matilde. She looked him up and down and seemed uncertain whether to express concern or be amused. She tried the former, but seeing he was unharmed, her natural good humour quickly bubbled to the surface and she started to laugh.

'You look like a ditcher,' she said, walking around behind him to appreciate the full scale of the mess he was in. 'How did you manage to end up in such a state?'

'I was listening to a conversation about Michael between Simekyn Simeon and a scholar from Oxford and I slipped. It must have been divine retribution for spying.'

'Ah, you mean William Heytesbury of Merton,' said Matilde immediately. 'He is in Cambridge to learn whether Michael is a blustering fool who wants certain information simply to secure the Chancellorship of the University next year, or a cunning negotiator who will use the information to promote Cambridge's interests over those of Oxford.'

Bartholomew gaped at her. 'How do you know that?'

Matilde smiled at his astonishment. 'Through the sisters, of course. Langelee feels guilty for his shameful tactics during the last election for the Master of Michaelhouse, and so will recommend that Heytesbury does what Michael suggests. And then, perhaps not next year, or even the year after, Michael will use Heytesbury's information to steal away from Oxford the patronage of some wealthy and powerful people.'

Bartholomew nodded. 'I gathered as much. But I thought his negotiations were secret. He certainly has told me very little about them.'

'But Heytesbury is not as discreet as Michael,' said Matilde. 'He had already unburdened himself to Yolande de Blaston. Michael is a clever man. Heytesbury should be careful.'

'Where are you going?' asked Bartholomew, suddenly feeling a strong desire to spend some time alone with her. 'Will you come with me to the Brazen George for a while? Now?'

'I certainly will not,' she said, beginning to laugh again. 'The landlord would not allow you in all covered in mud, and I have my reputation to consider.' She sensed his disappointment and leaned forward to touch his arm with a slender forefinger. 'But when you are clean and dry, I would welcome your company in my house. Will you come tomorrow evening?'

Bartholomew smiled. 'There is nothing I would like more.'

Michael's green eyes grew large and round when he saw the state of his friend but he said nothing. He followed the physician into his room, which still lay under a thick coat of dust from the collapse of the scaffolding, and Bartholomew felt a pang of regret when he realised that Cynric would not be in to help him clean it, or to leave fresh water in the jug on the floor by the table. He fetched his own, and went to the lavatorium, trying to sluice away the stench of the Ditch.

When he had finished, Michael was waiting, but the monk wrinkled his nose in disgust and went to fetch some of the coarse-grained scented soap they had seen in

Master Runham's room. It was not pleasant standing on the cold flagstone floor of the lavatorium while Michael threw jug after jug of water over him, and the soap was rough on Bartholomew's skin. But it smelled powerfully of lavender, and he imagined most people would consider it an improvement on the rank stench of the Ditch. He rubbed the soap in his hair, revolted by the brown sludge that washed out as Michael tipped water over his head.

Between deluges, he told Michael about the meeting between Heytesbury and Simeon. The monk was delighted that Simeon had underestimated him, and began speculating on the advantages Heytesbury's information would hold for Cambridge at Oxford's expense. He was especially gratified to learn that Langelee also had Oxford connections, and swore that the philosopher's hypocrisy would be exposed at some future time, when it would be most damaging.

'I will be Master of Michaelhouse yet, and Langelee will be sorry he ever crossed me,' he vowed, pulling a face when he saw that the filth of the Ditch still clung to Bartholomew's skin. 'This is going to take for ever. What were you doing, anyway? Making mud pies? And I am not sure that this reeking soap of Runham's is any improvement. You will smell like a whore, and Father William will think you have been rubbing up against Matilde.'

Bartholomew ignored him. 'Runham was not a man who seemed especially interested in hygiene. I wonder why he kept so much soap in his room.'

'He took it to Wilson's tomb,' said Michael.

Bartholomew regarded him uncertainly through his dripping hair. 'Like a votive offering, you mean? That sounds rather pagan.'

'That is what I thought, but I saw him doing it at least twice. If you look behind that altar, you will see it is packed with the stuff. It is the strong odour of this soap that always made me sneeze if I went too close – a good excuse for not praying there, I always thought.'

'So that is why Wilson's tomb always smells like a brothel. Sometimes the scent was so powerful that I could barely breathe – like when Runham demanded that I knelt next to him there the morning after the feast. What an odd thing for him to do.'

'Hurry up,' said Michael, pouring more water over the physician's head. 'Or we will miss our meal. And do not be shy with the soap. Runham will not be needing it to make his cousin's tomb smell pretty now.'

Bartholomew scrubbed vigorously, noting with distaste the amount of dirt that swirled around his feet. Suddenly he dropped the soap with a yelp of pain, clutching his arm.

'What now?' asked Michael impatiently, dashing the last of the water at Bartholomew as the physician inspected his arm. 'Never mind. That will do. Get dressed quickly before the bell rings. Agatha promised to make a mess of eggs and bacon fat today, to celebrate her return.'

'So that is the hurry, is it?' asked Bartholomew, shivering as he rubbed himself dry with a piece of sacking. He reached for a clean shirt. 'Runham's soap might be generous on scent, but it is as coarse as stone. That hurt.'

Michael picked it up from the floor, and was about to toss it in the empty water jug when he saw the faint glitter of metal.

'No wonder you howled,' he said. 'There is something in it.'

He rummaged in Bartholomew's medicine bag for a surgical knife, and poked about with it while the physician finished dressing. Eventually, he had prised an object free of the waxy substance, and spent a few moments paring the excess soap away so that he could be certain of what he held.

'I do not understand this,' he said, bewildered, as he inspected a small crucifix. 'This is part of the College's silver.'

'The silver that Runham sold to raise funds for his buildings?' asked Bartholomew, equally bemused. 'But what is it doing in his soap?'

'I think when we know the answer to that, we will understand why he died,' said Michael grimly.

'What about your eggs in bacon fat?' asked Bartholomew, as the monk started to stride across the courtyard towards the gate.

Michael faltered, then changed direction abruptly. 'You are right. I am a lot better at grave-robbing when I have a full stomach.'

'Grave-robbing?' asked Bartholomew in alarm. 'What are you talking about?'

'I am talking about retrieving the rest of the soap from Wilson's altar and seeing what else it contains,' said Michael. 'But first things first. I have not tasted Agatha's egg mess for ages, and you look as if you could do with a good meal. You are unnaturally thin these days.'

The bell had started to ring, so they made their way to the hall and ate a hasty meal, while Father William reported in great detail the lack of success of his own investigations into Master Runham's murder. Kenyngham, occupying the Master's seat again, did not pay the friar any attention, and gazed beatifically at one of the stained-glass windows, evidently reflecting on some religious matter that was uplifting to his soul.

Clippesby sat alone, barely eating and wearing the expression of a man hunted. Bartholomew wondered whether William or Suttone had been indiscreet in their surveillance of him, and that the Dominican knew he was under suspicion of murdering his Master. Bartholomew also wondered whether Clippesby could shed light on why Runham saw fit to keep the College silver in his soap. Was Clippesby Runham's seller – the man who took the purloined goods from their hiding place in the church and passed them to the blithely innocent, or to the less innocent who did not care as long as a profit could be made? Clippesby might not be entirely sane, but he was also cunning in his own way. He certainly had the intelligence to fence stolen goods.

Between Clippesby and William sat Suttone, trying not to let William's strident voice distract him as he read a psalter. His grimaces as he tried to concentrate suggested he was having serious doubts about whether Michaelhouse was the right place for him. Bartholomew sincerely hoped he would not leave, and made a mental note to try to spend some time with him, to convince him that Michaelhouse had a lot to offer.

Langelee sat at the end of the table, his nose buried in a cup that Bartholomew was fairly sure did not contain the customary small ale, but something a little stronger. As soon as he could, Michael made his apologies to Kenyngham and asked to be excused, leaving the other Fellows curious as to what could be so important as to make the monk rise from the table while there was still bread to be eaten and the egg-mess bowl to be scraped.

'We will go to St Michael's Church immediately,' said Michael, as Bartholomew followed him down the spiral stairs and into the yard. 'We will look behind this altar of Runham's, and bring any soap we find back to the College. And then we will decide what to do next.'

They were about to open the front gate when Walter came hurrying out from the porter's lodge, his gloomy face anxious. He was working days at Michaelhouse in the hope he would be reappointed. 'I would not open that, if I were you, Brother,' he advised. 'Some of your choir are outside.'

'So?' asked Michael irritably. 'What do you think they might do? Sing to me?'

'That would be a good enough reason to stay behind locked gates in itself,' said Walter without the flicker of a smile. 'But I do not think they have come to sing: I think they have come to fight.'

'Fight?' asked Michael. 'Why would they want to fight? I plan to reinstate them as soon as I have resolved this business with Runham. I should have done it before, but first I was ill, and then I was busy.'

'They do not know that, do they?' Walter pointed out. 'But they are outside, and they look as though music is the farthest thing from their minds.'

A flight of steep, narrow steps led to the top of the wall that separated the College from Foul Lane. Bartholomew climbed it quickly, and was startled to see that Walter was right: there was a large gathering of townsfolk outside the College gates. None of them carried weapons as far as he could see, and he supposed that they had only come to beg for the reinstatement that Michael proposed to arrange anyway. They did not seem to be the menacing throng that Walter had claimed.

'You should talk to them,' he said to Michael, climbing down again. 'Tell them that the next practice will be at the usual time, and I imagine they will disperse quite peacefully.'

'Very well,' said Michael, striding towards the gate. Before he could reach it, there was a tremendous hammering. He stopped and gazed at Bartholomew in surprise.

'Michaelhouse!' came a loud voice from the other side of the wall. 'Open up.'

'Who is it?' demanded Walter in an unsteady voice.

Standing well to one side, he eased open the small grille in the door that would allow him to see out.

'It is me and Adam de Newenham,' came Robert de Blaston's voice. 'And a few others who are prepared to stand by us and see justice done. We want our money for working on your buildings.'

'You said tomorrow,' said Michael, aggrieved. 'Then we will have a week's wages for every man at the rate agreed by Master Runham.'

'But we want all of it,' shouted Blaston. 'We want the entire month's pay in advance – today, not tomorrow.'

'Michaelhouse will pay you for a week,' said Michael firmly. 'That is already twice what you would have earned from Bene't.'

'We have heard rumours – put about by your own servants – that Michaelhouse was robbed when Runham died,' shouted Blaston. 'We do not trust you to pay us later. We want *all* our money now.'

Walter immediately started to inspect his fingernails, while one of the cooks who had been listening to the exchange seemed to be similarly guilt-stricken. Bartholomew did not blame either of them: they had been summarily dismissed after years of service, and it was only human nature to gossip and gripe about it in the taverns – and to speculate that the College did not have the money to pay for the services it had requested.

'It is not common practice to pay everything in advance,' argued Michael. 'We will pay you for the week of work that you have already done, and then you can return to Bene't. The scholars there are keen for you to complete their building first. You can finish ours later.'

'The rumours were right!' cried Newenham in disbelief. 'You do *not* have the funds to pay us what we are due.'

'I will not shriek out this matter with you like the

constable of a besieged castle,' snapped Michael irritably. 'I will open the door, and you and Blaston can enter. We will discuss this like civilised men, not like vendors at a fish market.'

Reluctantly, Walter opened the gate to admit Blaston and Newenham, flinching as though he anticipated the horde outside might come crashing in. Michael's beadle, Meadowman, was with them, white-faced and tense as he contemplated the widening rift between the University that paid his wages and the town in which he lived.

Curious scholars had gathered in the yard, and they ringed Michael and the two carpenters, watching the exchange with interest. The other Fellows arrived, too, Langelee in a foul enough mood to join in any fight going, and Clippesby and Suttone, unused to the occasional spats between town and University, looking nervous. William was gripping a heavy bible like a lethal weapon, and Bartholomew had the unnerving impression that he was either about to pronounce the start of a holy war or hurl the book at someone and brain them with it.

'Oh, hello, Doctor,' said Blaston amiably to Bartholomew as he spotted the physician. 'Did I tell you that my Yolande was very pleased with her ribbon?'

'What is this?' demanded William, glaring challengingly at Bartholomew. 'You gave Yolande de Blaston a gift? I thought she was a whore.'

'Only on certain nights of the week,' objected Blaston, offended.

'Then what is that smell?' demanded William, gazing around him with the glare of a fanatic. 'I detect the unmistakable odour of brothel!'

Bartholomew moved away from him.

'And how would you know, Father?' asked Langelee

archly. 'You have some personal experience of brothels, do you? Perhaps you can recommend me a couple.'

'Come into our hall,' said Kenyngham quickly to the craftsmen, sensing a confrontation in the making that had nothing to do with wages and broken contracts. 'Share some wine with us, and we will discuss this in a dignified way.'

'No, thank you,' said Newenham hastily. 'We hear that Michaelhouse has laid in a supply of Widow's Wine. I would not drink that stuff if I were dying of thirst in a desert.'

'It is a splendid brew,' said William indignantly. 'It is a good, honest man's drink, not this weak and watery rubbish that I hear is served in other Colleges. I must see about ordering more of it.'

'We did not come here to talk about wine,' said Newenham impatiently. 'We came because we want our money. We want the ninety pounds right now – for the supplies that we will have to buy and for our labour over the next three weeks, as well as what we are already owed.'

'It is not customary to pay for work before it is completed,' argued Michael again. 'I can assure you that our College—'

'Show us, then,' interrupted Blaston. Michael regarded him uncertainly. 'Give us our week's wages now, and show us the rest. We heard it was all in a large coffer in Master Runham's room. Show us this coffer, and we will be back within the hour with our tools to complete the work we started. We only want to make sure we will not be cheated.'

'Michaelhouse does not cheat people,' began William, offended. Kenyngham put a cautionary hand on his shoulder to quieten him.

'Please,' said Suttone, stepping forward and raising

his hands in a placatory gesture. 'Michaelhouse scholars are honest men, and none of us has any intention of cheating you.'

'No?' demanded Blaston. 'Then show us the gold.'

'We are clerics,' continued Suttone, in the same reasonable tones. 'Friars and monks. I promise you we are honourable men who will see you are paid what you agreed with Runham. Even if I have to work as a common scribe in St Mary's Church for the rest of my life, I assure you that Michaelhouse will make good its debts.'

Blaston gazed at him, aware of the sincerity in the Carmelite's voice. 'Then show us the gold, Father. Prove to us that you have it. That is all we are asking.'

'When Master Runham died, we thought it was unsafe to have so much money in one place,' said Michael smoothly, 'so we deposited it with various people around the town. We cannot show it to you, because it is no longer here.'

'Lies!' spat Newenham. He turned to Blaston. 'The rumours were true: Michaelhouse will not pay us at the rate we were promised. They want to give us a week's money, when we were promised four times as much. I am not standing here to have my intelligence insulted!'

He stamped towards the gate, which Walter hastily fumbled open. After a moment, Blaston followed. Before he left, he turned and addressed the assembled scholars.

'You will regret this, Michaelhouse. You are trying to cheat honest workmen. You will regret it.'

'No!' cried Suttone, distressed. 'Please wait! There is no need for violence that may lead to bloodshed. Come back, so that we can talk about this.'

But although Blaston may have believed that Suttone did not intend to cheat him, he was clearly not convinced of the honesty of the other Michaelhouse men. With an apologetic shrug to the Carmelite, he turned and stalked away. Beadle Meadowman grabbed Michael's sleeve and muttered in his ear before following.

'He means what he says, Brother. Michaelhouse had better show them what they want, or you can expect every working man in the town to fall in behind them to see justice done.'

'I hope you are not threatening us,' said William coldly.

Meadowman shook his head. 'I have been with these men for a week now, and I know what they think. I am only warning you that they mean what they say: pay up or face the consequences.'

He turned to run after Blaston before Walter locked the gate. Bartholomew climbed to the top of the wall and was relieved to see that the people assembled in the lane were dispersing. He was about to descend when Blaston turned and howled at the top of his voice.

'You have trouble coming your way, Michaelhouse!'

Bartholomew knelt next to the small altar near Wilson's tomb and tugged with all his might. Next to him, Michael was casting anxious glances up the nave, as though he anticipated that a horde of furious townspeople would descend on him at any moment. Not far away, and covered by a sheet of silk, was the body of Runham, lying in its own coffin – not the parish one that served everyone else – and looking as smug and complacent in death as it had in life.

'I keep thinking he is watching me,' said Bartholomew, glancing over at the body as he pushed and pulled at the portable altar. 'It is not a pleasant sensation.'

'Do not be fanciful, Matt. And hurry up! I do not feel safe here.'

'No one will attack the church,' said Bartholomew reasonably. 'It is Michaelhouse they want, and that has withstood attacks before – far more violent ones than a few masons, carpenters and out-of-work singers will manage.'

'Do not be so sure,' said Michael. 'You know how the apprentices love to join in any kind of rioting and looting. They will willingly add their numbers and their belligerence to the mob.'

'Then stop it before it starts,' said Bartholomew, easing himself into a better position and trying again. 'You have already warned the Sheriff's men and your beadles to be ready, but perhaps you need to call a curfew or close off St Michael's Lane.'

'I know how to attempt to prevent a riot,' said Michael stiffly. 'I am the Senior Proctor and have far more experience of this sort of thing than you do.'

'Well, stop fretting about it, then,' said Bartholomew. 'Come and help me with this. I think it must be mortared into place. I cannot budge the thing.'

Michael elbowed him out of the way and lent his considerable strength to prising the small altar from Wilson's tomb. With a snapping of ripped wood, it came free and they peered behind it. It was stuffed to the gills with blocks of soap, the scent so powerful that Michael backed away and immediately started to sneeze. Bartholomew removed one and began to pare the soap away with one of his knives. Concealed within it was a ring.

'That is the gold ring Sam Gray placed as a pledge in one of our hutches,' said Michael, taking it from him and wiping his running nose on a piece of linen.

Bartholomew gazed at him in confusion. 'I do not understand. I thought Runham had sold all those things. That list we found in his room told us how much he had been paid for each item.'

'We were wrong, Matt,' said Michael tiredly. 'In the light of what we have just discovered, I suggest that the list was not Runham itemising how much he *had* been paid, it was predicting how much he thought he was *going* to be paid.'

'But that means the chest in his room never contained ninety pounds at all,' said Bartholomew. 'It must have contained the thirty he borrowed from the guilds, the thirty he begged from benefactors, and some undetermined amount.'

'Do you think he planned to abscond with it?' asked Michael, turning the ring over in his fingers. 'It is possible, you know. Runham was very partial to money, as was his thieving cousin.'

Bartholomew sat back on his heels and considered. 'I wonder if the fact that the bowl of yours that Wilson stole later made an appearance in Runham's room suggests that Runham knew his cousin was a thief and came to Michaelhouse specifically to claim these ill-gotten gains.'

'I wonder,' said Michael thoughtfully, sitting on the damaged altar. 'It makes sense.'

'Does it?' asked Bartholomew, not absolutely certain he was right.

Michael nodded slowly. 'Runham came to Michaelhouse a year ago, and it seemed to me as though he always intended to make a bid for the position of Master when it became vacant.'

'But Roger Alcote, who died this summer, was generally considered Kenyngham's successor.'

'No one liked Alcote,' said Michael. 'I am not sure *I* would have voted for him, and I am very sure *you* would not.'

'True. But I would not – did not – vote for Runham, either.'

'But you might have done if the alternative was Alcote. We all knew Runham was smug and superior, but none of us knew how truly dreadful he was until he was in a position of power. He must have been hiding his real character all this time.'

'So, he presented us the charming side of his personality – his arrogance and condescension – for a year, and then made a bid for the Mastership?' said Bartholomew.

Michael nodded again. 'And all that time, the unworldly Kenyngham was residing in the Master's quarters. Stolen treasure could be dripping from the walls and Kenyngham would not notice. Do you remember Runham ordering Kenyngham out of his room as soon as he was elected Master?'

'He did occupy the Master's quarters with unseemly haste,' agreed Bartholomew. 'Usually, the outgoing Master shows a little respect for his predecessor by allowing him a few weeks' grace, but Runham wanted Kenyngham gone within a day.'

'And the reason was that he could not wait to search it, to see if he could find the treasure he knew Wilson had stolen. We assumed he was flexing his new muscles of power, but it was because he was desperate to get his greedy fingers on Wilson's room.'

'But the only evidence we have that Wilson was a thief is your little bowl,' said Bartholomew. 'I hardly think a man like Runham is going to bide his time for a year on the off-chance that a few crystal bowls might be hidden up the chimney.'

'You are wrong, Matt,' said Michael. 'There were other pieces I suspected Wilson had pilfered. Alcote lost some silver spoons, while the Oliver brothers – remember that dreadful pair, who were students during the Death? – had a purse of gold stolen. Wilson was seen near both rooms just before these items went missing, although this was insufficient evidence to confront him with.'

'Dunstan and Aethelbald, the rivermen, told me that

there was a rumour in the town that Wilson's room was stuffed full of stolen gold and silver when he died,' said Bartholomew thoughtfully, recalling what had been said when the choir had been dismissed.

Michael shrugged. 'There is often a grain of truth in some of these tales.'

'And then there were the last rites Matilde told me about,' said Bartholomew. 'She said Wilson absolved rich people who died during the plague, and then relieved them of as many of their worldly goods as he could carry.'

'Did he indeed?' breathed Michael, his eyes bright with interest. 'No wonder he caught the disease, if he went rummaging about in the houses of the sick looking for their treasure.'

Bartholomew recalled vividly the night Wilson had died – how he had been burning papers and leaving his business affairs in the way he wanted them found. He had probably been hiding things, too, secreting them away behind weak plaster or old wall hangings, perhaps even imagining that he might return from the hereafter to retrieve them.

'And then Runham must have started to spirit Wilson's goods out of the College to sell,' said Michael. 'He hid them in the soap so that he would not be caught red-handed. But it is already dusk. We should leave these items here – they have been quite safe so far, and I do not want to carry them back to the College in the dark – and prepare ourselves for our foray to Bene't tonight.'

Bartholomew sighed. 'I am not sure we are within our rights to—'

'We are perfectly within our rights,' interrupted Michael. 'We are doing well, Matt. We have found part of Michael-house's missing treasure, and by tomorrow we will have the Bene't murderer in the proctors' cells. And then all we need to do is to discover which of us killed Master Runham.'

CHAPTER 11

OR THE FIRST TIME IN MANY YEARS, BARTHOLOMEW was faced with a clandestine nocturnal expedition without the comforting presence of Cynric. He seriously considered asking the Welshman if he would go anyway, but knew that he had no right to make that sort of demand on their friendship. Trying to recall all that Cynric had taught him about sneaking around in the dark, he sat in the kitchen, watching Agatha mend one of his shirts.

It was good to see her familiar figure in her customary fireside chair, and to hear the creak and groan of the wicker as she rocked herself back and forth, her thick fingers deftly manipulating the tiny silver needle. Bartholomew sat on a stool to one side of the fire, poking it with a stick. When the College cat rubbed around his legs, he picked it up and put it on his lap, finding in its trusting purr a comforting respite from the twists and turns of the University's schemes. Michael was at the kitchen table with a pile of fresh oatcakes smeared with bacon fat, happily enjoying a little light refreshment to supplement the meal of pea pudding and bread he had already devoured in the hall.

'This is better,' he said, beaming at Agatha and Bartholomew as he rammed another cake into his mouth. 'The spectre of Runham is exorcised, and the College is gradually returning to normal. We have most of our staff back again, and there is food in the pantry and cool ale in the cellars.'

'But we still have a murdered Master, a half-empty chest from which we will need to pay the workmen—' began Bartholomew.

'A third empty,' corrected Michael. 'With the gold that was returned to you, we now have fifty-seven of the original ninety pounds.'

'—and the horrible prospect that one of our colleagues is a Master-killer.'

'Clippesby,' said Michael with certainty. 'He is the only one whose alibi is patently false. The Bene't men had nothing to do with Runham's murder, Matt. I know we thought they had a motive – to get their workmen back – but the more I think about it, the more ludicrous that notion feels.'

'But what about those intruders?' asked Bartholomew. 'They must have been people from outside Michaelhouse. If either of them had been Clippesby, there would have been no need for furtiveness.'

'Clippesby would have been furtive if he were smuggling a woman in,' said Michael confidently. 'I think the intruders who have bested you twice were Clippesby and his whore.'

Bartholomew gazed at him in astonishment. 'And how did you reach that conclusion, Brother?'

'It is all I can think of,' said Michael carelessly. 'But let me tell you what I think happened: Clippesby is a man who feels the need for female company – well, who does not on occasion? – but being a Dominican friar, he needs to be a little careful. One night, Runham – who we know crept around at night, hoping to come across people he could fine – caught him. Rather than risk exposure, Clippesby smothered Runham and then raided the chest to make the murder look like robbery, rather than a crime of panic.'

'And did he arrange for the scaffolding to fall, too?'

'That was a coincidence, as I have been telling you all along. Clippesby just happened to be escorting his whore out of the College when the thing collapsed. I was fortunate you made such a racket when you attacked them, or I would have been sleeping in my room at the time and would have been killed for certain.'

It all seemed far too convenient to Bartholomew; he could see no evidence at all that Clippesby had a penchant for the town's women.

'We have forgotten about Justus, Runham's dead book-bearer,' he said, changing the subject.

'That is because Justus was a suicide who dragged a wineskin over his head and killed himself. You said so yourself.'

'But that was before I discovered that Runham and Wymundham had also died from suffocation. It is too unusual a way to die for all three deaths to be coincidental.'

'Very well,' said Michael irritably. 'We will include Justus in our reasonings, if it will make you happy. But I must point out that you did not mention the presence of smothering cushions at Dame Nichol's Hythe when you found his corpse.'

'If someone had tied a wineskin over Justus's head to make it appear that he had killed himself, that person would hardly have left a tell-tale cushion behind,' said Bartholomew. 'But perhaps the most important point here is that Justus was killed *before* Clippesby arrived in Cambridge: thus we cannot blame Justus's death on Clippesby – and if not Justus's, then also not Runham's and Wymundham's.'

'No, Matt. Justus was killed *the same day* that Clippesby arrived,' said Michael. 'Perhaps that alone is significant. But you are wrong in thinking the deaths of Wymundham, Justus and Runham are connected. They are not: they cannot be. What could a gloomy servant, a gossiping Bene't Fellow and Michaelhouse's Master have had in common?'

'Justus was Runham's book-bearer,' said Bartholomew. 'There is one connection.'

'But not to Wymundham. I will accept that Runham's death and Justus's suicide may be related, but the business at Bene't is completely separate. Clippesby killed Runham, and your logic would have him slaying Justus, too. But I do not see why he would also murder Wymundham.'

Bartholomew sighed, knowing he would not convince Michael otherwise. 'So, what do you plan to do about Clippesby?'

'Nothing,' said Michael comfortably.

'Nothing?'

'Nothing yet. I will be watching him day and night – Walter, Agatha, William, Suttone and others will help – and when he makes a mistake, we will have him.'

'What kind of mistake?'

Michael shrugged. 'Spending large amounts of money, smuggling a woman into his chamber, an unhealthy fascination with cushions.'

'That is risky,' said Bartholomew anxiously. 'He might harm someone before you can stop him.'

'As I said, Matt, we will be watching him. If he makes a hostile move, we will strike.'

Bartholomew frowned, not sure that the monk's strategy of wait-and-see was a wise one. There was no doubt in his mind that Clippesby was verging on insanity, and to allow him freedom of movement when he might be connected to the deaths of three people seemed rash, to say the least.

'So, what will you do about Master Runham's fine north court?' he asked after a while. 'Do you really intend to send all the workmen back to Bene't, as you promised Heltisle?'

'I think we must,' said Michael. 'Then we can blame the fact that they will not get their bonuses on Bene't. That means we can use the money we have to repay the loans Runham took out with the Guilds of St Mary's and Corpus Christi, and also return some to our generous benefactors – unless I can persuade them to wait a while. Oswald Stanmore will not mind us keeping his five marks indefinitely, I am sure. And if there is anything left over, we can refill some of the hutches.'

'And what do we do with a half-built court and a half-repaired north wing?'

'Leave them as they are,' said Michael simply. 'Remove the scaffolding and return to the shabby elegance we had before.'

'That shabby elegance included leaking roofs and damp walls. And it may have escaped your notice, but a good part of the north wing is missing a roof and one room has been demolished.'

'The workmen will have to make good the damage their careless scaffolding did when it collapsed,' said Michael in a tone of voice that suggested he was bored with the conversation. 'But tonight I am more inclined to think about the Bene't murders than Michaelhouse. I feel certain I am close to solving those. De Walton will tell me all I need to know about that treacherous Simeon when we rescue him tonight.'

'There is a lot that can go wrong with this plan of yours to save de Walton,' began Bartholomew. 'It is full of risks – not just to us, but to Walter.'

'It will work,' said Michael. 'Walter will let us into Bene't while Osmun and that vicious Ulfo are asleep; we will rescue de Walton from where he is being kept prisoner by Simeon in the hut near the King's Ditch; and de Walton will tell us who killed Raysoun, Brother Patrick and Wymundham. Then we can concentrate on how to extricate Michaelhouse from the mess Runham left.'

'I do not know how I became involved in this,' said Bartholomew weakly. 'It is not my place to creep around other Colleges in the dead of night looking for murderers.'

'You would not let me go alone,' said Michael complacently. 'You know I need your help. None of my beadles would be good at this sort of thing, and anyway, Osmun has them all terrified out of their feeble wits.'

'How?' asked Bartholomew. 'The beadles are supposed to be the law enforcers in the University. It is not for the likes of Osmun to terrify them.'

'I agree. But when they arrested him for fighting with de Walton the other day, he put his time under lock and key to good use. He made all sorts of threats to my beadles and their families. Osmun is a violent, vengeful man, and they are all far too frightened to do anything that might attract his unwanted attention.'

'And this is the man you want us to slip past at midnight?' asked Bartholomew doubtfully. 'Maybe the beadles are right to stay out of his way.'

'They are. But is that the kind of person you want on the streets of your town, terrorising the law enforcers, assaulting Fellows and students, and generally defying the University's authority?'

'No,' admitted Bartholomew. 'Perhaps we should ask for Dick Tulyet's help – the Sheriff's men will not be afraid of a bullying brute like Osmun.'

'Tulyet cannot take part in a plan to break into the University in the dead of night,' said Michael practically. 'And it would not be fair to ask him to do so. But we will pit wits and cunning against brute strength, Matt, and by morning we will have Osmun and that plotting Simekyn Simeon – how did he ever acquire a name like that anyway? – safely secured in the proctors' prison.'

'You seem very sure that Simeon is responsible for the murders of Raysoun and Wymundham, but it seems to me as though the entire College is involved. De Walton himself, Caumpes, Heltisle, Osmun and Ulfo were also present in the church when Adela saw Wymundham's leg.'

'Adela said Caumpes was not there.'

'Right,' said Bartholomew wearily. 'Do you realise that you will make an enemy of the Duke of Lancaster by proving his henchman committed murder, Brother? I understand the Duke can be a dangerous man.'

'Not as dangerous as my Bishop,' said Michael smugly. 'And I sent the Bishop a letter this evening, revealing all. If the Duke tries anything nasty on me or Michaelhouse, he will find he has a very powerful churchman to contend with. But the Duke will disclaim Simeon, if de Walton's evidence exposes him as a killer. Loyalty to one's henchmen only goes so far.'

'But what will you do if de Walton declines to betray his colleague?' asked Bartholomew. 'He may be too frightened – like your beadles.'

'Master Lynton says de Walton has leprosy, Matt,' said Michael, becoming exasperated. 'He is already a dead man in the eyes of the world, and he will tell us exactly what happened that day in Holy Trinity Church when five Bene't men lined up to prevent Adela from seeing a body behind the altar. And he will tell me which of these five followed poor, terrified Brother Patrick and stabbed him just when he had reached the safety of his hostel.'

'How do you know Patrick was killed just as he reached his hostel?' asked Bartholomew sceptically. 'Adela saw these five men with the body in broad daylight, and Patrick must have been killed in the dark, or someone would have noticed his body in the grounds.'

'Not necessarily. Ovyng Hostel's gardens are extensive, and, unlike Mayor Horwoode, its scholars probably do not stroll there on a regular basis. But you are throwing up problems that are irrelevant. Tonight we will solve the murders of Raysoun, Wymundham and Patrick, and we will find that the culprit is Simekyn Simeon, because he is the one who is holding his colleague prisoner in the hut in Bene't's grounds.'

'Well, come on then,' said Bartholomew, standing up reluctantly. 'We should be on our way before Walter allows his sense of self-preservation to get the better of him and he declines to allow us past the sleeping Osmun and Ulfo.'

'He would not dare,' said Michael comfortably. 'I have told him that I will ensure he remains working at Bene't for the rest of his life unless he does as I ask. Walter will not let us down.'

With the unshakeable feeling that he was about to do something very stupid and dangerous that he would later regret, Bartholomew followed Michael across the courtyard to the front gate.

Carefully, as though the merest thud would wake the entire College, Michael removed the bar from the wicket gate and eased open the door to Michaelhouse. Both he and Bartholomew were dressed in dark clothes – Michael in his black habit and matching cloak; Bartholomew in dark leggings, a brown jerkin hidden by his tabard and a short black cloak. Bartholomew was about to precede Michael outside when he heard soft voices in the lane and saw two cloaked figures moving towards him. Stomach churning, he ducked back inside again, regarding Michael in alarm.

'It is them! The two intruders!'

Michael took Bartholomew's arm and pulled him into

the deep shadows at the side of the gate. 'Then let us wait here for them, and unmask Clippesby and his whore once and for all.'

'No,' said Bartholomew, trying to pull away. 'They have bested me twice, and I have no wish to engage in a tussle with them a third time. I have had enough of this; I am going to bed – where you would go, too, if you had any sense.'

'Matthew!' exclaimed Kenyngham with pleasure, as he eased himself through the gate that Michael had just opened. 'And Brother Michael, too! How thoughtful of you both to wait for Master Suttone and me to return from lauds and unlock the gate for us. I confess I was not sure how we were going to gain entry, given that we still have no night porter.'

'Perhaps Walter will come back to us,' said Bartholomew, relief flooding through him as he stood aside to allow his colleagues past.

'Matt and I are about to apprehend a killer,' said Michael, making it sound like a pleasant excursion to a country meadow in summertime. 'You can help us, if you will.'

'Us?' asked Suttone nervously, casting an anxious glance at Kenyngham. 'I am only a poor friar, Brother. I have no experience in wrestling with vicious killers in the middle of the night – nor do I want to gain any, thank you very much.'

'I am not asking for physical assistance, just for a little information,' said Michael reassuringly. 'The night Runham died, you and Master Kenyngham attended compline in St Michael's Church. It is what proved neither of you had a hand in his murder.'

'I wish I had not gone,' said Kenyngham sadly. 'I wish I had stayed here, so that I might have been able to prevent such wickedness.'

'If you had, the killer would merely have waited for another opportunity,' said Michael practically. 'But can you recall who else was at compline at St Michael's Church that night?'

Kenyngham and Suttone exchanged a mystified glance.

'I do not remember,' said Kenyngham, scratching his head. 'It was days ago, and I have attended many offices since then. They have begun to blur in my mind.'

'Well, there was that loutish bargeman who used to sing bass in the choir,' said Suttone, frowning thoughtfully. 'He spent the entire time pawing some woman in the shadows at the back. There were a couple of men from Ovyng, and a handful from Physwick Hostel – they use St Michael's regularly, as you know. Then there was that skinny fellow from Bene't, and I think it was Friday that some folk from the Market Square attended the service . . .'

'Which skinny fellow from Bene't?' Michael pounced.

'I do not know his name. He speaks with a Fenman's accent and has terrible teeth. When Master Kenyngham was at the high altar, he joined me near Wilson's tomb and we prayed there together for some time. We did not speak, and I do not know whether he will recall the incident or not.'

'Why did you not mention him earlier?' asked Michael.

Suttone shrugged. 'I did not want you hunting this man down, and then him claiming he did not remember me next to him. Think how it would have looked had he failed to corroborate my story. I would have looked as guilty and suspicious as does Clippesby.'

'I will give my full attention to Clippesby in the morning,' said Michael grandly. 'But first I am off to Bene't, to catch the villain who shoved Raysoun off the scaffolding; smothered Wymundham in Holy Trinity Church; and then stabbed Brother Patrick.'

'Who is it?' asked Suttone curiously. 'It is not that vicious Osmun, is it? I have heard stories about his brutality, Brother. Be sure to take plenty of beadles with you.'

'Matt and I will deal with this alone,' said Michael confidently. 'But we should be on our way. I want to make an end of it as quickly as possible.'

Leaving Kenyngham and Suttone to lock the gate behind them, Michael led the way up St Michael's Lane and began to head towards Bene't, his thumping footsteps very loud in the still town. It was a cloudy night, and there was no gleam from the moon to light their way. They moved slowly, wary of the water-filled potholes and of the slippery, sewage-encrusted drains that meandered down either side of the road. There was no wind, and the stench from the ditches was thick in the still air, overlaid with the smell of ancient animal dung, rotting waste that had been hurled from the houses into the street in the vain hope that it would be washed away by rain, and spillages from the tannery and the potters' workshops.

Michael stumbled in the dark, swearing viciously when he skinned his knuckles against a wall. Somewhere a dog barked furiously, warning its owner that someone was moving down a road that should have been deserted except for the beadles and the Sheriff's patrols. A window shutter opened, sending a sliver of golden light slanting into the street, but was then closed quickly when the dark shadows of Michael and Bartholomew glided by.

Eventually, they reached Bene't, a dark edifice laced with scaffolding, as though some skeletal hand had reached down from the sky and had seized it. Bartholomew shuddered, and tried to push such fanciful images from his mind.

'We are early,' whispered Michael. 'The bells have not chimed midnight yet. We should hide in St Bene't's churchyard and wait, or Walter might not be ready for us.'

'I hate this,' complained Bartholomew as he followed Michael through the long, wet grass of the cemetery. 'It is not normal for two respectable Fellows to be skulking among graves in the middle of the night.'

'It is no good leaving it until tomorrow,' said Michael. 'By then, Simeon may have killed de Walton, and I am not sure if we can rely on Walter to help us again. It is now or never. And do not tell me you would rather it was never. Do you not want to see the killer of Raysoun, Wymundham and Brother Patrick brought to justice?'

Bartholomew sighed. 'There is the midnight bell. Let us get this over with, so that we can go home and solve the murder in our own College.'

They walked stealthily back to Bene't's main gate and tapped softly on the wicket wood. Immediately Walter's white face peered out.

'I do not like this at all,' he whispered fearfully.

'You are not alone,' muttered Bartholomew. 'So, where is this hut in which Simeon is supposed to have de Walton secreted away? We need to release him, and take him back to Michaelhouse as quickly as possible.'

'But he has leprosy,' objected Walter in horror. 'You cannot take lepers to Michaelhouse! He will kill everyone he sets eyes on!'

'Leprosy does not spread quite like that,' said Bartholomew. 'As far as I can tell, it is passed—'

'Nevertheless, Walter is right,' interrupted Michael quickly, before the physician could deliver a lecture. He rubbed his chin, making a soft rasping sound in the darkness. 'We cannot take a leper back to Michaelhouse.'

'Why did you not think of this before?' asked Bartholomew in exasperation. 'You have been considering this plan all evening.'

'I cannot think of everything,' snapped Michael. 'You are the physician – you should have raised the point.'

'We will take him to the hospital near the Barnwell Priory,' said Bartholomew. 'But let us get on with this business before my nerve fails me and I go home.'

'Come on, then,' said Walter, pulling them inside and closing the door. He led the way through the gatehouse, and peered carefully all around the courtyard before turning back to them. 'You must cut across to the south-east door – I made sure it is open – and then take the path that runs through the vegetable garden to the orchard. Right at the bottom of the orchard, surrounded by nettles, is an old lean-to that is used for storing apples. De Walton is in there.'

'Will you not show us the way?' asked Bartholomew.

'No fear!' said Walter. 'That was not part of the arrangement. I will leave the main gate open so that you will be able to get out, but I am off right now. I will spend the rest of the night in Michaelhouse, thank you.'

He was gone before either scholar could object, scurrying out through the gate at an impressive pace and with evident terror.

'Come on, Matt,' whispered Michael. 'Follow me. We will keep to the shadows at the edge of the court – that is what Cynric would have done.'

'I wish he were here,' muttered Bartholomew, trying to walk softly as they moved across the slippery cobbles. A rat scuttled in front of him and he took a sharp intake of breath that made Michael regard him in weary exasperation.

The gate that led to the grounds behind the College was ajar, as Walter had promised. Wincing at the croaking squeak that sounded very loud in the silence, Michael eased it further open and stepped through, waiting for Bartholomew to follow. Once away from the half-finished buildings where the scholars slept, Bartholomew began to relax a little, thinking that he and Michael could always run to the end of the garden and scramble over the wall to Luthburne Lane should they be followed and challenged. It was also not so necessary to remain quiet, and they were well concealed from any sleepless Bene't scholar by the trees and fruit bushes that lined the path.

'There it is,' whispered Michael, pointing to a dark shape that huddled against the back wall. 'That is the hut Walter described.'

He started to move forward, but Bartholomew pulled him back, listening intently to ensure that they had not been led into a trap. There was nothing. Cautiously, he edged towards the hut, wincing as nettles stung his hand. A sturdy bar had been placed across the door; Bartholomew removed it quickly and pressed his ear to the wood. There was no sound, and he began to wonder whether the leprous de Walton was not secured inside it at all. He pulled at the door, but it would not budge.

'It is locked,' he whispered to Michael, pointing to the chain that had been looped through two iron rungs. The metal shone dimly, and Bartholomew supposed it had been placed there relatively recently.

'Break the chain,' whispered Michael back.

'How?' asked Bartholomew. 'I would need an axe, and we are trying to be quiet.'

Michael gave an impatient sigh. 'Give me those birthing forceps you have in your bag.'

'No,' whispered Bartholomew angrily. 'My forceps are delicate, and you will damage them.'

'Delicate!' spat Michael. 'They are about the sturdiest weapon I have ever seen. I will be more likely to damage the door than to put so much as a scratch on them. Give them to me, Matt. There may be a sick man inside this hut, and it is your duty as a physician to help him.'

Feeling as though Michael had scored a cheap hit, Bartholomew handed him the heavy instrument, and watched him insert one of its arms through the rung and begin to twist. With a sharp snap, the rung popped loose, and Michael removed the chain that secured the door. Carefully, he pushed it open and peered into the darkness within.

The inside of the hut was pitch black, and Bartholomew could make out nothing other than one or two rotten apples that lay on the floor near his foot. To one side, he heard the scrape of tinder as Michael lit a candle. Careful to shield the light from draughts with his cupped hands, the monk stepped into the shed.

A man lay on the rough wooden planking of the floor, heaped with blankets and with an unnatural pallor to his face. At first, Bartholomew thought that de Walton was already dead, but the man's eyelids flickered open. Bartholomew moved forward reassuringly, but the man struggled away from the blankets and regarded the dark shapes that stood over him with naked terror.

'No!' he shrieked loudly, making Bartholomew leap out of his skin and startling some roosting birds so that their agitated flapping added to the sudden disturbance. 'No! I will not tell!'

'Quiet!' hissed Michael urgently. 'I am the Senior Proctor, and I am here to rescue you.'

'Rescue me?' squeaked de Walton, in an unsteady, confused voice. He tried to stand, and Bartholomew could see the fading bruise on his face that Osmun had inflicted.

'Can you walk?' asked Bartholomew gently. 'I do not think we should stay here any longer than we have to.'

'No,' agreed Michael sardonically. 'Especially after that

unholy screech. He has probably woken the entire town.'

'But I do not want to leave,' whispered de Walton in alarm. 'I want to stay here, where I am safe.'

'You are not safe here,' Michael pointed out impatiently. 'You are in a freezing shack, locked in by a man who means you harm.'

'I will not go with you,' sobbed de Walton, leaning back against the wall and hugging his blankets to him. 'You cannot make me.'

'Is his illness making him deranged?' asked Michael curtly of Bartholomew. 'Give him something to make him see sense, Matt. We do not have time to argue.'

Bartholomew slipped an arm under de Walton's shoulders and tried to pull him to his feet, but de Walton gave another screech and began to pummel the physician with his puny fists.

'I have leprosy!' he wailed. 'Touch me and you will catch it, too.'

Bartholomew, like Master Lynton before him, had observed the faint lumps and blemishes that characterised the disease's early onset, but knew that leprosy was not as contagious as was popularly believed, especially the type that afflicted de Walton. 'Let me take you to the hospital near Barnwell Priory,' he said kindly. 'You will be well looked after there.'

'But I will not be safe,' said de Walton, trying to push Bartholomew away. 'I do not want to go.'

Exasperated, Bartholomew released him. 'But why? Simeon and Osmun have imprisoned you here against your will. Why will you not let us help you to escape?'

De Walton gazed at him. 'They did not imprison me; they put me here with my consent, so that I would be safe from the rest of them.'

'The rest of who?' asked Michael, confused and impatient. He went to the door and peered out into the darkness to check that no Osmun was bearing down on them. 'Who are you afraid of?'

'Go away,' said de Walton desperately. 'You reveal by your questions that you know nothing about what is happening in my College, and your meddling will only make things worse.'

'If I do not understand what is going on, it is only because your colleagues have spun me such a web of lies that I am unable to see the truth,' snapped Michael. 'Tell me what is happening, and then I will decide whether to leave you alone or whether to remove you to the proctors' prison.'

De Walton began to shake. 'Prison? But you said you would take me to Barnwell.'

'That,' said Michael harshly, 'depends on how co-operative you are.'

'Then ask Simeon,' said de Walton, casting an anguished glance towards the door. 'He understands the details better than I do.'

'Details?' demanded Michael. 'Is that how you describe the murders of Raysoun, Wymundham and poor Brother Patrick?'

'Who is Brother Patrick?' wailed de Walton in terror. 'And Raysoun was not murdered: he fell from the scaffolding, because he was drunk and the planking was unsafe. He liked to spy on the workmen, to make sure none of them slacked. He was a mean and miserly person.'

'Mean and miserly or not, Wymundham heard him whisper with his dying breath that he had been pushed,' said Michael. 'What have you to say about that?'

'Then Wymundham was lying,' protested de Walton. 'He was often untruthful, and you should not have believed anything he told you. He was using Raysoun's death to fan the flames of dissent among his colleagues.'

'Perhaps. But Wymundham himself was most definitely murdered,' said Michael. 'Why would he be killed if his claims regarding Raysoun's death were false?'

De Walton was so white with fear it seemed he was almost beyond caring. 'There are at least two very good reasons why Wymundham might have been murdered. Firstly, to prevent him from spreading lies about our College – such as that Raysoun was dispatched by one of his colleagues when he was not. And secondly, because he often pried into our personal affairs and threatened to expose us unless we paid him to keep silent.'

'You mean Wymundham was a blackmailer? Why has no one mentioned this to me before?' demanded Michael angrily.

'I imagine because no one wants you to find out what we paid Wymundham to conceal,' replied de Walton heavily. 'Perhaps someone decided Wymundham should not be allowed to continue his life of extortion.'

'And who is this "someone", who decided to kill, rather than risk his nasty little secrets being made public?' asked Michael. 'Simeon? He seems to be that kind of man.'

De Walton pressed himself further into the corner and remained silent, tears welling in his eyes. Bartholomew suspected that even the formidable figure of the Senior Proctor was insufficient to frighten the Bene't Fellow into telling them more, and was inclined to abandon de Walton to his dirty hut and his leprosy, and leave while he was still able. But Michael scratched his head, determined to persist.

'I do not understand any of this. You say Raysoun's death was as it initially appeared – an accident. Can you prove it?'

'Ask the workmen,' said de Walton in a small, tired voice, evidently sensing that the Senior Proctor was not a man to be easily deterred when in interrogation mode.

'They will tell you that Raysoun was a drunkard and that the scaffolding was unstable. It was only a matter of time before he missed his footing and plunged to his death.'

'Let us be logical about this,' said Michael, infuriatingly pedantic. Both Bartholomew and de Walton glanced nervously at the door, anticipating some enraged killer plunging in from the dark while Michael calmly tried to clarify the twists and turns of de Walton's information in his mind. 'You say Raysoun's death was an accident, so we will dispense with that for now. But someone definitely killed Wymundham, and my suspects are you, Heltisle, Caumpes, Simeon and the two porters, Osmun and Ulfo.'

De Walton laughed bitterly. 'Me? If only I could! Do you think a leper could overcome a healthy man like Wymundham and smother him?'

Michael and Bartholomew exchanged a glance. The fact that de Walton was aware that Wymundham had been smothered suggested that he knew more about the death than an innocent man should have done. Yet Bartholomew believed that he was right about his physical limitations: Wymundham had been small, but certainly not weak, and it was obvious that de Walton was a very sick, frail man.

'And Osmun and Ulfo were busy with College duties the night Wymundham disappeared,' de Walton continued. 'Ask any of the students. I would love to see Osmun and Ulfo hang for murder, but Wymundham did not meet his death by their hands.'

'Whose then?' pressed Michael.

'Ask the others,' pleaded de Walton. 'Leave me alone! I do not want to be accused of telling tales and punished for it. Just go away and leave me be!'

'We *will* question the others,' said Michael with quiet

determination. 'But now I am speaking to you. I am left with Caumpes, Heltisle and Simeon. One of them is the killer.'

'Simeon brought me here for safety,' said de Walton. 'He did not smother Wymundham.'

'Then it must be Heltisle,' reasoned Bartholomew, 'because Adela Tangmer told me that Caumpes was not present when she saw Wymundham's corpse in Holy Trinity Church. Caumpes was not one of the five who tried to conceal Wymundham's leg from her.'

De Walton gazed at him aghast. 'What?' he cried, shaking his head and almost weeping in his agitation. 'You think that Wymundham died in Holy Trinity? Thank God I did not leave this hiding place when you demanded! You know nothing, and I would be no more safe with you than I would in an open field!'

'Explain what happened in the church, then,' ordered Michael tersely.

De Walton swallowed hard. 'I thought we had succeeded in hiding Wymundham when Adela Tangmer burst in on us unexpectedly. But it was no corpse she saw in the church that day: what she saw was Wymundham drunk.'

'She saw a leg—' began Michael.

'She very well may have done,' interrupted de Walton. 'The man was in a terrible state – clothes dishevelled, wine spilled all over himself, and virtually insensible.'

'And what had driven him to make such a spectacle of himself?' asked Michael, unconvinced.

De Walton gave what was almost a smile. 'Heltisle. He had just paid Wymundham a handsome fee to encourage him to tell the truth about Raysoun's death – that the man had fallen. Wymundham took the money and bought himself enough wine to float a ship. Simeon spotted him going into Holy Trinity Church, and ran to fetch the rest of us before he could shame the College with his disgraceful behaviour.'

Bartholomew realised that de Walton was telling the truth. He knew that it was possible to buy cheap wine in Holy Trinity – he had been offered some there himself. Wymundham must have consumed his wine in the church, away from the disapproving stares of his Bene't colleagues.

'And what did you do?' asked Michael. 'Smother Wymundham while he lay insensible?'

De Walton sighed. 'Of course not. We bundled him up in a cloak and carried him home, telling anyone who asked that he was faint with grief for Raysoun. I do not think many believed us, given the terrible stench of wine that wafted from him. It was all very embarrassing.'

'But if Wymundham did not die in the church, where was he killed?' asked Bartholomew. 'And who stabbed Brother Patrick?'

'I know of no Brother Patrick, but I know where Wymundham met his end.' De Walton reached out and tossed a filthy cushion at Michael. 'That is what killed him. He died here, in this shed, just as I will, if you do not leave!'

Bartholomew took the cushion and inspected it in the candlelight. It was stained with something that might have been saliva, and there was a small tear surrounded by a brownish mark. He poked at it, and felt something hard embedded in the filling. More prodding with his surgical knife produced a small square of ivory. It was a broken tooth. He gazed from it to de Walton, and then flung tooth and cushion from him in revulsion. He recalled telling Michael that whoever had smothered Wymundham had pressed down so hard that one of the front teeth had snapped. It seemed de Walton was telling the truth.

'Were you present when this vile deed was done?' demanded Michael.

De Walton shuddered. 'No! But Simeon and I examined this shed when we realised it was the last place any of us had seen Wymundham alive – he used it as a venue to meet with the people he was going to blackmail. Simeon and I saw him wandering with feigned nonchalance – the way he always walked when he knew he had some hapless victim awaiting his extortions here – down the path the day before his body was found.'

'And?' pressed Michael, when de Walton paused.

'And the evidence of his death was here: the stains on the cushion, broken pots that suggested a struggle, and Wymundham's ring left on the floor. And now I have told you all I know, so please leave me alone. Your blundering investigations have not revealed my hiding place to the killer yet, so go, before it is too late.'

'Do you really feel safe here?' asked Bartholomew, glancing around uneasily, noting that some of the smashed pots still lay on the ground. 'What if the killer returns to the scene of his crime?'

De Walton shook his head with utter conviction. 'It will be the last place he will look. He will want to stay as far away from here as possible. Now go.'

'But you have not yet told us what we most want to know,' said Michael. 'Is Wymundham's killer Heltisle or Caumpes?'

'Work it out yourselves,' whispered de Walton. 'I do not want to be slain for betraying him.'

'Caumpes,' said Bartholomew suddenly, as something clicked in his mind. 'Both Robin of Grantchester and my brother-in-law told me that Caumpes likes boats, and whoever killed Wymundham would have needed a boat to take the body from here to Mayor Horwoode's garden.'

De Walton glared defiantly at him, and for a moment

Bartholomew thought he would not confirm his reasoning. Then the Bene't Fellow nodded, lowering his head to look at the lumpy, leprous patches on his hands. 'Caumpes is the only one of us able to row a boat. Like you, Simeon and I surmised that he took the body downriver and dumped it on Horwoode's land.'

'Why there?' asked Michael.

'Because it was dark and secluded, I imagine,' said de Walton. 'You do not want to row further than needful when you have a corpse in your boat.'

'And so it is Caumpes you fear,' said Michael. 'Not Simeon or those cursed porters?'

De Walton shook his head miserably. 'Caumpes is fiercely loyal to Bene't, and will do anything to protect it. I sympathise with him to a point: it was horrible to see the likes of Wymundham giving us a reputation for quarrelling and slyness, but I cannot condone murder for it.'

'Why did you not tell us this when Wymundham's body was found?' demanded Michael irritably. 'It would have saved a good deal of time – and a good deal of agitation on your part.'

'I was afraid. I hope to God you are able to prove all this and arrest Caumpes, because I am a dead man if you do not.'

'Who else knows he is the culprit?' asked Michael.

'Only Simeon. He said he would pay Osmun to help me leave Bene't safely, and then he would seek out more evidence that will confirm Caumpes's guilt before passing the matter to you. It was he who said that Caumpes will not think to look for me here.'

'Then Simeon was wrong!' came a sudden yell from outside. There was a crash and a thump, and with horror Bartholomew saw that the door had been slammed shut. He leapt towards it and thudded into it with his shoulder, but the bar had been replaced and all he did was bruise his arm.

'I told you to leave!' screamed de Walton in terror. 'Now he will kill us all!'

'He will not kill us,' snapped Michael impatiently, refusing to yield to the panic that had seized de Walton. 'If we make enough noise, someone will come and let us out.'

'But they might be too late, Brother,' said Bartholomew in a soft voice, looking upwards: smoke had began to seep through the loose planks of the roof.

Suddenly, there was a dull roar, as the pitch that had been used to render the roof watertight caught alight. Bartholomew ducked as burning cinders began to rain down on his head. Then, faster than he would have imagined possible, the whole ceiling was alive with yellow, flickering flames and the air was sharp with the acrid smell of burning.

'We are trapped!' shrieked de Walton. 'We are all going to be burned alive!'

Bartholomew coughed as swirling smoke seared the back of his throat. It billowed downward relentlessly, bathing everything in a dull grey so that he could not even see the candle Michael held in his hand. A burning timber smashed to the ground, just missing him, and immediately the floor began to smoulder. Flames flickered this way and that, running up the tinder-dry walls and licking at the pile of blankets that had covered de Walton.

De Walton began to scream, so that Bartholomew thought the flames were already consuming him. He snatched up a blanket and groped his way forward, but it was only terror that was making the Bene't scholar shriek; he crouched in his corner like a hunted animal, wailing and howling. Another timber crashed from the roof with a terrific tearing sound, and de Walton's yowls of fright grew louder still. Bartholomew groped around the walls, trying to find something he might use to smash open the door.

'Out of the way,' ordered Michael, hauling him back with a powerful hand. He took a deep breath, crouched down with his shoulder hunched into his side, and ran at one of the walls like an enraged bull. The wooden side of an ancient lean-to provided no obstacle for a man of Michael's strength, and he was through it and powering out into the fresh air beyond almost as though it did not exist. Bartholomew followed, dragging the hysterical de Walton after him by the scruff of his neck.

'That was impressive!' gasped Bartholomew, eyes smarting as he glanced back at the hole in the wall, now surrounded by a halo of flames.

'I recognised that voice,' shouted Michael furiously, gazing around him while Bartholomew bent over de Walton, who sobbed and retched in the grass. 'It was Caumpes!' He clutched Bartholomew's arm and pointed into the darkness. 'And there he is! After him!'

Peering through the gloom with watering eyes, Bartholomew could just make out dark shadows moving through the trees on the path that led to the College. Michael was after them in an instant, dragging Bartholomew with him. They ran blindly, barely able to see where they were putting their feet. Bartholomew stumbled over woody cabbages when he strayed from the path, then fell heavily when he lost his footing over the gnarled root of a pear tree.

'Got you!' he heard Michael yell in triumph.

He scrambled to his feet, his haste to help Michael making him more clumsy than ever. Someone grabbed him and he struck out, trying to dislodge the grip on his tabard.

'Bartholomew, stop!' he heard someone yell. 'It is me! Simekyn Simeon! Stop this flailing before one of us is hurt!'

Bartholomew could just make out the soft features of the Duke of Lancaster's squire peering at him. The man Michael had seized with such glee was Heltisle, who was gazing around him in confusion, not understanding why two Michaelhouse men should be attacking him in his own gardens.

'Damn! I thought you were Caumpes,' panted Michael, releasing the Bene't Master impatiently and scanning the surrounding trees.

'Caumpes is over there!' shouted Simeon, pointing to a shadow that was moving quickly and purposefully towards the opposite end of the grounds. 'And he is escaping!'

'I thought it was *Caumpes* I saw skulking in the trees,' snapped Michael, regarding him accusingly. 'But it was you.'

'We were not skulking,' objected Heltisle indignantly. 'This is my College. If anyone was skulking, it was you!'

'We have no time for this,' said Michael, leaning against a tree with a hand to his heaving chest. 'Caumpes is getting away. Chase him, Matt, or he will elude us.'

Wondering why Michael could not pursue his own villains, Bartholomew set off at a run across the grassy swath towards Luthburne Lane, the narrow alley that ran along the back of Bene't College. The shadow bobbed ahead of him, moving fast because he was on familiar ground.

Aware of footsteps behind him, Bartholomew glanced round to see Simeon on his heels. He slowed, uneasy with the Duke's henchman at his back, and certainly not keen on the notion of a knife between his shoulder blades. Caumpes may have ferried Wymundham's body to Horwoode's garden, but Bartholomew felt he had no cause to trust any of the Bene't men yet. The fact that it had been Simeon who had visited Langelee in Michaelhouse before the scaffolding had collapsed and almost killed Michael made Bartholomew far from certain that Caumpes was the only Bene't man with murderous inclinations.

Simeon shoved him forward. 'Do not stop! We can catch him. Quick, climb over the wall.'

He formed a stirrup of his hands, and Bartholomew found himself projected upward, so that he could grasp the top of the wall that surrounded the College. It was not as high as the one that protected Michaelhouse, nor as thick. He straddled the top, and leaned down to offer Simeon his hand. The courtier grasped it, and scaled the wall in a way that suggested he had not spent all his time playing lutes and writing poetry for the Duchess's ladies-in-waiting.

'We have lost him,' said Bartholomew, looking up and down a lane that was still and silent. 'I cannot see him any more.'

'There!' yelled Simeon, grabbing Bartholomew's arm so violently that the physician almost lost his balance. 'He is heading for the river. Come on!'

He leapt from the top of the wall and began to run. Reluctantly, Bartholomew followed.

'He will not be able to pass through the town gate,' he gasped, breathless from the chase. 'The soldiers will stop him.'

'He will use his boat,' yelled Simeon. 'We must prevent him from reaching it. Hurry!'

The foppish, effeminate scribe suddenly seemed a good deal more energetic than Bartholomew. He led the way along the path that ran parallel to the King's Ditch, towards where it passed one of the three main entrances to the town – the Trumpington Gate. Ahead,

Bartholomew saw a shadowy figure climb the leveed bank of the Ditch and drop down the other side.

'That is where we keep the boat,' shouted Simeon, running faster. Bartholomew struggled to keep up with him, his heart pounding and the blood roaring in his ears. He scrambled up the bank, feeling his leather-soled shoes slip and slide on the wet grass. He reached the top and saw a dark shape moving into the middle of the canal. Caumpes had found his boat and was about to escape by rowing past the gate to the river beyond.

'I will alert the guards,' said Bartholomew, tugging on Simeon's sleeve. 'They will stop him.'

'They will not listen to you,' said Simeon. 'But they know I am the Duke's man; I will go. You follow him along the canal bank, and grab the boat if it comes close enough.'

Bartholomew gazed at him in the darkness. 'I do not think that is very likely . . .' he began.

Simeon gave him a shove that all but sent him into the murky, sluggish waters of the Ditch, then tore off towards the guardhouse, yelling at the top of his lungs. Bartholomew regained his balance and began to trot along the top of the slippery bank, keeping his eyes glued on the dark shape that was being propelled steadily away from him.

'You cannot escape, Caumpes!' he shouted, knowing that Caumpes was very likely to escape if he reached the river before Simeon roused the guards.

'Damn you, Bartholomew!' yelled Caumpes, rowing furiously. 'Everything was beginning to come right until you and that fat monk interfered.'

'Stop!' yelled Bartholomew. 'You are a killer and you will not go free.'

Caumpes's bitter laughter verged on the hysterical. 'I am not the man you seek. I have killed no one.'

'But you tried,' shouted Bartholomew, thinking that if he could engage Caumpes in conversation, the man would have less breath for rowing. He could see Caumpes quite clearly in his boat, which was moving at a brisk walking pace along the still waters of the Ditch. It was only a few feet away from him, and if Bartholomew had not known about the treacherous currents that seethed in the seemingly sluggish waters and of the sucking mud and clinging weeds that lined its bottom, he might have considered leaping in and grabbing the skiff to prevent Caumpes's escape. 'That fire almost killed three people.'

In the faint glow of the lamps from the gatehouse, Bartholomew could see Caumpes close his eyes in an agony of despair. 'Stupid!' he muttered. 'It was a stupid thing to do.'

'Where will you go?' called Bartholomew, frantically searching for a topic that would slow Caumpes's relentless advance towards the freedom of the river. 'Your whole life is at Bene't.'

For a moment, Caumpes faltered, and the rhythmic pull of oars in the water was interrupted.

'Everything I have done was for the good of Bene't,' he said, his voice so low as to be all but indiscernible. 'Tampering with the Michaelhouse scaffolding was for the good of Bene't, so that the workmen would return to us and not waste their time on Runham's cheap courtyard. And I became embroiled in all this just so that I could raise the money for our own buildings to be completed.'

'Is that what all this is about?' asked Bartholomew. 'Money for buildings?'

'Do not judge me, Bartholomew,' cried Caumpes, agitated. 'I love my College. I swore a vow of allegiance to it, and if that entails using my skills as a buyer and a seller of goods to greedy town merchants, then so be it.'

'How can killing your colleagues be good for Bene't?'

'You are wrong about that,' said Caumpes. 'You will have to look elsewhere for your murderer.'

'I do not believe you,' said Bartholomew, but something in Caumpes's quiet conviction disturbed him. He felt as though all the answers he and Michael had reasoned out were slipping away from him, and that there was a darker, more ruthless plan than Caumpes's desperate attempts to protect a College whose petty rivalries and quarrels were tearing it apart.

They had almost reached the Trumpington Gate, and Bartholomew could hear Simeon's exasperated yells as he argued with soldiers loath to leave their warm guardhouse on some wild-goose chase thought up by scholars. Bartholomew saw that Caumpes was going to slip past them, and that would be that. Once he was on the river, he would be free: he could head north to the mysterious, impenetrable wilderness of the Fens, or he could travel south towards London. Or he could just disappear into the myriad ancient ditches and waterways that surrounded the town and lie low for a day or two until the hue and cry had died down.

Bartholomew gazed at the little skiff with a feeling of helplessness. He glanced around quickly, to see if there were another boat he could use to give chase. There was nothing except a length of rope that lay coiled on the bank. He snatched it up and, keeping a grip on one end, hurled the other as hard as he could towards Caumpes. It landed squarely on the Bene't man's head before slithering harmlessly to the bottom of the boat. Contemptuously, Caumpes shoved it away from him, and then began rowing for all he was worth.

He was already past the guardhouse, and the infuriatingly slow figures that walked sedately towards the bridge would never stop him. Bartholomew hurled the rope a

second time, feeling it catch on something. He heard
Caumpes swear and scramble about to try to disentangle
it. Bartholomew hauled with all his might, then stumbled
backward as Caumpes managed to free it. Bartholomew
threw it a third time, putting every last fibre of strength
into hurling it as hard as he could, while the little boat
bobbed farther and farther away from him.

Caumpes was ready, and caught the rope as it snaked
towards him. Then, while Bartholomew was still off balance from the force of the throw, he jerked hard on his
end, and the physician went tumbling down the bank and
into the fetid waters of the Ditch below.

Bartholomew heard the exploding splash and felt the
agonising chill of the Ditch as it soaked through his
clothes. He spat the vile-tasting water from his mouth
in disgust, kicking and struggling against the clinging
mud and weeds that closed around his feet and legs. In
the distance, he saw Caumpes's boat move a little faster
as it neared the stronger current of the river, and then it
was gone.

'Take my hand,' instructed Simeon, slithering down the
bank of the King's Ditch to Bartholomew, who floun-
dered and flapped like a landed fish. 'Do not struggle,
or we will never get you out. I saw a sheep drown here
only last week.'

Bartholomew stopped struggling and reached out to
grab Simeon's hand, trying not to snatch at it and pull
the Duke's man into the water with him. The mincing
courtier had surprising strength, and it was not long
before Bartholomew was extricated from the weeds and
mud of the King's Ditch to stand dripping on the bank.
For the second time that day, Bartholomew stank like
a sewer.

'When I said you should stop Caumpes, I did not mean

you to dive in after him,' said Simeon dryly. 'He is not that important.'

'He is a killer,' said Bartholomew, teeth chattering uncontrollably.

'Yes, he probably is,' agreed Simeon. 'But even so, it was foolish of you to jump into the water to stop him. I will track him down anyway.'

Bartholomew spat again, trying to clear his mouth of the revolting taste of sewage and refuse. He wondered whether he would fall victim to the intestinal diseases that plagued those of his patients who drank from it. The sulphurous taste made him think that people who preferred it to walking a short distance to one of the town's wells were probably insane, and beyond anything he could do for them.

'We should go back to Bene't before you take a chill,' said Simeon, unfastening his cloak and draping it around Bartholomew's shoulders. 'Come on. A brisk walk should warm you.'

He led the way at a cracking pace along the High Street to Bene't College. Osmun answered his hammering, furious because the new porter Walter was nowhere to be found.

'I will wring his neck when I find him,' Osmun vowed, his face a dark mask of fury. 'He was paid a week in advance, and he still owes us two nights. I will kill him!'

Bartholomew made a mental note to tell Walter to repay the outstanding sum unless he wanted Osmun to claim it back in blood and broken bones. Simeon shot the enraged porter a cool glance of dislike before taking Bartholomew across the courtyard to where Michael and Heltisle waited in the hall.

'Caumpes escaped, then?' said Michael, eyeing Bartholomew's wet clothes. His evident disappointment was tempered by amusement that the physician had once again muddied himself in the King's Ditch, although he could scarcely reveal to Simeon that it was Bartholomew who had overheard his conversation with Heytesbury earlier that day.

'It was the fault of those soldiers,' muttered Simeon angrily. 'It was like trying to rouse the dead. They were so agonisingly sluggish – putting on their helmets and buckling their swords before they would leave the comfort of their little guardhouse – that by the time they reached the bridge, all we could see was Caumpes rounding the corner on his way to freedom. I will have words with the Sheriff about that band of worthless ne'er-do-wells.'

'I do not believe this,' said Heltisle miserably. 'I have known Caumpes for years. He has never struck me as a murderer. And now he has fled, and will continue to damage my poor College from afar.'

'No,' said Simeon. 'Caumpes will not harm Bene't because it was his devotion to it that led him into all this in the first place. And anyway, we will catch him sooner or later.'

He placed a stool near the fire for Bartholomew, whose clothes began to steam, and handed him a cup of mulled wine. The physician took a hearty mouthful, and then felt his stomach rebel at its powerful flavour, which even copious amounts of sugar and cloves could not disguise. Thinking it impolite to spit it on Bene't's fine floor, or even in the fire, he forced himself to swallow, flinching as the wine eased its fiery way down to his stomach. Simeon smiled at his reaction, as though it was a prank he had played before. Bartholomew did not find it amusing, however, and glanced at Michael, wondering whether he, too, had recognised the acidic, tarry taste of Widow's Wine.

The monk nodded to his unspoken question. 'It is the same foul brew that incapacitated most of Michaelhouse on the night that Runham was elected Master.'

Simeon's eyes grew round with wry astonishment. 'You used Widow's Wine to celebrate Runham's election? After all your claims about the fine cellars that Michaelhouse keeps? That, my dear Senior Proctor, is the most flagrant example of hypocrisy I have ever encountered!'

'It was not just any Widow's Wine,' said Michael. 'It was stronger – more potent.'

'I did not think there was anything in Christendom stronger than Widow's Wine,' said Simeon, laughing openly. 'The Duke's cooks use it for sluicing the slop drains.'

'This tastes strong and potent to me,' said Bartholomew, setting it down on the hearth and declining to drink any more.

'Exactly,' said Michael softly. 'While I do not make a habit of imbibing Widow's Wine, if it can be avoided, I am familiar with its flavour. The one served at Michaelhouse that night was more concentrated than any I have tasted before – rather like this one, in fact.'

Simeon seemed about to object to the implied accusation, but Heltisle shook himself from his gloomy reverie and replied instead.

'So that is what happened to it,' he said morosely. 'Two hogsheads of the stuff went missing from our cellars nine or ten days ago. I wondered where they had gone – even students would have to be desperate to steal that for their revelries.'

'Apprentices seem to like it well enough,' said Michael.

Heltisle shook his head. 'Not this brew. You are right – it *is* stronger than usual. I order it that way because it is good for preserving fruit from the orchard. We do not usually drink it, though – except on rare occasions when we need something powerful to warm us.'

'Like now,' said Simeon, still smiling. 'You can see how it drives out the chill.'

'We usually disguise the flavour with sugar and cloves,' continued Heltisle. 'We would never drink it raw.'

'Caumpes must have taken it,' said Bartholomew. 'He just admitted to being one of the two men who tampered with the scaffolding at Michaelhouse. He must have stolen this horrible brew from Bene't and smuggled it in to be used at our feast, so that everyone would be too drunk to notice what he was doing.'

'What *was* he doing?' asked Simeon.

'We do not know,' said Michael with a sigh. 'Late on the night that Runham was elected, Matt and I encountered two people leaving Michaelhouse who were clearly up to no good. When we challenged them, they ran. We wondered from the start whether strong wine had been deliberately provided, in order to allow some dark deed to be done with no witnesses.'

Simeon gestured to Bartholomew's cup. 'Are you telling me that everyone in Michaelhouse drank this stuff – that no one did what any human being with a sense of taste would do, and decline it?'

Michael scrambled to prevent Michaelhouse from gaining the reputation of a community of drunkards who would down anything as long as it was in a goblet. 'You must understand that our minds were concerned with more important matters. We had just elected Runham as Master.'

'And you had the audacity to pretend to be a man who knew his wines when you came to visit us earlier?' said Simeon, regarding Michael askance. 'Yet you drank Master Heltisle's pickling agent without demur? I can believe that of Ralph de Langelee, but I expected more of you, Brother.'

'Of course. I had forgotten Langelee was a familiar of yours,' said Michael.

'Hardly that,' said Simeon distastefully. 'But we have

known each other for a long time, and he invited me to Michaelhouse last Sunday to take a cup of wine in his chamber, although he certainly did not give me Widow's Wine. I would have objected most strenuously.'

'Is that all you were there for?' asked Michael. 'Wine and some none too intelligent conversation?'

'Yes,' said Simeon, genuinely surprised by the question. 'Why else would I be there?'

'The end of your visit coincided with some collapsing scaffolding,' said Michael pointedly.

'I heard about that,' replied Simeon. 'But I can assure you that it had nothing to do with me.'

'Caumpes has just admitted to doing that,' said Bartholomew tiredly. 'Simeon and Osmun's visit was no more than a coincidence.'

'If you think I would sully my hands by tampering with timber, nails and other dirty objects, then you *have* been drinking too much Widow's Wine,' said Simeon.

'I do not make a habit of drinking the stuff,' Michael objected stiffly.

'We can debate wines another time,' said Bartholomew, sitting as close to the fire as he could. 'What we need to discuss is what to do about Caumpes.'

'There is nothing we can do tonight,' said Simeon practically. 'We will search for him tomorrow. He will not be far. He has lived in this town all his life, and he will not know where else to go.'

'Are you sure it was Caumpes who killed Raysoun, Wymundham and Brother Patrick?' asked Bartholomew of Michael. 'Only he denied it, you see.'

'Well, he would, Matt,' said Michael, wearily. 'Perhaps he knows he will be caught sooner or later, and is already planning his defence.'

'Caumpes did not kill Raysoun,' said Simeon. 'He fell from the scaffolding while drunk.'

Bartholomew sighed. 'Wymundham said Raysoun whispered with his dying breath that he had been pushed.'

'Any of the workmen will tell you that there was no one anywhere near Raysoun when he fell,' replied Simeon. 'Almost before Raysoun had breathed his last, Wymundham had started rumours that he had been murdered, but they were lies, intended to create disharmony and suspicion among the Fellowship.'

'While in prison, Osmun told Robin of Grantchester that Wymundham had stabbed Raysoun,' said Bartholomew, trying to sit even closer to the fire.

'Osmun would believe anything of Wymundham,' said the Duke's man. 'They hated each other. But I saw Wymundham arrive at Raysoun's side, and the builder's awl was already sticking out of him. And much as I would like a neat end to all this, and have Raysoun's death blamed on that scheming weasel, I know it is not true. Raysoun fell and the awl pierced him as he landed.'

'But why would Wymundham want his colleagues accused of murder?' asked Bartholomew.

'Wymundham was not a pleasant man,' said Heltisle. 'He was bitter and twisted, and resented anyone else's good fortune. As I told you before, I was not sorry to hear that he had died, although I did not wish him murdered.'

'We knew Wymundham's lies about Raysoun's death would be damaging to Bene't,' said Simeon. 'Even though the workmen were prepared to swear it was just a tragic accident, you know how people are – they would much rather hear about a murder than a boring accident.'

He glanced significantly at Bartholomew, who realised that despite the claims of honest men, like the carpenter Robert de Blaston, he had been more inclined to believe the unsubstantiated claims of Wymundham. And all the time, evidence that Raysoun had been drinking had been staring him in the face: he himself had smelled wine on Raysoun, and he had seen the wineskin that Raysoun had dropped when he had fallen.

'And even though there was a crowd of people around Raysoun as he died, it is curious that only Wymundham heard these last words, is it not?' Heltisle pointed out.

'I certainly did not, and I was kneeling next to him, giving him last rites,' added Michael.

Bartholomew recalled his surprise that Raysoun had spoken, given the extent of his injuries. Now it seemed that Raysoun's broken back had indeed robbed him of consciousness. Wymundham *had* been lying.

'So, the remaining Fellows had a meeting, to decide what to do about Wymundham's behaviour,' said Simeon. 'I suggested we pay him to tell the truth. Buying men off usually works at court.'

'It was a dreadful idea,' said Heltisle mournfully. 'It gave Wymundham the means to indulge in a drinking spree. As soon as the coins had left my hands, he went to Holy Trinity Church to buy some cheap wine.'

And that explained why Wymundham had appeared furtive when entering the church, thought Bartholomew: he was about to embark on a binge that the University would condemn, because he had known about Holy Trinity's wine-seller who offered cheap drink that had been illegally exempted from the King's taxes.

'I spotted Wymundham staggering around the church and went to fetch the others,' continued Simeon. 'When Caumpes saw Wymundham lying in a drunken stupor wearing his Bene't tabard, proclaiming to the world which College he was from, he was livid.'

'I had to order Caumpes back to the College while the rest of us dealt with Wymundham,' added Heltisle. He gave a grim smile. 'Actually, he was ready to rid us of Wymundham long before that day. In September, he and I overheard him with that Brother Patrick of Ovyng, exchanging nasty snippets of gossip as they strolled in the water meadows one Sunday afternoon. Caumpes was furious, and almost had his dagger out then, too.'

'Well, he had his wish,' said Simeon. 'Caumpes killed Wymundham in the hut you just saw burned to the ground. And then he must have rowed the body to Horwoode's land and dumped it there because it is the most isolated spot on the King's Ditch.'

'Why did you not tell me this before?' asked Michael. 'It would have saved a lot of trouble.'

Simeon sighed. 'We had been to some trouble to protect the College from Wymundham. Why would we reveal to you what we had been to some pains to hide?'

'But it is out now anyway,' said Michael, slightly gloating. 'And all your subterfuge has been in vain. I am not the gluttonous buffoon that you believe me to be, Master Simeon.'

Simeon gaped at him and then began to laugh. 'So that was you eavesdropping on me near the King's Ditch earlier? I would not have thought you agile enough to scale it! But as it happens, that is not what I think of you at all. I have listened to stories of your previous successes, and I know you have a formidable mind. But I swore an oath of allegiance to Bene't, a Cambridge College. Do you think I would not take advantage of Oxford by spinning Master Heytesbury a few misguided opinions?'

Michael's fat face slowly broke into a wide grin. 'I like that. And I am beginning to like you!'

'What are you two talking about?' demanded Heltisle impatiently. 'Whatever it is, we would be better discussing Caumpes and his wicked deeds.'

'Caumpes must have killed Brother Patrick, too,' said Michael, reluctantly dragging his thoughts back to the more mundane matter of murder.

Simeon looked puzzled. 'Who is this Brother Patrick that everyone keeps mentioning?'

'I do not know why Caumpes should kill Patrick,' said Heltisle. 'I know Wymundham and Patrick liked to gossip together, but with Wymundham dead, Patrick was irrelevant.'

'Brother Patrick was seen running from Holy Trinity Church, having observed all of you standing around what we thought was Wymundham's corpse,' explained Michael to Simeon.

'Oh *him!*' said the Duke's man in sudden understanding. 'That was Patrick, was it?'

'Do you know him?' asked Michael.

'He ran errands for Wymundham – including collecting money that Wymundham had extorted from people. Patrick was not a nice man, either. If he was seen running away from the church, it was probably because he did not want to be caught with his drunken comrade.'

'I suppose Caumpes killed him after he had dispatched Wymundham, to ensure that the secrets Wymundham had discovered remained secrets,' said Michael, in the tones of a man who felt he had resolved the last of the mystery.

'If you knew Caumpes was a killer, why did you do nothing to stop him?' asked Bartholomew of Simeon. 'Why did you let him remain at large where he might have posed a threat to de Walton – among others?'

'Because we had only just reasoned it out,' said Simeon. 'Heltisle, de Walton and I each knew a little, but none of us had the whole story. And although we suspected a Fellow had put an end to Wymundham, none of us knew which one. Needless to say no one was inclined to risk his own life by confiding his suspicions to a possible killer. It was only when I took the risk of approaching de Walton that we began to suspect Caumpes.'

Heltisle sighed. 'Caumpes was thorough, I will say that.'

'He was,' agreed Michael. 'And cool. It takes some nerve to linger where you have just tried to incinerate three people, and then wait for two of them to leave so that you can deal with the third.'

'What do you mean?' asked Bartholomew, confused. 'What did Caumpes do to de Walton?'

'He stabbed him, while we were chasing shadows,' said Michael. 'De Walton is dead.'

It was almost dawn before Bartholomew and Michael left Bene't College. Bartholomew's clothes had dried by the fire, but they had a stinking, pungent aroma to them that made him feel grubby and tainted. He felt even more unclean when he thought about Caumpes and the College he loved so much that he was prepared to go to any lengths to serve it – even committing murder. While Simeon went to the Castle to organise a search for Caumpes, Bartholomew and Michael trudged back to Michaelhouse.

'What a filthy business,' said Bartholomew gloomily. 'It was Wymundham who tore that College apart, driving wedges between his colleagues and using the sordid secrets his nosiness uncovered to cause bitterness and dissent.'

'And Matilde and her sisters were right about Patrick,' said Michael. 'He was a vicious gossip who became involved with another like-minded man – and died for it.'

'And now we are returning to our own College where matters are not much better,' Bartholomew pointed out. 'We also have a murderer in our midst.'

'Look on the bright side, Matt,' said Michael. 'We will be back in time for breakfast, although I would ask that you change your clothes before you sit next to me. You smell of the Ditch.'

Bartholomew glanced nervously up at the repaired scaffolding before ducking into his room. Blaston and his apprentices had been at work to render it safe, but Bartholomew knew he would never trust scaffolding again.

For the second time in less than a day, he scrubbed himself with Runham's soap, while Michael fetched pail after pail of lukewarm water from the kitchens. The soap reminded him of Runham's hoard, awaiting collection in St Michael's Church and, still shivering, he followed Michael up the lane pushing a small handcart borrowed from the vegetable garden to retrieve it while most of the town still slept.

He sat at the base of a pillar, and watched Michael haul the altar away from the wall and begin to toss the soap blocks into the cart.

'I suppose Runham must have used accomplices to help him with this,' said the monk conversationally as he worked. 'I do not think he would have known how to sell these things on his own. The answer must lie in the cloaked intruders we keep almost catching in the College.'

'No,' said Bartholomew. 'Caumpes admitted to tampering with the scaffolding, which accounts for one of those times. But . . .' He paused as certain things became clear in his mind.

'But what?' asked Michael impatiently.

'Caumpes,' said Bartholomew. 'It was Caumpes who sold the treasure that Runham recovered.'

'Really?' asked Michael uncertainly. 'How do you know?'

'Two reasons. First, I saw him. One afternoon, I watched him visit Harold of Haslingfield, the goldsmith. Later,

Harold told me that Caumpes had provided him with a number of items recently, although he said none were stolen – he checked with his Guild and with Dick Tulyet.'

Michael scratched his chin thoughtfully. 'Yes, but if Wilson garnered his ill-gotten gains during the Death, then there are a couple of points we should remember: dead people cannot identify their own property or register it as stolen; and we are talking about thefts committed five years ago. It is not surprising that the goldsmiths and Dick did not recognise these items as stolen.'

'And the second reason I know Caumpes must have been Runham's accomplice is that Oswald informed me that Caumpes dabbles with the black market. Harold told me, too, and, come to that, so did Caumpes himself – he made money for Bene't by buying and selling things.'

'So, Runham commissioned Caumpes to sell items that belonged to Michaelhouse, such as the contents of our hutches and the College silver, along with the valuables he recovered from Wilson's hoard,' said Michael, frowning in thought. 'Runham hid them in the soap for Caumpes to collect and dispose of at his leisure, and the memorandum we found in Runham's room was a listing of the amounts Caumpes told Runham to expect for each item.'

Bartholomew nodded. 'The only problem I can see in all this is that Caumpes hated Michaelhouse for poaching Bene't's workmen. Why should he then act as Runham's agent?'

'The building work started last Wednesday, and two days later, Runham was dead. The answer is simple: as you have said all along, smothering is an unusual way to kill someone. Wymundham was smothered, and we *know* Caumpes killed Wymundham. Runham was also smothered. *Quod erat demonstrandum.*'

'I suppose so,' said Bartholomew uncertainly. 'But Caumpes said he did not kill Wymundham.'

'Murderers do not make honest witnesses, Matt, and you should never believe what they say. Anyway, Caumpes would do anything for his College, so we have reason to assume that he would swallow his dislike of Runham in order to raise money for Bene't's buildings. We know Bene't was having financial problems, with the Duke tightening his purse strings and the guilds less generous than they had been.'

'So, we were right last night when we surmised that very little was stolen from Runham's chest?' asked Bartholomew, turning his attention back to the soap-stuffed altar. 'We assumed that about forty-five pounds was missing, but we were wrong because Runham's chest never contained the ninety pounds he needed for the building.'

'Right,' said Michael. 'Runham must have assumed that Caumpes would be able to raise the outstanding amount by the time the builders were to be paid. But Runham's list mentions books, chalices and other items too large to be concealed in soap. He must have those hidden elsewhere. And then we must not forget the twelve pounds that was so kindly returned to you the other morning. Now there is something I do not understand.'

'Nor me,' said Bartholomew. 'It is unlikely to have been Caumpes.'

'Clippesby!' exclaimed Michael suddenly. 'I *knew* he would be involved. There is your second cloaked intruder – Caumpes and Clippesby, both wandering Michaelhouse at night, breaking our scaffolding and murdering our Master.'

'But Clippesby had no reason to creep around in the dark,' said Bartholomew. 'Michaelhouse is his College, and he has every right to be in it.'

'Michaelhouse is his *new* College,' corrected Michael.

'He probably did not feel confident to demolish scaffolding and murder his Master without donning some sort of disguise. Matt, someone is coming! Quick, put this piece of soap in your bag, while I hide the rest.'

Michael was still heaving at the broken altar when Suttone walked up the aisle. The Carmelite smiled benignly at them, his red face friendly.

'It is my turn to say the daily prayer for the soul of our founder,' he explained. He saw the damaged altar and the redness drained from his face, leaving it white and shocked. 'What are you doing? That is sacrilege! You have damaged a sacred altar!'

'It needed some repairs,' said Michael smoothly, leaning against it so that Suttone could not look too closely.

'It did not!' cried Suttone, aghast. 'What have I let myself in for at Michaelhouse? It is a College of murderers and desecrators!'

Michael sighed, then moved away from the altar so that Suttone could see it. 'I am sick of secrecy, and you will know everything soon anyway.'

'Know everything?' echoed Suttone in alarm. 'I am not sure I like the sound of that.'

'We have discovered who is behind all this,' said Michael. 'A previous Master called Wilson was a thief, and Runham was his cousin. Wilson hid stolen goods in his room, and when Runham was elected Master, he set about seeing which of his kinsman's ill-gotten gains were still there.'

'What sort of ill-gotten gains?' asked Suttone anxiously.

'Items stolen from his colleagues and from people who paid him for last rites during the Death. Runham then started to move the property out of Michaelhouse to sell, using tablets of soap, so that he would not be caught with the goods on his person.'

'You are not on mass duty this week, Suttone,' said Bartholomew, puzzled. 'I am.'

'Runham had an accomplice,' Michael went on. 'We have reasoned that it is Clippesby, who with the assistance of Caumpes, helped to murder Runham because their game started to go wrong.'

'Clippesby?' asked Suttone quietly.

'I imagine that unholy trinity – Runham, Clippesby and Caumpes – intended to make themselves rich on Wilson's stolen treasure. The other two killed Runham when he disagreed with them over some matter.'

'No, Brother,' said Suttone softly, drawing a long, wicked knife from his sleeve. 'You have this all wrong. All terribly wrong.'

CHAPTER 12

'NOT YOU!' EXCLAIMED MICHAEL, EYEING IN horror the knife that Suttone wielded in St Michael's Church. 'Surely *you* were not Runham's accomplice in this filthy affair?'

Suttone closed his eyes. 'It has all gone wrong. I cannot imagine how matters have spiralled so far out of control.'

'Then put down the knife,' said Bartholomew, standing up slowly. 'Stop this before it goes any further.'

'Stay where you are, both of you,' said Suttone, snapping open his eyes and gesturing that they were to sit on the remains of Wilson's altar. 'We must talk about this. There are things I wish you to know.'

'Put down the knife first,' said Bartholomew.

Suttone sighed, standing sufficiently far away to prevent any surprise lurch from Bartholomew and holding the knife as if he meant business. 'Where in God's name do I start with all this?' He answered his own question. 'With Wilson, I suppose.'

'Wilson was dishonest, and secreted stolen items in his room,' said Michael promptly, seeking to engage the man in conversation to distract him from the long and sharp-looking knife. 'There was some suggestion at the time that the University might not survive the plague, and I imagine he was lining a nest for his future, should the worst happen and he find himself Collegeless.'

Suttone nodded. 'He skulked in his room by day, avoiding those with the disease, but at night he slipped

out to see his lover in the Convent of St Radegund. On
his way, he stole from the dead and the dying. He stole
from a person very dear to me – a relative.'

'Is that what all this is about?' asked Bartholomew.
'Revenge on Wilson because he stole from someone you
loved?'

'Not revenge,' said Suttone. 'All I wanted to do was
recover this wealth and return it to its rightful owner.'

'You became a Michaelhouse Fellow just to get someone's money back?' asked Michael warily. 'But why not
claim it through the courts – legally and openly?'

'No court in the land would act on my claim, and
especially not against a powerful institution like Michaelhouse. When I saw Kenyngham was Master, my hopes
rose, because I knew he was a man who would see justice
done. But he resigned before I could take him into my
confidence, and Runham was elected.'

'You voted for him,' Michael pointed out.

'I thought I would fare better with him than with that
fanatical William. I was wrong.'

'Runham immediately started selling the items he had
recovered from Wilson's hoard,' said Michael. 'Like my
crystal bowl. And you knew you would have no help
from him.'

'He stole from you, too?' asked Suttone. 'Then you
must understand how I feel.'

'I do,' said Michael. 'That bowl was very dear to me – a
gift from my grandmother. Put the knife down, Suttone,
and let us discuss this in a civilised manner.'

'Everyone was surprised when Runham suddenly produced the finances for his new buildings,' said Suttone,
still fingering the weapon with unsteady hands. 'None of
you knew where it came from. But I did.'

'You guessed that Runham would use Wilson's treasure, some of which belonged to your friend, to build his

College,' said Michael, trying to sound sympathetic as he eyed the knife.

Suttone nodded. 'I decided to approach him before he could spend everything. I told him that not all of Wilson's fortune was obtained honestly, but he refused to listen. At first he denied that he had recovered Wilson's hoard, but then he started to gloat that he would use it for the good of his cousin's soul.'

'And you did not want your relative's possessions adding to the glorification of the man who had robbed him in the first place,' said Michael, hoping to calm the man.

Suttone clutched the knife harder, and Bartholomew saw sweat beading on his forehead. 'It was obscene! It was not Runham's to dispose of – and certainly not to be used for purifying Wilson's diseased soul!'

'So you smothered him,' said Michael. Bartholomew jabbed him in the ribs, certain that bringing the discussion around to murder was unwise. Michael ignored him. 'You took a cushion and you pressed it over his mouth until he stopped struggling.'

Suttone gazed at the floor, and Bartholomew tensed in readiness to spring an attack, grasping his medicine bag like a shield to protect himself from the blade. He glanced at Michael, who gave an almost imperceptible shake of his head.

'I am not sorry Runham is dead, God rot his soul,' said Suttone softly. 'But I am sorry it was I who did the deed.' He glanced across to Runham's body, lying under its fine silken sheet.

'And are you sorry that you and Caumpes endangered the lives of your colleagues by causing the scaffolding to fall?' asked Bartholomew coldly. 'Had Michael been in his room, he would have been killed, and he has nothing to do with this business of Runham's.'

'I did not touch the scaffolding,' said Suttone. 'I thought that was an accident – that it fell because Runham did not pay for it to be assembled safely.'

'But Caumpes said—' began Bartholomew.

'Then Caumpes acted alone,' interrupted Suttone firmly. 'I had nothing to do with it. I killed Runham, but I did not touch the scaffolding.'

'And are you sorry you killed Wymundham, too?' asked Michael. 'If you killed Runham, then you also killed Wymundham. Both men were smothered with cushions.'

Suttone did not reply, and Bartholomew tensed again, poised to strike. Michael tugged the physician's sleeve, urging him not to move. Bartholomew was uneasy that Michael was content to let Suttone continue their discussion waving a knife, when there was a chance to disarm him, but knew he would not be able to break Michael's grip and be able to launch a surprise attack on Suttone.

'Yes,' said Suttone eventually. 'I was sorry I had to kill Wymundham. But he had discovered what I had come to do, and he threatened to expose me.'

'How did he find out?' asked Michael, puzzled.

'I have no idea,' said Suttone. 'Perhaps he consorted with witches or fortune-tellers.'

'Surely you do not believe that,' said Michael doubtfully. 'You are a friar!'

'Caumpes told me about the evil things Wymundham did – how he drove his lover Raysoun to drink and then lied about his dying words; about how he blackmailed de Walton over his harmless admiration of Mayor Horwoode's wife; and how he threatened to reveal that Caumpes's father was not the wealthy merchant he always claimed. It would not have surprised me to learn that Wymundham was in league with the Devil.'

'So, he deserved to die,' said Michael flatly. 'He was an evil man whom no one would mourn.'

'You are putting words in my mouth,' said Suttone. 'No one deserves to die, before they have had the chance to repent their sins. And Brother Patrick did not deserve to die, either.'

'Did you kill him as well?' asked Michael.

Suttone shook his head. 'But he saw me kill Wymundham. He was Wymundham's apprentice, busily learning dark secrets that he could use to his own advantage in the future.'

Bartholomew recalled that Heltisle had said the same. 'So did Wymundham try to blackmail you about your plan to return Wilson's ill-gotten gains to their rightful owners? Did he ask you to meet him in that shed in Bene't's grounds, where you put a cushion over his face and smothered him?'

Suttone nodded. 'And Patrick was stabbed when we realised he had seen what I had done.'

'We?' pounced Michael. 'Who is we?'

Suttone smiled sadly. 'I will confess everything else, but never that. Too many lives have been tainted by men like Wilson, Runham, Wymundham and Patrick already. I will not see more people fall victim to their plague.'

'Is it a woman?' asked Michael bluntly. 'You must think highly of her, given that you are prepared to kill and steal for this person.'

Suttone looked shocked. 'I am a friar, Brother. I have committed many sins, but breaking my vows of chastity is not one of them – unlike you, I should imagine.'

'We are not discussing me,' said Michael haughtily. 'But you had an alibi for Runham's murder. How did you manage that?'

Suttone smiled. 'Poor Master Kenyngham is too good and honest for this world. You know how he is – every office is a deeply religious experience. I was present at the beginning of compline that night, but he did not notice me leave in the middle of it, and he did not notice me return later.'

That rang true, thought Bartholomew. Once Kenyngham was into the business of praying, very little could impinge on his consciousness. And anyway, Bartholomew recalled, Kenyngham had stayed after compline to pray at the high altar, while Suttone had said he had prayed at Wilson's altar. Since Wilson's altar was nearer the door, it would be entirely possible to slip out and back in again without being seen from the high altar at the other end of the church.

'And it was not Kenyngham who provided you with your alibi ultimately,' he said. 'It was Caumpes.'

'Caumpes was there,' said Suttone. 'He showed me the latest pieces Runham had asked him to sell, but none of them fitted the description of the jewels my relative had lost. In despair, I went to speak with Runham again. It was then that I killed him – when he mocked me for my desire to see justice done.'

'And then you just returned to the church to finish your prayers?' asked Michael. 'That was cool-headed!'

Suttone ran the blade of the knife along his fingers, as if testing its sharpness. 'I returned to ask for forgiveness, but not for me – for Runham.'

'Why Caumpes?' asked Bartholomew. 'I do not see why you chose to go into partnership with a Fellow from another College.'

'Why not? Would you have volunteered your services? I met Caumpes just after my first encounter with the blackmailing Wymundham, and he was kind to me. We struck up a friendship. He is a man of integrity, a virtue that seems lacking in most people I have met at this University.'

'So, the arrangement was that Caumpes would show you all that Runham gave him to sell before he disposed of it?' asked Michael. 'Why did he do that? What was in it for him?'

'Nothing,' said Suttone heavily. 'As I said, Caumpes is a man of integrity. He knew of the wrong perpetrated on my relative, and was keen to see it rectified.' Michael looked patently disbelieving, and Suttone allowed himself another small smile. 'And my relative offered to make a donation to Bene't to ensure Caumpes's co-operation.'

'That I can believe,' said Michael. 'So, did Caumpes kill Patrick?'

'Caumpes has killed no one.'

'But he killed de Walton,' said Bartholomew. 'Stabbed him.' He glanced uneasily at the knife, and wondered whether that had been a wise thing to say.

Suttone rubbed his head. 'I do not believe you. All Caumpes has ever wanted was to protect his College. He is not a murderer.'

'Caumpes provided Michaelhouse with the Widow's Wine on the night of Runham's election,' said Bartholomew. 'He stole it from Bene't cellars.'

'He sold Langelee a couple of hogsheads of it, so that everyone would be drunk and I would be able to search Kenyngham's room should the worst – or what I then imagined would be the worst – happen and Father William be elected Master. I knew I would never have another opportunity. Unfortunately, you and Michael left before the feast was over and almost caught us as we were leaving after our unsuccessful search.'

So, thought Bartholomew, it had been Caumpes and Suttone with whom he had first struggled, and who had pushed him into the mud of St Michael's Lane. But searching the Master's room for hidden gold and intoxicating the entire College with Heltisle's pickling agent had not been all the pair had achieved that night.

'You poisoned the salve I use for infections,' said Bartholomew coldly. 'You knew I would use it on Michael's stung arm. You were plotting murder even then.'

'I exchanged your pot for one with stronger ingredients, guessing that you would use it, because Michael was scratching himself like a dog with fleas,' said Suttone. 'I was afraid his injury would render him sleepless, and that he might see Caumpes and me searching the Master's quarters. But the salve was not poisonous. It was intended to make him sleep.'

'It might have killed him,' said Bartholomew. 'And later, you stole it back again.'

'I retrieved it from your bag when Runham started making unpleasant accusations,' said Suttone. 'I was sure the salve I gave you was safe, but I did not want to provide Runham with the means to persecute you, should I be wrong. I took the salve to protect *you*.'

'Thank you,' said Bartholomew icily.

'I am not a bad person,' Suttone insisted unsteadily. 'I started with the most noble of intentions, and, through no fault of my own, ended up a murderer.'

'You started a murderer,' said Bartholomew, recalling another death that could be attributed to Suttone's preferred method of killing. 'Like Wymundham and Runham, Justus was smothered.'

Suttone sighed and his eyes took on a distant look, as though the memory were a painful one. 'I smothered him, and then put a wineskin over his head to make it appear as if he took his own life. He was senseless with drink at the time. He felt no pain; he did not even struggle. And I did conduct his requiem mass for no charge.'

'A kindly killer,' said Michael softly. 'But why? What had Justus done to you?'

'I am not an evil man, Brother,' repeated Suttone, ignoring the question. 'I only want justice. When I realised that the money I had seized from Runham's chest exceeded the amount my relative had lost, I gave the balance back. I passed it to Bartholomew in the churchyard.'

'So that was you, was it?' asked Michael.

'I keep telling you, I am not wicked,' said Suttone. 'It is Runham, Wilson and Wymundham who are the real villains in this story. It is with their selfishness and greed that all this starts.'

'So put the knife down,' said Bartholomew. 'If you are not evil, you will not be committing any more murders, and especially not in a church.'

There was a sudden crash at the back of the nave, and Cynric appeared with his weapon at the ready. Stanmore and Father William were at his heels, along with a white-haired Carmelite friar. Cynric faltered when he saw the knife Suttone held.

'More murders?' asked Suttone, as though the thought had not crossed his mind. He looked from Cynric to the dagger he held in his hand, and then gave a slow, sad smile. 'You misunderstand me, even now. It is not you I came here to kill, my friends. It is me.'

And he took the knife and drew it in a quick slashing motion across his neck.

Bartholomew dived towards Suttone as the friar collapsed slowly on the floor next to Wilson's altar, tugging the knife from the inert fingers and flinging it away in disgust. He rammed the sleeve of the man's tabard against the pumping wound in his neck, but he knew it would do no good. Even pressing as hard as he could, the blood dripped and spurted beneath his hands, and the rosiness gradually faded from Suttone's face to be replaced by the waxy whiteness of death. Just as the feeble pulse began to flutter into stillness, Suttone turned his head and gazed at the sheeted form of Runham's corpse, regarding it with a weary resignation, as though he considered that neither of them had won.

Michael had dropped to his knees to begin intoning prayers for the dead. The white-haired Carmelite, who had entered the church with Cynric, Stanmore and William, hesitated, but then joined him. William did nothing but turn his bewildered gaze from the blood that flowed in a shiny red puddle across the chancel tiles to the damaged remains of Wilson's altar.

'What has Suttone done?' he whispered hoarsely. 'It is a dreadful sin to take the life God granted him in God's own house, but to desecrate His altars, too? He is hell-bound for certain!'

'Just pray,' snapped Michael, taking a handful of William's unsavoury habit and jerking the friar down to kneel next to him. 'Suttone was a man who allowed friendship and loyalty to those he loved to cloud his judgement. He deserves our pity, not our condemnation.'

'He is bound for the fierce fires and boiling brimstones of the Devil's domain . . .' began William, who relished voicing his extraordinarily vivid predictions of the nature of Hell.

'Pray, Father, or I will see you join him there,' hissed Michael venomously.

Unused to such naked hostility from the equable monk, William quickly bent his head and began reciting the offices for the dead, taking a small phial of holy oil from his scrip to anoint Suttone.

Bartholomew stepped away from the clerics, and walked outside, breathing deeply of the cool morning air with its scent of wet grass and the richer aroma of river. He was wiping his bloodstained hands on some moss when Stanmore came to join him, Cynric at his heels.

'How did you know where we were?' Bartholomew asked, recalling their timely entry.

'We thought you were in dreadful danger, Matt,' said Stanmore unsteadily. 'Cynric and I were riding into town after making a delivery of cloth to Barnwell Priory, when that Carmelite asked us the way to Michaelhouse. We fell to talking as we went and he told us that he had been delayed in taking up a new appointment in your College by an accident.'

Bartholomew looked up at him in dull resignation. 'And I suppose his name is Thomas Suttone? The Carmelite friar who was due to be admitted as a Fellow of Michaelhouse at the same time as Clippesby?'

Cynric nodded. 'He was attacked as he journeyed south from Lincoln, and his arm was injured. He was obliged to wait for it to heal.'

'Lincoln,' said Bartholomew flatly. 'Justus came from Lincoln.'

'What of it?' asked Stanmore. 'So do a number of people, I should imagine.'

'But not the man who has just slit his own throat,' said Bartholomew. 'He had probably never been to Lincoln, which is why Justus had to die. He could not risk Justus asking him awkward questions, and Justus might even know the real Suttone. Lincoln is not a very big place.'

'Justus was murdered?' asked Cynric. 'I thought he had killed himself with his wine and his morose reminiscences.'

'That is what we were supposed to think,' said Bartholomew, looking down at the reddened moss at his feet, where he had wiped Suttone's blood from his hands. 'So who was Suttone? The false Suttone, I mean, not the real one.'

'A man prepared to injure an innocent friar in order to take on his identity and conduct nasty business in Michaelhouse,' said Stanmore angrily. 'We saw the false Suttone – and he saw us – as we rushed into the College to tell you about him. By the time we had found William and he suggested you might be in the church, we realised that was probably where this impostor had headed, too, knowing his game was over.'

'I thought we might be too late, boy,' said Cynric unsteadily. 'And you did not have me watching out for you in the shadows as usual.'

'Suttone never intended to harm us,' said Bartholomew wearily. 'Michael sensed that – it was why he would not let me try to wrest the knife from him. I saw only a murderer, but Michael saw a tortured soul.'

'He was a tortured soul who made an end to Master Runham, by the sound of it,' said Stanmore unsympathetically. 'Well, at least it is all over now. I heard this morning that you identified Caumpes as the man who killed the Bene't scholars, and now you have the culprit for the Michaelhouse murders. It is over, Matt. Finished.'

'I do not think so,' said Bartholomew with a sigh. 'We have Suttone's confession that he smothered Justus, Wymundham and then Runham; and it seems that Raysoun's fall from the scaffolding was exactly that – an accident. But Suttone claims he did not kill Brother Patrick or de Walton, and Caumpes says he did not either.'

'As I have told you before,' said Michael, emerging from the church and coming to stand with them, 'murderers do not make for reliable witnesses, Matt. Suttone and Caumpes were lying.'

'Suttone smothered his victims,' said Bartholomew, leaning against one of the church's buttresses. 'But both Patrick and de Walton were stabbed.'

'Then stabbing was probably what Caumpes did well,' said Michael in exasperation. 'Caumpes was certainly in the vegetable garden when de Walton died – and he almost turned you and me into human torches while he was at it.'

'What about this wronged relative of Suttone's?' asked Bartholomew. 'Perhaps he stabbed Patrick and de Walton.'

'Listening to Suttone's confession has unsettled you, Matt,' said Michael. 'Let it go.'

'Why were you so sure Suttone would not kill us?' asked Bartholomew of the monk. 'You would not even let me try to disarm him.'

'I wish I had now,' said Michael. 'I did not think he would kill himself, either. I sensed he had come to confess, but I did not anticipate it would be a dying declaration.'

'There are still some things I do not understand,' said Bartholomew. 'For example . . .'

Michael tapped him on the shoulder. 'Leave it, Matt. What we need to do now is to try to think where Runham might have hidden the rest of his treasure. If we can find it and show it to those workmen today, we might yet save Michaelhouse from harm.'

'I think it is too late for that, boy,' said Cynric nervously. 'A mob has been massing in the Market Square since dawn. And it means to tear down Michaelhouse stone by stone.'

While Stanmore hurried back to his business premises to make certain the rioters did not shift their attentions to the wealthy merchants' properties on Milne Street, Bartholomew, Michael and Cynric, with William and the new Carmelite trailing behind, ran back to Michaelhouse with the cart full of soap.

The atmosphere of the town had changed since

Bartholomew and Michael had hurried through the darkened streets to the church earlier that morning. Then, the city had slept, silent and peaceful. Now, distant voices could be heard on the wind, angry and demanding. Sensing that Cambridge was about to degenerate into one of its frequent spells of anarchy, people had closed the shutters on their windows, and their doors were locked and barred against attack. The High Street, which usually thronged with traders and travellers, was virtually deserted: its residents were either barricaded inside their homes to wait out the chaos that was to come, or had joined the crowd in the Market Square.

'Oh, Lord, Matt!' groaned Michael, as a sudden roar of furious voices reverberated around the empty streets from the Square. 'We should not have wasted time listening to Suttone's confession. Now we are too late to prevent this riot – and it is Michaelhouse's fault!'

'It is,' agreed Cynric uncompromisingly. 'You should not have dismissed the choir and the servants or tried to cheat the builders.'

'Will the town really attack us?' asked Bartholomew. 'Is there no way to prevent it?'

'Yes,' replied Cynric. 'You can give the workmen their due. Nothing less will spare Michaelhouse from being stormed by a good part of the town. They mean business, and I am not sure that even your strong walls will protect you this time.'

They arrived at the College to find that Langelee had not been idle. He had barricaded the back gate and set a guard of servants to watch it, and had soldiers from the Castle lined up along the front wall with bows and arrows at the ready. The students were prepared to defend themselves and their College, too. They were armed with a vicious assortment of sharpened sticks, short swords and even a mace. Deynman and Bulbeck, directed by

Clippesby, were dragging parts of the scaffolding to pile against the main gate, while Gray lined up the others like some kind of military parade.

While Michael briefly outlined to the other Fellows what had happened to Suttone and about the treasure Wilson stole and Runham sold, Kenyngham scuttled back and forth in dismay, appalled that once again his College was to be the scene of violence. The new Carmelite – the real Suttone – took one look at the preparations that were underway and promptly fled, claiming he had left something at the friary on Milne Street. William watched him go with considerable disapproval.

'Typical!' he spat in disdain. 'Carmelites are always far more interested in saving their own skins than in doing their duty. If he had not been so feeble over his injured arm, we would have known that the other Suttone was an impostor a good deal earlier. And then Runham might still be alive.'

'Then thank the good Lord he is a malingerer,' said Langelee fervently. 'It was a black day for Michaelhouse when that evil tyrant was elected Master. If everyone had voted for me, then none of this would have happened.'

'Never mind that,' said Michael impatiently. 'What we should be thinking about now is how to protect Michaelhouse.'

'Michaelhouse will come to no harm,' said Langelee confidently, laying a thick, calloused hand fondly on the creamy yellow stones of the front wall. 'The rabble of builders and music-makers who plan to attack us will not make much headway against this.'

'Music-makers?' asked Kenyngham, startled, looking up from where he knelt among the pile of soap parings and recovered jewellery.

'Forgive me, Master Kenyngham,' said Langelee. 'I had forgotten that the word "music" is not one that is usually associated with that gaggle of caterwaulers who like to be known as the choir.'

'They are improving,' said Michael, offended. 'But I am sure my choir is not part of this mob.'

'They are, Brother,' said Cynric. 'You have not reinstated them as they expected, and they are only too willing to vent their ire against Michaelhouse.'

'We must find the rest of that treasure hidden by Wilson and Runham,' said Michael urgently. 'If we can show the mob that we do indeed possess ninety pounds, then they might disperse before any fighting begins. How much can we lay our hands on now?'

'Probably about seventy pounds with the soap jewellery,' said Langelee.

'It is not enough,' said Kenyngham. 'These are not stupid men – they will know we are short.'

'Ask Agatha to clean these baubles off,' said Langelee, glancing down at the soapy bracelets and necklaces that lay on the ground. 'If we pile them in the chest, the workmen may think we have more than we do.'

Kenyngham shook his head. 'They will want to see irrefutable evidence that we have the entire amount in cash – not a few pounds and a heap of trinkets.'

'True,' said William, picking up one of the pieces and inspecting it briefly with an experienced eye. 'Many of these items are of little value – gilt and coloured glass.'

'Then we must find where Runham stored the rest of his treasure,' said Michael. 'The only problem is, I do not know where to start.'

'His room, of course,' said William. 'That is where Wilson hid a lot of it, you say. I will take a couple of students and start looking there right now.'

'I will come with you,' said Langelee, running after him. 'The Master's room is the finest chamber in the College, and I would not like to see it destroyed because you are impatient or unable to see that some of the furnishings are delicate. Kenyngham says he will resign again soon. The new Master will have to live in that room – and it might be me.'

'Over my dead body,' muttered Michael, as he left.

'I suspect that Runham has removed anything easily recoverable from his room already,' said Clippesby hesitantly. His hair, greasy and unkempt, stood in a spiky circle, so that with his staring eyes he had the look of a frightened cat. 'And then he put them in the church, just as you told us. So, I think it would be better to look elsewhere for the rest.'

'I agree,' said Michael, barely looking at him as he desperately tried to think of ways to convince a furious mob that Michaelhouse was not twenty pounds short. 'Where did you have in mind?'

Clippesby looked blank for a moment, but then brightened. 'He may have buried it in the orchard. I will go there.'

'The orchard is a large place,' said Bartholomew, regarding him uncertainly. 'How will you know where to look?'

'Voices,' said Clippesby mysteriously. 'I hear voices. They will tell me.'

He strode away towards the small gate that led to the gardens. Bartholomew gazed after him, wondering whether to fetch him back.

'That man is not sane, Matt,' said Michael. 'Voices indeed! Who does he think he is? The Virgin Mary?'

'Remember what Runham said about him?' asked Bartholomew. 'That he was ill before he came to us? I imagine that the stresses and uncertainties of these past few days have unbalanced him, and that we have made the poor man ill again with our accusations and suspicions.'

'Is it safe to allow him in the orchard, do you think?' asked Kenyngham, wringing his hands in despair as he saw yet one more problem to contend with. 'Are you sure he will not ram a spade through the skull of one of the students?'

'I do not think so,' said Bartholomew. 'It is best to leave him to his own devices. We will only distress him if we try to prevent him from doing what he wants.'

'Very well,' said Kenyngham unhappily. He pushed Clippesby from his mind, and turned his attention to the matter of the hidden gold. 'I will look in the attics in the south wing.'

'Take Deynman with you,' suggested Bartholomew, his immediate thought to put his slow-witted student in a place where he might be safe if the mob attacked. 'Gray and Bulbeck will stay here and ring the bell if the mob starts to mass outside.'

'I do not think this treasure is in the College, boy,' said Cynric in a low voice to Bartholomew.

'Where is it, then?' demanded Michael, overhearing and coming towards the Welshman. Cynric seldom ventured an opinion about such matters that was not worth hearing.

'Do you remember giving me a document to look after when we were in Suffolk this summer? I hid it in a place where I said you would not think to look.'

'Yes,' said Michael, peeved. 'I had to give you a shilling when I lost a bet that I would be able to guess where it was. And you have never told me where you put it.'

'I put it under Master Alcote's corpse,' said Cynric. 'In his coffin.'

Bartholomew and Michael stared at him.

'What are you suggesting?' asked Michael uneasily. 'That Runham hid the treasure in St Michael's parish coffin?'

'Not in the parish coffin,' said Cynric. 'In Master Wilson's coffin – inside his tomb.'

'But he would not dare!' exclaimed Bartholomew, revolted. 'Wilson died of the plague. Even a greedy man like Runham would not open the grave of a man taken by the pestilence.'

'Are you sure about that?' asked Cynric.

Michael scratched his face, fingernails rasping on his bristles. 'You may be right. Runham was certainly prepared to use the space in the altar to hide his ill-gotten gains. What was to stop him from storing the rest inside the tomb itself? It would certainly explain his unhealthy fascination with it.'

'And the strong-smelling soap served not only to smuggle riches out of the College and into the church, but to disguise the stench from the open tomb,' said Bartholomew.

'That is an unpleasant suggestion, Matt,' said Michael, wrinkling his nose in disgust. 'But you are probably correct. And when Runham was kneeling at that grave, pretending to pray for his cousin, he was hiding his treasure for Caumpes to collect.'

'When any of us saw him at the tomb, our immediate reaction was to avoid him,' said Bartholomew. 'None of us wanted to be invited to join him at his prayers, and I think we were all made uncomfortable by the devotion with which he revered Wilson's memory.'

He recalled Runham kneeling at the tomb the morning after his election, when he had fined the physician for being late. Bartholomew's assumption that Runham had arrived early to catch him was wrong: Runham had arrived early to place some of the treasure in the church for Caumpes. He had not been cleaning when Bartholomew had arrived, but hiding his loot.

'And Wilson and Runham did not even like each

other,' said Cynric. 'Father Paul said that they had always been rivals, and that he was surprised Runham should be so determined to build a tomb for a man he hated.'

'He was not building a tomb,' said Michael. 'He was building a strongbox for the treasures he anticipated would fill it when he finally became Master.'

'We should go,' said Cynric. 'The lane is clear at the moment. We should be able to sneak out without being seen by the rioters.'

'But what happens if the mob attacks Michaelhouse while we are gone?' asked Michael. 'I do not like the notion of being outside its walls when the trouble comes.'

'Then we will have to be quick,' said Bartholomew. 'The whole point of the exercise is to prevent the riot from starting. Those archers on the walls will not hesitate to shoot, and I do not want to see men like Blaston and Newenham hurt.'

'Or my choir,' added Michael. 'Isnard the bargeman, and the rivermen Dunstan and Aethelbald, are good people whom Michaelhouse has wronged. Come on, then, Cynric. Lead the way.'

With a grin of pleasure, delighted to be back in his role of assistant to the Senior Proctor, Cynric slipped the bar on the wicket gate and led the way up the lane towards the church.

The High Street was still deserted, although Bartholomew could hear the ominous rumble of voices emanating from the Market Square. He heard individual voices, too – that of Sheriff Tulyet, ordering people back to their homes, and of Mayor Horwoode making an appeal for peace. He and the others jumped to one side as a group of mounted soldiers thundered past, swords already drawn in anticipation of violence. Bartholomew and Michael exchanged a horrified glance and hurried on.

Bartholomew wrenched open the door to the church, swearing loudly when the sticky latch played its usual tricks. The building was silent and shadowy. Runham still lay under his silken sheet in his coffin, and the altar that Bartholomew and Michael had prised from its moorings remained on its side. As far away from Runham as possible was the fake Suttone, covered hastily with a sheet and lying on two planks. Below him was a bowl, strategically placed to catch the blood that still dripped from the body.

Wilson's grave had once been a boxlike affair of grey stone, topped by a simple and attractive piece of black marble. Since Runham had arrived, the box had been encased in some elaborate wooden carvings, while the life-sized gilded effigy of Wilson, sneering at the world as it rested on one elbow and gazed across the chancel, had been grafted over the marble slab.

'I do not like this, Brother,' said Bartholomew, pausing with a metal lever poised over the tomb. 'Supposing opening this grave releases the contagion again, and the plague returns?'

'Runham probably had it open, and the Death did not strike him,' Cynric pointed out. Bartholomew could not help but notice that the book-bearer was nevertheless keeping a respectful distance from the tomb and its contents.

'But what if you are wrong?' he asked, hesitating. 'What if Runham hid the treasure elsewhere – with a friend, for example?'

'Runham did not have any friends,' said Michael, exasperated. 'And people will die unless we are able to produce this damned treasure soon. I cannot think of anywhere else Runham might have stored the stuff, and we do not have time to hold a disputation over it. All we need to do is lift that slab and have a quick look underneath.'

'All right, all right,' said Bartholomew. 'Stand back, then.'

He began to poke around with his lever, seeing that the mortar had been loosened all along the back. Cynric was right: someone had been inside the tomb. Bartholomew began to heave. The slab lifted slightly, and then dropped back. He tried again, but it was too heavy with the brazen effigy reclining on top of it.

'We need to lift this thing off first,' he said. 'We will never get the lid open with this revolting carving weighting it down.'

Cynric and Michael watched him chip away the mortar that held the effigy in its place, but made no move to assist when he staggered under its weight.

'It is curious how loath I am to touch it,' said Michael, reluctantly stepping forward and wrapping his hands in his sleeves before he handled the statue. 'It reminds me so much of Wilson himself, that I want nothing to do with it.'

'If you are not squeamish about opening the man's grave, I hardly think you can be fastidious about touching his graven image,' said Bartholomew. 'Put it on the floor, over there. We do not want to damage it and then have more of Wilson's cousins coming to rectify matters.'

'We do not,' said Cynric with a shudder.

Once the effigy had been removed, prising open the slab was easy. The silence in the church was broken by the noise of clattering hooves. More soldiers were hurrying to the escalating confrontation between Sheriff and mob in the Market Square.

'Quickly,' urged Michael, white-faced. 'If Cynric thinks these rioters mean business, then Tulyet will not be able to control them for much longer.'

'I will hold it up, while you slip your hand inside the

tomb and see what you can feel,' said Bartholomew. Michael and Cynric exchanged a nervous glance.

'We will feel bones, boy,' said Cynric with a shudder. 'We will not do it, will we, Brother?'

'We will not,' said Michael with firm conviction. 'Just lever the whole thing off, and then we can look inside with no need for poking about with our hands.'

'It is too heavy,' said Bartholomew. 'And if we take it off, we will never get it back on again. We cannot leave an open grave – of a plague victim, remember – in the church where our friends come to pray.'

'Then we will lever and you can feel,' said Michael, snatching the metal rod from him. 'You are more used to that sort of thing than us.'

Bartholomew sighed, wanting the whole matter over and done with. 'Hurry up then, before I change my mind.'

Cynric and Michael leaned on the bar, and Bartholomew peered into the dark space within. He could see Wilson's coffin, already beginning to crumble and crack with age, and he fancied he could detect the paler gleam of bones within it. It stank of dampness and mildew and ancient, rotting grave clothes, and he felt himself gag. Before he could lose his nerve completely, he thrust his hand inside, careful not to touch the coffin, and felt around. Triumphantly, he emerged with one of the College's silver chalices. He rummaged again, and found two silver patens and the lovely thurible that the founder had left to Michaelhouse in his will.

'You were right,' he said, smiling up at Cynric. 'This is exactly where Runham hid his treasure!'

'Now why did I not think to look there?' said a voice from the shadows of the nave.

Bartholomew rose to his feet fast, holding the thurible like a weapon that could be hurled and looking around him for the owner of the voice. Cynric and Michael seemed as bewildered as he was.

'Now, now, Matthew,' said Adela Tangmer, stepping out from the shadows and giving him one of her open, cheerful grins. 'Put down that lovely work of art before you damage it. Thomas Caumpes has his crossbow loaded, and he will not hesitate to use it, if I ask him – which I will if you start throwing around goods that I intend to sell.'

Michael gazed at the vintner's daughter in astonishment. 'You?' he exclaimed. 'You are the secret relative whom Suttone was prepared to kill for?'

Behind her was Caumpes, still wearing the blue tabard that marked him as a Fellow of Bene't College. He was white with shock and fear, and Bartholomew noticed that the crossbow was unsteady in his hands. His eyes looked haunted, and Bartholomew suspected that the traumas and anxieties of the past few days had made him unpredictable, and that his shaking fingers might even loose a quarrel by accident.

Adela beamed with her long teeth. 'And why not, Brother? Do you think I am insufficiently attractive to warrant such devotion?'

Michael clearly did: he gaped at the woman's plain features, her baggy brown dress and practical riding cloak, at a loss for words. More horses pounded past outside, indicating that Sheriff Tulyet intended to quell the rebellion with all the resources at his disposal.

'Are you leaving the town?' the monk asked, gesturing to the saddlebag thrown over Adela's shoulder. 'I do not blame you. A riot is brewing. But if we can get this silver to Michaelhouse, we may yet prevent trouble.'

'My leaving has nothing to do with that,' said Adela. 'My father is driving me to distraction with his insistent whining about marriage. I might be obliged to stab him if it goes on much longer, and I do not want to do that.'

'Stab?' asked Bartholomew, appalled. 'So, it was *you* who killed de Walton and Brother Patrick, not Caumpes?'

'I told you it was not me—' began Caumpes. Adela silenced him with a wave of her hand.

'When you escaped from Bene't's burning hut, I thought our game would be over,' she said. 'But then you started chasing shadows that were nothing to do with us, and Caumpes acted as decoy to lead you away from where I hid in the trees. I was able to escape – after I made an end of de Walton, of course. I did not want him talking before I was ready.'

Bartholomew thought it likely that poor de Walton had known very little. He was sure the man had not guessed it was Adela behind the plotting that had so damaged his College.

'And Patrick?' asked Michael. 'He saw Suttone smothering Wymundham, so you killed him, too?'

Adela gave a careless nod and pulled a handful of metal spikes from her saddlebag. 'I stabbed him with one of these – the implements I use for plucking stones out of horses' hooves. And I will kill you with them, too, unless you do as I say.'

'So that was why the shape of the wound was so unusual,' said Bartholomew, recalling the round injury in Patrick's back.

'But why did you tell us about Patrick fleeing from Holy Trinity Church?' asked Michael. 'We know now that it was no corpse that made him run away.'

'She wanted to make us look more closely at Bene't, so that suspicion would be removed from her,' said Bartholomew, before Adela could answer. 'It was a ruse.'

She gave a quick grin of begrudging approval at his

deduction. 'Patrick did flee the church – but because he was afraid of being associated with Wymundham's drunken state, not because Wymundham was dead.'

Michael began to edge away from the tomb. 'I see. But much as I would love to have the answers to this mystery, there are more pressing matters to attend. If we do not return to—'

'Stay where you are,' said Adela sharply. She jumped, as a sudden roar of angry voices came from the Market Square.

'Listen to them,' said Michael, desperately 'Those are the workmen Runham hired to build his new courtyard. They plan to destroy Michaelhouse unless we can—'

Caumpes released a sharp bark of laughter. 'Then there is some justice in this mess! Michaelhouse will pay for what it did to Bene't.'

The reminder of the wrong perpetrated on Bene't seemed to steady Caumpes. He took a firmer grip on his crossbow and his expression changed from miserable bewilderment to bitter determination.

'Let us go,' said Bartholomew, appealing to Adela. I do not want to see good men like Robert de Blaston killed by the Sheriff's soldiers.'

'No,' said Adela. 'I have no intention of handing over what Wilson stole from my dying mother to pay Michaelhouse's debts.'

'Please, Adela,' pleaded Bartholomew. 'Too many people have already died for Wilson's treasure.'

'You are wrong,' said Adela harshly. 'Not enough people have died – including you, Brother.'

Michael seemed startled to be singled out for such venom, but then he nodded slowly. 'Matt's suspicions were right about my recent illness. You told Suttone to exchange the salve Matt usually applies to infections for a more potent one, and you persuaded Caumpes to tamper with the scaffolding near my room. But what have I done to earn such hatred?'

'I did not want you to investigate Patrick's death before Suttone had had the chance to retrieve my mother's stolen treasure.'

'Do you feel no remorse for Suttone's death?' asked Bartholomew softly.

'Suttone was a fool,' said Adela. 'He knew nothing about horses and thought the reward for retrieving my stolen goods was my marriage to him. And him with great fat legs like a pig!'

'Whom will you marry? Caumpes?' asked Michael.

Adela regarded him askance. 'Do you think I would go to all this trouble just to put my now considerable wealth at the disposal of some man to drink and gamble away?'

'Was it Caumpes who betrayed Suttone to Wymundham?' asked Michael. 'Wymundham knew all about Suttone – that is why Suttone smothered him.'

'I did not—' began Caumpes, casting an anxious glance at Adela.

Adela silenced him by raising her hand. 'Actually, I told Wymundham about Suttone. Not deliberately, of course, but he fed me some of that disgracefully strong brew that Bene't uses to drive out the cold – tastes like horse liniment.'

'Widow's Wine,' said Bartholomew heavily. 'That stuff seems to crop up all over the place.'

'It should not be allowed to crop up at all,' said Adela. 'Anyway, I became a little indiscreet – at a respectable guild meeting, too, held in Bene't's hall! I embarrassed my father dreadfully, but I do have a weak head for wines.'

'You mean you betrayed Suttone because you were drunk?' asked Bartholomew, astounded.

'Basically. I did not mean to, but the wine was strong and Wymundham was an attentive listener.'

There was another yell from the Market Square. Bartholomew cast Michael an agonised glance. Unless they acted soon the rioters would march on Michaelhouse and people would die.

'We must—' he began.

'As long as Michaelhouse is under attack, this church will be safe,' interrupted Adela. 'We will remain here until the violence is over.'

'Let us go,' pleaded Bartholomew. 'We may be able to—'

'Enough!' snapped Adela. 'I do not want to hear any more about this wretched riot.'

'The way Suttone spoke, I thought he referred to someone who had died in the plague,' said Michael in the brief silence that followed.

'Something of me did die during the Death,' said Adela softly. 'I learned that it is unwise to love someone who might be snatched away without warning. It is that knowledge, more than anything else, that makes me determined to put myself in a position where I never have to marry.'

The triumphant braying was gone from her voice, and Bartholomew saw that, yet again, the pestilence had a good deal to answer for; it had stolen away people with whom Adela might have led a contented life.

Caumpes, meanwhile, was nervous again. He was sweating profusely and his hands shook almost uncontrollably. Bartholomew glanced at Cynric, but the book-bearer's shocked, disgusted face suggested there would be no help from that quarter.

'So what did Wilson steal from you?' asked Michael, breaking into Adela's soulful introspection.

'During the Death, I persuaded Wilson – who was on

his way to visit his lover in St Radegund's Convent – to give my mother last rites. When he had finished, I noticed he had relieved her of all her jewellery. What kind of man steals from the dying?'

'I suppose he thought she no longer needed it,' said Michael. 'Things seemed different during the pestilence, when no one knew whether they would live another day, or which of their friends or relatives would die before sunset.'

'That is irrelevant,' she hissed angrily. 'The jewellery was not his to take. My mother might not have needed it, but she did not intend it to end up in the vile claws of a corpse-robber. She wanted it to be mine.'

'So, what will you do when you have it back?' asked Michael. 'You cannot stay here.'

'I will go to Ireland, where I will not be pestered by proposals of marriage. But my plans are my business and none of yours.'

'Quite,' said Michael hastily. 'But the day is wearing on, and you should be on your way. If Master Caumpes will kindly lower his crossbow, we will—'

'Oh, no!' said Adela. 'Caumpes's crossbow remains, thank you. But there will be no need for violence. If you co-operate, I will let you go. I have one question to ask and as soon as I have the answer, I will leave under the cover of this riot. My trusty steed Horwoode is waiting outside. You can do what you like.'

But her steely gaze told Bartholomew that, if things went according to her plan, he, Michael and Cynric would not be leaving the church alive, one question answered or not.

'What is your question?' asked Michael, his eyes fixed uneasily on the quaking Caumpes and his wavering crossbow. Bartholomew swallowed hard, wondering what would happen first – his death at the hands of Adela, or the attack on Michaelhouse that would see a bloodbath in which scholars and townsmen would die.

'I want to know where Runham hid his treasure,' she said. 'I see you have some of the College silver there, but what have you done with the rest of it?'

'Suttone took only what he considered to be yours,' said Michael in sudden understanding. 'He even returned the excess to Matt later, because he did not like the notion of stealing.'

Adela grimaced. 'That just shows what happens when you engage a friar to help you. A word of warning, Matthew – if you ever decide to commit a robbery, choose Cynric to assist, not your friend the monk. Clerics have scruples that you would find frustrating.'

'I am not so sure about that,' muttered Bartholomew, who knew Michael much better than she did. 'But who *was* Suttone?'

'A Carmelite friar, just as he told you,' said Adela. 'He left his Order because he found his brethren lacking in morals. We are distantly related, and he came to my father's house to beg for work. Before my father could set him to carrying wine barrels, I suggested something that appealed to his sense of justice. I asked him to take the place of one of your new Fellows, so that he could rectify a great wrong.'

'Then he chose the wrong man to impersonate,' said Michael wryly. 'The real Suttone was a thief, according to Master Runham.'

'That upset him terribly,' said Adela. 'But you are trying to distract me. Where is the rest of the treasure?'

'Most of it is at Michaelhouse,' said Michael. 'Wait here, and I will go and fetch it.'

Adela laughed. 'I know there is about seventy pounds at Michaelhouse – the money Suttone returned to you, along with some promissory notes and baubles that Runham found, begged or borrowed. But that is nothing compared to what Wilson really had. Runham boasted to Suttone that Wilson had at least a hundred pounds in gold coins hidden away. So, let us not play games here. Where is it?'

'A hundred pounds?' exclaimed Michael, astonished. 'As well as the seventy pounds in College?'

'Yes,' said Adela impatiently. 'And do not pretend to be surprised: it is common knowledge that Wilson's room was stuffed to the gills with gold after he died, so you cannot fool me with your feigned innocence.'

'But I am telling the truth,' protested Michael. 'Believe me, if I knew where to find a hundred pounds, we would not be poking around in Wilson's tomb for treasure to show angry builders.'

'Liar!' snapped Adela. 'Tell me where it is, or Caumpes will shoot you.'

Caumpes was quaking like a leaf, and Bartholomew inched forward. It was a mistake.

'Caumpes!' Adela's ringing no-nonsense voice made the agitated scholar jump and his finger trembled on the trigger. 'Pull yourself together!'

'I did not mean for this to happen,' said Caumpes in an unsteady whisper. 'All I wanted was to protect my College from wicked men like Wymundham and Brother Patrick, and to make sure Michaelhouse did not poach our workmen. That is all. I wanted no part in murder and theft.'

'But you sold stolen goods,' said Michael, unmoved.

Caumpes turned a tortured gaze on him. 'No! Do you think I would risk having it said that Bene't scholars peddle stolen property? Everything I sold was honestly obtained. Ask Sheriff Tulyet or the Goldsmiths' Guild.'

'Then why did you throw in your lot with her?' asked

Michael, casting a contemptuous glance at Adela. 'And with Runham?'

'I told you,' said Caumpes miserably. 'I wanted money to finish Bene't's buildings, because the Duke and the Guilds of St Mary and Corpus Christi are becoming reluctant to pay.'

This time the yell from the crowd was hoarse and angry. It sounded as though it were closer, as if the mob had left the Market Square and was already on the move.

'The treasure,' prompted Adela, gazing purposefully at Michael. 'Where is it?'

'Caumpes will not shoot,' said Michael, although his voice was uncertain. 'He has said all along that he is not a murderer, and he is right.'

'Caumpes!' snapped Adela again. 'Kill the servant. Show them that you are a man, and not a snivelling, cowardly rat.'

'Caumpes is not a murderer,' said Michael again. His conviction wavered slightly as Caumpes swallowed hard and brought his crossbow to bear on Cynric. 'And it would do you no good if he were, madam, because we do not know where Runham hid his gold.'

'I do not believe you,' said Adela. 'Shoot him, Caumpes.'

But Michael was right: Caumpes had no intention of shooting anyone. He hurled the crossbow from him in revulsion and started running up the nave towards the door. Before Bartholomew could react, Adela made a quick, decisive movement, and Caumpes fell, scrabbling helplessly at the metal that was embedded in his back. She turned to Bartholomew, Michael and Cynric, showing that she held another four or five shining silver spikes in her hands.

'I am good with these,' she said. 'I advise you to stay where you are.'

Bartholomew gazed at Caumpes who was gasping for

breath on the patterned tiles of the nave, and then watched him painfully continue his journey to the door. The physician guessed the wound had pierced a lung, and doubted whether Caumpes would survive. How many more people would die in their church, he wondered, before the curse of Wilson's stolen treasure was exorcised?

A short distance away, the cheated workmen and the wronged singers were definitely making their move. The shouting was louder, and Bartholomew could hear ringing curses from carters on the High Street as the rioters began to stream from the Square towards Michaelhouse, blocking the road. Caumpes had reached the church door and opened it, allowing the sounds to drift in more clearly. A horse neighed in panic at the sudden increase in noise.

'Horwoode!' exclaimed Adela in alarm, glancing at the door.

'He sounds panicky,' said Bartholomew quickly, seeing an opportunity to break the stalemate. 'Perhaps someone is trying to steal him.'

'No one in this town would steal a horse of mine,' she said, raising her throwing hand to warn Bartholomew against moving. She glanced towards the door in agitation, then snapped her attention forward again as Bartholomew braced himself to stand. 'They would not dare.'

'Then perhaps it is an outsider,' said Bartholomew. 'To a poor man with a starving family, Horwoode would be well worth stealing.'

'And eating,' added Michael. 'After all, it could not be sold, given that it is so distinctive, but it would keep a family in meat for a week.'

It was enough. Without a word, Adela turned and raced up the nave, her mind fixed on the rescue of her horse.

Bartholomew followed her, ignoring the warning cries of Michael and Cynric to let her go. By the time he reached the door, she was mounted and the horse was prancing skittishly among the graves. She pulled back her arm, and Bartholomew ducked back inside the porch. One of her spikes thudded into the door.

'Stay away!' she yelled. 'Let me go – we have a pact to help each other, remember?'

'I would not have made it had I known what you planned,' he shouted back. His medicine bag caught on the door latch, and as he struggled to free it, he felt the smooth metal of his new childbirth forceps. He hauled them out and held them like a weapon. Adela gave a bitter smile.

'What will you do, Matthew? Club me off my horse with the implement you use to save women's lives? Believe me, I will kill you before you close half the distance.'

To prove her point, another of the silver missiles appeared in her hand, and her arm came up as she prepared to throw. A furious yell from the mob unnerved Horwoode. Hooves flailed and Bartholomew took the opportunity to dash to the back of the bucking horse. It did not like the sensation that someone was behind it, and began to prance and rear even more frantically. Despite her skills as a horsewoman, Adela was having difficulty in controlling it. Meanwhile, Caumpes had reached the High Street, and was clinging to the churchyard gate for support.

Bartholomew dodged this way and that, trying to get close enough to knock Adela from her saddle. Horwoode became more agitated, and a sudden sideways skip made the horse collide with Bartholomew, causing him to drop the forceps to the ground. The metallic clatter and the sight of something shiny under its feet was the last straw. Horwoode bolted.

At that precise moment, Caumpes released his grip on the wall that supported him and began to lurch forward, following some final desire to make his way back to the College he had loved. Startled by another movement under its front legs, the horse jolted backward, rolling its eyes in terror, and then fell.

Caumpes was crushed under the falling body, while Adela lost her grip on the saddle and slid to the ground. She recovered herself quickly and maintained her grip of the horse's reins, but the horse was on its side with its hooves flailing wildly. There was a sickening crack as one of them caught her on the side of her head. She stood immobile for a moment, and then crumpled to lie twitching on the ground. The horse scrambled to its feet and darted off along the High Street.

Bartholomew dashed forward and knelt next to her, but he could see she was beyond anything he could do. The hoof had cracked the skull at the temple, and crushed the brain inside. Despite her convulsive struggles, her eyes already had the glassy look of death in them.

'The horse killed her,' whispered Cynric, coming to stand next to Bartholomew. 'She was killed by one of the animals she loved.'

Adela's uncontrolled shuddering ceased as the brain relinquished its damaged grip on her body.

'The horse has killed Caumpes, too,' said Michael, who crouched next to the scholar from Bene't. 'He is dead.'

'This is no place for us,' said Cynric urgently, grabbing Bartholomew's tabard and hauling him to his feet as an ear-splitting howl echoed through the churchyard. 'The mob is here.'

Dragging Bartholomew behind him, and with Michael following with uncharacteristic speed, Cynric darted to the back of the graveyard and hid among the tangle of bushes and small trees that grew there. They had been wrong when they had assumed the mob would go straight to Michaelhouse. The gaggle of workmen and singers had known perfectly well that they would be unlikely to make an impression on a sturdy foundation like the College, and had marched instead on that most prominent piece of Michaelhouse property – St Michael's Church.

From his frighteningly inadequate hiding place, Bartholomew watched the rioters pour into the churchyard. At the head of them was Osmun. He faltered as he saw Caumpes's body, and his pugilistic features hardened. He jumped on a tombstone to address his followers.

'This is the body of Master Caumpes of Bene't College!' he howled in fury. 'Caumpes was a good and honest man, and it is obvious who killed him – Michaelhouse men!'

'Why is that obvious?' piped up old Dunstan the riverman from the front of the crowd. The question was not put in such a way as to question Osmun's authority, but in a manner that suggested the old riverman merely wanted the information.

'Because his murdered body lies in the graveyard of the church Michaelhouse owns,' yelled Osmun, spittle flying from his mouth in his fury. 'Use your wits, old man!'

'I do not see that proves anything,' said Aethelbald, Dunstan's brother, scratching his head in genuine puzzlement. 'Anyone could have killed your Master Caumpes and left the body here.'

'Michaelhouse hates Bene't scholars,' fumed Osmun. 'Poor Caumpes was killed only because he wore the blue tabard of the College I serve.'

'In that case, why is Adela Tangmer also dead?' asked Robert de Blaston the carpenter. 'She was not a scholar from Bene't.'

'And anyway, those Michaelhouse men are a cunning brood,' said his friend Newenham knowledgeably. 'They would not leave the bodies of people they killed on their own property.'

Osmun was not stupid. He could see that the crowd's fury was fading as he argued with them. He gave a warlike whoop and waved a long, gnarled stick in the air. There were some answering cries and a few weapons were rattled, although it all seemed rather feeble to Bartholomew.

'To Michaelhouse!' shouted Osmun. 'We will tear it stone from stone to its foundations!'

'We have been thinking about that,' said Dunstan uneasily. 'If we destroy Michaelhouse, we will never be invited to sing in a choir again – none of the other colleges would have us.'

'Will you let music interfere with justice?' yelled Osmun, outraged. 'To Michaelhouse, lads, and all its ill-gotten wealth will be ours!'

'But that is the problem,' Blaston pointed out. 'It does not have any ill-gotten wealth. If it did, we would not be here now, using the tools of our trade as weapons. We would be working on their north court. Michaelhouse is destitute.'

'Hardly that,' muttered Michael indignantly. Cynric jabbed him hard in the ribs to silence him before he gave them away.

'To Michaelhouse!' yelled Osmun, ignoring the carpenter.

'It is all that Runham's fault,' said Dunstan, climbing unsteadily on another tombstone, using his brother as a prop. '*He* dismissed the choir and *he* made the deal with the craftsmen that he knew he could not fulfil. It is not the fault of the other scholars – only him.'

'Where is Runham?' screamed Isnard the bargeman from the back of the crowd. 'It is him we will tear apart! And then we will march on Michaelhouse and demand our bread and ale.'

'He is in the church, God rot his wicked soul,' said Dunstan, addressing the crowd from his little pulpit, just as Osmun had been doing. 'He is lying under a lovely piece of silk – unlike his own book-bearer, whom he left to rot for days. Justus would still be there now if Doctor Bartholomew had not arranged his burial.'

'When was that, then?' asked Isnard conversationally. 'I would have attended Justus's requiem mass had I known when it was going to happen. I like a good funeral.'

'Justus was my cousin,' yelled Osmun. 'I had to plead and beg on bended knees for Michaelhouse to honour his poor remains and do its duty. Bene't would never have left a man unburied for more than a week.'

'Why did you not bury Justus, then?' asked Dunstan. 'If he was your cousin—'

'March on Michaelhouse now, and demand all they have!' shrieked Osmun, sensing he was losing control of his small crowd to the old man. 'We will have their silver and gold, and their rich cloaks and fine food.'

'Michaelhouse does not have fine food,' said Isnard. 'You are thinking of Peterhouse. Michaelhouse is the College with the worst food in Cambridge.'

'I think you will find that honour goes to Gonville Hall,' muttered Michael indignantly. Cynric prodded him again.

'And the food has got worse since Runham was made Master,' shouted Dunstan, although there was no reason why he should be privy to such facts, now that he no longer earned his Sunday bread and ale. 'And it was bad food that made Brother Michael ill. Runham tried to starve him to death!'

There was an ominous, angry rumble from the members of the choir, although the craftsmen appeared sceptical, and Bartholomew buried his face in his hands so that Michael would not see him smile. He wondered whether

any of the crowd would question why Michael should be
made ill with bad food, if Runham was starving him.
None did.

'And Runham was going to stop Doctor Bartholomew
coming to visit the sick,' continued Dunstan, now enjoying his role as spokesman for the underclasses. 'How can
we afford the high fees of Master Lynton when we are ill?
We need Doctor Bartholomew, and Runham was trying
to take him from us.'

The angry rumble increased in volume. Dunstan had
succeeded where the aggressive Osmun had failed.

'And Doctor Bartholomew gave my Yolande a green
ribbon, too,' added Blaston, drawing the bemused glances
of several of the choir. 'He is a kind man who is fond of
his patients – us.'

'To Michaelhouse then,' shouted Osmun, waving his
stave, 'to avenge all these wrongs.'

'No!' wailed Dunstan in his reedy tenor. 'To St Michael's
Church to where that vile Runham's corpse lies. We will
string it up.'

This time, the yell of approval from the crowd was
distinctly more enthusiastic.

'What for?' demanded Osmun, startled. 'Hanging a
corpse will do you no good. Looting the College will
bring you fortunes beyond your wildest dreams.'

'How many more times do we have to tell you?'
demanded Blaston, shoving the porter out of his way.
'Michaelhouse does not *have* this great fortune you keep
talking about. And it is Runham we want. Runham is
responsible for all our troubles.'

'Wait!' shouted Osmun, as the crowd surged forward
and elbowed their way into the church.

But no one paid him any heed, and there was no more
for him to do than to pick up the body of Caumpes,
sling it over his shoulder, and be on his way. Smashing

sounds came from inside the church. Bartholomew leapt to his feet and tried to move forward, but Cynric held him back.

'Are you mad, boy?' he hissed. 'They will see a Michael-house tabard and turn their rage on you.'

That was certainly true, thought Bartholomew, easing back into the cover of the trees. He had almost been the victim of the choir once before in St Michael's Church.

'But they will destroy it,' he whispered. 'And they will take the church silver.'

'I have that here,' said Michael, holding up Adela's saddlebag. 'And there is nothing else to steal. The only thing of any value in that poor church is the silk sheet that is draped over Runham's corpse – and they are welcome to that.'

'But they are smashing things. I can hear them.'

'Only the vase that contains the flowers Runham left for Wilson,' said Michael. 'And that has been empty this past week.'

There was some angry shouting, and the crowd began to emerge from the church, carrying Runham's coffin with them. Dunstan, wearing the silk sheet around his thin shoulders, led the strange procession like some bizarre priest. Behind him, Runham shuddered and bumped as he was carried head-high along the High Street, willing hands reaching up to be part of the grisly celebration. Not far behind, the gilt effigy of Wilson was being given similar treatment, joggling in grabbing hands as it was borne away towards the Market Square.

It was not long before the church was empty. Fearful for it, Bartholomew darted from his hiding place and through the door. But Michael had been right, and the only thing that had been smashed was Runham's clay vase. He started in alarm when the door clanked open.

'Where have they gone now?' asked Sheriff Tulyet

wearily. 'I thought that by showing them all my soldiers, armed and willing to use force, I had convinced them to go home peacefully. They were perfectly calm when I left them, and then I heard the whole thing had started again.'

'Osmun from Bene't was whipping them into a frenzy,' said Michael. 'Or was trying to. They do not seem a particularly frenzied mob to me – just people who have been badly treated.'

'So where are they?' said Tulyet. 'I have better things to do than chase around after frustrated choristers. I will have that Osmun in my gaol for his role in this.'

'Quite right, too,' agreed Michael. 'And then he can enjoy a spell in the proctors' prison – that will cure his riotous fervour for a while. But the mob snatched Runham's corpse and Wilson's effigy and were heading off to the Market Square with them.'

'Oh, horrible!' exclaimed Tulyet in distaste. 'What do they plan to do? Have a spit roast?'

'There would be plenty of lard to baste the meat if they did,' said Michael, unaware that he was not in a position to criticise the fat of others. 'I think they intend to lynch him.'

'Lynch a corpse?' asked Tulyet uncertainly. 'Oh well, it is better than lynching a live person, I suppose. Come on. Let us put a stop to all this madness before any real harm is done.'

He made as if to inspect the crumpled figure of Adela as he passed, but Bartholomew took his arm and hurried him on, thinking the Sheriff's duties lay with the living first; he could deal with the dead later. Michael and Cynric followed them the short distance along the High Street to the Market Square.

'That was Adela Tangmer,' said Tulyet as they ran. 'What happened to her?'

'She fell off her horse,' replied Michael tersely. 'I will tell you the details later. Right now, it is more important to deal with these rioters.'

'We can only deal with them if we know what they are doing,' said Tulyet, skidding to a halt as they reached the Market Square. 'And I have no idea what they plan to do.'

He was not the only one. Standing next to him, Bartholomew regarded the scene warily. The crowd, having reached the Square with their intended victim, was suddenly at a loss at what to do. Without the yells and encouragement of Osmun – and Dunstan was too old to have kept up with the main body of the mob and was still huffing his way from the church – they milled around like lost sheep. The body of Runham in its fine coffin was set down gently near the fishmonger's stall, while the effigy was propped nonchalantly against the water pump that stood in the centre of the Square.

'I think the answer to your question is simple,' said Bartholomew. 'These people do not know what they are going to do, either. Tell them all to go home, Dick.'

'Michaelhouse will not press charges over this?' asked Tulyet. 'You would be within your rights to do so. Snatching the corpses of scholars is not generally regarded as good civic behaviour.'

'Depends on the corpse,' said Michael. 'But Matt is right. The sooner this incident is over and forgotten, the better. Tell them to disperse and that there will be no reprisals from Michaelhouse.'

'Right,' yelled Tulyet, striding forward and taking control while he had the chance. 'I want eight volunteers to transport Masters Runham and Wilson back to St Michael's Church, and then we will say no more about this disagreeable spectacle.'

Several of the choir shuffled forward, and Runham

was heaved off the ground to begin his return journey. Aethelbald was one of the ones who volunteered to lift the effigy, but it was heavy, and his frail old arms were not strong enough to take the weight. With a crash that echoed all over the Market Square, it slipped from his grasp and smashed to the ground. The head rolled in one direction, the legs in another, while the torso cracked in two. And out from the breaks rolled Master Runham's hidden treasure.

For a moment, no one moved, and the tinkle of coins flowing from the statue was all that could be heard. And then there was chaos. Runham was rudely dropped to the ground, where his corpse flopped from its coffin and his white shroud became splattered with dirt. The crowd surged forward, Michael among them, and uncountable hands reached, grabbed and snatched for the bright gold that lay in the mud. People were trampled, hair was yanked, clothes were ripped, and faces were slapped and thumped. Bartholomew watched it all aghast, while Tulyet used the flat of his sword in a hopeless attempt to try to restore some sort of order.

News that there was gold to be had near the fish stalls carried faster than the wind, and more people raced to join the affray. Those staggering away from the chaos found themselves mugged for their new acquisitions, and Bartholomew was wrestled to the ground by two apprentices who were certain his pockets were stuffed with coins, but backed off when Cynric came to his rescue.

'Come away, boy,' the Welshman urged with distaste. 'This is no place for honest men.'

'But we cannot just leave,' said Bartholomew, appalled both by the display of naked greed and by the fact that the gold that was being spirited away in a hundred different pockets was stolen property and would never be returned to its rightful owners. 'Some of that gold belongs to Michaelhouse.'

'Not any more,' said Cynric with a grin.

EPILOGUE

THE FOLLOWING DAY, WHEN PEACE HAD BEEN restored to the town and Master Runham's body had been restored to St Michael's Church, Bartholomew and Michael sat in the conclave with Langelee, William and Kenyngham. It was a lovely afternoon, with a pale winter sun shining in a clear, cloudless sky that bathed the room with its warm brightness. A merry fire crackled in the hearth, and Agatha had just brought a platter of freshly baked oatcakes for the Fellows to eat while they waited for the bell to call them to supper. The students were all gainfully employed removing the last of the scaffolding under the watchful eye of a shame-faced Robert de Blaston, while Cynric moved around the room refilling goblets with wine. Michael was happily contemplating a resumption of his hoodwinking of William Heytesbury of Merton College, while Bartholomew was anticipating with pleasure his meeting with Matilde that evening.

'It is good to have you back, Cynric,' said Michael, holding out his cup. 'The College was not the same without you.'

'A life of evenings at home is very nice,' said Cynric, 'but I found I missed the occasional adventure with you. I have decided to work at Michaelhouse during the day and return to Rachel at night – unless you have any prowling or fighting you need done.'

'I hope that will not be necessary,' said Bartholomew in alarm. 'I have had more than my share of that sort of thing for a while, and I do not think Rachel would approve of us leading you astray.'

'She wants whatever makes me happy,' said Cynric with smug contentment. 'You always claim you do not like these adventures of Brother Michael's, but I think you do, really.'

'I do not!' began Bartholomew vehemently. 'In fact—'

'Has anyone seen the real Master Suttone today?' asked Langelee, downing his wine in a single draught and holding out his cup to Cynric for more. 'Or is he still skulking in the Carmelite Friary?'

'Is that how he will be known from now on?' asked Michael, amused. 'The real Master Suttone?'

'It is better to be clear on this matter, Michael,' said William pompously. 'Or who knows what confusion might arise? On the one hand we had a man prepared to lie and kill for a woman, and on the other we have a weaselly coward who ran away the first time his College needed him, and who remained in his bed for nigh on two weeks with little more than a scratched arm.'

'Do not despise the real Master Suttone for his cowardice, Father,' said Michael comfortably. 'He may have done more for Michaelhouse than he will ever know – it was because of him that we are now rid of the dreadful Runham and his wicked deeds.'

William gazed at him. 'Then perhaps the real Master Suttone should have stayed away longer still. Then we might have been able to rid ourselves of that mad-eyed Clippesby, too.'

'We believed the mad-eyed Clippesby had killed Runham,' mused Michael. 'Now it seems that the man is innocent – he just happens to be insane.'

'He is not insane, he is disturbed,' said Bartholomew. 'He has delusions and is unable to view the world in the same way as a rational man.'

'The sedate, calm life of a scholar should heal him, given time,' said William, following Langelee's example and downing his wine so that he could have more.

'Perhaps he should go elsewhere, then,' said Kenyngham anxiously. 'The events of the last few days have indicated that Cambridge is not the place to be if you desire a sedate, calm life.'

'Are you saying that one of the Fellows is genuinely insane?' asked Cynric, not sounding as surprised as Bartholomew thought he should.

'Not insane,' Bartholomew corrected. 'Disturbed. And if he has the support and care of his colleagues, he may overcome the problem.'

'So, only one of the Fellows is officially a lunatic,' muttered Cynric with a puzzled frown. Bartholomew was not sure whether he had heard him correctly, but was too grateful to have the Welshman back again to begin an argument over it.

Clippesby entered the conclave, looking more haunted and nervous than ever. Bartholomew smiled at him and made room near the fire. Timidly, like a deer taking an apple from a hunter, the Dominican edged forward, as if he imagined the proffered stool might suddenly move of its own accord – or that he might discover it was a figment of his imagination. Finding it was not, he sat quickly and looked around at his colleagues with his peculiar eyes.

'What happened to the false Suttone?' he asked shyly in the slightly awkward silence that followed his entrance. 'Somehow I seem to have become confused by all the chaos of yesterday.'

'I am not surprised,' muttered William. 'I was confused myself, and *I* am sane.'

Cynric chuckled softly as he replenished the Franciscan's goblet. 'It is good to be back,' he said ambiguously.

'Four years ago,' Michael began, 'a Master named

Wilson decided to gather himself a fortune, lest the University flounder after the plague and he find himself without employment. He stole from a number of dying people, including the mother of Adela Tangmer. Hatred festered in the daughter after Wilson's own death, and eventually, goaded by her father's constant nagging that she should marry, she embarked upon a plan to get this money back. The wealth would also allow her to become independent from her father, and give her a life of freedom.'

'The false Suttone was the key to the plan,' said Bartholomew. 'He incapacitated the real one and took up the appointment instead, careful to kill the one College servant – Justus – who, like the real Master Suttone, was from Lincoln and who therefore might be in a position to expose the false one as an impostor.'

'Meanwhile,' continued Michael, 'arguments and dissension were bubbling among the Fellows of Bene't, exacerbated by a spiteful-tongued blackmailer called Wymundham. Wymundham used like-minded men, such as Brother Patrick of Ovyng Hostel, to uncover embarrassing secrets about his colleagues. When Wymundham's friend Raysoun fell from the scaffolding, driven to drink and despair by Wymundham himself, Wymundham claimed he had been pushed.'

'Why?' asked Clippesby.

'No reason other than malice,' said Michael. 'He was bored by the life of a scholar, and sought to liven it up by creating a few scandals. Then he took money from Master Heltisle, as a bribe to stop telling lies about Raysoun's death, and immediately set off for Holy Trinity Church to buy some of that cheap wine that we all know can be purchased there of an afternoon.'

'Wymundham blackmailed people to buy wine?' asked Clippesby, confused.

'No,' said Michael impatiently. 'I have just explained Wymundham's motive to you. The wine was a bonus, but not the main purpose of his actions. Do pay attention, man.'

'Meanwhile, Adela became drunk at a Bene't feast, and told Wymundham that her kinsman Suttone planned to infiltrate Michaelhouse with a view to reclaiming the goods that Wilson stole,' said Bartholomew.

'I remember that,' said Langelee, thoughtfully. 'I was at that feast, to meet the Duke of Lancaster. The woman had to be carried home, if I recall correctly. Her father was most embarrassed, and so was Master Heltisle, who had no business serving Widow's Wine to his female guests.'

'So Wymundham decided to blackmail Suttone,' said Bartholomew. 'He arranged to meet Suttone in the shack behind Bene't, where he found his intended victim waiting not with a purse of gold, but with a cushion.'

'And Adela followed Patrick, who was a witness to the murder, and stabbed him with one of her horse picks in the grounds of Ovyng Hostel,' said Michael.

'One of her what?' asked Clippesby, bewildered.

'A tool for removing things from horses' hooves,' explained Michael. 'Sensing that time was running out, Suttone confronted Runham and demanded back the jewellery Wilson stole from Adela's mother.'

'But why did he not just take it?' asked Clippesby. 'Runham was not in his chamber all the time.'

'He tried,' said Michael. 'He searched the Master's room the night Runham was elected – with Adela herself – while most scholars were drunk on an exceptionally powerful brew of Widow's Wine, provided by Caumpes. Matt and I almost caught them as they left. A week later, after Runham declined to part with Adela's money, Suttone smothered him with the cushion Runham had stolen from Agatha's chair.'

'Agatha, the laundress,' said William in sudden glee. 'That reminds me. How *is* Osmun, by the way?'

'He will live,' said Bartholomew. 'Although he will be scarred for life.'

'Why?' asked Clippesby, open-mouthed. 'What did she do to Osmun?'

'She bit him,' said Bartholomew. 'After Osmun had taken Caumpes's body to Bene't, he returned to the Market Square and tried to agitate the crowd into marching against Michaelhouse again, arguing that there was more gold hidden here. Agatha suggested he might like to be quiet. Rashly, he did not take her advice and she bit him in the ensuing mêlée.'

'With those pointed teeth?' asked Clippesby, awed. 'Did she bite anything off?'

'Almost,' said Bartholomew.

'We were talking about Suttone,' said Michael, irritated by the interruption. 'After he had smothered Runham, he removed a certain amount of money from the building chest. But he was not comfortable keeping what he knew was not Adela's, and he returned the balance to Matt in the churchyard before mass one morning. I suspect that was the turning point in their relationship. Suttone had agreed to right a wrong – to help Adela retrieve jewellery stolen from her mother by Wilson on her deathbed. But Adela wanted *all* of Wilson's fabled wealth.'

'Once or twice, when I was in the Master's chamber, gold coins rolled from the chimney,' said Kenyngham with a vague smile. 'And another time, a ring fell from behind one of the tapestries. I wondered where they had come from.'

'Did you investigate, to see whether there were more of them?' asked Michael, astonished.

Kenyngham shook his head. 'I care nothing for such baubles, Michael, you know that. I gave them to the poor and put the matter out of my mind.'

'So, the walls and chimney were dripping gold and you did not think to look into the matter?' asked William in horror. 'Really, Father! Michaelhouse might have been rich had you bothered to tell anyone else about this.'

'I thought you also despised baubles,' said Bartholomew, raising his eyebrows at the indignant friar. William's mouth set into a grim line, and he stared stonily in front of him.

'Meanwhile,' said Michael loudly, growing tired of the interruptions, 'Caumpes had been happily selling jewellery for Runham, left for him in Wilson's altar. Caumpes was probably telling the truth when he said he thought it was legal.'

'But it was not,' said Clippesby.

'No,' said Michael. 'It was not. It was taken from dying people by the avaricious Wilson, and Runham knew this. Perhaps he really did believe that building a new courtyard in Wilson's honour would assuage the sin, but I suspect he intended to make his mark on our College and then leave – along with whatever remained of Wilson's treasure trove.'

'But surely Caumpes was suspicious with an arrangement that necessitated leaving treasure hidden in soap?' asked Clippesby. 'Why evolve such a plan if the whole business was legal?'

'Because the townsfolk do not like scholars dabbling in trade,' said Michael. 'Caumpes was tolerated because he was once a merchant himself, and he is a local man. But Runham could not afford to be seen to be involved in the buying and selling business. Such secrecy was not necessarily an indication of any wrongdoing.'

'So Caumpes was in league with Runham?' asked Clippesby. 'I thought he was working with Adela and the false Suttone.'

'He was,' said Michael. 'Adela always liked Caumpes

more than the other Bene't Fellows, and Caumpes, like Suttone, was a victim of Wymundham's blackmailing. They formed an alliance. Caumpes sold Runham's jewellery, and he told Adela exactly how much the old miser was making. Doubtless the thought of all that treasure going to pay for a building to honour the man who stole from her dying mother was a bitter pill to swallow, and it made her more determined than ever that Runham should not have it.'

'Caumpes's motive, however, was not to get his hands on Wilson's gold for himself, but to raise money for his College,' said Bartholomew. 'He went with Adela to tamper with the scaffolding at Michaelhouse one night, thinking that its collapse would drive the workmen back to Bene't. Adela, though, had different intentions: she wanted the scaffolding to fall on Michael, because she did not want him exposing her before she had a chance to locate the rest of the gold.'

'Speaking of murder, Adela also tried to kill me and Matt in the shed at Bene't,' added Michael, rather indignantly, 'and she succeeded in stabbing de Walton with one of her horse picks, while Caumpes acted as a decoy.'

'Why did she kill de Walton?' asked Clippesby.

Michael sighed. 'Because de Walton would have been a valuable witness in convicting Caumpes. Simekyn Simeon sensed that de Walton was in some danger, and so hid him. Like fools, Matt and I led Caumpes and Adela right to him, and he died for our mistake.'

'Oh, I do not think you should see it like that, Brother,' said Clippesby, fixing the monk with his fanatical gaze. 'It was not your fault that Caumpes and Adela were murderers. It is they who are to blame for the death of de Walton, not you. Especially her, I would say.'

'True,' said William. 'The woman was a maniac.'

'I appreciate your support,' said Michael. 'Then Suttone

came to confess his role in the affair to me in the church, intending from the outset to kill himself; and Adela and Caumpes appeared, wanting Runham's treasure. The rest you know.'

'Poor Runham was only doing what he thought was best for his cousin's soul,' said Kenyngham, who always searched for the good in people, even in thieves and murderers.

'You can believe that if you will,' said Michael. 'I think he came here a year ago intending to have himself elected Master at the first opportunity. I also think he conducted a preliminary search of the Master's room and learned that the rumours were true, and that there was indeed gold hidden in it. And I believe he regularly slipped into it while you were out, and that he has been leaving bits and pieces for Caumpes for a lot longer than the period of his Mastership.'

'I agree,' said William. 'Although most of the stolen treasure has surfaced relatively recently. I saw a set of silver spoons that Alcote lost during the plague for sale some months ago. Runham must have found them on one of his foraging missions and passed them to Caumpes to sell.'

'He evicted you from your room with indecent haste,' said Langelee to Kenyngham. 'He could not wait to give the chamber a really thorough search. And he was well rewarded, it seems. I think that once he had satisfied himself that he had recovered every scrap of Wilson's inheritance and the buildings were completed, he would have left us, taking with him the coins he had hidden in the effigy. They were never intended for Michaelhouse or for Caumpes to sell. They were set aside for his personal use.'

'The effigy was a cunning place to hide them,' said Michael. 'When I examined the smashed pieces, I saw a small slit in the top of Wilson's head, so that the coins could be dropped through it as and when they became available. They would have been safe for years. None of us could bear to be near the thing, let alone inspect it closely.'

'That was why Runham was so keen for the building work to be finished quickly,' said William. 'All he really wanted to do was complete his new court and then leave Michaelhouse to live a life of luxury.' He folded his arms and pursed his lips to show his disapproval of such worldly temptations.

'But why bother with the building at all?' asked Clippesby. 'Why did Runham not search out the gold and run away with it immediately?'

'Immortality,' said Michael. 'Every man wants to be remembered. Runham desired to be revered as the Master who built the north court. He did everything on the cheap, but the new court – even if we had been obliged to rebuild the whole thing – would have been called "Runham's Court". He would have been remembered by generations of Michaelhouse scholars, and doubtless, before he left, he would have arranged to have masses said for him, too, like our founder.'

'Ingenious hiding place, though,' said William reluctantly, his mind still fixed on Wilson's gold, despite his alleged dislike of material possessions. 'Who would have thought of looking there?'

'It did take a certain amount of cunning on my part,' said Michael, not looking at Cynric.

'It is a good thing you were there when the effigy broke,' said Clippesby shyly to Michael. 'The money you recovered was just enough to save Michaelhouse from disaster.'

'But only just,' said William gloomily. 'We may have paid the workmen, reimbursed our would-be benefactors and returned the loans from the guilds, but our hutches remain empty.'

A shriek from outside brought them all to their feet, and Bartholomew felt his stomach turn upside-down, anticipating some dreadful accident involving the students. But it was only Gray, howling with laughter as Deynman gasped and shook water from his hair from the bucket that had 'accidentally' fallen on him.

'Kenyngham is a saint, putting up with students like that year after year,' said William, returning to his place near the fire. 'Disgraceful behaviour! Well, I want none of it.'

'Is this your way of saying that you will not stand as Runham's replacement?' demanded Langelee with keen interest.

'It is,' said William firmly. 'I do not want to become embroiled in plans to raise buildings we do not need, nor do I want to be smothered with cushions by discontented colleagues.'

'That does not trouble me,' said Langelee eagerly. 'I will do it.'

'Then you have my vote,' said William in disgust.

'Wait,' began Michael in alarm.

'And mine,' said Kenyngham tiredly. 'I am just grateful to pass the responsibility to someone else. I have no stomach for this kind of thing, either.'

'No!' cried Michael, struggling to heave his bulk out of his chair so that he could protest more vigorously.

'I will vote for you, Langelee,' said Clippesby shyly. 'I do not like Franciscans, such as Father William, but I will vote for you.'

'But . . .' spluttered Michael, horror making him uncharacteristically inarticulate.

'Good,' said Langelee, rubbing his hands. 'I am elected, then. We do not need the real Master Suttone, because technically he is not a Fellow yet, given that it was his impersonator who was admitted. Paul has resigned, so we cannot ask him. That only leaves Michael and Bartholomew – and since I have three votes already, what they think is irrelevant.'

'Oh, my God!' breathed Michael in horror. 'He has done it! Langelee is our next Master.'

hISTORICAL NOTE

MICHAELHOUSE WAS FOUNDED BY A WEALTHY lawyer called Hervey de Stanton in 1324. After his death, Stanton's will provided funds for his College to purchase a house that became known as Ovyng Hostel, among other properties, and he left the scholars a collection of church silver, including a thurible. He also drafted a set of statutes, which were read aloud to any prospective Fellow, who was then obliged to swear to abide by them and exchange a kiss of peace with his new colleagues. Some of these statutes, translated from the original Latin, are the ones Kenyngham read to Suttone and Clippesby.

By 1353 Thomas Kenyngham had stopped being Master of Michaelhouse, although the records do not say why. However, he is mentioned in documents dating to the foundation, so he was no longer a young man: it is likely that he either died or resigned. The next Master in the records is John Runham, who was succeeded in 1353 by a man called Ralph de Langelee. Again, the records do not say why Runham ceased to be Master.

In 1353 Michaelhouse was engaged in buying some land, and the eventual purchase was made in the names of Ralph de Langelee, Thomas Suttone and John Clippesby, all of whom were Michaelhouse Fellows.

Nothing remains of Bartholomew's Michaelhouse today. The foundations of a later hall are buried under the handsome eighteenth-century block called the Essex Building in Trinity College's Great Court. St Michael's Church, rebuilt by Stanton when he founded Michaelhouse, still stands on what was once called the High Street, but is now Trinity Street. A scheme was launched in March 1999 to restore it as a community centre for the University and the people of Cambridge, and to call it Michaelhouse.

Michaelhouse, like many of the other Colleges, operated a system of 'hutches', whereby students were loaned cash in return for a pledge of equivalent value. Some of these were solely for the use of students, others for the use of Fellows. Their contents were sacrosanct, and for any master to borrow from them illegally would have been considered a dreadful breach of trust.

Bene't College – or the College of St Mary and Corpus Christi, to give it its full official title – was founded in 1350 with generous donations from two town guilds: St Mary and Corpus Christi. For many years the institution was known as Bene't College, because it was close to the Saxon church of St Benedict (usually abbreviated to Bene't), although it is called Corpus Christi today. The first Master was a man named Thomas Heltisle (or Eltisley) and the first two Fellows to be admitted were Thomas Caumpes and John Raysoun. John Wymundham was appointed as the College chaplain.

Bene't College had some powerful and wealthy patrons. Among those who appear in the benefactors' list in the 1350s was the Duke of Lancaster. His squire, a man with the odd name of Simekyn Simeon, was also mentioned as helping the College in 1350, along with one Henry de Walton. College records tell that two of the carpenters employed to build Bene't College were called Robert de Blaston and Adam de Newenham.

In the town, Henry de Tangmer was a wealthy merchant and a burgess, who was also in the Guild of Corpus Christi, while William Horwoode was a member of the Guild of St Mary, and town Mayor. The Tulyet (or Tuillet) family were a powerful force in the town and were burgesses and mayors throughout the fourteenth century.

Meanwhile, one of Oxford's most famous thinkers in the fourteenth century was a nominalist called William Heytesbury, who was a member of Merton College. His texts on philosophy were well known in contemporary universities, and were still in use in the fifteenth century. Heytesbury's best-known work was *Regulae Solvendi Sophismata*, in which he lent vague support to the controversial scholar William of Occam (of razor fame).

Out now

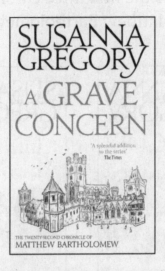

SUSANNA GREGORY

A GRAVE CONCERN

'A splendid addition to the series'
The Times

THE TWENTY-SECOND CHRONICLE OF
MATTHEW BARTHOLOMEW

Identifying the murderer of the Chancellor of the University is not the only challenge facing physician Matthew Bartholomew. Many of his patients have been made worse by the ministrations of a 'surgeon' recently arrived from Nottingham, his sister is being rooked by the mason she has commissioned to build her husband's tomb, and his friend, Brother Michael, has been offered a Bishopric which will cause him to leave Cambridge.

Brother Michael, keen to leave the University in good order, is determined that the new Chancellor will be a man of his choosing. The number of contenders putting themselves forward for election threatens to get out of control, then more deaths in mysterious circumstances make it appear that someone is taking extreme measures to manipulate the competition.

With passions running high and a bold killer at large, both Bartholomew and Brother Michael fear the very future of the University is at stake.

Go back to the beginning

Discover the first three chronicles of
Matthew Bartholomew

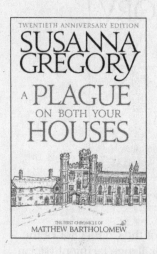

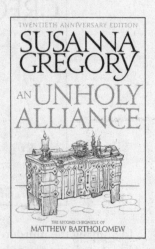

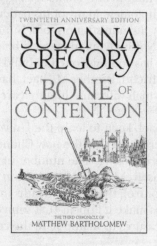